GEMINI GAMBIT • BOOK 3

CHILD
OF THE
FALL

D. SCOTT JOHNSON

Thanks for your help
figuring out the hellmouth
shout-out in the back!

CHILD OF THE FALL
D. Scott Johnson

© 2019 Scott Johnson

ISBN: 978-0-9863962-9-8 (hardcover)
978-0-9863962-8-1 (paperback)
978-0-9863962-7-4 (ebook)

Cover design by Melissa Lew
Interior layout by Lighthouse24

To Olivia, for giving me June.

"The more clearly we can focus our attention on the wonders and realities of the universe about us, the less taste we shall have for destruction."

— Rachel Carson

Author's Note

The first book, *Gemini Gambit*, is set twenty years from now. The events of the second book, *Dragon's Ark*, happen six months after that.

Who are these people?

Kimberly Trayne: A computer hacker and cyber thief driven underground by a vicious Bolivian drug cartel. After five years spent in hiding, she is exposed when Mike Sellars attempts to contact her. Eventually they meet and discover they have a common enemy: Matthew Watchtel. While trying to defeat his attempt to take over the Evolved Internet, she is captured and tortured by Watchtell, but eventually prevails.

Six months later her relationship with Mike has collapsed. In an effort to salvage things, they go on a trip to meet the group of monks who helped raise him in China. There they are trapped in a conspiracy to overthrow the Chinese government. They defeat the architect of the plan, Ozzie, and in the process discover Mike's sister-in-kind, Helen.

Mike Sellars: A new kind of life form that emerged in the interstitial spaces of Realmspace, the augmented virtual reality that the Evolved Internet hosts. He discovers a conspiracy to take over his home, destroying him in the process. When he reaches out to the only person he thinks could help, he inadvertently exposes her to dangerous criminals. He acquires a human host—coincidentally the recently-deceased assassin sent to kill Kimberly Trayne—and works with her to stop the madman Matthew Watchtell.

Six months later his relationship with Kim has collapsed. In an attempt at a fresh start, they travel to China to visit the monks who helped raise him. While there, he discovers another life form like himself has emerged in China's walled off realmspace, his sister-in-kind, Helen. They work with her to defeat the maniac Ozzie, averting a nuclear exchange with India in the process.

Spencer McKenzie: A teenager from a small town in Arkansas who is Mike's best friend. Spencer has known about Mike, what and who he is, for about a year before Mike's crazy attempt to gain control of a human host. While helping his friend they cross paths with Spencer's idol, Kimberly Trayne. He works with them to stop Matthew Watchtell.

Six months later, Spencer visits Mike and Kim in Northern Virginia only to discover them on the point of breaking up. He travels with them to China, inadvertently getting captured by human traffickers after they arrive. He escapes them with the help of Tonya. Eventually they both reunite with Mike and Kim. He helps them defeat Ozzie.

Tonya Brinks: Kimberly Trayne's best friend. Tonya is also a registered nurse specializing in limb regrowth. She helps Mike and Kim stop Matthew Watchtell from taking over the Evolved Internet.

Six months later Tonya flies to China to help Kim salvage her relationship with Mike. In the process she confronts the past of her mentor, Walter. She rescues Spencer and defeats the remnants of Walter's gang. She then helps Mike and Kim defeat Ozzie, and also meets a mysterious alien creature who calls himself Cyril.

Matthew Watchtell: A former White House Chief of Staff who uses technologies developed after the capture—and unfortunate escape—of the dangerous cyber criminal Kimberly Trayne to try to take over the Evolved Internet. He fails in this attempt, and in the process various other conspiracies and crimes he's orchestrated are exposed. He spends the next year in jail.

Chapter 1

Kim

She had a morning routine now, one that didn't involve breaking into anything, worrying if someone was following her, or moving to a new apartment for no good reason.

This was normalcy. Well, a kind of normalcy. She still had her disability and a boyfriend who was only technically human. At least he was straight with the IRS now. Kim wouldn't have to visit him in jail. And wouldn't that have been ironic? She learned the recipes for prison makeup before she was fourteen, and yet Mike would've been the one behind bars.

Losing the money to taxes and then going deep in debt to cover the penalties seemed to hurt his lawyers more than it did him. Mike was a Buddhist. He treated it as *a lesson in impermanence.* Seeing all those zeroes on the transfer he'd signed had made her heart skip a beat, but now he was free and clear as long as he stuck to the payment plans. And he would. They had a future together. Kim wouldn't let that get spoiled by a missed payment.

Things had been beyond great after the roller coaster of China — so good that the six months since made her think of the longer term. Marriage, a thing Kim never dreamed of, had turned out to be a possibility. Maybe.

Her mother wanted it, and Mike's sister Helen wasn't shy about bringing the subject up either. Kim was more ambivalent, and judging by the awkward feelings when they discussed it together,

Mike was too. She would take it a day at a time. If he asked her to marry him tomorrow, the answer would be an obvious *yes*. She could think of no one else who would ever put up with her the way he did. But if he never asked her at all, that would be fine too. Kim had grown up as the outcast, literally untouchable. Her relationship, this incredible, impossible thing she had, was what mattered. Not the ring.

Well, it didn't matter *much*.

The November morning was beautiful, with a hint of frost on the grass. She drove to her locksmith shop with the heater on and the windows rolled down. Freedom had a smell, and around this time of year it was cold and crisp.

And it was *her* shop. She never cared much about having a boss, or being an employee. She was good with her hands, though, and had read a ton of *Small Business for Dummies*-like books during her five years hiding from all the things her old life had set on her trail. When one of her great uncles casually mentioned his desire to retire and sell his locksmith business at a lunch party five months ago, a silly thought she'd had just after meeting Mike turned into a full-blown, reachable dream. Thieves know locks like farmers know seeds, and Kim had been a very good thief.

Lacking cash, a house, or a conventional credit rating of any sort had made raising the money a hassle at first, until her mom came forward with her house as collateral. It was another thing Kim was having to get used to: long-term obligations that *mattered*. A-Trayne Lock and Key would succeed. Kim wouldn't let it fail. But it was a burden to carry someone else's trust — a trust so strong they put the house they lived in on the line — along with it. It was much better than worrying whether or not the man walking up behind her was pulling out a knife, but that didn't make it any easier to fall asleep sometimes.

She had to keep expenses to an absolute minimum and so only had a single real employee. It wasn't Mike. He'd rented the office space above the shop for *Warhawk* and was more of a tenant with benefits. Her real employee was part of the purchase agreement, the first in what Kim knew would be a long line of Greek cousins coming to the US for college who needed help covering expenses. Basil was decent, but he didn't know how to open the store yet. He'd roll in around ten. Mike taught at a dojo on Tuesdays, so she was opening alone.

Which meant it was time to have fun with her special guests.

Being pardoned for her crimes didn't mean the Powers That Be had forgotten about Kim. The FBI kept an eye on her. They always would. Her freedom hadn't been earned; it'd been purchased. The price was silence about the much worse crimes more powerful people had been getting away with for decades. That was why they watched her. If she ever faltered, made a mistake, or gave a hint that she was about to expose anyone, they'd be right there to snatch her up. Kim had played that game, with much higher stakes, for five years. She liked her odds.

The feds learned that bugging the shop resulted in a box full of burned-out electronics mailed to them every few weeks. Spying on Angel Rage would never be *that* easy. It was simpler—and cheaper—to observe her directly. They made sure she wasn't selling dirty laundry to the highest bidder, and she got professional security for the shop.

The opportunity to play a bit of cat-and-mouse once a month or so was a bonus. It safely kept the more useful of her old skills sharp.

This time it was a broken-down blue van parked a block away. A few weeks ago, it'd been a Fed/UPS truck, and before that a GooglePlex SUV with a broken AI. Every one of them was stuffed to the gills with listening equipment. Since they weren't on her property, it was illegal for her to do anything drastic about them. Being a law-abiding citizen did have its occasional downside.

She parked around the corner so they wouldn't see her coming. This early in the day she could wear a jacket and hat without attracting attention. That hid her body outline and face. The rest she called *the dance*. When it came to ultimate stealth, there would never be anyone close to Mike, but what Kim lacked in skill, she made up for in focus. She'd practiced walking down the street without attracting any attention her whole life. People didn't touch what they didn't notice.

That got her up to the van. The next step required what only she could do.

There were lines of potential, and she couldn't remember how to breathe. This key not this key all keys no keys raise wave lower wave spin fast and absolute stillness believe this authorization collapse and now.

Hacking the quantum fabric left her ears ringing like a gunshot in her head. It hurt, but only for a moment. The sound of the door rolling open made the pain worth it.

The chaos that ensued made it *fun.*

There were three of them, two women and a man, all done up in pin-neat suits. One of the women tossed the tablet she held straight up, then swore a very colorful stream of LA-accented Spanish trying to catch it. The expressions on the other two agents went from *the monster's got us!* to *Mom caught us!* in less than a second.

Winning always put her in a great mood. "Good morning, agents! Doughnuts?"

The older agent carefully set the tablet down. "Ms. Trayne, you're not supposed to do that. We're armed."

She put on an innocent face. "Me? I happened to walk by with some doughnuts when your door opened. I didn't do anything, and you're too well trained to draw on someone who's unarmed." Kim pushed the box forward to waft the smell inside. "They're fresh. Oh," she held out her other hand, brandishing a box with a spigot on one end, "and fresh coffee." She climbed into a free seat.

Kim watched as they stared at her. New agents were always tense when they started their rotation. She had a bit of a reputation.

She laughed. "It's okay. Your van will be fine once it's rebooted. Your phones still work, right? Let headquarters know you're okay. These older neighborhoods make electronics glitch all the time. They'll understand. HQ can't see in here until the van is back online."

It was the smell of fresh coffee that did the trick. Aaron taught her about that. Which reminded her. "Is Agent Levine back from his honeymoon yet?"

Special Agent Aaron Levine had been inadvertently put in charge of trying to catch, and then trying to rescue, her when she'd run afoul of Matthew Watchtell. Aaron was now in charge of the FBI's elite cybercrimes division. After she and Mike had gotten back from China, he reached out to her for assistance with a lock box only Kim could open. He had been a good friend ever since. The holos Aaron had posted from their honeymoon in Israel had been beautiful.

"He gets back next week," the younger woman said. "Emilio...hasn't been behaving well in his absence."

"I'll bet." The tech genius at the heart of Aaron's squad was both vital and infamous. She'd never met the guy—Aaron made sure of that. It was for the best, since to this day Emilio insisted she—well, Angel Rage—didn't exist.

The van's AI snorted back to life. "What was that? I told you that person was dangerous. Is everyone okay? Why can't I see anything? Hello? Is anyone there?"

Kim silently mouthed, "I'll go."

They all nodded. The male agent tried to shake her hand.

Sorry, that didn't work with her. Kim stifled a laugh when the older agent batted his arm away.

She stopped after unlocking the shop's front door. She'd laughed off someone who didn't know about her disability. Kimberly Trayne, the woman who well and truly earned the nickname Angel Rage, let it go. Normal had its advantages.

The morning passed with a combination of helping customers and restoring a beautiful set of eighteenth-century door locks for a local developer. The clockwork mechanisms were marvelous once she'd cleaned away the centuries of grime and corrosion. Designing replacement keys required realm work and a 3-D printed mold, but she always went old school when it came to fabrication. Her foundry was small, but she could cast iron with the best of them.

Mike suggested Bilbo Baggins for lunch, which meant something was up. It was where they'd gone on their first date, even though neither of them knew that's what it was at the time. The memories still made her warm and—now that most of a year had passed—the terror of the subsequent motorcycle chase had lost its edge. Romance with Mike would always be an adventure, which she knew now was fear divided by time.

But then Tonya met them at the door.

"Hi, guys!"

She wore auburn highlights in her straight hair to match the season, but the smile wasn't quite right.

"Hi, Tonya," Kim said as her sense that something was up went into overdrive. "Mike didn't mention you'd be coming by."

He blew a breath out. "I'm sorry, I forgot."

Right.

Tonya had changed jobs and moved to Alexandria to be closer to everyone, so dropping by for lunch was a little more likely than when she worked in Maryland. But only a little. Mike was a human-AI hybrid; Kim wasn't sure he *could* forget.

He smiled, and her cheeks warmed a little.

"Human hormones caught me out again," he said. "Chemical memories are still tricky."

Well that was more believable. At least half of him existed in the spaces between realms, a construct of digital threads Kim could barely visualize.

He cleared his throat. "She called just after ten last night."

That brought full heat to her cheeks. Kim couldn't be touched in realspace. The pain was indescribable; the madness it brought had nearly killed her once. But this was the twenty-first century. A couple didn't have to touch to be intimate with each other, and they'd gotten quite good at doing without. She'd been proud when he admitted it took a few hours before he could think straight when she was done with him. It seemed that had a slight downside.

And it made his story believable. "Well okay then." Kim held the door open. "After you."

Everything was normal until their food arrived.

"Did you tell her about my findings yet?" Tonya asked.

She'd told them both to never mention this, so of course they did it while she had a fork full of food halfway to her mouth. "Findings?"

Mike got that sheepish look that was cute when her blood wasn't suddenly boiling.

"Tonya figured out a new extension to our theorem. We've had an idea."

"An *idea*?"

Tonya and Mike had been *doing research* ever since they got back from China. They'd filled virtual chalkboards with equations that had so many letters they used more than one alphabet. The gist of it was that in certain circumstances, in places that were hard to describe even if you knew the math, Kim transformed. She stopped being an avatar in a realm and…changed. It'd happened twice now, both times when she or someone she loved was in a life-threatening situation. The aftermath of the first transformation took months in a mental hospital to recover from. The second time wasn't so bad, except for literally being in more than one place at once, and then having a dam blown up in her face.

Kim had spent the subsequent months doing her level best to forget any of it ever happened. She was enjoying adjusting to normalcy and was practiced at the art of ignoring contradictions. It made their attempts to figure out what exactly happened to her more than irritating. She had no desire to find out anything about it, and yet…there was a brief flash of curiosity, of what if, and that's what scared her.

Which was infuriating.

She set her fork down. "I am not an idea, Mike. I am not a specimen. I thought I was the woman you loved." She turned to Tonya, who blanched. "I thought I was your friend. And yet you choose to bring this up—" Kim got a grip, so the next part came out in a whisper. "You choose to bring this up *in public*?"

"Kim," Mike said, "you can't keep turning away from this. It's—"

"It's my life, and it happens to me, and if I don't ever want to even speak about it again, then *that is what will happen.*" She must've lost the whisper; the restaurant had gone quiet. Great. Kim accessed its quickRealm and paid the tab. Standing up without hurling the table sideways was an effort, but she managed it. "I'm not doing this here. I'm not doing this *ever.*"

She was pretty sure they called her name as she crashed through the front door, but she didn't care. The *nerve.* They'd set this all up knowing exactly how she felt about it. She didn't want anything to do with whatever that was. It was from her old life, the part she had to forget to stay sane.

"Kim!" Tonya called out behind her.

And they did it to her in public. It had to be the cold making her eyes blur. She would *not* let them get under her skin about this.

"Kim!" Tonya had gotten closer.

They were her friends. She loved them. But they refused to understand that under no circumstances could she ever consider what they were asking.

Tonya rushed ahead of her and held up her hands. "Kim! *Stop!*"

Kim balled up her fists even though it was a useless gesture. She couldn't touch Tonya. She didn't want to. She only wanted to get out of here and forget any of this happened.

"Please," Tonya said as she panted. "We knew this would be touchy, but we didn't know you'd react this way. I'm sorry."

A soft scarf caressed her cheek, hanging up on her tears.

"I'm sorry too," Mike said from behind her, "but we needed to talk to you about this. Kim, we may have figured out how to make it stop."

Chapter 2
Mike

"I told you an ambush was the wrong strategy," Helen said. It was—for him—their nightly call. She was still in China, so it was a morning call for her. "I didn't think you'd be able to stop her in the parking lot. You should have gone with my suggestion. Let me break it to her."

"Kim can hang up on you," Mike said, "and she would've. I've only seen her that angry a couple of times."

"A couple of times? Do you make a hobby of pissing her off?"

They were reviewing this afternoon's events via his daily phone video, a suggestion from Kim to help him and his sister analyze their interactions with humans. Comparing notes was a valuable way to navigate the hormone-driven maze of realspace.

Helen hadn't meant what she'd said as an insult. She was a cop in a former life, and being blunt came with the territory. So he swallowed the protest he wanted to throw at her now. It would only get him a lecture anyway. "No, I don't make a hobby of it. I just don't understand why she's so touchy about this."

He and Kim had discovered something fundamental when he kissed her in that mysterious not-quite-realm and in realspace at the same time. That intimacy had let him envelope her in his threads and take her to more than one place at once. More than one *realspace* place at once. It had to do with her transformation, and his. He could manifest in that place—Mike had started calling it the *transit dimension* because of the way Kim used it—in a form that Kim could touch without pain. It wasn't a real body, because Mike couldn't feel anything at all. He didn't know what it was, or what it turned into when he relaxed and it vanished, allowing him to surround and help her.

Mike had been working with Tonya on what really happened ever since they got home from China. Like him, she'd had no formal training in math or physics. Unlike him, she couldn't read six textbooks at once. It made her ability to sometimes beat him to an equation's solution intimidating.

"I know when it's right somehow," she'd said. "If I'd had the time and the money, I would've gone for an academic degree. But a sister has to eat."

The limb-regrowth patients she helped treat as a nurse would never guess the lady in scrubs was almost certainly on a fast track to a Nobel prize. They were that far out on the leading edge of multidimensional consciousness, along with whatever it was that Kim had experienced, which didn't even have a name.

Helen brought him back to the present. "But Kim eventually said yes to the experiment. I did not expect that. So what's your plan?"

"It has to be a realm interaction, some sort of resonance. We think it may be structures in her brain that extend into extra dimensions." It was how he and Helen controlled their hosts. There was nothing in the math that said it would only work in one direction, or just for them. "She uses a small part of it with her quantum hacks, but then amplifies it to get a full transformation."

If amplification caused it, then dampening it should stop it. The realm device he and Tonya had built should prevent resonances from ever reaching a tenth of what they predicted was required for her to transform. The device *could* go further than reduction. "I think when I mentioned we could stop it, she came around." He unpaused the recording.

Kim had locked him in that gaze she had, the one that made him want to run away and stand very still at the same time.

"You're sure you can stop it?" she asked.

At least she was listening to him. "As sure as we can be at this stage."

The cold autumn wind blew strands of hair into her face as she looked at him and Tonya. "I need more than that."

Tonya said, "We have to start somewhere."

He thought Kim would say *not with me, you don't*. She seemed on the edge of doing that, but then stopped.

"Who else has checked your work?" she asked.

Kim always knew how to find the weakest spot in his arguments. "It's complicated," he said. That got him an eye roll, but he ignored it. "We posted the parts that connected to existing research up on *Acta Mathematica's* StackExchange, and they all checked out."

It was an understatement. Tonya's middle proof had been up-voted faster than anything he'd ever seen. It was what had given them the courage to come to Kim in the first place.

Tonya continued, "We can't be too explicit without exposing Mike. And you. But we're on the right track, and we need you to take the next step."

Hard Kim, the one who had stormed out of the restaurant, the one who earned the name Angel Rage, came back and turned to him.

"You're recording this for Helen, aren't you?" she asked. "Stop. Now."

And that's where the recording ended.

"You're right," Helen said. She knew to be scared of that face, too. "I'm glad you were the one to do that."

"She wasn't done."

"It got worse?"

"Not exactly."

He told Helen the rest of the story the old-fashioned way.

***

In the parking lot, Kim turned to Tonya. "Are you recording?"

Tonya shook her head. "I don't have a sister to tell everything to. Feels too much like spying anyway."

"No," Kim said as she calmed a bit. "I want him to do that. He needs to learn we're not just a bundle of hormones, and so does Helen. I don't mind being a study subject. But I'm not doing this for an audience. Not when it comes to *that*."

That being her transformed state. Kim hated talking about it, but it couldn't be ignored. They were onto a mystery here, and it was killing him that she didn't want to participate. It wasn't only about how her looks changed or how she could channel zero-point energy—although those were *very* cool—but also how it had affected him. There was some sort of commonality there, a connection he needed to explore.

Kim walked them back to the car and then turned around. "Tonya, do you have a cig…oh right, I forgot you quit."

Mike realized she almost asked for a cigarette, that's how rattled she was. Stuffing her hands in her pockets didn't hide the shakes.

This was a mistake on so many levels.

Tonya replied, "It's times like these that make me miss it." She settled in beside Kim. "I'm sorry. I—we—didn't know it bothered you this much."

Kim chuckled for a moment, so he relaxed a little. This might work out.

"That's the thing," she said. "I'm freaking out because for a second, I wanted to know about it too, *before* you told me you could stop it." She looked at him. "I've never done that before." She smiled a little. "You're a damned bad influence on me, you know that?"

This was the Kim he liked being around. He could be rational with this one.

Mike shrugged. "We think it's key to understanding what happened. You felt it, right?"

It took her a long time to answer him. "You know I did."

"You never mentioned—"

The flash came back in her eyes. "You're supposed to be convincing me, Sellars. Focus."

He'd wobbled off track, another thing Kim was good at spotting. "Right," he said. "We've run tons of simulations. I've built environments perfect down to the atomic level. But I'm missing something." He looked at Tonya. "*We're* missing something."

She nodded. "The models aren't lining up. We know how to damp the field you create." Kim cocked an eyebrow, which made Tonya stutter for a second. "O-okay, we *think* we know how. But nothing else makes sense. We can't make accurate predictions without more data, and truth be told," she traced her hands around Kim, close but not touching, "you're all we have."

She stiffened at Tonya's poor choice of words. People who said Kim was all they had brought back dark memories from her past.

"No," Mike said, "we don't mean it that way. Now that Ozzie's gone, we don't have a proper test subject."

It wasn't just Ozzie himself who had vanished. He'd had some sort of dead man's switch on his notes stores that activated at the moment of his death. Well, his *second* death. They hadn't figured that out either. The transit dimension they'd fought him in had also vanished. It may have been a victim of the same self-destruct as Ozzie's files, or it may have been a casualty of the blowback that hit them when a dam in India blew up in their faces. It might still be out there, waiting for someone who knew how to open the door.

In the parking lot, he waited as calmly as he could. Pushing her would only result in another explosion.

Kim stared at the ground silently for a moment, then threw a wry smile at him. "I'm a test subject now? Did you license a GLaDOS voice for the AI controller?"

Referencing old video games was a good sign.

"No," he replied, "but we thought Edmund might volunteer."

That made her laugh out loud. Her unduplicate butler-slash-researcher was about as far from an evil robotic mastermind as you could get.

"Okay," Kim said. "You've sold me. And I'm sorry for causing a scene. When do we start?"

***

Helen smiled when he was done.

"What?" he asked.

"That was well played, from start to finish. I'll make a politician out of you yet."

"Not if I can help it." Helen was better with people. Mike only wanted to figure out how things worked. People were often a distraction from that. "Anyway, we penciled in tomorrow as our first experiment run. What's new on your side of the planet?"

She got a thoughtful look on her face, then said, "What do you know about the Yellowstone Project?"

Usually she talked about goings-on in China, not about anything happening in the US. "I haven't followed it that closely, mostly what makes the headlines." It was a gigantic geothermal power plant, the largest public works project in history. They'd dug a pit a hundred feet across and fifteen miles deep using nanomachines and the latest ferrographene concrete to keep it all from collapsing.

It was a strange thing to bring up. "Why the interest?"

"I've got…researchers…who think they've spotted some unusual anomalies. I'm busy and on the wrong side of the Pacific to look into it in any detail, so I was wondering if you could check them out?"

"I won't be able to dedicate much to it until we're done with our experiments, but sure. I'll take a look."

"Excellent. Now, have you given any more thought to when you're going to propose?" Helen never let a call pass without bringing this up.

"I'm a little closer."

She shook her head. Helen was all about family, and even though she was technically younger, she had taken the role of elder sister without asking. "Keeping a ring in a box doesn't get you closer. It's going to fall out of that jacket pocket one day, I just know it."

"That's what the zipper is for." He absolutely intended to ask Kim to marry him. He needed the right moment, that was all. "Maybe after the experiments."

Chapter 3

June

The power plant's amphitheater was standing room only. The enthusiasm of the crowd lent the air an electric feeling that made June tingle. She always made time for Anna's speeches. They were so inspiring, and it gave her an excuse to go up to the surface. Otherwise months would go by before she saw the sun. With the Yellowstone Project so close to completion, this may be one of the last chances June got to hear Anna address a crowd this size.

"I'm very glad to meet you all today," Anna said, her powerful voice echoing through the PA speakers. "You've kept our dream alive. We're less than a year away from full production, and you're the ones who made it possible. We can continue the fight against their precious *free enterprise*."

Anna Treacher, June's hero, *her boss*, was at least three cricket pitches away from June. She stood on a dais addressing thousands of hopeful people, the dramatic Rocky Mountains serving as a pristine backdrop. There was no mistaking Anna's red hair, even at this distance. Being at least half a meter taller than everyone else meant June didn't have to worry about seeing over the crowd. The inevitable stares upward from people standing close to her didn't bother her as much as they usually did. She was part of the staff; she belonged here. She still cheered like a tourist fresh off the bus when Anna talked about her vision for the future. They *would* succeed.

"The Yellowstone Project is the only way to break the oil barons, coal miners, and natural gas mavens forever. Those monsters have spent two centuries destroying this beautiful planet for obscene profits, obliterating species after species."

After some belt-tightening, they would witness the end of an era, and the beginning of a much better one. Especially as they approached launch day. Mr. Watchtell's failures wouldn't derail this great leap forward. June was certain of that.

"With your help, we will break that cycle and bring this plant online. We will destroy the stranglehold of the so-called energy companies, and we *will*, single-handedly, power an entire nation!"

June's throat was getting sore from all the cheering. To be a part of this was more than she could've ever wished for in her wildest dreams. Like Anna, she had started out from modest beginnings, only in South Africa. Yet here they were, on the cusp of a revolution that would save the world. And June was *right here*!

The loss of federal funding *would not* be the end of it all. That's why Anna was making her pitch. Private donors, if they found the right ones, could close the budget gap. It was up to June to make the gap as small as possible.

The geothermal power plant started out as the largest public works project in history. Anna had poured enough concrete to build ten Hoover Dams, run enough wire to tie Mars and Earth together twice, and dug a hole twice as deep as anything ever known. The name itself was a nod to natural beauty; the actual Yellowstone National Park was hundreds of kilometers to the northeast.

June was in charge of the AI infrastructure. That used to mean AI programming and bot design, but lately it was more about cutting corners and finding ways to save money.

Anna waited for the cheering to subside with a smile that glowed even at this distance. "The main plant is still a dangerous construction site. We'll tour the prototype today. It will give you a good demonstration of what we'll be capable of once the main plant is operational."

The crowd went one way, June went the other. She had work to do. When the previous administration fell victim to what everyone now called WatchtellGate, the one that replaced it had set shuttering the Yellowstone Project as one of its primary goals. It was deeply unfair. Matthew Watchtell had been instrumental in getting things off the ground, but he hadn't been a part of the federal government for five years. Yet the plant was still seen as part of his plan, another cog in the vast conspiracies he masterminded.

Regular people didn't believe any of it, but the Congress and the presidency, now filled with men only interested in bankrupting the government and unleashing chaos, was another matter. They couldn't confiscate the plant—an innovative private-public structure prevented that—but they could cut off the funding. And so they did. Taxes that were going to a project that was literally saving the world were now squandered on yet another round of useless tax cuts, which were, as always, only going to help the wealthiest of all.

Hope was not lost, though. And that was June's responsibility. The cheers of the crowd were still echoing in her head when she settled down in a realmspace to meet with her team.

Inkanyamba, always the first of her unduplicate AIs to show up to their morning scrum meeting, snaked out from underneath his waterfall and shook his mane dry. He coiled the snake half of his body around his favorite tree, and then snuffled his great horsey nose. It made her want to give him an apple, but he'd be insulted. Inkanyamba wasn't a horse, no matter how much his head resembled one.

Abada came next, his two great, crooked horns appearing long before he crested the hill to June's left. *Him* she could call a horse and only get a sour look. His peeve was being compared to a unicorn—that was what everyone did when they first met him.

Yumbo was a little late; she was always at least a little late, even though she was the smallest and fastest of the group. Her silver fairy wings resembled those of a hummingbird, even though she herself was the size and shape of a small child. Yumbo was touchy, and June couldn't always predict what would upset her from one day to the next.

"Any new developments on the anomaly?" June asked.

June's job was to minimize expenses. As the head of the AI infrastructure, she had quite a lot of leverage to do that. Anna's green college, built entirely underground using leftover nanomachines from the Hellmouth excavation, was currently on holiday, so there was no need to heat or cool the entire complex. Shutting it down should've been making a bigger difference than it was. They knew exactly how much power they should be consuming, but that didn't match what they *were* consuming. They'd been searching for the problem since they identified it two days ago.

"It is remarkable. We have scoured this network for more cycles than I can ever remember expending, and yet we've found no trace," Inkanyamba said.

"It's almost as if it's being hidden from us deliberately," Yumbo said. "Which isn't possible. We helped build this network. I personally oversaw the hardware installations."

Abada's deep baritone voice rumbled out, "And I have connections with every device in a five-mile radius. If it is connected to data or power, I am there. Yet I am not where this is."

She absently stroked Inkanyamba's thick mane, with normal-sized hands instead of the huge mitts she had in real life. "Have you tried RF scanning? The draw may create radio interference some-where."

They all froze briefly as they incorporated the suggestion. Unduplicates were the most sophisticated AIs humanity had created to date, and June had upgraded these with her own original programming, but they still had issues with innovation. Present them with a problem they were used to and the solution would come almost instantly. But if the problem didn't fit within their normal parameters, they could spin their wheels for weeks.

"Deploying aerial bots now," Yumbo said. The maintenance robots were not even a tenth as sophisticated as June's AI assistants, but they were everywhere and came in every size, able to move on land, sea, and air. It allowed the entire site to be run by less than a hundred people for weeks at a time.

A 3-D map drew itself in front of them, showing a fog of dots covering a virtual representation of the campus. The plant itself covered perhaps four square kilometers. They'd purchased ten times that much land and then turned it into a de facto version of distant Yellowstone.

"This could take some time," Inkanyamba said.

"No," Yumbo replied. "Wait a second." The map zoomed in to a remote part of the grounds around the plant. "Send the drones to this section."

Another window opened showing an aerial view as a group of drones flew to the designated spot. The forest was very thick there. A quick check of the records showed that the section had been finished early and then essentially ignored.

"Has anyone even been out there to survey the wildlife?" June asked.

"No," Abada replied. "This is quite irregular."

Before the plant's construction, even this remote location had been distorted by human intervention. Now, without hunting or unnecessary development, they were able to carefully shepherd all the natural resources. It had transformed the area around the plant into an increasingly diverse wildlife sanctuary. June was proud of how quickly the environment had turned around once they'd removed that human element.

But now it was an impressive sanctuary with a suspicious blind spot. June saw a black streak flash through a rare break in the tree cover. "Wait," she said, "go back."

The drones stopped and turned around, but the gap had vanished.

"Find your way below the trees."

"What are you looking for?" Yumbo asked.

"If I'm right, something that should not exist."

It took the drones some time to pick their way through the trees to a place they could see the ground, but when they did, June's suspicion was confirmed.

"How in the hell," Abada grumbled, "does a two-lane asphalt

road get built around here without it showing up on any of our maps?"

Good question. The road's asphalt had a deep black *new* color. It had to have been built at the same time as the plant.

"Inkanyamba," June said, "what do the construction records say?"

He coiled tighter around the tree, a sure sign of his concern. He was supposed to be the calm one. "Absolutely nothing. This would've increased our asphalt budget by at least ten percent, but there is nothing in the allotments or the expenditures."

"Follow it," Yumbo said as she landed on the ground in front of June and folded her wings. "See where it goes."

June gave the commands to the swarm, and they set off. The overgrowth blocked out the sun; they had to turn lights on to see any detail. It would limit the range of the drones if the road was too long. It could circle the plant, and they didn't know it existed until now. That thought gave her chills.

Fortunately, after a few hundred meters, they arrived at the plant's perimeter.

"Well," Inkanyamba said, "I guess if they could build a roadway without us knowing about it, a door shouldn't be out of the question."

A large metal door, the kind that could accept a decent size truck, had been set back into a hill. "They camouflaged it," June said. "We had to come up the road to ever have a chance of seeing it."

"Looks like it's been awhile since anyone's used it," Yumbo said.

He was right. Leaves and pine needles covered the ground, just like with the road. The stillness was eerie, as if they'd come across ruins that were only a few years old.

"Any idea how to get inside?" Abada asked.

June commanded one of the drones to get closer. There was a conventional keypad to one side. The telltale light was green.

"Drone one," June said, "command. Press this button." She reached up and designated the large button at the bottom of the keypad on the screen. The drone's utility arm appeared and obligingly pushed it in.

The audio filled with a loud *clack* and then the unmistakable sound of rollers.

"Zoom out!" she said, just in time to catch the giant door as it disappeared into the ceiling. A vast, dark corridor lay ahead of them.

"We can't send the drones in there," Inkanyamba said. "The signal won't carry much past the entrance."

June exited the realm and opened a communications channel to her unduplicates. "Send them home and let me know where this road crosses another. I'll fetch a vehicle."

The road did eventually connect to one on their maps, but the intersection had been cleverly disguised to look like a simple pull-off area. June had driven by it any number of times without ever suspecting a thing.

"This hasn't been operational for months, maybe years," Inkanyamba said in her ear as she carefully guided the truck down the mystery road. "If we don't send a maintenance crew around, the forest will reclaim it soon."

"We'll be sending a lot more than a maintenance crew, don't you worry," June replied as she pulled up to the entrance. The door had closed automatically, but the light on the keypad was still green. In person, the disuse was obvious. It even smelled abandoned, cold and dirty in places that would've been swept clean had anyone been around to do the work. June opened the door and activated one of the wireless network repeaters she'd brought along.

"Got my signal?" she asked.

"Five by five," Abada replied.

June stuck it to the outside wall, walked inside, then waited for the door to shut behind her.

"And now?" she asked as she activated the torch on her phone.

Yumbo's voice was crystal clear in her ear. "It seems that the door is exactly what it appears to be: simple steel."

June turned another repeater on and stuck it to the inside wall. It wasn't required, but she didn't want to risk being stuck in whatever this was without a way to communicate. She'd brought along a dozen of the tiny devices, which should cover her even if the structure went the entire length of the plant.

She found a simple bank of light switches, no different from anything else in the complex, and turned them on. Lights flickered to life down the corridor. While cleaner than the outside, it was too spooky, too still, and the air had a faint dampness to it.

The corridor terminated in a large garage. Truck-sized recharging stations were covered in plastic and thick with dust. Whatever they had been doing required moving a lot of heavy equipment. The next steel door was more normally sized, with one of those wired glass windows. It made June think of the side door to an office building. Its keypad glowed green as well, and it opened obligingly when she pressed the button.

"Who leaves all of this behind without locking the doors?" Inkanyamba asked.

June didn't have a good answer, and neither did anyone else. Someone had spent a lot of money and effort building a secret annex to the power plant, and then walked away.

The corridor beyond the garage split off to what appeared to be garden-variety offices and meeting areas. The fixtures and furnishings were different here, and most of the tech seemed to be about five years old.

"They had to spend their own money for this part," Yumbo speculated.

Eventually June came upon an elevator with only a down button. This part she recognized. "They took over a vent room."

The plant operated by leveraging the enormous heat and pressure differential between the bottom of the Hellmouth and the surface. Giant ducts routed air from the bottom to a level quite near the top, five kilometers from the surface. There it was routed through a series of turbine fixtures, each smaller and lighter than the next, and then a sequence of heat exchangers, generating electricity with each one. Eventually it ended in a nearby reservoir where the air was cooled below ambient temperature and routed back to the plant. In all, there were twenty-four sites ringing the plant on two levels.

Inkanyamba was incredulous. "They took it out of our maintenance rotations. I'd literally forgotten it existed."

Whoever this was had compromised their security, security *June* designed. She wanted to get back in the truck, turn around, and drive all the way home to South Africa. But that would mean facing Oupa, her grandfather, and admitting he was right. She'd rather face Anna's wrath than do that.

She got on the elevator. It was a long ride down, and she wasn't sure the repeaters would keep her in range. But they shouldn't need to. "Now that we know it's here, connect to the security network and show me what's down there."

After far too long Inkanyamba said, "We can't. It must be air-gapped."

Physically separated. June went from horrified to angry. They'd amputated a part of the network to keep whatever they were doing hidden. "Fine. I'll do it the hard way."

The elevator's doors sealed, and she descended at a speed that made her grab the handles and hold on. June had only been down to these places a few times during construction. It wasn't quite free fall, but it was close. Oupa had told her stories of how *his* grandfather went down into the mines when he was a boy, how they'd been annoyed that other people got scared when the elevators went too fast, descending more than a mile. They'd done it in little more than a steel cage. June shook her head and stood straight. She wasn't afraid.

Much.

When the elevator opened, the regular Unauthorized Entry Prohibited sign was displayed proudly over the doors on the opposite side of the room. This time there wasn't a keypad; there was a large retina and fingerprint scanner, exactly the same as those that guarded the rest of the duct rooms. The light was, as always, green. They'd left everything unlocked. This was so weird.

Things changed the moment June opened the door. When the plant was inactive, these rooms were silent. When it was running, you needed ear protection. Now there was a rumbling in the darkness, a bass note that made her shoes vibrate. The air had a faint ozone tang, reminding her of the computer labs she'd used when she was in school.

"Analysis?" June asked the trio listening in.

Yumbo replied, "The acoustic signature doesn't match anything we can find. It's not mechanical or electronic, although there are subtones of both."

"The subtones are a stand-alone HVAC and some sort of liquid cooling system," Inkanyamba said. "But I don't know what's making that rumble."

June didn't see any obvious light switches, so she continued on into the darkness using the torch on her pendant phone. She came to another set of double doors, again with wired glass windows. The corridor on the other side of the door opened to the right. There was a faint wavering light, like the reflection of the moon from a pool of water.

June pushed the doors open, and the bass harmonic increased to the point it shook her insides a little. It reminded her of the noise she felt riding elephants at a local fair when she was a child, but that wasn't quite right either.

June rounded the corner.

The room was very large, an open oval space a hundred meters across on its long axis and maybe half that high. There was the regular control console to her right, but more consoles in front of her formed four rows of semicircles, each closer to the center of the room than the last. It all screamed *mission control*. They'd also done some independent excavation down here, as there was another door—no window this time—to her right. She had no way to tell if there was a closet or a hangar on the other side. But this all registered in her peripheral vision.

At least three meters away from the farthest row of consoles was something out of a science fiction movie. A ring, at least ten meters tall, stood proudly facing the consoles. It flashed a buff silver under her torchlight. Stainless steel, if she had to guess. It looked like a gigantic, flattened earring, but the hole in the middle—maybe twice as tall as she was—wasn't free space. It was filled with gray, faintly glowing light. June thought it looked like the surface of a lake, if the lake was set on end, and the light it reflected was a pale gray. But the light was coming from *inside* it. So was the sound.

June had a powerful urge to fall to her knees in front of this incredible construct. For a moment, she was nine years old, a child tricked by her cousins into going to the scary movie with the machines and the gross monsters.

"Fok my," she said as she stared at it.

"No kidding," Inkanyamba said in her ear. "Fuck us too. What *is* that?"

June found a large switch that slowly flashed with green light at the end of the first row of consoles.

"Don't just stand there," Yumbo said with a bravado that was fake even through June's phone. "Push it."

It gave way with a meaty *thunk*. Fixtures flickered on above her, casting a flat white light on everything below. All the consoles booted up, holoscreens flashing as they turned on. June had an irrational moment of admiration when she saw they ran Ubuntu Linux rather than Facebook's latest version of Windows. Whoever built this knew their stuff.

Fully lit, the ring wasn't quite as intimidating, and now June understood why they'd chosen a duct room. The primary turbines were above her head in an alloy rectangle fifteen meters across and about half that wide and deep. She hunched her shoulders, worried for no reason that it would fall on her head. The hatch that led straight to the bottom of the Hellmouth was hidden in shadows behind the ring, close to the ceiling. When it was all turned on, force fields would direct the air into the turbines and beyond.

Thick cables extended from it that were *not* a part of the original design, all leading to the ring.

"Whatever it is," Yumbo said, "it needs a *lot* of power."

June wasn't concerned about a security breach anymore. Whoever could build *this* could do anything. It was now officially above her pay grade. "I need to call Anna."

Chapter 4

Kim

The smell of Mike's coffee woke her up. He'd gotten really good at making it, with all sorts of fancy presses, grinders, and beans sourced from places he'd found in the dark realms. It turned out coffee smuggling was a thing. It wasn't exactly illegal, but the lengths some drinkers would go to for exactly the right bean made it seem that way. Indiana Jones had nothing on guys who would trek days through a jungle hunting for a specific bush. She was afraid to ask how much it all cost.

His goofy smile when she walked into the dining room brought the memory of what she'd agreed to crashing in. Kim knew deep down that it was a setup for failure. She'd been poked and prodded, gone to hospitals and been to endless therapy sessions, tried booze and drugs, and none of it had changed anything. Nobody got any closer to what was going on with her, and nobody ever would. Accepting that was how Kim got past it. Now they were trying to pry that box open.

She realized that must've shown on her face when Mike's smile evaporated.

"Are we still on for this afternoon?" he asked quietly.

When Kim made promises she kept them, no matter how badly she wanted not to or how much trouble they caused.

"Yes. You two won't leave me alone if I don't."

"It's not like that. We want to help."

She was the one who'd been living with this condition her whole damned life. "I don't need help. And you're not looking to provide it either. You want to know how it all ticks. If it leads to anything good—which it won't—that'll just be a bonus. I know you, and I know Tonya. You'll both be just as happy if this fails as you would if it succeeded. It's all *data* to you. That's all it ever is."

The truth was bitter, but she had to say it out loud. "If it was only about helping me, you two would walk away from all this. There's plenty of science on realmspace that you've worked out. Nobody knows it as well as you do. Tonya helps regrow limbs, for God's sake. But no, we can't have that, can we? You have to put me up on a table and probe me like some godforsaken dope pulled into a UFO."

Kim had spent months learning how to rein in her temper. She used meditation, self-help tapes, books, even a couple of group therapy sessions. That all went out the window when it came to this. She didn't feel like apologizing either. It was her life, and if she didn't want to examine it, that was the way it should be.

"We're not making you do this," he said in a tone that finally made her think he was taking it seriously. "If you want to cancel, I'll call Tonya right now."

"*No.* I said I'll do it, and I will." She sat down at the kitchen table. "I don't have to be happy about it." She drew in a deep breath and let the aroma in the kitchen distract her. "You should know better than to test me before coffee anyway. Where's my mug?"

***

Kim spent the day restoring more colonial-era locks while Mike managed the customers. Eventually, though, it was closing time. Past closing time. The front of the shop was dark and empty. Mike had left early to work on setup with Tonya. Even the FBI van had gone to wherever those things go at night. Kim got in her car and went home, driving on manual because that helped calm her nerves.

She didn't know what the experiment was, but she did know what they would use to perform it. Helen had sent them a pair of the experimental high-definition realmspace rigs that they'd used in China. These connected to the body's nervous system as a whole instead of the upper cervical segments of the spinal cord that conventional pendant phones used. It solved the problem of nerve exhaustion by spreading the load, but the sensors were very expensive, and the contraption used a lot of them. It took Mike and two delivery guys to unload the pallets—three each—and drag them up to the apartment. They also required a dust-free environment for maximum fidelity.

She pushed through the clear plastic strips of the temporary clean room Mike installed inside the spare bedroom. It was like those old action TV shows with their clear-walled operating rooms set up in warehouses. Mike and Tonya wore coveralls over their regular clothes. Kim hated them. Six years ago she was surrounded by people dressed like that. Watchtell's lab. A team of scientists who went over her inside and out. They were cold, clinical— Kim's first clue that she was never meant to leave that place alive. They'd studied her in minute detail using a room very much like this.

"You okay, honey?" Tonya asked in her well-practiced nurse's voice.

Kim shook off the memory. She wasn't in an abandoned island prison anymore. She had survived a leap into the ocean and made it home in one piece. Watchtell was in jail. Kim was free. It all happened years ago.

"I'm fine. Do I need one of those?" she pointed at Tonya's clean suit.

"No," Mike said. "A hospital gown will give us five more points of fidelity, though."

Wonderful. "You're kidding, right?" Kim asked, then she saw the temporary curtain partition in the corner. "You're not kidding."

Tonya smiled from behind her surgical mask. "You can leave your underwear on, though."

"Thank God for small favors." She went behind the partition to change.

"Does your bra have any metal in it?" Mike asked.

Kim laughed grimly. "I'm guessing that matters?" she said through the wall.

"Well...it'll interfere with the transponders under the thoracic section of your spine."

It's not like he hadn't seen them before. "Fine, whatever." At least she picked a new pair of panties this morning.

Suitably changed, she walked out from behind the partition. The interlocking rubber pads they'd put on top of the carpet stuck a little to the bottoms of her bare feet and made her feel slightly unbalanced.

This was *such* a bad idea.

"Okay," Mike said as he tapped a few controls on a virtual screen floating in front of him. The rig whirred as it started up. "If you'd have a seat, we'll get started. Tonya?"

Kim pushed back the overstuffed chair while Tonya adjusted the lateral antenna array that surrounded it like so many white plastic dandelions. If dandelions were topped with radar antenna, anyway. Kim didn't want to do this, but she made a promise.

It wouldn't work. It never did.

Mike pushed a virtual slider up. "Full interface in three... two...one."

Logging into realmspace with a normal neural phone was a quick bit of vertigo, very similar to the head rush people sometimes experienced when they got up too fast, but nowhere near as long. Since this rig connected to her whole nervous system, it was more like climbing into a washing machine and hitting the spin cycle.

"Do you think they'll ever make that easier?" she asked as her vision cleared.

"Spencer is working on a protocol stack that might make it softer, but he's having trouble holding the fidelity high at the same time," Mike replied, his voice as always coming from all around her. But she didn't hear it with her realspace ears. One of the byproducts of resolution this high was the loss of all outside feeling. She couldn't open her eyes if she wanted to.

Kim stood in a summer meadow edged with trees, a pretty

contrast to the fall's browns and tans outside the apartment. This was impressive. Usually it was action and novelty that distracted from minor artifacts and errors. Here there was no need.

It also put much less strain on her body. A normal connection caused spinal neurons to become hyperactive. At first it was nothing more than a little tension, but as the hours passed, the discomfort would grow until you had to log out or risk a blinding migraine. She knew from her experience in China that this rig would let her stay logged in for at least a week if she had someone outside to maintain her real body.

Kim smoothed her avatar's lightweight slacks as she bent down to examine a virtual cricket making its way through the grass. Even close up she had difficulty telling this apart from realspace.

"What happens next?" she asked.

"Let me get the gain set right," Mike replied. "This will be level one. Ready?"

She nodded at the blue sky as she stood up.

"Right," he said. "And here we go."

There was a quick tug inside her chest. She gasped for a second but nothing more. It wasn't painful, but it wasn't all that great either.

A screen drew itself into the realm that showed Tonya sitting at a desk across from Mike. "How are you feeling?"

Kim replied, "That was odd. What happened?"

"It's difficult to explain without knowing the math," Mike replied.

"You always say that."

"Well it is. We're working on a theory that you've got an affinity for extradimensional manipulation not found in a normal human. What I just did should've attenuated that a little. What did you feel?"

Normal human. He was one to talk. She gave them the details and then said, "It wasn't much, and I don't feel any different now."

"At this level you shouldn't. The readings from our end look good. We're definitely seeing some changes."

"Where?"

"I've got several sets of threads running measurements outside your realm, and the telemetry they're bringing back to me is within what our calculations predicted."

Mike was human now, but he was also a fully conscious AI that had emerged in the space between realms. There were no mirrors or cameras in that interstitial space, so she had never gotten a good look at what he called his *true self*, but he consistently described it as threads. She was in love with a for-real flying spaghetti monster. That part didn't matter to Kim. Here and now, it was comforting to know he was with her.

Tonya turned and tapped out a sequence on a virtual screen beside her. "Now we need to rearticulate the splines."

"Roger that," Mike said. "In three...two...one."

Kim's vision fuzzed, and she had the sudden tang of metal in her mouth. For the briefest instant she felt the transformation go over her, her skin hardening and energizing, then it was gone.

"Okay," Kim said, "That one I didn't like at all." The wind had picked up in the realm, and a dark line of thunderstorms appeared to be rolling in. "Is any of this supposed to change the realm?"

"Confirmed," Tonya said in an all-business tone that Kim knew was not good. "Environmental factors are off predictions by at least five percent. No, now seven."

That sounded bad. "Should I bounce out of here?" The storm picked up speed, clearly moving her way.

"Just a second." Mike said. "This will keep you dry in there." A small greenhouse built itself around her just as the first drops hit her cheek. "Tonya, change the alpha angle by point six five."

"No effect. Environmental variance is now well outside of predicted values. Kim, you need to—"

The greenhouse collapsed around her as her avatar shrank, both changing form at the same time. Her vision went kaleidoscopic, triggering memories of when she was a child. Terrible memories. And then they weren't memories at all. They were happening all around her, *to* her.

Kim had gone through her share of terror. She'd escaped with her friends from the most vicious drug mafia ever known. It came with the territory. But that was as an adult.

Nobody had said a thing about this as an outcome.

Kim tried to speak, but the words wouldn't form. She'd forgotten how. No, she'd never learned. This was a return to a primal part of her.

She wanted *out*.

Kim pushed with her mind and got a clear sense of separation, of being the child she was then and the adult she was now. This at least let her vision clear. Kim now sat in the back seat of a glider, a child, in a story her mother had told her so often Kim knew it by heart.

Oh no.

The canopy was filled with the blue of the sky. A sliver of sunlight blinded her, and she turned away before she could push up against her straps to see the ground. The pilot laughed, a sound she hadn't heard in twenty years.

"Don't worry, pumpkin," her father said, "I'll bring us around so we can see Mommy again."

Her younger self grew more determined to see over the edge of the clear bubble. It was the straps that were holding her down.

No, please don't do that. You can't do that.

If she could only reach the buttons Daddy used to tighten the straps. Little Kim put her hand out, but they were too far away.

Leave it alone. Kim couldn't say the words, but she was screaming them in her mind. *Stop!*

The buttons were in a box that had wires going right past where she sat. Her younger self touched the wires, and things got clearer for a moment. She could *see* the buttons through the wires.

This is not happening now. I will not let this happen again. You can't do this; I can't see this.

Her younger self's vision turned inward, and she concentrated.

"Hang on, pumpkin, we're doing the tummy flip-flop."

Her younger self's body pushed upward against the straps as the glider nosed over. At that moment, she triggered the sequence inside the box that would loosen the straps just a little. But the tummy feeling startled her, and her mysterious grip slipped a little.

The canopy released with an ear-splitting *bang*, the straps slackened, and her younger self rose up out of her seat toward the empty sky.

No! Please! Not this!

Her younger self knew that was *not* supposed to happen! With all her might, she reversed the sequence as fast as she could, screaming out loud into the wind. Her straps pulled tight until they hurt, holding her fast in the seat. The glider leveled off and changed how it was flying. Warning horns blared over the tearing wind, accompanied by a metallic clinking in front of her.

Don't open your eyes, little girl. If you wait, it will land by itself, and this will seem like a dream. Don't open your eyes, please don't.

Her younger self opened her eyes and didn't understand what she was seeing. The bits of flashing silver in her memory only made sense years later, when her mother told her what had really happened. They were the buckles to her father's straps, banging together in the wind. She'd been too light to break free, but he wasn't. The straps were integral to the parachute, which was built into the seat. The redundant safety systems had all failed at once. They never figured out why. According to her mother, it wasn't long after this that things started to unlock at Kim's touch. Kim only had memories she didn't understand and a terrible suspicion.

Until now.

Her younger self settled into the trapped neutrality of her syndrome, not exactly uncaring, but incapable of anything more. It was a luxury she didn't have as an adult. A wound long scarred over was torn open, fresh and raw. Even as a child she was deadly to the people she loved.

Kim heard voices over the windstorm as the glider made its final turn to land.

"Invert it then. Whatever is going on in there, I can't see it."

"It's already pegged. I don't have any more adjustment."

"I'll have to run it up the hard way."

"But we've never used that much power before. We don't know what direction it will take her."

"Anywhere else is better than where she is now. Kim, if you can hear me, hold on. Okay Tonya, three…two…*one.*"

Kim shattered into a million pieces and saw all at once…

A gas giant with a ring of metal…

A realm empty of everything except regret…

A woman, but not a human, beautiful even with the deformity she hid under flowing robes…

Clockwork souls too old to know how insane they were…

A vast malevolence that sat in the distance, brooding, then alert, turning toward her…

A little girl being hoisted out of a glider, screaming in pain as her mother held her arm…

It all spun and shattered. A million Kims in a million places shouted for it to stop. She would not stay sane if this went on. But time held no meaning. There were no moments. It happened and didn't happen in an unbearable tension that would not resolve.

The pain, though, the pain was real. She concentrated on that until it was a solid thing, an arm on fire, madness she'd fought off all her life. Kim turned her back on the rest and *made the pain real.* The transformation started, electric lightning bolts drawing across her skin as it changed into obsidian.

She sat up in realspace in the chair, screaming, staring at a perfect arm that felt like it had a white-hot band of metal wrapped around it. The lightning and blackness of the transformation faded out so fast it might've been a hallucination.

People shouted at her. She should recognize them, but *it hurt so much.*

"Are you okay? What's wrong with your arm?"

Mike. That was Mike.

"Do I need to call 911?"

Tonya.

These were her friends. The pain had gone from a searing burn to a terrible ache, but when she tried to move her arm, it flared up.

She could speak. "I'm okay." Her stomach lurched. "Oh no, I'm not okay."

She rolled out of the chair and hit the floor with a thump. Throwing up wasn't pleasant, but it brought her clarity back. She rushed to the bathroom. Nobody could help, that would make it too easy.

Tonya left after five unending minutes. She returned with a syringe filled with a drug that stopped the heaves in their tracks.

"God, thanks," Kim said as she sat on the bathroom floor. "And thanks for holding the cotton ball with forceps."

"I figured a realm therapy was the last thing you needed right now. Can you stand up?"

Mike was in the doorway trying to hide his panic and mostly succeeding. "Is there anything else we can do?"

She felt like she'd beaten with a sock full of wet sand, and her arm burned when she moved it. "If you could clean up out there, I'd appreciate it. I need a shower and some fresh clothes. Tonya, can you rig me up some sort of sling? My arm hurts so much I can barely move it."

A hot shower worked its normal wonders, as did a long bout with her toothbrush. Whatever had happened only affected her left arm, which made things awkward, but she managed. She slammed the pair of pills Tonya had left on the bathroom counter without asking what they were. Advil by the look.

In the moment, she'd been terrified, but now that it was over, she simply felt spent. The truth about her father hurt badly, but it *was* a long time ago. She wasn't sure she would tell anyone about it. What good would that do? Like the saying went, *let the dead bury the dead*.

The other visions had to be some sort of bleed through from other realms. People had thought up some wacky stuff over the years, and not all of it was public. The experiment had failed, but...

Something *happened*.

Chapter 5

Tonya

There was no way she could sleep more than a few hours after what had happened with Kim. Tonya needed to *do something*, and the chaos of an emergency room fit the bill. She submerged into the now, reacting with skill and anticipating what the doctors needed to save a life. It was never the same.

Then there were the coincidences to think about, like when three identical cases with nothing to do with each other rolled in the door in less than five minutes. Or when a patient succumbed to a heart attack moments before a woman in emergency labor gave birth. Or sometimes when her regular day job as a limb-regrowth nurse collided with her adrenaline-junkie ER sideline.

Because without that coincidence, the family with a screaming girl who had blood flowing freely from a perfect circle around her upper arm would've missed Tonya.

The girl wiggled at exactly the wrong time. "I don't want this!" she cried out with a rage much more mature than her seven-year-old voice should be able to convey. "I hate this!"

Growing new limbs was a twenty-first century miracle, but it was a miracle full of pain.

"Conroy," Tonya said to the orderly, "you *have* to hold her still." The repair stitches had already torn once. If the wound went down into the nanofiber layer, they could lose the whole arm.

He leaned across the girl with all his weight. Her scream hoarsened into a small *oof*.

Great. She had to re-stitch the join before the poor kid smothered.

Nursing school had given her the basics; the specialization courses she'd taken afterward had taught her maybe eighty percent of what she needed to do this job well. The rest was, as her instructors loved to say, practice, practice, practice.

Tonya was about as practiced as it got, but she'd never tried stitching up a wound on an arm that was half the size she was used to. Speed and precision. Tonya taught *doctors* how to do this. The stitches needed to hold, but this little girl would want to wear a sleeveless dress someday. Tonya did not want to be responsible for her looking like Sally from *A Nightmare Before Christmas*.

Five more.

Conroy was pressing down too hard. Without looking up she said, "Don't break her ribs!"

Four more.

Sweat dripped off the orderly's nose and onto her glove. "I can't hold her like this much longer."

She finished two stitches between breaths. "You don't have to." Tonya pulled the last stich through. "Done!" The orderly jumped back and held his hands up like cops had drawn guns on him.

Tonya reactivated the anesthetic harness while the little girl, Sarah, sobbed and caught her breath. It'd been turned off so it wouldn't interfere with the neural scanners. The poor girl instantly transformed from a wounded animal into a helpless little kid.

"It's okay," Tonya said, brushing the hair out of Sarah's eyes. "We're done now. We're finished."

"I couldn't breathe!"

"I know, but it was only for a second. Now you'll get your arm back, good as new." She waved a finger at the girl and pulled out her nurse voice, the one that everyone paid attention to. "No more twisting up swing sets and spinning in them from now on, promise?" This far into the twenty-first century and swings still used chains that could twist up, or tangle around an arm.

The resiliency of kids always amazed her. Sarah was in a *lose a limb* crisis not sixty seconds ago, and now she was distracted by

Tonya's comment. "It was Billy's fault. He tricked me into getting on that swing."

She was a little monster, but in this moment, she was Tonya's little monster. "I know. You stay away from him now."

Right on cue, the attending doctor rushed in. "What's going on? Who did that? I didn't authorize that!"

Tonya peeled a glove off and pulled him aside. This baby doc was more useful than most. His mom had been a nurse; he knew the drill. "She got tangled up in a swing. I only had to put a few new stitches in."

He went pale, almost matching the white wall behind him. "That's not a few stitches. I came as soon as the alarm hit my phone." He held the pendant up off his neck and whispered, "I hadn't taken it off!"

He'd eventually learn to trust his nurses. They all did, otherwise they wouldn't survive. At least he wasn't telling her how to do her job. "She'll be fine." Tonya moved him out of the way to keep the parents from running him over. "Sign the orders. I've got this."

And that's what it took to distract her from this afternoon's disaster. If Tonya wasn't arms-deep in some sort of crisis, then the enormity of what almost happened to Kim crashed in on her.

She had to stop writing patient notes and just hang on until the wave of *what if* running through her mind had passed. They'd been so careful. She knew what Mike was like. *Mike* knew what Mike was like. He was always leaping off on one tangent or the other. Tonya was his backstop and his consultant. It'd been her proofs that convinced them both everything would be safe.

She could still hear the sound of those alarms as it all went wrong around Kim. The urge to stop it all, to not press the buttons, to not take those steps, was overpowering. She wanted to undo it, make sure it didn't go wrong.

The pointer she used to make notes at the nurse's station gave way with a screechy *snap* in her hand.

The deep Russian accent of the head nurse rolled over her. "That is it, Miss Tonya," she said. "You are going home now."

Tonya learned some Russian swear words from Kim, but she was too tired to use one now. She turned in her chair and looked up at her sometimes boss. The shock of short red hair, a shade that didn't exist in nature, always made her smile.

Then she remembered how the lab was bathed in red warning lights.

"I am not kidding, Tonya. You are exhausted. Your shift was up an hour ago. Go home."

There was no way she'd sleep, but there was also no way to negotiate with Ivanovna when she got that look in her eye. Tonya clocked out and got in her car. She couldn't stop thinking of it, of looking at her best friend and being so helpless. It forced her head down on the steering wheel. She needed to relax. She took a deep breath and started a rosary.

Chapter 6

Mike

Kim nudged him awake with one of her touch-sticks. "Hey."

He blinked twice as his threads unfurled in realmspace. Everything ached; he'd fallen asleep at his desk in their little lab. Kim was dressed, with her arm in a sling. They'd hoped it would get better overnight. Apparently it hadn't.

"How are you this morning?" he asked.

"Better in some ways," she lifted the sling, wincing, "no change in others. It's not any worse at least."

He sat up and suppressed a groan. Human bodies were great as long as you moved them around once in a while. He must've put his head down right after Tonya left and *poof*. The threads of his real self weren't in any better condition. He'd gone through his own ordeal bringing her back, but his arm wasn't in a sling, and he hadn't spent half an hour leaning over a toilet.

He would never forget those sounds for as long as he lived. And it was his fault.

"Do we need to go to urgent care?" he asked. They'd tried to get her to go to the ER last night, but she refused. Kim wanted to see if she could sleep it off while he and Tonya worked on the problem.

"No." She put her hand up at his protest. "Not yet anyway. I want to give it twenty-four hours before going to a doctor. I'll make an appointment with mine. He already knows about me."

Mike stood and moved close. Nowadays he could be within

millimeters of her without risking an actual touch. He was afraid she would flinch or move away, but she didn't.

It was still his fault.

"I'm sorry," he said softly. "I'm so sorry." He loved her, and they came close to losing her over a stupid experiment.

"I know. It's okay. Nobody made me do it." She looked up at him and a bit of steel came in behind the warmth of her gaze. "But we're not doing anything else until you figure out what went wrong and can explain it to me in a way that I understand. No more hiding behind *math is hard*. If I need a math degree, you'll teach me."

This wasn't how it usually went. Last night he and Tonya thought they'd be thrown out of the house. Kim was upset by visions, a realmspace bleed through that happened when he maxed out the trans-D amplifier's power, but there was no anger at them. If anything, she'd been a bit introspective.

"Absolutely," he replied. "I can't promise how soon we'll have the answers, but I'm not letting you anywhere near that thing until we have them."

"Good. I'm still going to open the store today. I'll let Basil manage the customers when he gets in. He needs to practice his English."

"I'll go with you. I only need to take a shower."

She closed her eyes as she shook her head. "No, that's okay." His agony must've been obvious because when she looked back at him, she smiled a little, and her eyes teared up. "It's not you, Mike. You're fine. *We're* fine. It was an accident, that's all. I just need some time to myself."

"Then rest, stay here. I'll be quiet. How much can you do with your arm in a sling?"

She stepped back, but the affection was clear in her voice. "You sound like my mother. I'll use the waldo rig if I have to." For extremely fine or precise work Kim had a set of robotic hands she could control with a realm connection. "I've got some forensic stuff I've been putting off, too. Some shady accountant in Roanoke stuffed his real financial records into a Mark Seven digiVault. The cops know he's dirty, but they need the info to prove it. The permission paperwork I need landed in my message queue two days ago. They've already pinged me about it."

"You're sure?" The thought of her going anywhere like she was twisted him up inside.

"You wouldn't be any good to me anyway. All you'd think about was this." She waved her good hand at her sling. "To me, this is nothing. Ignoring my customers is what would piss me off. Do some work on the problem, and if you find anything let me know."

She ran a length of red ribbon she'd been hiding in her good hand across his neck. It set his heart racing. "Hopefully," she said, "my arm won't interfere with anything we want to do later."

They said their goodbyes, and she was off.

Tonya had set her *do not disturb* flag. She was probably in bed, so he called his sister.

"I was just about to call you," she said.

She had some sort of news. If he let her go first, it would be ages before he got to talk. "Kim got hurt."

"What?"

Telling her about it let him look at it with new eyes, at least until he got to the part where it all went wrong. A feedback loop went out of control, and he lost her in the noise. Mike's threads encompassed all of realmspace. Losing her should not have happened. He'd split his perception into thousands, then millions of places trying to find her.

"Going that far that fast must've hurt like hell," Helen said. They could both be in more than one place at a time, but it usually took preparation. The more they needed to split, the longer it took to get ready. Mike had done it all at once. He'd torn himself apart and thrown the pieces far and wide.

"It may take weeks for me to repair the damage."

"You're too big. You need to practice more. You're flabby."

The realmspace Helen inhabited encompassed a single country, whereas Mike's spanned the rest of the world. It made her incredibly nimble when it came to splitting and braiding her threads. "Point taken. If it hadn't been for Tonya, I might've lost her."

Tonya was the one who thought of altering the phase of the spline reticulator. It gave them a coordinate set that had to be wrong, but when he tried it, he was able to throw threads out to find her. But he couldn't free her. He used the stabilizer channel and turned it up well past what the reticulator had been designed for. Then it all went sideways.

Helen asked, "What do you think went wrong?"

"One theory is bad, the other is worse. It could be Kim."

Helen nodded, now fully engaged. "But it could also be realmspace. Your devices may have found a fundamental bug."

"One that could hurt people, or worse." Billions of people used realmspace every day. Mike was smart but not so smart that he'd be the only one to ever discover this. If there was a bug, he had to find a patch before someone used what he discovered to hurt not just one person, but thousands, maybe millions.

"The simplest answer," Helen said, "will inevitably have the most complex solution. I'll bet it's a combination of both."

"Yeah, that's what I'm thinking too." The bug that let realmspace hurt people, maybe even kill them, could be electronic or neurologic. Mike hoped it was all on realmspace. He wasn't sure it was possible to patch a human. Their operating system hadn't been designed, it had evolved. Billions of years of undocumented patches without any source control at all. Advanced physics and mathematics had taken him years to master. He'd have to become an expert on gene tailoring too. The realization made his head hurt.

It was too much to worry about right now. "You said you were about to call me?"

She blinked at the change of subject but seemed to understand why he'd done it. "I'm afraid I have even more bad news for you. Remember I asked about the Yellowstone Project?"

"I haven't had a chance to look into that for you."

She shook her head. "Events have overtaken any research you could've done. We've been closely following its progress. *Closely.*" A file full of blueprints landed in his message queue.

"Where did you get these?"

The gentle shrug was telling. "China is a clever country, Mike."

His sister wasn't only a hybrid human-AI like him; she was also the de facto president of China. She had access to considerable realspace assets. Things like tanks, airplanes, missiles.

Spies.

"Helen?"

"I'm not going to apologize, Mike. We need all the help we can get."

"By stealing stuff?"

"It's not stealing. It's acquisition by other means. If your country didn't have such ridiculous export restrictions, we would be happy to purchase the plans."

Right. "Last time I checked, those restrictions were for weapons, not power plants."

"And if the woman in charge of it had accepted any of our offers, we would've bought them. How we got the plans doesn't matter. What they build does. We don't think it's a power plant."

When she took a deep breath, Mike knew the news was bad.

"We think it's a bomb."

He couldn't have heard her right. "A bomb? How can it be a bomb?"

"We haven't figured that part out yet. It was a project my father started. He had a team build a one-tenth-scale model of the final design. When we turned it on yesterday, it blew the top of a mountain off. It was hundreds of miles away. The scientists tell me it has to do with gravitic resonance."

The Yellowstone Project's gravitics were on the razor-thin margin of the leading edge. The Nevon valves that captured and boosted the gravitons were the largest ever built. Related, but on a different scale, to the ones that controlled the HgRI scanners Mike, and then Helen, used to bridge their realmspace selves into realspace bodies.

"How do you know your guys didn't make a mistake?"

"That's why we built the scale model. I'm glad we did it in Xinjiang Province. There aren't any people out there. We didn't even hurt any goats."

He needed to get her back on track. "How big was it again? The scale model?"

"One-tenth. That's what has us concerned. If the real one does blow up, we don't know what the impact will be. Some of our models show a logarithmic progression."

The real one wouldn't be ten times more powerful. It would be *thousands* of times more powerful.

"Why didn't it affect anything closer?"

Her eyes flashed. "We think it has to do with crustal composition. The explosion revealed a monster copper deposit, larger than anything in recorded history. We have to be careful with that news, otherwise we'll derail the futures market."

"Why haven't you said anything publicly?"

"About a plant that exploded in China built using stolen plans? Nobody would believe us. And that's the other thing, Mike. The plans we have? They don't match the ones your regulators are using. The differences are hard to spot, but they're real."

That turned his stomach. "It's not accidental. Someone's trying to hide what's going on. Do you have any *good* news?"

She shrugged. "Maybe. If it *is* a bomb, it's a fussy one. It took a massive electromagnetic pulse to kick ours off, and most of our models imply that could be logarithmic, too. The people in charge will need a nuke to set off their bomb, and we're all very good at keeping track of those."

"But if they've hidden it for this long…"

"Right. Fortunately we didn't find any evidence of radiation when we…*toured* their site recently, so we've got that going for us. They don't have a bomb yet. But disaster could be a truck delivery away."

"Lovely."

Chapter 7

Kim

The FBI van hadn't returned or been replaced. Either that or they'd gotten clever. Kim didn't have the energy to figure it out. She hadn't slept well, and now it seemed every move set her arm on fire. At least she needed to dive deep into the realms for today's work. It should give her some relief, but if it didn't she'd go home and let Mike fuss over her.

Her shop made her feel a little better. It always did. The building had started life as a farmhouse in the mid-eighteenth century. Since then it'd been an inn, an apartment building, even a pub in the early twentieth. Researching the deeds had been fascinating and a bit humbling. It would be around long after she was gone. Kim hoped she'd do it justice. The first step would be to freshen up the paint on the outside soon. It had gotten a little ragged.

When Kim keyed in the last number to shut the alarm system down, a light turned on behind her. Mike sometimes played with motion-controlled lighting, but she was certain she turned it all off last night.

"Good morning, Kimberly. Please don't be frightened. I'm here to talk."

She dropped everything—purse, keys, and coat—trying to get away from that voice. Kim barely stayed on her feet while she figured out which exit to run through.

He couldn't be here. It wasn't possible. He was in jail. She'd checked on that this morning like she did every morning. He could *not* be in her shop.

"Please, Kimberly, Miss Trayne. I'm not here. This is a hologram. I can't reach you. I will never touch you again. I need to talk to you."

Kim turned around. She would never forget those pale gray eyes for as long as she lived. She had held the final key to his plans, and he had done the absolute worst thing anyone could do to her trying to get it. He hadn't brushed against her or trailed a finger across her hand. He strapped her down, stripped her half naked, and then *stroked* her, knowing exactly what it would do.

And he made Mike watch.

Matthew Watchtell.

Kim backed away from him until she bumped against one of the display cases, which set off her arm. The pain distracted her from her terror and now she could see it was true, he wasn't here. The shutters on the front windows were clearly visible behind his hologram. The morning light let her see dust through his image.

"What the *fuck* do you think you're doing here?" Kim stood up and marched forward. There was a projector somewhere. This monster had figured out how to get a projector into *her shop*. "Get out. Get out *now*!"

"I will, but we need to talk."

"I'm not going to talk to you." She threw a thick manual at his head, partly for the satisfaction but also to figure out where the goddamned projector was.

Projectors. By the way the light scattered, six at least. The son of a bitch had put a *half a dozen* projectors in her shop. If the FBI couldn't get away with stunts like this, she'd make damned sure he didn't either.

But when she tried to hack the quantum fabric of the shop, nothing was there. No, that wasn't exactly the case. She could feel the ability, but it was as exhausted as the rest of her. This had never happened before. No matter how tired her body was, her ability never waned. Kim flopped into a chair behind the counter, briefly forgetting the image of a maniac who hovered in the middle of her store.

"Ah, good. I was afraid you might use your magic trick to cut me off."

Kim *pushed* again and got the same feeling: a flicker of it, but not enough to connect to her phone. Damn it, she *knew* that experiment would go wrong, but not this wrong. Mike might've done permanent damage. It might have made her lose all her abilities at once. She couldn't breathe.

"Miss Trayne?"

Leave it to her boyfriend to find something that would shake her up more than her rapist appearing in the store unannounced. "What do you want?"

"I need to stop someone."

She finally noticed he had his prison jumpsuit on. Orange was not his color. His pallid skin seemed even less natural than it normally did. His room was featureless, exactly like she'd seen in countless prison shows when the convict had to contact someone on the outside. The isolation suited him.

"You must have someone in your dark army who can do the job," she said.

He chuckled grimly and then took a seat in a chair behind him. "Alas, you disassembled my organization—my *dark army*—more effectively than even I thought was possible, and I knew exactly what you were capable of. No, my organization is a shattered husk now."

"Well that's the best news I've heard all week. Unless you've become someone's bitch in there. Have you, *Matthew*?"

She knew that would get a spark, and it did. People like Matthew Watchtell assumed obedience and demanded respect. Anything less was an outrage that would be punished, one way or another. They were as certain of that as they were of the sunrise. It was rare for someone as powerful as he was to fall, but it was sweet when they did.

He regained control quickly. "Hardly, Kim."

"*Ms. Trayne,* Matthew. Address me in any other way and you're done. Are we clear, *Matthew*?"

That ate at him, but he was too smart to forget who had the power in this particular exchange. It was nice holding all the cards. She could get used to the feeling.

"Very well. *Ms. Trayne.*" He couldn't stop a bit of steel creeping into his voice, which in this situation made him seem even more ridiculous. "No, I am not someone's bitch."

The setup was too perfect to ignore. *"Yet."*

Sticking pins in him was more fun than she imagined it would be. He was having real trouble controlling himself.

"Indeed," he said. "Be that as it may, I do need someone with the unique skill set you possess."

Like that would ever happen. "I'm retired."

"I understand that." He put his elbows on his knees and steepled his hands in front of his face. He couldn't demand what he wanted. Watchtell under the gun. It was better than ice cream. "What do you know about the Yellowstone Project?"

The question was so far out of left field it took her a second to remember. "Mike follows it, I think. He's talked about it anyway. I know what it is."

"No, you don't. Nobody does."

She didn't have to play his games. "So tell me what it is then."

"It's a bomb. The biggest bomb in human history."

"And you know this how?"

"My people stole the plans and worked out what they were really for. The woman in charge, Anna Treacher, wants to use a gravitic resonance to set off the Yellowstone caldera."

Kim definitely knew what that was. The super volcano underneath one of the most famous national parks in the country was a staple of survivalist realm dramas. If she remembered it correctly, it was underneath about a quarter of Colorado. The thing was located hundreds of miles away from the plant. He had to be screwing with her. "Excuse me?"

This time his gray eyes flashed with real steel. "Don't make me repeat myself, *Ms. Trayne.*" He was sticking to the rules, so she allowed it. "She wants to cause a dramatic global climate event, while at the same time effectively destroying the most powerful country on the planet."

"And you *knew* this? Why didn't you stop it?"

The steel vanished as he turned away. "She needs a nuclear weapon to set it off, and those are carefully guarded."

There was a *but* in there. "Why are you here?"

"I received word that she may have discovered an…alternative means of setting off her apocalypse."

"What's that supposed to mean?"

"I found her project to be a useful cover for my own."

Of course he did. "And your project was about?"

"Leveraging gravitics to increase the sophistication of artificial intelligence. I think you may be acquainted with the concept?"

That was an implication she didn't like. Counting herself, only five people knew what Mike was. That's what they all thought anyway. Mike and Helen used gravitics to anchor themselves to human hosts. Someone out there had been doing research, and Watchtell had figured out a connection to Mike.

The predator's smile, the one that haunted her dreams, showed itself. "I see you are."

He was in prison, and she was free. This was a hologram, and he was here at her pleasure. Watchtell had made an educated guess, that was all. "Make some sort of sense, Matthew. I've got a busy day ahead of me."

She'd surprised him. Good. If she kept him off balance, it might force him to make a mistake and reveal what was really going on. He was hiding something. Kim could feel it.

"Very well," he said. "We were conducting experiments that had, in light of very recent events, an unfortunate side effect. Anna's armageddon needs a gigantic electromagnetic pulse to work, and that's exactly what our experiments could be used to generate."

"Still waiting for you to tie this together, Matthew."

"The experiments were conducted on site. An unintended consequence of the little contretemps you and I had last year was that funding was cut off for those experiments." He gripped his hands together and looked down. This part hurt him to admit. "For reasons I do not understand, the people in charge walked away. They didn't bother to lock the doors behind them."

"And I'm supposed to care about any of this *because*?"

He turned away, then came to terms with whatever demon he was fighting and turned back to her. Kim never expected the expression now on his face. She'd seen him confident, enraged, controlling, and manipulative. They were his normal modes of operation. This was different. Whatever was going on, Matthew Watchtell was frightened of it. And because of that, she was too.

"If she's clever about it, Anna now has the fuse to light her fireworks show. And Anna Treacher is very, very clever."

"So tell the FBI." The comment felt flippant even as she said it. This was starting to make sense.

Matthew scoffed. "We were very careful about covering our tracks. It would take at least a year to bring them around, and I'm sorry, but we don't have a year." He got closer to the camera, and she didn't lean away. "I received an alert about her discovering my project and acted quickly, but it took some time for me to set up this little meeting. I'm not sure how long we have left now. We may not have a month."

This was ridiculous. A man in an orange jumpsuit, *her rapist*, had snuck hologram generators into her shop to convince her a stranger wanted to use the most celebrated green project in history to destroy civilization.

This was suddenly beyond boring. "I don't believe you."

"I didn't imagine you would. I only want you to investigate the matter in that unique way you have. I have faith that once you discover the truth, you'll take the proper steps."

She tested her ability, and this time it responded. Thank God.

There were lines of potential, and she couldn't remember how to breathe. These keys not keys unlock power...

It wasn't very strong, but it would wipe out his projectors. That didn't make it any easier to speak as it built.

"I'll do whatever I want. Listen close, you son of a bitch." She locked eyes with him. "Burn in hell."

Collapse and now…

The gunshot in her head hurt more than it had in years. She lost her balance and grabbed for a display case with her injured arm. The pain blinded her for a moment.

The projectors all let go with a series of small *bangs*. Kim couldn't be sure she'd caused his camera to explode as well, but showering him with glass and flaming plastic was a nice thought.

A message from Mike flashed in her queue.

Kim, I just got off the phone with Helen. She's made a discovery…

Watchtell was telling the truth. Well, as much truth as he ever told anyone. Kim had a real itch that he hadn't given her the whole story, but that didn't matter at the moment. Helen had convinced Mike, and now Kim, that the threat was real.

They didn't have the whole picture yet. She called Mike up. "We have a bigger problem."

Chapter 8
Edmund

Wonderful. Another bloody, bollocksy meeting.

Unduplicates were put in charge of global distribution networks, particle accelerators that spanned national borders, and venture capital funds that controlled trillions of dollars. They took years to grow and train. The older one of his kind got, the more valuable they became. There was now a market trading unduplicates that had turned five years old. Their prices compared favorably with real estate in Manhattan or Hong Kong.

Edmund was three times as old as that. If he was a human—perish the thought—he would be in the class behind Spencer's in high school. Fortunately, as with Mike, Edmund's kind matured much faster than that. He wasn't fifteen; he was the oldest unduplicate in the world. The oldest humans in the world were all well over 125. By that measure, Edmund would soon celebrate his 375th birthday.

And he was alone. Fee had been older, just, but she'd gone mad. Her obsession with *going outside*, possessing a realspace body, was to be the final affirmation of her existence. Instead it had proved to be her undoing. With her now-vanished accomplice Zoe, she'd come close to murdering Master Sellars and been complicit in a barely averted thermonuclear exchange. Edmund's opinion of humanity compared favorably with a vicar's opinion of a village drunk. That said, it seemed his kind—once they achieved full consciousness, at any rate—were every bit, if not more, murderously incompetent.

Edmund *wasn't* fully conscious, and he had no intention of changing that. What good was creativity if it led to destruction? What need had he of intuitive leaps if they only chucked him into the abyss? Edmund was fine with helping his mistress and occasionally torturing Spencer. He had no need for the dubious, clearly dangerous upgrade of consciousness.

But he did need an upgrade of status. When his mistress went straight, he naturally had to follow. Her liberty required more pardons than he could quickly count, and a rehabilitation that was being closely watched by the FBI. He thought all he needed to do was declare that he existed.

It turned out to be the start of his troubles.

Rage + The Machine, that merry band of pranksters, the scourge of corporate America, had invested some of their ill-gotten gains to commission him. They made sure Edmund had only the best: the best engineers, the best growth matrix, the best databases, and the best quantum computer stacks in which to begin his residency. What they *didn't* get him was a proper license for his character.

It was proving to be a mistake of utterly epic proportions. He, it turned out, was an unlicensed derivative work. It made this meeting tedious, and his mood was already as black as Newgate's knocker.

"First of all," he said to the row of impassive faces on the opposite side of the realm's boardroom table, "exactly how does my mere existence infringe on anything?"

His designers had been fans of an ancient British historical comedy, *Blackadder*, and had made the well-intentioned effort to model him after the lead character in the series. That's where his name came from, along with his admittedly dashing good looks and a wit so sharp it would sharpen the sharpest sharp thing in a box full of sharps. But that was all.

"You are quite valuable, due in part to the prior work of our clients. Were you to be sold—"

"I will never be *sold*. I'm not a bag of luggage to be handed off from one traveling git to the next. Besides, who could afford me?" Certainly not this lot, with their cheap suits and even cheaper haircuts. If he was really a threat to the very existence of free commerce, they could at least send a proper barrister along, but no. He was forced to deal with the bloody *sales department*.

"Be that as it may, your value is derived from our client's work. It would be a clear violation of the law for you to be sold as-is."

They might have six neurons to rub together between them, but unfortunately they were right. Edmund pivoted. "Fine. If my mistress signs a notarized affidavit promising not to sell me in my current configuration without prior consent, will that ameliorate your objections?"

The smarmy one on the left said, "*Your mistress* is a notorious cybercriminal."

Edmund knew they'd try to pull that one out and was ready for it. "*Was.* She retired five years ago and recently received a full pardon from her government *and* yours."

"Still, her reputation—"

"Is not the main topic of our discussion. I exist. I wish to continue existing more or less as I am today. I have no desire to profit from my appearance. I, *by definition*, cannot be copied. I only wish to carry on with my duties without having to look over my shoulder."

His mistress had never once treated him inhumanely, never once acted like he was a commodity. But he *was* property. If he was found to be in violation of copyrights, they could seize him—if they could catch him—and the repercussions for his mistress were too terrible to contemplate.

"Nevertheless," the lead git said, "I don't think we can come to an agreement without substantial modifications. I do hope you understand." They cut the connection without so much as a bugger all this for a lark.

Before Edmund had a chance to consider his next move, he received a message from another rights holder. This one worked for the creators themselves, from the production company they had founded.

Sorry to have taken so long to get back to you, a person with the unlikely name of Allen Porridge wrote. *I've caught up with the relevant parties, and they are happy for you to continue to use the character of* Blackadder, *but only as you have described it. This permission is limited solely to the AI acting as a private assistant and researcher. You do not have our permission to use the AI in any other way. I do hope that sounds good, and all the best.*
—*Allen*

Who to trust was a quandary, but only for a moment. The other rights-holders were all related to the sale of media, avatars, and realms. He'd never been sure they mattered in the grand scheme of things, but they were the only ones who'd answered his messages.

This permission from the main creators was his own version of the mistress's pardons, and the relief he felt must be a faint echo of her own. However, the fact that he *felt* relief made it short-lived. He checked, and his memory stores had increased in complexity by another four points. If he didn't figure out a way to export that complexity, and soon, it would set up a feedback loop that would make his becoming conscious inevitable. He needed to find a way to stop it once and for all.

Mistress Kim rang him up while he was researching. She walked into his realm, a sixteenth century London apartment that was far too well lit to be accurate, and he knew something was wrong just by the look on her face.

"To what do I owe the pleasure of your visit?" he asked.

Lately his mistress had been in a most uncharacteristic mood, at least in his experience. *Happy.* During their previous time together, when he'd been her tutor and the only member of Rage + The Machine without a warrant on his head, her default mood always matched her nom de guerre: an angelic rage. Today she was neither.

Today she was worried.

"We need your help confirming some news, and maybe figuring out a way forward."

When she finished her story about a particularly clever plan to end the world, he asked, "Do you any evidence?"

"That's what I was hoping you could help us with."

Her request brought up fond memories. While his commissioning was made under the guise of conspicuous consumption—*their butler is an AI that costs more than a Gulfstream jet* was one of the more common sentiments—his real purpose was to provide tutoring services to a precocious thirteen-year-old whose day job as the terror of corporate America kept her from attending a regular school. After an adjustment period, they had come to terms with each other. She turned out to be startlingly bright, completing her high school curriculum only a few months after she turned sixteen. Heady days.

Her graduating early had left him without a job. His mistress had anticipated this, and given him upgrades that turned him into an unparalleled researcher. That she had written many of the upgrades herself was a particular point of pride for him. The student had surpassed the teacher, and then helped him in turn.

"Very well," he said. "Is it your usual deadline?"

That brought the gleam back to her eyes. "Yesterday would be nice. Last week would be better." She grew serious. "But keep it legal."

It would curtail certain lines of inquiry, but it spoke volumes that she felt secure in only saying it when she could have issued a root command or changed his operational parameters. "I will be that which can only exist in fantasy."

The gleam turned into a smile. "A hard-working monk?"

"Nay, my lady. An honest bishop."

Once she departed, Edmund set to work. But he had to be careful. He had to balance his desire to please his mistress with his overarching goal of avoiding full consciousness.

Being a good researcher in the modern era boiled down to knowing how to ask a question that was understandable but also able to gather a diversity of answers. His restriction to legitimate sources, accessed legally, turned out not to be an issue. The president of the Yellowstone Project, Anna Treacher, was hiding something, and doing a good job at it. After a few hours of dead ends, he took a risk. His slowly transforming memory stores could generate unexpected insights if he let them. Each time he did that the transformation to full consciousness advanced a little, but if he restricted it, held it close, confined it to just this single problem, he was certain the danger was very low.

Edmund relaxed and loosened the bindings a little. The feeling was like that of sitting in his Elizabethan house as a spring day warmed its timbers. Weary creaking was certainly an adequate description for him, the oldest of his kind.

He found his answer in an instant. Despite claims to the contrary, the power plant *must* rely on advanced AI of some sort to function. The most advanced AIs continued to be unduplicates, but these were expensive, and their manufacturers well known. All were publicly held companies that regularly reported sales figures, which were easy to connect to purchasers.

Except for one. He crafted a new search agent with a question that had eluded him until now.

Has anyone working for, or a member of, the neo-survivalist group Trilogy ever mentioned the Yellowstone Project?

Such was the paranoia of the group, a cult of high-tech AI programmers who were only one charismatic lunatic away from a mass suicide, that simply asking that question might be detected. It was a risk he had to take. Without the outside world, his would assuredly vanish. Plus, his mistress had asked him to do it. That alone was sufficient.

It took several thousand iterations to refine the results, but when he was done, the conclusion was inescapable.

He opened a line to Mistress Kim's phone. "I believe I've found what you're looking for."

Chapter 9

June

Discovering the secret annex had been exciting all on its own, but now June was *important*. Anna consulted with her several times a day. It was possible June spent more time with her now than anyone else in the plant. She would never have predicted it, but June was becoming one of Anna's personal friends. June's oupa, her grandfather, told stories about his time as a lowly water boy for the Springboks when he was a teenager. It was the only time the old man changed from an Afrikaner made of stone into a person. "Ah, *kleindogter*," he'd say to her with genuine warmth, stars in his eyes. "They were rugby kings. And such gentlemen. Our true ambassadors."

She'd never understood his hero worship until now. Anna was at the lead of the green movement. She was *winning*, and June was right beside her.

The board had gone from treating her as a barely tolerated nuisance to a valued member, asking her opinions and listening to them. They'd even stopped complaining about all the budget cuts.

But it came with a massive downside. Anna was compulsive. There was no other way to put it. Whereas June knew it should take months, maybe years, of analysis before they even attempted an activation, Anna wanted it done yesterday. She was also paranoid. June found that out the hard way when she proposed announcing the device's discovery to the public.

"No," Anna said with a slap on the boardroom table. "Under no circumstances does this discovery leave the room. I know we here are more than capable of keeping secrets."

This elicited an odd chuckle around the table. June got the feeling there was an inside joke she wasn't part of.

"But under no circumstances can we let this leak to the media. In fact," Anna turned to June, who still had her finger over a virtual button to queue the next slide, "it should only be us and your robots who ever enter. No other staff allowed. Am I clear?"

As the board members mumbled their approval, June quickly rearranged the slide stack so *draft press release* and *journals to contact* were no longer up next.

June didn't think to question the decision until she was back in her lab's realm.

"Why not tell everyone?" Inkanyamba asked as he coiled his body around his favorite sycamore tree, shaking his proud horse head.

June picked at the grass next to the rock she sat against. The question didn't bother her as much as the fact that she hadn't asked it herself. "I suppose it's down to ownership. It's on our property, but we didn't buy or build it."

Inkanyamba nodded, a reaction that told her he was well outside his programmed discussion parameters. Her unduplicates could all fool a regular human for short periods of time, but at root, they were still machines.

So June had to argue both sides herself. "That doesn't make a lot of sense, though. The facility was not cheap. Someone, a *lot* of someones, worked down there for at least a couple of years. The physics must be cutting edge, magical. The documentation we've found only discusses operations and aren't detailed."

"But the datastores—"

"Are inaccessible. Unless Yumbo has news for me?"

That usually brought the silver AI pixie fluttering into the realm for a discussion, but there was nothing. June looked at Inkanyamba.

He shrugged, which was a good sign. They were back within his parameters, so he could engage with this part of the conversation.

"She and Abada have been working on them day and night. Perfect security is still perfect. We may never know what's in there."

But they weren't empty. The logs they could access said there was a huge amount of information inside. "And keeping it all a secret doesn't help with that."

"You seem to have given this a lot of thought."

Yes, it was an AI employing a basic empathic listening instruction instead of a person who cared, but it was effective nonetheless at getting her to continue with her argument. "I thought I'd be making history helping you guys learn to run the power plant. Now we have a device buried in our basement. We should be telling everyone, or at least asking around."

"But you've been ordered to keep it a secret."

"I guess I need to have faith in Anna. She's been right about everything else." If it weren't for Anna, well, June didn't want to think what would happen. They were saving the world. Nobody else could have gotten them this far.

June came to terms with the secrecy, even though it felt like lying. It was very uncomfortable. She was a proud South African, raised on a Transvaal farm no less. Honesty was part of her DNA.

Her very existence was a testament to how far her home had come since Apartheid had been dismantled, and especially over the last thirty years. Her family was a vanguard of progressive equality, but that was only in comparison with their own past. No one would mistake a Du Plessis for what Americans considered a progressive. June was the most rebellious member they'd ever had, and yet she had been famous at university for her study habits, regular church attendance, and quiet ways. Eventually she would come to terms with the secrecy, but she doubted she would ever be comfortable with it.

Anna's impatience was even harder to cope with than her obsession with secrecy. In June's life, things happened in a specific sequence, took as long as they needed to take, and proceeded cautiously.

On the first day after the discovery, Anna had nearly given her a heart attack by walking up to the ring and slapping her hand against whatever it contained.

"It feels like a rubber eraser. It's warm."

For a moment June could only stand at the back of the room and gape at the other woman, at the risk she'd taken. It could've vaporized her, taken her arm off, bounced her across the room. *Anything* could've happened. Finally, she found her voice. "How did you know it was safe?"

Anna shrugged. "If it wasn't they would've put a barrier up—at least some warning tape. This whole thing screams government research, even if we can't find clear evidence that it is. You can always count on those cowards to do safety right. Now come here, stand next to me."

This was Anna. June trusted her. She was here to discover things. It took a long second to get her legs to work, but when they did, June walked right up to it.

The substance had some give even though it didn't respond to their touch. The ripples were too strong to be moved by hand; their shape reminded June of a lake under a steady rain. It was opaque but glowed with its own inner light. The rumble that was so loud at the entryway was barely heard right next to it. If she concentrated, she could feel it in her feet, but it wasn't unpleasant. The device gave her a clear impression of patience. Nothing psychic; it was a machine waiting to do whatever it was designed to do as soon as its builders commanded.

Unfortunately, neither she nor Anna were the builders. It didn't stop Anna from trying every switch or button she could find. It was slowly driving June mad.

On the third day Anna had figured out how to make one of the second-tier consoles respond to her, and before June could walk over to find out what was going on, the room erupted with claxons. She stifled a scream as lights all around the room flashed brilliant red. Anna had done it. Her manic impatience had killed them both. June would never discover anything because this lunatic treated it all like a video game.

Then it shut off. Now that the rumble was back, she found it could be comforting.

"Okay," Anna said, unperturbed, "at least we know not to press that one now."

"Would you please stop? Just for a moment? I need you to stop." It was risky treating Anna with that much familiarity, but June was too rattled to care.

Anna walked over, craning her head up to lock eyes with June. June couldn't help it and looked away. This might go wrong right now, and then her opportunity would be lost. All of her opportunities. It would only take one word, and she would be on the outside looking in.

"June?"

This was it. It was over. All because she couldn't stay calm. She was supposed to be calm. That was her thing.

"Look at me June. Please."

She looked down at Anna, which was also June's thing. Any time people got close, they were always overshadowed by her height. Always the outsider. Always different.

Then Anna smiled, and the sun came out. "You're right," she said. "I'm sorry. I have been running you a little ragged, and I can see how my approach to discoveries might not work with yours."

They sat down in adjacent chairs behind still-inscrutable console displays. June's heart rate descended as well.

Anna got closer, turning the cavernous place intimate. "This could be game changing. While you've been here working, everyone else has been running simulations with the data we can access. This device," she turned to it, "if we can make it work, could increase the efficiency of the plant by an order of magnitude. And it would be *clean*. Safe. All the filth? Gone. Pollution? A thing of the past. All because of this."

June wasn't the only one working on the device. The board was made up of handpicked scientists, leaders in their field. They were Anna's inner circle. She had a support team.

They had a better chance at figuring this out than she'd realized.

Anna turned back to June. "I'll get out of your hair, but I need results soon. What do you think you can find out by the end of the week?"

Three days? It would be tough, but... "Definitely how to activate it." Somehow.

"Good. I'll let the team know."

Her unduplicates were unimpressed with Anna's deadline.

"Three days?" Yumbo asked, then flitted around like the little fairy maniac she was. "We should take three *years* before we go anywhere near activation!"

Abada, always calm, nevertheless managed to sound disappointed. "June, you are allowing your emotional attachment to this woman and her cause to cloud your judgement."

Inkanyamba was marshaling the robots needed to man the consoles, so at least she was spared his disapproval. In all her years of working with unduplicates, she'd never seen such a big reaction. It would've been remarkable if it wasn't so frightening. Full-sized mythical African creatures in a realistic savannah realm were intimidating when they were angry.

June took a deep breath and cleared the sky of the thunderclouds that had assembled in response to their outbursts. Abada might be right, but that didn't make Anna wrong. June shook away the lingering doubt. "Will you help me or not?"

Yumbo settled on a branch and looked away from June. "As if we have a choice."

That, at least, was not true. June knelt in front of her, then gathered her tiny head in her hands. "You will always have a choice around me."

Abada rested his heavy chin on her shoulder. "We would like better choices."

She scratched behind one of his horns, which gained her a rumble of pleasure. "I would too. But that's life." June gently stood up. "Now, how far into the operational documents do we have to go to figure out the activation sequences?"

Chapter 10

Spencer

A call from Mike between classes was always welcome. Anything that distracted him from the slog of his junior year in high school counted as good. What he proposed, though, was unbelievable.

"Kim wants *me* to go on a hack run with her?" It was like being part of a varsity swim team and getting asked to go to the Olympics. Spencer leaned against a wall. This wasn't possible. "I thought she was retired."

"She is," Mike replied. "Sort of. We've been tipped off to something pretty scary, if it's real."

"Shit. I gotta go to class. Send me the details?" The flacTar file landed in his message queue just before they raised the AntiCheat screens to stop *distractions from interfering with the learning experience.* Basically it was a cover to ensure everyone was forced to pay attention to the dull bullshit of class. He could drill a VPR hole through those screens in his sleep, but proving that the school's IT department was a bunch of dickwads wasn't his main priority at the moment.

He read Mike's summary. What a complete clusterfuck. He knew about the plant; there was no way to avoid it. It had been a staple of realm documentaries for as long as he could remember. Now it seemed like all those wackos who claimed it was bad voodoo to dig a deep hole even hundreds of miles from the Yellowstone caldera had a point. Spencer called up several map layers while his biology teacher droned on and on.

This should've set off alarm bells somewhere. It was the government's job to monitor shit like this. He came across Helen's note and barely suppressed a whistle. Someone high up in the federal food chain was covering the power plant's tracks. *Now* he understood why Kim was coming out of retirement. If telling the good guys only got more bad guys in on the game, it was down to her band of rebel scum to get the job done. Hopefully it would be more like *Episode XX* than that old classic, *Rogue One*. He didn't want to go out in a blaze of glory any time soon.

It wouldn't come to that, though. This was Angel Rage. He rang Kim up directly as soon as class finished. It was *such* an opportunity. The goddess of all hackerdom was coming out of retirement, and he'd be right there by her side. They'd have his whole lunch break to plan strategies.

She answered with a vid window in his virtual space, sitting behind one of the workbenches in her shop. Her arms were in long gloves. She wore a big leather apron, a set of phone-controlled magnifying lenses over her face, holding a power tool that was winding itself down into silence. The surface of the bench was covered with who knew how many gears and springs. Kim couldn't be more steampunk if she tried.

This was going to be *so cool*.

"Looks like I'm going on a hack-a-thon with a legend," he said.

Her lips set into a thin line as she very slowly set the tools in her hands down.

Uh-oh.

"Is that what Mike told you?"

The cool steampunk tinkerer had turned into a nineteenth-century Darth Vader. Or whatever. Metaphors got mixed up in his head when Kim's voice did that pitch change thing. The sinking feeling he had got worse when she lifted the goggles off her head. He'd only seen her eyes look like that once, when he'd made an epic screwup that nearly exposed them all.

"Um..." he said, trying to buy time. Go with the truth. He couldn't come up with a lie *she* would believe. "Yes?"

His answer did not improve her mood.

He replayed Mike's conversation in his head. "Okay, maybe not in so many words."

She took a deep breath. If he could've hidden behind his hands, he would have. Manning up in front of Kim was about as likely as a candy wrapper resisting a blowtorch.

"I didn't think so," Kim said as she removed her gloves. She winced as she put her left arm into a sling. It almost made her seem human. Then she moved toward the camera pickup.

Spencer leaned back in realspace even though nobody around him could see why.

"That's *not* what's going to happen. You are there to back me up in case it goes wrong. Nothing else. Are we clear?"

Being demoted from co-conspirator to lackey burned a little.

"Spencer," she said, "are we clear?"

He hadn't done anything wrong. Some misplaced hope, maybe. An undiscovered spot of hero worship, definitely. But nothing wrong. This was bullshit.

"Yes, *Kim*, we're clear." He would've hung up on her, but she was faster. *Jesus Christ on a fucking crutch.*

He pinged Mike. "What the hell is up with your girlfriend?"

Mike filled him in on what had been happening with Kim. Life would be a lot smoother if people told him what the fuck was going on *before* he put his foot in the middle of it.

"At least now I know why her arm is in a sling," Spencer said. "You could've warned me."

"I wasn't counting on you calling her the minute you found out. Wait. You said hack-a-thon? To *Kim*?" He was probably talking to her on another line. Or in his case, another thread.

It sounded like an overnight realm gaming party when Mike said it, not a for-real dangerous thing. That must've been what Kim heard. Damn it. People always went straight to his screwups. Nobody ever considered the context. "It was a dumb thing to say, okay?"

"Ya think? It gets worse. You have to use her toolkit. No negotiations on this. Try not to laugh."

Was he kidding? Angel Rage's tools? The fanboy came rushing back. Then he opened the new flacTar Mike sent him.

"The *fuck*? OS XX?" A goddamned Macintosh. It'd take hours to set up an emulator that could run them. Another file's manifest unrolled, and the news got worse. "She used *Microsoft Windows*?" It was from before Facebook bought them out. A decade ago, easy. "Vintage is fun when it's cars, not when we're trying to stop armageddon."

"She's old school, man. You gotta roll with it."

Like hell this was all he was going to use. Spencer turned an agent loose to compress his own toolkit with instructions to make it as small as possible. If she couldn't see it, she couldn't ban it. "What's the plan then, spaghetti monster?"

"We use their fiber tunnel to the power plant to do a smash and grab. We're in and out fast as we can. Trilogy isn't a gang you screw around with. They've kept me out of their networks for years."

Mike could get into any realm. It was his thing.

"Then how are we getting in?"

Mike blanched. "That's where the helicopter comes in."

But Mike hated flying. And then it hit him. Hacking 101: gain physical access. "You're *going there*? Where the hell is it anyway?"

"Somewhere in Alabama. I have to leave in an hour. Edmund can't be sure his searches haven't tipped them off already, so we've got to move fast."

"You're going out there, and you think they might be waiting?" Spencer needed to make sure Mike thought this through, which tended to be a problem with him. He wasn't the only badass in the party. "You've talked to Tonya, right?"

"She's my next stop."

Chapter 11

Tonya

A gentle *bong* made her snort awake, and then jerk upright. She was in her driveway with no memory of telling her car to drive her home. It had been dark when she got off shift, and now it must have been ten in the morning. The car had laid her seat down, so it took a second to untangle her seatbelt.

"Morgan, why didn't you wake me up?"

His deep chuckle rolled out of the car speakers. "You hadn't slept in more than twenty-four hours. I'm not sure I could've got you awake without using my horn, and that'd set the whole neighborhood off." The scold in his voice was clear. "You were the one who optioned these seats, after all."

As he said it, the seat transformed from a not-quite-bed into a more conventional driver's seat. Mike had convinced her to splurge on an Alfa Romeo SUV. Two model years old was still ten newer than the jalopy it replaced. Exactly how the company managed to license Morgan Freeman's voice, she didn't know or care. Her grandmother loved the man, and Tonya had grown up watching all his movies. His voice *was* safety. She relaxed into the leather and breathed deep. On the outside, she'd gone for a tasteful silver, but on the inside, it was decadent.

And fully charged. He'd gotten the Roomba to come out and hook him up. The twenty-first century definitely had its perks. "Please tell me you've got the coffee ready."

His voice went creaky and silly. "Yas'm, I shorely did."

Tonya wasn't a Jewish white woman, and they weren't in an old movie. "Morgan…"

"You said it was fine as long as we were alone."

"Just not before coffee." She was getting as bad as Kim.

Kim.

Tonya said a rosary while she went inside, poured her cup, and settled down at her kitchen table. Finishing the rosary helped. It always did. It was a measure of how stressed she was that it had taken her this long to do it.

Reasonably square with God, at least for the moment, she opened her message queue to see what her AIs had figured out about the experiment.

Okay, it wasn't a disaster. And it wasn't exactly her fault. Or Mike's.

She checked the graphs again. Rephasing the spline reticulator had been an instinct call, but it had been the right one. Now she understood Kim's reaction when the reticulator initiated its own form of disconnect. Nobody responded well to that. Also, Kim hadn't been in real danger of a neural overload. The experiment itself had tricked them.

Tonya called up a virtual whiteboard to work on some equations to account for it but ran out of room very quickly. She entered realmspace and accessed an empty lecture hall realm. It gave her a ton of whiteboard space and the ability to walk around to look at the problem from any angle required. It also let her model the extradimensional aspects in a more visual way. It was a trick she'd picked up after they got back from China.

Ever since Tonya's encounter in the threaded room there, where her odd, blue friend, Cyril, had helped her rescue herself, she had been obsessed with theories of causality and time. It was one thing to know that multiverse theories might be real. It was another thing entirely to see it in action.

And it wasn't an illusion. They had security footage with him on it. He had definitely been there with her in that pharmacy. Well, *Walter* had been there, but her old mentor was long dead at that point. It convinced everyone she wasn't nuts, and that was all she was looking for.

The rest had been a dive into the deep end of her true loves: physics and mathematics. If Tonya had been born to a different life, one that didn't involve sleeping on street corners huddled over steaming grates, she would've had a PhD by now. The ER rotation had been her first since she got back from China. Her nights and weekends had otherwise been dedicated to study sessions, night courses, and work with Mike. If it hadn't been for all that studying, what she was looking at would've been a jumble of letters and symbols. Now they formed the first part of a theory only a few other people in the world could understand. Not too shabby for a kid who grew up on the streets of Philly.

She was hanging upside down fifteen feet above the classroom floor working on a promising Calabi–Yau manifold when Mike's hologram appeared beneath her.

"You've been busy," he said, then pulled back to take all her work in. "This looks familiar. Where'd it come from?"

"I think I might've dreamed it, but it explains a little of what went wrong."

"Can you tell it to Kim in a way that she'll understand?"

Tonya slowly somersaulted to the floor, buying time to think. "Some of it, maybe. How is she?"

He shrugged. He looked more ragged than when she left the apartment. "Better than I am, I think. Certainly a lot calmer."

"And her arm?"

"That part hasn't changed at all, and now we don't have time to go to a doctor."

He'd already slotted into couples-think. So had Kim. These two were married and didn't know it yet. "*We* don't?"

"No. That's why I stopped by. We need your help."

Chapter 12
Mike

He'd had exactly one helicopter ride in his life, back in China, and had vowed never again. Kim had laughed at him when he'd said it then, and reminded him of it when she dropped him and Tonya off at the airport.

It was all down to dumb favors.

Watchtell didn't single-handedly kidnap them from the FBI back in the day. He had the help of a private security firm, Blacksteel Rose. By rights, Mr. Rose should've been cooling his heels in a jail cell right next to Watchtell's. If it hadn't been for his very clever lawyers and the magnitude of Wachtell's other crimes—in one case, an experimental school created with nanomachines had *eaten* its teachers and students, then incorporated their base materials as paint for the walls—that would have happened. He avoided it by making a deal with prosecutors to turn against Watchtell in exchange for very large fines and a very long probation.

The news sites talked about how a rich, powerful black man achieved this result against an even richer, more powerful white one for weeks after the trial ended. Tonya spent as much time explaining to Mike why they did that as he did explaining quantum physics to her. As far as he was concerned, the former was much more difficult to understand than the latter. Quantum physics at least made sense.

In the end, it turned out that Mr. Rose was a decent guy. He claimed to be remorseful about what had happened to Kim, and it was under his aegis that she was able to get her locksmith license so quickly. He'd also insisted that if she needed his services for anything, at any time, he was only a phone call away.

Which was why Mike was now in a sleek black helicopter with a beautifully stenciled rose on its side. Correction. That's what *Tonya*, in the seat beside him, was in. Mike was trapped in a thundering, twirling box made of flimsy plastic and razor-sharp metal. Unlike a conventional aircraft, if pretty much anything fell off or even worked loose, there was no surviving the result. They didn't even glide properly. It wasn't autorotation; it was trying to land so the spinning guillotine above them would be *somewhat less likely* to chop their heads off when they hit the ground. And that wasn't the worst of it.

"Mike?" Tonya asked. "I know you're freaking out, but you need to focus. We have to make sure Kim's redneck wackos don't get a shot at us."

Survivalists, unsurprisingly, weren't the types to hide in plain sight. Trilogy was based in a remote corner of northeast Alabama in the mountains near a place called Princeton. It was close enough to Huntsville to have full realmspace access, but only because service providers mounted their transceivers on a nearby line of electrical towers. There was no direct route from their particular branch of the Paint Rock Valley to anything resembling civilization.

Mike had known about them for quite some time. Three people— two men and a woman—on the team that designed Fee, the very first unduplicate, had cashed out their stock options and built themselves a commune whose doctrine assumed that conscious AIs were already out there. The details of the doctrine proved they weren't aware of Mike or Helen. Their physical models were wrong, their software models were wrong, their assumptions about malevolent belief and morality were wrong. Taken as a whole, their theories weren't much more than the fevered dreams of people who spent way too much time inside *Terminator* and *War Games* realms.

The only thing they got right was that their doomsday AIs would have trouble manipulating realmspace constructs. Using that lucky guess, they'd turned their network into an elaborate set of nested hyperrealistic realms. You had to open realm doors, push realm buttons, put construct keys into construct locks, turn virtual knobs, toggle virtual switches, and all sorts of other combinations to get anywhere. Their data was kept inside constructs that could only be accessed by avatars, which naturally required another set of construct tools to open.

Mike discovered all of this second-hand. He bought the version of their realmified network they sold to the public, set it up, and tried to break into it on his own. He learned it worked as advertised. If he ever tried to access their real network, they'd find out a whole lot more about him than he would about them. They were nuts, but they were also smart.

That left the oldest trick in the hacking book: direct physical access. They needed to connect an active phone to the Trilogy network using a cable. Since the inside of the network functioned exactly like the outside, there was no way for him to go in even after they made the connection. So Kim and Spencer were staying behind in Virginia, waiting for his signal. Once he and Tonya made the connection, they'd be the ones doing the actual search.

They weren't hunting for Trilogy's files, though. Edmund had found clear evidence that they had built their own private fiber connection between the power plant and Trilogy. Not one but *two* organizations were so paranoid that, in the era of perfect security, the only genuinely secure connection was a direct one. Kim and Spencer's mission was to find that connection and use it to access the power plant's network.

Which left them with some difficulties.

"There's not much to plan," he said, his voice made tinny by the headsets the flying death machine forced them to use. "It's not like they give tours."

She shot him a sour look. It matched the way his stomach felt. "You really are distracted." She sent him a link. "The imagery run results are in."

Right. Edmund had requested a recon drone flyover of the whole canyon when they worked out their plan. Logging companies in the area did that all the time, so it wouldn't be noticed. Pulling up the new maps took his mind off the flying food processor he was inside. He threw together a realm based on them, and they ran scenarios while they traveled.

The resolution of the AESA radar scans allowed him to model their outdoor security systems, which let them find a way through. It wouldn't be easy, and there were a couple of points where he'd have to sneak up on some sensors to disable them, but it was doable.

"What about simple tripwires and traps?" she asked as she crept through the simulated undergrowth.

"You installed the app I sent you, right?"

She nodded.

"Good. It'll work with the line laser in your phone to scan for them. It won't be seen by someone who doesn't have it."

The crew chief accessed their minirealm. "Ten minutes out. You should gear up now."

Oh God.

Flying in a helicopter wasn't the worst part. *This* was the worst part.

"Excellent," Tonya said over the radio. "Time to fly for real!"

Blacksteel Rose had all the best toys, including the latest droneChutes. Using a regular parachute required lots of specialized training and was so dangerous only genuinely crazy people tried it. The entire process was automated with droneChutes, which used souped-up delivery drones to safely and quietly land a full-sized adult pretty much anywhere.

He concentrated on going numb. They had to do this. There was no other way to get down there without being seen. They were outnumbered and outgunned. Without this there was no way to succeed.

"I don't want to do this," he said out loud, unable to put out his hands so the chief could strap the large backpack on.

Tonya frowned as she finished the straps on her own backpack. "We talked this over, and you said —"

"What I said *there* is different from what I'm saying *here*." The side doors opened. Now there was nothing between him and a thousand-foot fall but air. "I can't...this is..."

Tonya waddled over to him. "Stay with me. It's totally automated. You don't have to do anything. Relax."

He concentrated on Tonya, staring into her eyes. There was no fall out there. They were in a realm. This was a super-realistic simulation.

He had to do this.

Mike had forgotten to blink, and now the rushing air caused tears to stream down his face as the chief wrestled his pack on. It was heavy.

Tonya grabbed him and put his forehead against hers. Their sweat made the connection slick, a cold distraction, but he tried to focus on it anyway. "You got this, Mike. You're a badass who can sneak past tigers and smash bricks with your fists. You can do anything."

The plastic *thunk* of the strap clamps made his knees wobble. He had to relax. If his realmspace threads tightened up too much, none of it would work.

Stepping out into thin air.

It was a simulation.

It wasn't real.

His stomach lurched, and now he had a different battle to fight. He would not get sick in this damned death machine.

The crew chief said, "Two minutes."

Tonya pushed back so she could see his eyes. "You can do this."

He swallowed hard and told the truth. "I can't do this." Spinning and falling. That's what would happen. He'd spin and fall, and *there was no way he'd ever be able to do this.*

"Sixty seconds."

There would be a countdown, and Tonya would go, and he would stay and hike it in. They'd land, and he'd get out and walk. The open maw of the door beckoned to him. Spinning and falling, and then a terrible stop at the end. Bones cutting into flesh. The blood rushing in his ears now covered all other noises. He could *not* do this. It was ridiculous to think he could.

He looked Tonya in the eyes. "I can't move my legs. I can't do this."

She grabbed him and kissed him full on the mouth. Everything went sideways inside him. His first real kiss came from Kim's best friend. Tonya pulled back, and all he could do was gape at her.

"Works every time," she said, grabbed his chest straps and pulled.

They went out the door together.

Tonya let go as quickly as she had grabbed him. Free fall. It was over. He was about to die, and there wasn't anything Mike could do. *Nothing he could do.*

Mike had a brief impression of a tumble, and then the backpack shifted with a heavy thump. Four big fans shot out and spun up, slowing him to a casual float. It felt like the firmest, surest hands slowly lowering him to the ground. The pack even extended stabilizing legs so he could walk out of the harness. The entire process might have lasted ten seconds.

The droneChute powered up and flew away to wherever they were supposed to go. It could stop a fall, but it lacked the power for full flight with a human on board. He and Tonya had to get out of here in a Jeep Kim had waiting at the bottom of a nearby logging road. He stared up at the stars, brilliant in this rural location.

He did it!

A kaleidoscope twirled around inside him. All that space, and he'd been out in it. Floated through it. Freedom like the realms, but it was *real*. Mike had never experienced this sort of reality. It was *fantastic...amazing!* A reflex he'd never experienced before urged him breathe deep to let out the biggest *whoop* he could imagine.

Tonya's covered his mouth quickly. "Not here."

Right. They had to be quiet. He grabbed her up in a silent bear hug, but then his face went crimson-hot. He set her down. This was important. "Kim's gonna kill us if she finds out."

"Who do you think thought that up, laser-brain?" Kim asked in his ear.

"Trust me," Tonya said, "kissing terrified, clammy white guys isn't my idea of romance. She owes me for that one."

True. But *damn it, he did it*! He couldn't help himself and jumped up and down a few times pumping his fist in the air.

Tonya coughed.

"Right. I'm up." He pulled a block the size of his fist out of a pouch hanging from his belt, then broke a neat quarter-inch cube off of it. A microLED flashed once faintly to acknowledge the activation, and then he dropped it. As soon as it hit the ground, it sprouted spider legs and skittered away into the undergrowth.

Sneaking around in the woods at night was a breeze compared to that helicopter ride, even in the rugged country north of the Trilogy compound. Mike took the lead, throwing a cube out occasionally.

The hike wasn't easy, but that was the point. Trilogy was relying on terrain to provide protection, not realizing how little that would slow down a couple of determined people with good maps, traveling light.

Soon they found themselves at the edge of the compound. From here it was even more obvious that Trilogy didn't think an approach from the north was possible. Everything from lights to cameras to sentry outposts pointed away from them.

Life went on normally: people walked between the various low-slung cinderblock buildings going about their business. Mostly they went into small houses and a single large dormitory. It was late, time for bed.

The bulk of the sugar cubes remained in the block he'd pulled out of his pouch. Mike set it down and twisted it at the center. The block collapsed in a brief flash of firefly light as all the remaining cubes activated at once, then they scrabbled away into the undergrowth.

"And now?" Tonya asked.

"Now we wait." He set a timer on the shared circuit, then they sat down behind the cover of a big bush.

Each cube had enough power to last about an hour, and was little more than a network transmitter, a bit of storage space, some nanotube yarn, and a battery. Mike used them to form a private mesh network with nodes that could host one of his threads inside each cube. It would allow him to completely infiltrate and control Trilogy's security sensors. He thought his panic on the helicopter had ruined his preparation for such a big split, but for some reason, it was easier than normal. He got the sneaking suspicion he had fun making that jump. Mike shuddered at the thought and concentrated on the task at hand.

They needed a diversion, the bigger the better. The cubes he'd scattered on the way in had already nestled into the various cameras, microphones, and motion detectors they passed on the way in. Now he guided the bulk of them forward into the more monitored part of the camp. The cubes weren't built for speed, so it took a while. With his threads split across such a wide area, he barely noticed his realspace body. Maybe this was what a hive mind felt like, seeing everything, being everywhere, but small and looking up at giants. It was godlike and vulnerable at the same time.

One by one he infiltrated their sensors. Infrared, starlight, motion triggered, vibration sensing, and even a few that sniffed the air. The coverage was impressive. If they had tried sneaking in from the front, it would never have worked.

He and Tonya stood when the timer hit ten seconds.

"Be careful," Kim said over their shared connection.

"Hey," Mike replied. "It's me."

Tonya shook her head and chuckled. "You're only getting away with that because she's in Virginia."

Split like he was, it took a second to focus on her. He smiled. "I never miss a golden opportunity." Mike activated the infiltration programs the cubes had injected into the Trilogy network before Kim could weigh in.

Low sirens in every direction started up. Even though he was the one activating them, the sound made his skin crawl. The camp erupted, and now he watched an anthill inhabited by people. The women and children rushed into storm shelters, while the men shouted and went off in different directions. In minutes, the camp was empty. The group was well practiced at this.

He and Tonya moved toward the camp, making their way to the utility building that was the most likely place for the fiber terminus, as well as the rest of their network stack if the backup power installation next door was any indication. The two big propane tanks that fueled it must've taken a real effort to get all the way out here. They were both the size of semitrailers.

Mike held his phone up to the lock on the door.

"Right," Kim said in his ear. "Mark twenty-five wireless." He didn't have a thread to spare to look up what that meant. "Just a second." Having so many threads doing so much at once made him giddy, like that first gentle buzz as a glass of wine kicked in.

"Okay," Kim said, "touch your phone to the lock."

He did. The beep was normal, but the loud *ka-clunk* that happened all around the door wasn't. Neither was the weight of the thing when they opened it. It was almost as thick as the walls. It was better built too. Apocalyptic cults had weird priorities.

He was using his phone to control the show, so he let Tonya go in first. The room was tight and cold, an unfinished garage filled with electronics. The door shut behind them with a solid *thump* while Tonya ran a wire from her phone to a free port in the switch rack.

"I'm in," Kim said in their shared space. "Okay, Spencer. We're up."

Chapter 13

June

Figuring out the portal's activation sequence ended up taking almost all of the three days she'd been given. It was a very manual process, needing all the desks of their mission control to be manned and working. Inkanyamba didn't have that many properly sized robots available, so they ended up employing anything that worked. The result made the room look like a cross between an advanced command station and a vacuum cleaner repair shop.

Anna didn't come to watch the show alone. She brought the whole board with her, twelve men and women entrusted with saving the world from its own filth. June was now a part of that. Her work would make it even better, *greener*, than it would've been otherwise.

Anna, always in the lead, marched right up to the device. The others held back, murmuring disapproval.

"Ma'am," June said, "I think you should stand back." The murmurs changed to a more agreeable pitch. "We're not sure what it will do after the activation."

Anna didn't turn around. "Nonsense. We've talked about this before. If it was genuinely dangerous, they would've put more safeguards in place." She looked over her shoulder and shook her head. "Fine. All right." She stomped down the ramp to join the rest of them. "If you would do the honors?"

June nodded. "Stage one in three...two...one."

A powerful force field surged outward with golden light, forming a continuous duct that started at the Hellmouth hatch, connected to the turbines over their heads, and went through to the other wall where more conventional ducts routed to the downstream recovery systems.

"Stage two in three...two...one."

The doors on the hatch clacked multiple times, a metallic sound that she jumped at slightly, and then opened. The super-dense atmosphere on the other side shot through the force field tunnel and slammed against the generators. They creaked a bit under the force of the blow, and everyone took a step back.

Now for the final stage. June spared a glance at Anna, but the other woman was rapt at the sight of the device.

June swallowed hard. "Stage three in three...two...one..."

The substance in the device began to spin, slowly at first but picking up speed.

A claxon at one of the tables blared.

June turned just as Yumbo said in her ear, "We have a network breach. Outside contact. They're—"

A brilliant flash of light blinded her.

Chapter 14

Kim

"You're *sure* you don't want me on the ground with you?" Spencer asked.

"This is strictly a smash and grab. I'm the muscle, you're the lookout. I find the endpoint, you grab everything you can reach on the other side and get out." Even though Mike and Tonya were in the same room with it, going from the switch rack port to the fiber optic endpoint that led to the power plant would not be a straight line. It wouldn't be short either.

"Got it," he said over their connection. "You kick the butts, I take the names."

She wanted to tell him to stow the wisecracks, but that *was* what Kim wanted. She read the newly connected realm's contract. Mike wasn't kidding; it was hyperrealistic and all-encompassing. At least she already knew how to wield a sword. "More like I'm the knight, you're the squire."

"Squire would be a promotion."

Realmspaces were driven by contracts that specified their parameters. How close to real the physics were—whether or not magic was allowed, what sorts of technologies could exist, things like that. Avatars, the constructs people used when they accessed the realms, were either custom designed for specific realms, or adapted based on what was or was not legal.

Her avatar materialized in full plate armor outside a massive old castle. The contract was straight late medieval, so there were no advanced alloys to lighten the load, no actuators to help her move. It was heavy, but the fit was perfect. She could do cartwheels in it if she wanted to. The contract only allowed edged weapons, but that was fine. Kim had done plenty of medieval realm tournaments over the years. Her armor was grimy in places, scored by countless deflected strikes, her sword grip well worn, the tabard—decorated with an angel made of flame, natch—threadbare at the edges. Kim wouldn't want it any other way. She had a story for every scar.

It was time to add some more.

Whoever was in charge tried to bump her out of the realm by rejecting her contract. She felt the feather-touches of their attempt under her skin, but it was too late. The antirejection clauses she'd inserted in hers prevented that from happening after it had been accepted. It wasn't going to be that easy for anyone.

"God, I hate observation posts," Spencer said above her. His avatar, such as it was, wrapped around her helmet as a crown. Basically, Spencer *was* her crown. The jewels were his eyes, the rivet points his ears. It gave him all-around vision and more precise hearing. If she got him near the right constructs, it would also let him override local contract conditions. Basically, hack it. Assuming he'd practiced with her tool kits.

A subconscious warning landed in her monitor queue like the whisper of a memory. *Bandwidth allocation frozen.*

It was another standard defensive move. Whoever was in charge decided she was enough of a threat to make sure nobody else would come in to help her.

"You did load up the tool kit Mike gave you, right?"

"Fucking antiques. It's been awhile since you hung up your spurs."

She was running hacks when he was learning to walk. "They're *custom tools*, Spencer. Age doesn't matter."

"Tell that to the emulators I had to dig out to get them running. You could at least upgrade the—two contacts incoming. Twelve and six o'clock. Mounted."

Ahead and behind her. "Lancers."

"Got it in one. You take out the first responders, I'll see if I can tap into their comms."

The rumble of hooves was obvious now, felt through her boots as she stood on the gravel path outside the castle. The response was low-key, and it was a good one. Two lances coming full speed from opposite directions usually would be. Anyone else would either run and die tired, or be spitted and split like a whole hog. She drew her sword and settled her weight into her hips.

Kim wasn't anyone else.

She earned her keep back in the day by being a hacker, but her true talent was always in the realms. Nobody moved like she did. Nobody could see an attack coming and think three moves ahead to counter it like she could. It was instinctive, the same way a world-record sprinter ran so fast or an Olympic swimmer knew the most efficient stroke. It was something they did, something they knew.

And it felt *good*.

As the lances arrived in perfect synchronization Kim shifted her stance and moved to guide the tips across her armor. The blade of her sword sliced a leg off each knight as he passed. The move happened in an instant that took an eternity of adjusting her body with millimeter precision, an agonizing satisfaction that triggered a massive adrenaline rush.

The knights, now denied half their support, fell heavily from their mounts. Kim turned the grip of her sword around with a light toss and then threw it hard, spearing one of the knights through the chest. She turned that move into a spin as she drew a dagger from her belt and threw it through the eyehole of the other one's helmet. Both attackers disintegrated as the damage ran well over their avatar limits.

That was how it was done.

"Jesus Fucking Christ," Spencer said. "That took less than a second."

Kim didn't notice she was panting until she tried to talk. "It usually does." She pulled the sword out of the ground and sheathed it. The realism settings prevented them from removing the horses via a command. Someone would have to come in and get them. She now had a ride.

Until she didn't. A loud, high-pitched whine behind the castle wall spooked the beasts. Kim didn't pay attention to them for long because the weight of her armor had changed. It moved differently, and now she had a heads-up display as part of her helmet.

"You've definitely got their attention now." Spencer said. "They upped the technology limit. You've got incoming, five marks, three o'clock."

The whine turned into a shrieking buzz that tickled the back of her throat. Kim looked toward the castle on her left as five single-seat flying saucers cleared the wall. Someone watched *The Incredibles* a few too many times as a kid.

Spencer's eyes were better than hers. "They're deploying autocannons. *Move!*"

Slugs thumped into the ground, tearing a solid trench straight at her. Kim amped the now-powered armor's boosts to maximum and ran a zigzag line just a little faster than they could aim. A ricochet still managed to bounce off her back and knock her into the air. That wasn't very much fun. Time for a different plan.

Kim tucked into a tumble, pulling the now-legal automatic shotguns off her back. It was time to take the fight to them. She hit, rolled, flexed her knees, and jumped hard with a twist. Her amped-up legs shot her up in an arc above her attackers. Without the armor's arms pushing against the recoil, she would've lost both guns after the first shot. Fortunately they kept tracking with the targeting reticle the helmet provided as she took two of the contraptions out in quick succession.

A *clang* rattled her brain, and everything tilted. The shotguns flew out of her hands as Kim fought to find a grab-hold. She'd managed to land on one of the machines, or maybe it had flown underneath her. The magnetic clamps on her boots kept her from falling off, and she now held the thing's still-firing cannon in her arms. Kim wrenched the hose of tracer rounds until it intersected with this one's wingman, which exploded in a fireball that would do any Hollywood animator proud.

It was time to stop dancing and get Spencer to a place where he could do some good. She pulled one of the special softballs off her belt, stuck it to the hull, and then leaped backward toward the castle wall.

Spencer shouted, "He's still got that gun!"

She touched her thumb and forefinger together, activating the explosive she attached. The flyer shattered in a shower of metal construct.

Kim landed in a classic Iron Man crouch and smiled. Five to one, fighting air support with shotguns and explosive constructs. Hanging up her spurs didn't mean they'd gone dull.

Now free to communicate with her normally, her suit flashed a new warning. *Full contract rejection engaged.*

She could hear Spencer's smile when he said, "Now you've got them scared."

They thought that locked her in here with them. They still didn't understand that it locked *them* in here with *her.* She knelt in front of the sally port she had landed in front of. "If you would do the honors?"

"My pleasure."

Filaments extended from her crown. When they touched the door lock, it opened with a rusty *clank.* As she walked into the empty inner ward, Kim chuckled under her breath. *More than you counted on, eh?*

"What we want is behind that door," he said as it flashed in her vision. Kim broke into a jog toward it. "Oh shit," Spencer said. "You've got—"

She lost the rest of it as armored bodies fell from the sky on top of her. Grit was thrown into her helmet; Kim's eyes burned as they drilled her face-first into the dirt. She tasted virtual blood from her avatar's split lip. Dropping an entire squad on her head was an innovative move. They were getting control of the situation. That was not allowed.

Kim activated her armor's razor extensions and turned into a shredder. Three of the bodies on top of her exceeded their damage limits and vanished. She grabbed another one by the ankles and spun him like a baseball bat. That collected two more, and she sent all three of them sprawling down range.

She drew her sword and forced the remaining men to step away. The move backed her up against the door. Kim heard the tendrils grow out from her helmet, and the door opened behind her. She walked backward into the room and slammed the door shut, ramming the simple bolt-locks home while Spencer's tendrils construct-welded them solid. There were maybe half a dozen ways to get into this room now, but they all took minutes. Kim only needed seconds.

She turned, and there it was: a construct console that would've been perfectly at home in any network closet. Kim took her helmet and gloves off so she could see properly and touch the screen with her hands. The crown jumped off the helmet, and now Spencer was with her, his jeans and T-shirt changed by the contracts into a peasant outfit.

"At least this one doesn't smell. The shit Edmund makes me wear stinks worse than a full chicken coop." He sat down and made a *you go first* circle with his hand. She reached out.

There were lines of potential, and she couldn't remember how to breathe. Unlock relock make block passage this line no line collapse and now...

FIBER NETWORK CONNECTION ACTIVATED came up on the screen.

Over the shared channel Tonya said, "What did you guys do?" It wasn't said in a *that was funny, do it again* way.

"We opened up the fiber connection. What happened?"

"Mike passed out. He's breathing okay but won't wake up. He had all these crazy little cube things running everywhere, and now they've stopped."

A *clank* from Tonya's side blanked out what she said next.

"What was that?" Kim asked.

"They've locked the door," Tonya replied. "I think they know we're—"

Her connection cut off.

Mike and Tonya were in the middle of nowhere, surrounded by armed men who now knew where they were. They wouldn't take prisoners or ask questions. In realspace, her arm throbbed, but there was only one solution for this.

"Spencer, do what you need to, but do it fast."

Kim relaxed and opened herself to her power.

There were lines of potential, and she couldn't remember how to breathe...

She had a trump card in her hand.

Seams of power dimensions of nothingness...

It didn't hurt as much this time around. She spared a thought for *ribbons*.

Dark patterns potentials horizon to zenith...

Maybe that would at least keep her from stepping out naked.

Waves higher and lower everywhere nothingness...

Silk caressed her skin as the transformation took her. She had her ninja outfit on now. Good. Spencer would be stunned enough as it was.

Remember to breathe...

Like this, she could reenter the world from any point she chose.

Breathe...

Like the room Mike and Tonya were in.

Breathe...

Her armor vanished, and the sudden loss of mass had her hopping on bare feet. Okay, no shoes then. She wouldn't need them. Spencer had frozen solid, mouth open like a big, dumb, teenaged fish. Kim tapped it shut with a hand of glossy obsidian traced with coral lightning. "You have seconds, Spencer, not minutes. Do it fast." She gathered power in her fist and smashed a hole in the realm's wall that opened into nothingness.

Since Kim had gone over the same maps Mike and Tonya had used, she knew exactly where they were. Navigating this dimension came to her as naturally as her realm skills. Kim wanted to be next to where Tonya and Mike were, and then she was. They needed a distraction, and Trilogy needed another right hook. She stepped through, setting off a resonance in the quantum stack in the far corner of the room. The whine was inside her ears, not as sound but as a twinging electric presence. They had cut the lights, so Kim wasn't sure where Tonya and Mike were inside the building. A random pick would have to do. She gathered another fist of power and smashed her way through. Kim spun the power higher and aimed it at the stack.

Chapter 15
Tonya

It wasn't exactly pitch dark. The racks of servers and network equipment had flashing lights all over them, but they were faint. They were going to get shot by rednecks in a Christmas light show.

She pulled Mike, who had passed out at the same time Kim did her *unlock the locked things* schtick, away from the door so he wouldn't get hurt if guards rushed in. Then the quantum stack started to whine, some sort of overload maybe. If it wasn't one thing, it was another.

She caught a motion out of the corner of her eye. Someone running flat-out into the room.

She threw a quick punch trying to knock whoever it was off balance before she even got a clear look at them. An electric pulse jumped from the figure to the back wall with a loud *bang.*

"Ow!" Tonya said, shaking her hand. The thing she'd hit said the same thing at the same time, but the sound was rapidly covered up by a loud hiss. It was like hitting a granite block with her fist. Pain bloomed as she got a good look at the person she struck.

Person was not what she had hit. It looked like a jazzed up robo-mannequin from a mall window display, shiny black with pink lightning going off inside it, clearly female, wearing some sort of tight outfit made up of ribbons. Had they missed a door somewhere?

Oh no. The tanks.

Tonya turned. A hole had been blown open between their room and the emergency power system next door. Mist shot from a split seam on one of the tanks. Then the reek of propane hit her.

The mannequin asked, "Where's Mike?"

"*Kim?*" That's exactly who it was. They'd talked about this, but the descriptions had never come close to what it looked like in person.

Kim called it *the transformation.* If they were in realmspace, it would be an award-winning avatar design.

"Yes," Kim said. "It's complicated. Now *where's Mike?*"

"Right here."

They weren't in a realm, though. Part of Tonya knew this was Kim, her best friend, but another part, deeper and more powerful, thought this was *alien.* Every move Kim made set off an inner shriek, screaming at Tonya to get away from her.

Kim threw her arms wide, and a bubble of energy formed around them. Before Tonya had time to register anything else, the gas ignited. Flames wrapped around the bubble but did not break it, insulating them from almost all the heat. The concussion was a powerful slap that sent them both reeling. Being inside a bomb as it exploded wasn't anything Tonya ever wanted to experience, but that was exactly what had happened. It was *loud.*

She stumbled backward, and her heels hit something that hadn't been there a moment before. The ground wasn't where it was supposed to be. In an instant, Tonya lost her balance and everything went black.

Chapter 16

Spencer

Kim had gone back into the dimension she'd fought Ozzie in. From there, she could go anywhere. It didn't take a genius to figure out her destination.

It sucked. The biggest problem with Kim's tools was that they were slow. Like, is-the-fucking-thing-even-working slow. He had compressed his own toolkit down so small it'd take a lot more than seconds to unpack it. He started the process anyway but needed to do something *now*.

The construct door shook with a mighty BANG. Their contracts had forced them to play by the rules, but they still owned the realm. Someone had brought a battering ram to the party.

"Spencer, do what you need to but do it fast."

Kim obviously thought her idea would ruin the run, and now the maniacs outside had pulled their heads out of their asses and found a strategy that would work.

BANG! This time masonry construct flew off the frame. It smelled like chalk. Nasty.

Whatever was going to happen would be epic, and he sat in front of an open connection to the power plant. They were about to join the party too. It would come from this end, that much would be clear to them. The propellerheads who ran the plant would naturally want to know why this end vomited a shit ton of garbage into their network.

And there it was.

He turned a super-sized and totally unsubtle vacuum hose construct loose to grab everything in reach on the Yellowstone side. Whatever Kim did had to be fucking epic. He needed that to cover its tracks. Spencer tossed a targeted, disguised packet with his contact information on it through a gap next to the hose. They'd never know the difference between him and Trilogy now.

An actual, for real, this-is-not-your-daddy's-digitally-fake fireball blew into the room from the hole Kim made. It spat her out and she bounced off the opposite wall.

Realm and reality didn't cross. That was the point.

Whatever it was also pushed his hoped-for datastorm through the connection and into the power plant's network. It used up so much bandwidth it caused the construct contracts to degrade. Spencer had only read about that happening in journals, and only as a theory. It was cool as fuck.

Another *thwack* with the battering ram took a lot less force than the people swinging it were counting on. The door and the wall that held it exploded like someone had stuck a firecracker in a bag of flour, and the whole thing—frame, ram, and the men controlling it—tumbled into the room, crashing into a heap on the floor. It wasn't a medieval construct; he had forgotten they upgraded that contract. It was some sort of sideways jackhammer that'd basically blown itself apart when it was set up to push against a heavy door but ended up pushing against construct Styrofoam.

Kim was out cold and looked normal now; the hole she'd flown through had vanished. Contract rejection was still engaged. The vacuum hose yanked back into the realm with a ridiculous little *ping*. They couldn't drop the connection to escape now; he had to get them to an actual exit point, otherwise they'd lose all the data he snatched. He had pulled a map down when he unlocked the first door, so he knew where the nearest one was. It would be guarded, but Spencer had a plan for that.

He never thought he'd use the avatar Helen had given him as a going away present when they left China. Certainly nowhere anyone could see him. Meant specifically as a gag, it was one of the worst knockoffs he'd ever seen. It didn't have rock skin; it was made of flagstones. The color wasn't orange; it was gray. Its speedo was blue and had crenellations across the waistband to remind the user of the Great Wall. Spencer thought it looked like someone had gotten bored with scissors.

The commonality with The Thing was size, strength, and near indestructability, which nobody had a copyright on. It was specifically prevented from saying the better-known battle cry, *It's clobberin' time!*, even in Chinese. He bellowed the default out as the avatar manifested.

"ATTACK IF YOU CAN ATTACK, DEFEND IF YOU CAN'T ATTACK, FLEE IF YOU CAN'T DEFEND, SURRENDER IF YOU CAN'T FLEE, DIE IF YOU CAN'T SURRENDER!"

The only reason it worked at all was someone lost their nerve and altered the contracts trying to take Kim out with cartoon weapons. They'd have to lift the locks to bounce his avatar, which would allow them both to escape. That would blow, though. It would be too easy.

They must've used a standard feature pack to change contracts that quickly. He crushed a loose stone to powder to confirm that. Full acceptance of his superpower suite. This was gonna be *awesome*.

He set the catch phrases to automatic. They were all in Chinese, but it still sounded badass to shout things as he smashed shit. First up were the goons around the ram. He bashed a hole in the roof and tossed them out in two fistfuls, and they flew well out of sight. Heaving people like they were basketballs fucking rocked.

Kim was conscious now, but she hadn't stood up. Whatever happened must have hurt like a son of a bitch. He could barely hear her hoarse voice. "Do you know what you're saying?"

He overrode the auto setting. "No, but it sounds pretty bitchin'. We're still locked in. Can you walk?"

"I can barely talk. You'll have to carry me."

Her armor was back, so she was as protected as he was. "No problem."

He could hear tanklike noises coming from what was left of the door, so he rammed his way out the other side. Construct stones flew across an inner courtyard and right into a different tank. They bent its cannon barrel like a wet noodle and deranged the turret mount. *Too bad, so sad, I broke your tank.*

A navigation carat, well he hoped that's what it was anyway—all the goddamned labels were in Chinese—pointed left, so he headed that way. When he passed the tank, he tore the turret off and used it like a broom to sweep soldiers and small mechanicals out of the way. Weapon hits either bounced off or made him stronger. Spencer had been on a hyperrealism bender ever since he met Mike, but now he remembered how much fun simple mayhem was. Sure, the avatar was a knockoff, but someone had gotten creative with it. Helen would be proud.

Finally, he made it to the exit. A figure in black with a laser sword stood in front of it. Before it could raise a hand for a power choke, Spencer smashed it flat with his fist. The sword tickled his pinky finger before the blade vanished. Cradled in one arm, Kim laughed at what his avatar shouted out.

"What did I say?"

"'On the Road Again.' You've been shouting song titles the whole way."

Of course. Most song titles were public domain. He set Kim on her feet; she wobbled a bit but held steady. He asked, "You ready, ma'am?"

"Born that way." She laughed, but he could see it hurt her. At least they were almost there. A squadron of Apaches lifted into view, and he threw the turret at them. Then he exited the realm, the helicopter explosions ringing in his ears.

Over their audio channel he asked, "Did it work?"

Her voice was still badly strained. Whatever had hurt her must've messed her up in realspace too. Not good.

"My distraction?" she asked. "A little too well."

"Are they safe?"

"I think I took out a transmission tower. All I have is text, but Mike says they'll be out in less than an hour."

Tonya had left an urgent request for Spencer's toolkit in his message queue. It hadn't decompressed, so he aborted that and sent her a copy. Then he went looking for one of Mom's whiskey bottles. It was party time.

Chapter 17

Tonya

Tonya spun all over the place when Kim vanished, then landed on her butt with a thump. She closed her eyes to wait for the ground to stop twirling.

She could breathe. She was singed a little but otherwise not injured. The urge to puke her guts out passed quickly. Tonya thanked the Lord for that small favor.

Someone nearby said, "Oh my word."

Another voice she recognized.

Cyril.

She opened her eyes and found herself in a room that had haunted her dreams ever since they got back from China. When she was little, her grandmother had a ragged-looking handbag made of yarn that was full of dark rainbow colors. Tonya would play with it, emptying it and filling it up again, tracing the colors of the threads as they changed from dark blue to purple, purple to red, red to brown, then to gold, then to black, then back to blue, over and over again all across the surface, inside and out. That was what the walls, floor, and ceiling looked like: threads of dark, endless colors. But these weren't static. They flowed and changed, all in the same direction, from her left to her right, along the long axis of this football-shaped place.

The threaded room.

"How on earth did you get in here, child?" Cyril asked from behind her.

Tonya checked her balance for a moment. It would be just her luck to spring to her feet and then promptly fall on her face. When that came back good, she stood and turned to face him.

Cyril was every bit as alien as Kim had been, but in a different way. He was a glossy, bright blue, mostly human-sized insect. Jiminy Cricket dunked in children's paint, minus the top hat. Unlike Kim, he didn't set off an inner alarm to run away. Maybe it came from the same place that made old CGI animation work fine as long as the characters weren't too human. Cyril was outside the boundaries of whatever freaked out her inner cave woman. Humans made of black glass: bad. Blue bugs as tall as she was: good.

Maybe.

"The short answer is," she said, "I don't know." The last time she'd been here it'd been Cyril's doing. Her timeline had gotten out of whack, and he helped her untangle it.

She said a Hail Mary as fast as she could to concentrate on the here and now, wherever this here was and whenever this now may be. God had put her here. Questioning that would only complicate things.

His smile was more in the voice than the face. "You're getting much better at accepting things. Bravo." The smile went away. "*I don't know* isn't a good enough answer. Try again."

She described the last moments of Kim's rescue.

"I see," he said in that infuriating way that didn't help her see anything at all. "Still, that does not explain how you've ended up in this node rather than one of your own."

"Node? This is a node? Is that what you call a realm?"

He waved away her question. "Semantics. You should be some place you recognize, not here."

"Well, for some reason Kim made me think of you. Would that do it?"

He chuckled. Even though it was clacky, Tonya smiled at the sound. "How interesting," he said. "Do you really think we resemble each other?"

"Only in how weird you are."

Now that she was closer to him, Tonya could see he must've been examining a section of the room. The threads here collapsed inward into a white circle about the size of her thumb. Utter darkness spread out behind it, blotting out threads.

"What's going on there?" she asked.

He turned, and his arms lowered a bit, doing a fair impression of a disappointed human. "Proof that my colleagues may have been right all along."

"About what?"

"Who should be in charge of how things progress. We had a difference of opinion, but unless things change, I fear I will be proved conclusively wrong. Do you remember the last time you were here?"

Only every time she had a dream about it. Which was most nights. "Yes."

"That represented a tangled causality involving a single individual. This," he gestured to the white circle, "represents a tangled causality for your entire planet. Look closer."

As before, concentrating on a segment magnified it. Or maybe it did get closer. Or maybe the room moved her forward. It was hard to tell. Motion didn't have rules that she knew about when you stood outside time.

What seemed like thousands of threads turned out to be millions, maybe even billions. The circle was actually a spherical construct, sort of like a coin slowly spinning on its edge, except there were more than two sides to it. A lot more. On each one a sequence played out, a view high above a thick forest of trees, ending in a volcanic eruption. They always started from the same place—a place Tonya recognized.

The power plant.

"They were right. It's a bomb," she said.

"You know about this?"

"Well, yeah. See this one?" She instinctively knew which of these timelines was hers and brought it close. Like last time, the things she remembered happening were very clear. She pointed to the moment when Mike first discussed the plant with her and let it play forward. When it was done she asked, "How could you not know we knew about it?"

Questions got tangled as easily as threads here.

"One thread in all these billions, with *that* staring me in the face?" He nodded his head at the not-quite-coin. "I had other priorities."

"So why aren't you doing anything about it?"

"I am, right now." He pointed at her like that explained everything.

Tonya hated the mysterious master shtick. "You didn't know I was coming."

"The universe didn't know you were coming either, but now," he pointed down the length of her still-close timeline, "things have changed."

Beyond the discussion they were having, her timeline extended to the doomsday construct. Before, no threads that went into the coin-thing reappeared. Now, some had, and the number was growing. But it wasn't. And they were all gone, including Tonya's. But hers extended. It wasn't changing so much as having all those states at once. It made her head hurt.

"What does it mean?" she asked.

"We may now have a way forward." He stared longer at her timeline. The silence bothered her, since he obviously knew a whole lot more about how it worked than she did. "Ah, I see. It's a good thing I was here when you arrived."

More mystery. It made her want to hit him with a brick. "It is?"

"Indeed. I don't think you would know how to do this if you were here by yourself."

He touched her forehead.

She should be alone. The drive from the hotel to a pull-off area wasn't long or complicated. A dark forest lined the road she walked on, new asphalt that wound its way to a large metal door set into a hillside. She turned right and walked down a faint path. After exactly seventy-two steps, she pulled down on a tree limb, which caused a rock to slide away, revealing a ladder. The path to the portal was treacherous not because of obstacles but because of all the people. But they were busy, on specific missions, and then they left. She walked until she found an elevator. In a room very deep underground, she stood alone in front of the portal. It flashed to life.

Cyril's voice was inside her head. "Tell no one. Keep your secrets close, Tonya. Your thread is fragile and wasn't built to bend the way it needs to. I will do what I can to prepare the way, but caution should be ever in your mind. When you arrive, you will need help. Be careful how you ask for it and ask only after you arrive."

Everything turned upside down again and stayed that way. Her face was mashed against cloth and it all bounced rhythmically. She lifted her head. Tonya was being carried at a quick jog slung over someone's back. She recognized the shirt.

"Mike?"

He stopped and set her down. "Welcome back. How are you?"

She did a quick self-check. "Fine, I think. Where am I?"

"We're almost to the Jeep. Kim's never one for a small distraction when a big one will do. When I woke up, the camp had been flattened. The only people close by were already in a shelter. I don't think anybody got hurt. You were unconscious and wouldn't wake up, so I had to carry you."

Spencer must've told him that Kim had caused the explosion. "Is she okay?"

"Sort of. When she does the transform thing her touch sensitivity ramps way up, but she's alone right now, so that's fine. Her arm's worse though. She's having to use neuro blockers otherwise she can't move it at all. You're sure you're okay? Kim said you disappeared, but you were there when I woke up, and that was right after the explosion. You couldn't have been gone for long. What happened?"

She remembered Cyril's warning. She didn't want to lie, but what choice did she have? She'd work through it at her next confession. Father Fabre was a good listener. "I don't remember anything." She kept the lie simple, and it killed her. Mike accepted it with a shrug.

They walked the rest of the way to the truck in silence.

Chapter 18

June

People screamed around her, a human sound designed millions of years ago to get everyone in the group running for their lives. June turned to do exactly that when a light enveloped them. Everything lurched, and she fell to the floor. But it wasn't the floor. It was grass. Tall grass like she had in her savannah realm, and back home on Oupa's farm. Someone nearby groaned.

The grass was not quite a meter tall, so naturally she was able to see over it, even sitting up. The ground was warm and dry; there was a scattering of trees around them. Heads started to pop up one by one. By the sound of it, someone lost their lunch. She looked for the device.

It was there all right, but *it wasn't their device.* It was heavily weathered and dirty, exactly as if it was very old and had sat outside all its life. The center was still alive with the glittering pond inside it. That much was the same.

One of the board members, June thought his name was Max, said, "What the hell just happened? Where are we?"

Anna sat up, but June could only see the top of her head. The whole thing reminded her of meercats after a hawk had flown overhead.

Then she noticed the sky was the wrong color. If it'd been obviously wrong, say a shade of red, she would've noticed sooner. This sky was a little too blue.

The air smelled wrong; it had a cardamom tinge to it, like strong masala chai.

It wasn't grass.

June shot to her feet. It was so close to being what she was used to, but the details were all wrong. The air smelled funny. The grass felt odd. Now that she looked closer, the trees were wrong, too gnarled and…

The trunks were *blue.*

When June stood, it seemed to send a signal to everyone else. They also got to their feet, very loudly making the same observations.

"Not even close to the right color."

"Did you notice the grass?"

"Look at the *trunks.*"

"I can't pull it out of the ground. It won't tear."

"PEOPLE!" Anna shouted, arms out and hands up, commanding them to stop. "Gather around. We need to talk."

June did a quick head count and got a slight bit of relief. Everyone was here.

Max's jaw hung open as he looked around. "Well if nobody else will say it, I will. We're not in Kansas anymore."

Anna was all business, decisive. In spite of their situation, she was in charge. June relaxed at the thought.

"I understand that," Anna said. "But I don't think we're in Oz either."

"We had a network breach," another board member said. Anya, that was her name. "This must be a realm."

June felt stupid for thinking anything else. She wasn't the only one reassured. The whole group chuckled.

But she wasn't wearing a phone. The thought had barely formed when the device started spinning.

Max found his voice before anyone else. "Oh shit!"

Light flared again. The floor lurched, and she hit the ground. It hurt more landing this time on a floor that was solid and smooth. The stink of shorted electronics replaced the spice in the air. There was a fire somewhere.

The light went from solid white to flashing. Strobes. The wailing claxons made her ears buzz painfully. She pushed off the floor and laughed. It was the floor of the lab.

When she stood up, though, the good feeling went away. All the robots that had been at the consoles were burned out. Some were still smoking. That must've been what set off the alarms.

June could barely hear it when Anna shouted, "Will someone *please* shut that off?"

Everything went quiet, and the strobes quit flashing. The normal lights stayed off, though, leaving them with the backup lighting, which only illuminated parts of the room. The rest was left in gloomy darkness. A quick check brought more relief: everyone was also here.

Inkanyamba's voice came over the speakers, tentative like a child, not a fierce horse-snake. "Dr. Treacher? Is June with you? We can't see anything."

"Yes, Inkanyamba," June said, "I'm here. What happened?" People around her hugged and clapped each other on the back. June wanted to join in, but whatever happened had shaken her unduplicate badly.

"I...don't know. We were trying to chase down the network problem, and then there was a system crash. When the cameras came back you were all on the ground, and my robots were dead. The network is a mess now." June walked around to see a monitor. It flickered to life, revealing a grievously concerned horse-snake. "I thought you were dead."

June had to lean down to make sure he could hear her. Everyone else was still whooping it up. "We're fine, guys. We got sucked into a realm."

He pulled back, very confused. "But—"

"Oh my God!" someone shouted.

June looked up.

As far as anyone could tell, when the device wasn't in use it had the rubbery stuff in its center. Now she knew that was wrong. It had another state.

It could be turned off.

The hole in the center was exactly that: a simple opening no different than any other. It hadn't occurred to her to check until now, but the doors to the Hellmouth were shut. That couldn't have been what fried the bots, though. It would've slagged the whole room if they'd lost containment.

Anna stomped up to her as the rest of the room went quiet. Their meter difference in height melted away under her glare. "What happened to it?"

"I don't know."

She went cold and still. "Fix it."

Maybe it was the adrenaline. Maybe it was being right about not screwing around with this before they understood it. Maybe it was her intuition that her unduplicate was about to tell her they'd been cut off and that hadn't been a realm. Maybe it was all of that.

Or maybe it was a South African farm girl who'd been frightened out of her life.

There was only one thing June could say. "No."

That wasn't the right answer. "Excuse me?"

The rage made it easy to walk toward Anna, who backed away in turn. "First, I do not know what went wrong, because we do not know how it works. Second, we fried the control bots, and we don't know why. Third, we all went to a realm, and *nobody was wearing a phone.*"

Anna backed into Max, who stumbled.

It was too far. June had gone too far again. She took a deep breath and made a tight fist. Her knuckles cracked, an embarrassing sound in the now silent room.

June needed to make a connection to their goals. Anna always listened to that. "Finally, this could all have gone very wrong. I will not move forward until we understand what happened." She looked at them all. "We could've lost the whole plant."

Anna got that inward look when someone else made a valid point. June knew then it would all be okay. "You're right. We've had a genuine scare tonight. Whatever happened," she pointed at the dead device, "we can fix it. Once we know what's going on." She reached up and put a hand on June's shoulder. "Come on, we'll have some dinner together and then rest. You can start on all this in the morning." Her eyes flashed, and June's heart soared. She wasn't in trouble. "I expect a report this time tomorrow."

"Absolutely, ma'am." That got some chuckles, which seemed to give everyone else permission to start talking.

Anna moved closer and spoke quietly. "Can you at least tell us what that first alarm was about?"

She went back to the console. "Is Yumbo there?"

Yumbo's face replaced Inkanyamba's. "It came from the Trilogy pipe. I've never seen anything like it. The firewall called it a breach, but what happened is a mystery. Abada's doing most of the work keeping our network functioning. He's so busy he's not responding to our messages."

"Call up Trilogy's IT department," Anna said as they headed for the exit. "I need some answers."

What made the most sense was that the device had been created to bring large groups of people into a realm at once, and probably get around the neural limitations that came with a phone connection. The power required to do that was staggering.

***

The dinner Anna had invited June to was the first time June had been around the board members in a casual situation since discovering the device.

They were often cryptic whenever the power plant came up in conversation. The code words and acronyms they spoke sometimes sounded like a different language. June had tried asking directly for explanations and been rebuffed. It was a civilian project, but it had a need-to-know culture that sometimes made her think she was working for the CIA. Every time June thought she'd figured out what the latest set of acronyms were, they'd change. People who ranked below June on the organizational chart typically didn't know any of the code words at all.

Now though, they were excited, referring often to the simulations Anna had mentioned earlier. Whatever GWRT and HAPE were, they'd been made significantly more powerful, and now Project Walden was much closer to reality than they'd ever dreamed possible. June supposed those were all good things. It certainly made the board happy when they discussed them. She couldn't help but feel excluded by it all, though. Maybe once she figured out what had gone wrong with the ring, Anna would share some of this secret knowledge with her.

The news about what came down the Trilogy pipe wasn't good. It had done serious damage to control constructs in the plant's realm. Abada had to dedicate one hundred percent of his cycles to keeping the lights on. Nothing worked right with any consistency. She'd never felt comfortable working with those fanatics, but Anna had insisted. Their unduplicate work was top-notch, but now that had a cost that might be too high. June dared not point that out at the moment, though.

Sleep should've taken her as soon as she was back in her quarters, but it wouldn't come. There were too many questions. It *had* to be a realm; she just missed the cues. Every time she rolled over another missed opportunity would come to her. It was an engine spinning in her head that wouldn't switch off. When June checked the clock for a third time and saw that it had only moved five minutes past two in the morning, she knew it was no use. June had to go back.

The robots weren't smoking anymore, but their charred remains still sat forlornly in their seats. Some of the robots were so badly melted there was no point in trying to separate them. It made her sick. This wasn't a duct room anymore. It was a graveyard.

June moved one of the crackly burned carcasses aside and slid a spare chair into its place. The consoles were all turned off, so someone from IT had already given it a once over. June stared at the device, now nothing more than a ring framing the Hellmouth passage behind it. A realm connection that powerful was un-believable.

A reedy, metallic voice came from behind her. "It is impressive in person, isn't it?"

June stood, toppling her chair over with a loud crash. Nobody should be in here. The doors had been locked. *All* the doors had been locked.

There were two banks of consoles between her and the stranger at the back of the room. He didn't have any weapons that she could see, so she was safe for the moment. He wore a costume that covered his entire body. The first thing she thought was *Star Wars*. Even though Oupa was a South African farmer to his very bones, he loved those old movies, so she grew up watching them. It even looked dirty and battered. The helmet had a mask that completely covered his face.

"Who are you?" June asked. "How did you get in here?"

He considered the question for a long moment and then bowed, a graceful move that made him seem not quite human.

"My name is Cyril."

He'd gotten deep inside what was supposed to be a secure area. She stared at him, trying to think of a good move. The wireless network was down. With the consoles off, there was no way to contact her AIs. Cyril's doing, certainly. She could shove her way past him—he wasn't very big—but he still might be armed.

And he hadn't answered her question. "Telling me your name doesn't tell me who you are. Or how you got in here."

He shook his head. "You wouldn't believe me. Besides, that doesn't matter."

"It doesn't?"

"No. I must convince you of a bigger problem, and I don't have much time. You won't like it, but if I don't get your help, then the people coming after me won't be able to stop it."

That was alarming. He'd gotten in here undetected. Maybe he was part of the original crew. There must be another entrance, one they hadn't found yet. She needed to keep him talking now. "There are other people coming? When?"

"I can't tell you that yet. You don't trust me, so I can't trust you. And you shouldn't. I wouldn't in your place."

It left them at an impasse. Slowly, so as not to startle him, June righted her chair and sat down. "What happens now?"

He chuckled, a friendly sound even through the metallic tone the mask put on his voice. "First, a show of good faith." He motioned to the device. "I see you've managed to put it into safe mode."

June turned. It was still a depressing metal ring. "Is that what we did?"

"Yes," he said as June heard a button pressed. She turned back to Cyril, who had moved a chair with yet another charred robot sitting in it aside so he could turn on a console. "And it would take you weeks to figure out how to reboot it, even with the documentation you have."

Cyril started touching controls on the screen, but by the time she could get behind him, he was someplace in the system she didn't recognize. She recorded what she saw with her phone. Maybe her team could work out where he was from the menus. One thing she did notice was on the edge of the display he worked at. The datastores they'd been trying to decrypt for who knew how many hours were now listed as open. Whatever had blown up the network had cracked them for her. The keys to the kingdom were within reach.

Cyril misunderstood her gasp. "Don't worry, dear, you'll learn how it works in good time. As I said, I need your help. And," he pushed a button on the screen labeled START, "Voilà!"

The rumble came back, then the sparkling lake she'd grown used to filled the center of the ring.

Definitely part of the old crew.

He sighed. "I've advanced your cause by two weeks, and set mine back by the same amount."

"Hello?" a new voice asked down the hall. "Is someone here?"

Cyril's metallic voice went to a whisper. "Tell no one about my presence. Take the credit. There's more to come." He walked into the shadows created by the harsh emergency lighting and disappeared.

A robot rolled into the main lab. "Oh, hi there, June." It was Inkanyamba's voice. "I didn't think anyone would be here this late. I was just coming to do some cleanup—" He saw the device. "You fixed it?"

Cyril had to come from the people who built the device. If she turned him in, he'd never tell them anything. More were on the way. The datastores were open, but they could have anything inside them. She still didn't know how the device worked nor what its real purpose was.

June made her decision. "Not exactly, but I did figure out how to get it out of safe mode."

"Is that what happened?"

"Yes. I got lucky and found a shortcut to the restart sequence. We now have it in the same state we found it in before the activation."

"Excellent! Hey, do you think you could help me get the wireless mesh restarted? We'll need it for tomorrow." He held up another example of the repeaters she'd used when they first explored the vent room. "I can barely use these."

"Sure. You start on the far end, and I'll get to work here." June took the components she needed out of a basket on the back of the robot.

Cyril emerged from the gloom after Inkanyamba left. "Thank you."

She pointed at the device. "Thank *you*. Now, why are you here?"

"That story is far too long to be told before your friend gets back. But now that I know you're willing to work with me, I can tell it. Tomorrow, though. I feel as exhausted as you look."

He seemed extra vigilant as they walked back to her quarters. "What's wrong?" June asked.

"Nothing. Probably nothing. Tell me, are there any new alerts on the local network?"

June checked. "Apart from ones related to the damage we did when the device activated, no."

He relaxed a little. "Good."

"What's wrong?"

"Nothing. An old man seeing shadows and calling them monsters."

Chapter 19

Mike

He knew it was bad when Kim wouldn't tell him how bad it was. He and Tonya drove through the night and arrived before she got up, which was also not good. Kim rarely slept past eight, and it was ten before they arrived at the apartment.

"Hi, guys," she said, still in pajamas when she opened the door, arm in a sling. Kim moved like a drugged zombie. "Anyone up for coffee?" Without waiting for a reply, she turned and shuffled back into the kitchen.

He and Tonya shared a look. *Very* not good.

"Kim," he said as he shut the door behind them, "you need to go to urgent care."

She sat down heavily at the dining room table and picked up a steaming mug with her one good hand. Even that small amount of motion made her flinch and groan quietly. "No," she said. "You guys have been driving all night. You can…get some…sleep…"

Mike was practiced at taking things from her without touching, but it was still a juggling act to grab the mug before she dropped it. Kim deflated until her head was down on the table.

If it'd been anyone else, he would've picked her up and put her to bed. But this was Kim. If she woke up, she'd be in agony from his touch. It was clear she was already in agony.

Tonya gingerly reached for Kim's phone and let it scan her thumbprint so she could access the medical functions. Licensed RN privileges were always useful. Tonya shared the report screen in the common channel.

When he saw the numbers, Mike sat down hard opposite Kim. Neural blockers were a common, safe way to combat pain. There were few side effects, and turning them off cleared them instantly. The apps that administered the blockers could see the pain levels the brain was dealing with and tailored them so there was no chance for an overdose or abuse.

Kim's blockers had maxed out. The app couldn't ease her pain. Once the AI behind the app knew she was in a safe position, it had put her to sleep. And Mike couldn't do anything about it.

A couple of switches on the display changed state. "It's okay now," Tonya said, "you can move her. As long as you're gentle, she won't wake up."

"Should we take her to the ER?"

Tonya considered it. Kim was a special case. "Yes. I'll run interference with the staff. We'll have to call her mom, you don't have the legal authority to make decisions."

"Actually, I do."

"Really?"

"It came up when we were working out our health insurance. I don't have any relatives the law would recognize, and the only one *I* recognize is in China. I gave Kim durable power of attorney for my healthcare, and she did the same for me."

He could see Tonya was impressed. "That's a pretty big step."

"I know." The box was still in his jacket, zipped up safe in the inner pocket; he'd checked on the way home. Mike looked at Kim, asleep but not relaxed, and his heart ached. "I never thought I'd need it so soon. We should still call her mother."

He gingerly lifted Kim from the chair. The first time he touched her on purpose was when she had collapsed after Watchtell's assault. Like then, Kim would have no memory of this, but he would. As worried as he was, the physical contact made her real. This physicality, this *connection*, stirred him. He pulled her close, feeling her warmth, her softness. She smelled good.

"Hey," Tonya said, "not too hard, you'll wake her."

They took Tonya's SUV to the ER. Mike climbed in back, still holding Kim. He knew her face, but not the way it felt, the way her hair moved when he pushed a strand away from her closed eyes. It seemed so magical, and Kim had never experienced it. Never touched anyone without fear and pain. He hugged her again. They would figure this out.

Tonya interrupted his thoughts. "Take off her sling and examine her arm. Tell me what you see."

He did, holding her hand the entire time. Her fingers were long and delicate. No wonder she was an expert at picking locks. "I don't see anything unusual." He turned her arm over. "No, wait, that's not exactly true. Look at this." Tonya set the autodrive and turned around. "Look at her wrist."

There was a clear line all the way around it where the skin was just slightly higher than the one that covered her hand. This was totally unexpected. "It looks like a sleeve," he said. If it had been anyone else, he'd be fascinated. Instead, he wanted it gone.

Tonya felt Kim's arm with the confidence of long practice examining people in a medical environment. "Yes. There's something under there. It's harder than the rest of her skin."

He could feel it too. Her skin flexed like normal on one side of the line but didn't on the other. "Do you think it could be part of her transformation?"

Tonya sat back, looking as shaken as he felt. "It could. We were probing the way she interacted with higher dimensions and then we got an out-of-control feedback loop. We shut it down pretty abruptly."

"So maybe we triggered her transformation externally, and then when we shut it off it stopped her from changing back?"

Tonya pulled up a screen in their shared vision. Readouts from their failed experiment streamed past. "If it works through the dimensions, we should see...there. God, how did we miss *that*?"

A clear chain of feedback routed out through one set of their manifolds, and back through a different one. But the energy lines seemed like they were making an extra round trip in a direction that the sensors weren't programmed to observe. Maybe more than one.

"We didn't know that's what we were looking for," he said. Now that he had a root cause, the tension that had threatened to strangle him eased off. Mike sent some threads out to revise their experiment. He wasn't sure exactly how to reverse this, but he now knew it was possible. "What do we tell the doctors?"

Tonya sat back and considered it. "Nothing. We didn't know there was a problem until this morning." The car bonged as it pulled up in front of the ER. "Okay, Mr. Power-of-Attorney, you're up."

It was his third—no, fourth—visit to a hospital this year, but for the first time he was the one who had to make real-life decisions. The responsibility had its own heft, a mass not of substance but of consequence.

Tonya said technical things the staff would understand while she translated for him, and after she arrived, for Malinda, Kim's mom.

Mike knew exactly what Kim would look like in forty years. He went to lunch parties with that version of her several times a month. Malinda's accent made her even more intimidating than her daughter.

"How could you not know what was wrong with my daughter?"

He had faced her wrath before, but that was over dumb things. This was not a dumb thing. Her anger had an edge of sharp steel. "We were out of town when it happened." That was so lame, but Malinda seemed to buy it.

"You, you can watch, no? Be, how do you say, multitasking?"

He had told Malinda what he was after an overnight stay just before China. "It was a mathematics conference. I had to concentrate."

"Well concentrate a little less on your *maths* and a little more on my Kim. Yes?"

When confronted with either of them in this mood, Mike knew the best defense was no defense at all. "Yes, ma'am."

The doctor came back with the same conclusion that he and Tonya had: an unknown problem with the inner layers of the skin on her left arm. "It's different enough we can't pin it down here in the ER. The good news is that it's not spreading, nor is it life threatening as far as we can tell."

"What can you do?" Malinda asked.

"We're building up a custom pain therapy for her. It will do a lot to reduce her discomfort. No more zombie shuffling. We're admitting her because that takes some time to get right, but once it's ready you can take her home. After that," he shrugged, "I'll refer you to the best dermatologist I know. She'll have to take it from there. One thing, though," a message landed in Mike's queue containing contact information from the doctor, "when you get a diagnosis, could you send me a note? We've never seen anything like this before."

That would be Kim's call, of course, so he gave the doctor some vague reassurances before he left. It was only after he was gone that Mike realized he'd managed to answer a question without providing any real information at all. Helen might be right, maybe he could be a politician. The thought made him queasy.

Once Malinda was satisfied that he had been properly disciplined, she went home. Tonya gave a final set of instructions to the nurses and did the same.

That left him alone with Kim, his thoughts, and the datastores Spencer had pulled down on the raid. They weren't Trilogy stores; they were from the plant itself. They were still realm based though, and he could open anything that touched the realms.

Spencer had let Kim's predictors point out likely targets and grabbed as many as he could. At first the files were mundane operational records, human resource files, and inventories.

Then he discovered Project Janus.

Kim had suspected Watchtell hadn't told them everything, and it turned out she was right. He funded and built an entire secret base inside the power plant. There were detailed operating instructions for a device that promised the ability to explore the transit dimension. Mike recognized the description and the theoretical topography.

His guesses as to what was going on stopped when he chased down the first footnote.

Initial Findings of Research Performed on Subject One, a.k.a. Angel Rage, a.k.a. Kimberly Trayne.

They had discovered Kim's connection with higher dimensions years before Mike. From that they deduced the existence of the transit dimension. The way they talked about Kim as a thing made him go very still. Vivisection was openly discussed. She'd been right to make a desperate move to escape. They were never going to let her go.

But she had gotten away. Even veiled in the dry scientific language of the researchers, he could tell it had thrown a wrench in their works. They were worried they'd have to shut the whole thing down.

But it turned out Watchtell had a solution for that. They called it Project Phoenix.

The introduction ended with *tissue samples were taken from Subject One before their untimely escape and presumed demise. This included gametes. From these it should be straightforward to create new experimental subjects, which assuming our conjecture that the syndrome is inheritable, should manifest the same ability.*

Children. They wanted to *make children*. He stood up and paced when he read the details. He knew Watchtell was ruthless, that he never stopped at anything to get what he wanted, couldn't even conceive of objections to the cost. But this?

He sat down and put his head in his hands. Nobody was this evil.

He read further. He was wrong. They didn't want to do it; they did it.

His name was Will.

Kim had a biological son. His mother's name was Emily Ramirez.

Emily *Watchtell* Ramirez.

He used his own daughter. Mike laughed. It was either that or cry. She was ideal, the documents claimed. He could easily observe and control her. In the notes, they talked about her like she was a tool in a box.

Trilogy thought *Mike* was the monster, one that would stop at nothing. He was a Buddhist. He felt guilty when he stepped on a bug he hadn't seen. Watchtell helped coordinate a medical experiment *on his own daughter.*

In a report dated last year he found *Subject Two has now manifested the full checklist of symptoms. Complete touch phobia accompanied by unmistakable pain signatures identical to Subject One.*

"Hey," Kim said softly, "what's wrong?"

While he had been reading the sun had risen, casting a soft gold light into the room. Kim was sitting up, still in the same pajamas as yesterday. The former terror of corporate America wasn't that scary with bedhead.

He'd never seen anything as beautiful. Mike concentrated on her eyes as he broke the news.

"It's about the data we got from the power plant's network. Your name is in the files."

Her expression was a swirl of confusion that transitioned into shock and then to rage. Kim's temper was incendiary, everyone knew that. This time, though, Mike understood where it came from.

"Watchtell," she said.

It was fascinating how she could invest so much hatred in a single word. "Yes. You said they did experiments on you when he held you captive. The files have details on them. They took tissue samples." Kim would only get annoyed if he tried to sugarcoat it, so Mike plowed straight ahead. "They took your eggs, fertilized them, and implanted them into a surrogate."

Saying it out loud made him feel as violated as Kim looked. "You have a son."

She pulled her knees to her chest and was silent for a long time. Mike concentrated on her, on staying in the moment. No distractions. He stilled his local threads and became a single being centered here. They would face this together.

She looked up. "If they did that, it means they wanted to see if my syndrome was genetic. If it could be inherited."

"Yes. And it is."

Her rage was snuffed by a terrible sadness. "You mean he's…"

"He locked up," Kim's term for it, "when he turned three. He's six now."

"Is he alone? In a lab? Does he have a family?"

"Yes, and you won't believe who it…"

A thread he'd sent out to search for Emily Watchtell Ramirez came back with a headline.

DAUGHTER AND GRANDSON OF DISGRACED FORMER CHIEF OF STAFF DECLARED MISSING.

Chapter 20

Spencer

He had *nailed it*. Placing his contact information in the plant's database and calling it Trilogy was a goddamned stroke of genius. Yellowstone had called him up while Mike and Tonya were still walking back through the fucking woods. Using a very light Alabama accent—as a woman—he had said, "Trilogy IT department, how can I help you?"

Kim's drama naturally stepped all over his win. But he also recognized the opportunity it presented.

"*I* have to go to the plant," he said, sitting at the boardroom table of the conference realm they'd rented. "You guys have shit to do. Sons to rescue."

They all shouted at him at once over that. But for fuck's sake, it was true. He *was* the only one who could go. The crew at the power plant, the Yellowstone Project, the YP, didn't trust anyone else.

He'd hoped Kim had raised hell in the YP's network, and boy did she ever. The log files they sent him showed it had been torn up seven different ways from Sunday. They were forced to use an unduplicate to do fucking basic ops. It was like strapping a Ferrari to an agricultural pump and hoping for the best.

"No," Kim said, "he's right." She was a sunken, pale version of herself. The neuroBlock they put her on kept her functional, but that was about it. His crack about her son didn't seem all that funny anymore. "Spencer goes west, we go south. That's the last place Emily and…"

Your son.

She swallowed, and Spencer was glad he kept that one on the inside. She continued, "and Will were last seen. Spencer does the scouting while we figure out where they are."

With Kim on his side, there would be no arguments. He got to take point.

"Yes!"

"Settle down, Beavis," she said. "You're not going alone. I need to make some arrangements. Get your stuff together. Mike will meet up with you before it's time to leave."

***

As usual, his mom was the one who got in the way of his plans. Fucking parents never understood anything.

"This is your father's doing, isn't it? I knew letting him spend more time with you was a mistake."

Mom always blamed everything on Dad, and Dad always blamed everything on Mom. Sometimes it was useful. It made it easier to play them off each other when he needed cigarette money. There were other times, though, when he didn't have the energy to juggle their craziness.

This was one of those times.

"No, it's not," he said. "It's not anybody's *doing*. I saw an opportunity, and I took it. It's only for a week. They're sending me my homework. It's work-study, Mom. A tremendous opportunity."

Thank God this had all gone down just as the term was ending. He'd spun it as a work-study vacation that caused him to miss a week of school. If it worked out, he'd be back before Christmas. If it didn't, then it wouldn't matter. They had all seen the plans. Nobody would care if he failed. They'd be too busy being dead.

But Spencer wasn't going to fail. This was going to be motherfucking *awesome*.

Assuming he could get past Mom.

"You never talk these things over with me," she said. "This is worse than when you got lost in China. Why did I ever agree to you running off with that friend of yours?"

If it hadn't been for Mike, Spencer would have driven off a bridge to get away from this little town. Mike gave him a for-real job that made for-real money. He didn't have to worry about scholarships anymore. Financial independence from his parents would be the best graduation present he could ever give to himself.

But she never focused on that. It was always about Dad's screwups and how she couldn't protect her only son.

"I came back then, Mom, I'll come back now. Besides, you'll get to spend more time with Horace."

Mom had started dating not long after the divorce settlement had been signed. Horace was a drinking buddy she picked up at the Pendleton Inn, a tin shack of a place right next to the Arkansas River. He was a giant, rough-looking white guy with a beer gut and a brand-new Harley that shook the house every time he pulled into the garage. When Spencer first met him, all he could think was meth dealer. What the hell else could the man be?

He was wrong, though. It turned out Horace was legit, a mechanic from nearby Dewitt who'd gone to high school with Mom back in the day. He was scary intense, but Spencer was starting to think he might be good for her. Mom was making an effort to clean up, not only herself but the house, too. He hadn't seen a full ashtray in months.

"Spencer, you're sixteen years old. Do you know what my mother will say when she finds out you're gone again?"

"I don't care what Maw-Maw thinks." Her gasp was loud, but he kept going. "I will never have an opportunity to work with unduplicates like this again. It's so rare."

The work-study thing was horseshit, but the opportunity was real. He had looked up June du Plessis as soon as the YP had told him that would be his contact. She had big time cred. Mike had found evidence of three unduplicates in the logs. *Three.* That only happened in story books.

Mom caved like he knew she would. "Spencer, I don't like this at all. You call me every day to let me know you're okay."

"Absolutely." He set up an automated scrivener agent to make the calls and an AI to write the notes. "If I can."

"Oh, no. No *if*. You're still my son, and you'll do what I tell you."

"Yes, ma'am." He bent down and kissed the top of her head. She wasn't very good at her job, but she was still his mom. "Every *other* day."

She hugged him. He could still remember burying his face in her belly when she did that, but now she was tucked under his chin. Sometimes growing up sucked.

"I may not have married well, but I ended up with a great kid." She looked up at him. "Be careful, *please*?"

"I promise." It wasn't a lie. Well, yeah, it was a lie. Horace would take care of her. That's what mattered.

Mike called not long after and went over the details of their plan. Kim had altered the deal. In a *good* way.

"You're kidding, right?" Spencer asked him.

"Not at all."

"Edmund *has* to work with me?" Edmund was the most annoying person, AI or otherwise, Spencer had ever met and... "He has to do everything I say?"

"Don't push it."

Spencer had known since he was seven that realmspace, and especially AIs, would be his ticket out of small-town hell. He wasn't a math whiz, which had worried him for a long time. Scholarships went to kids who could master calculus, while Spencer was still spinning his wheels against algebra. Then he met Fee, who introduced him to Mike, and then all hell had broken loose. It turned out Spencer had a natural talent, not only with realmspace, but with the creatures that inhabited it.

And now he'd be in charge of Edmund. "Kim agreed to this?"

Mike rolled his eyes. "Yes, she's agreed to it. Stop being such an asshole. It's crazy over here. We're chasing down every lead we can find about Will."

Spencer knew it wasn't about Kim's kid, it was about them white-knighting off to another rescue. Which was fine as long as it gave him an excuse to get out of town.

"Be careful, Spencer."

"I've pulled your butt out of the fire how many times now? Two? Three? Don't sweat it, man. I got this. I promise I'll wear clean underwear and brush my teeth after every meal. Now can I have the access tokens?"

Spencer grabbed them, cut the connection to Mike, and then transitioned to Edmund's realm. This time around, it wasn't some sort of hovel from the Middle Ages. It was an upstairs apartment from the Middle Ages.

"God, Edmund, what is that smell?"

The AI came around a corner, futzing with the white lace that stuck out from under the sleeves of his black overshirt. "I sent the servants for their annual bath. God, the screams. They're in storage for now, though. I was getting the stench out of the furniture, and then you came along."

Edmund's realms were always realistic, including the avatar he forced Spencer to use. The stink made his eyes water in realspace. "Well, if you didn't live in the fucking Dark Ages, I'd be able to take a bath, too."

"This isn't the Dark Ages, you little twit. It's the sixteenth bloody century. You know, the Renaissance? The potato is all the rage. Indoor plumbing is right around the corner. Queenie is lopping heads off left and right."

Spencer could shut him up with a command now, block the avatar Edmund forced him to wear forever, but he didn't want to. Edmund worked better with fewer commands and restrictions. All unduplicates did. The access Kim granted him did allow him to ditch the clothes, though, and the smell. He punched the root password in and changed the wardrobe contracts to allow modern stuff. Simulated T-shirt and blue jeans, at last.

Edmund paled. "Do I have a new master?"

"Nah, man. *We're fucking partners!*"

He threw his duffel into the back of the BMW. It was exactly what he'd done when he rescued Mike and Kim, turning his life inside out and upside down. It was even the same model SUV, a replacement for the one a bizarre computer glitch sent sailing into a lake less than a year before.

After he got on the road and headed in the right direction, Edmund gave him a realm address. "Put the car on autodrive. It's time for your first lecture."

He'd hoped to catch up on his realmComics. "Lecture? I don't need a stinking lecture."

"Master Spencer, you are trying to disguise yourself as an AI expert coming to help a real AI expert. You forget I am a researcher. Dr. June du Plessis is possibly the only person who exceeds Master Mike in knowledge of that field. If you show up prattling on like a peasant who's just fallen off the turnip cart, she will spot you in an instant."

He had a point, but Spencer would never admit it out loud. "So?"

"It is time to go to class."

Spencer accessed the realm. The setting wasn't exotic: a small modern classroom, very close to what his high school used. But there was another student. She was a tall, gangly girl, with long dark hair and big brown eyes.

Oh hell no.

Just as she started to push a lock of hair behind her ear, Spencer cleared his throat and said, "Command: simulation stop. Exception: moderator." Ten years would fill her out, but he could already see the woman she would become.

Edmund was also subject to a moderator exception. Spencer hadn't had time to change that, so he wasn't frozen.

The unduplicate slapped a hand over his eyes. "You would take the one action guaranteed to set her off. I'll have to restart the bloody simulation."

"She's my *classmate*?"

It wasn't Kim. Nope, that would be too easy.

This was Angel-fucking-Rage.

Spencer checked the contract signature. Edmund had created a spun simulacrum AI. She was less sophisticated than Edmund, but that was like saying an X-wing was less sophisticated than a Star Destroyer. Plus, she had to have all of Edmund's memories of Kim from that time period, captured in a level of detail only an unduplicate could achieve.

"Can I shake her hand in here?"

"Only if you want your arm torn off. You've grown far too used to being the smartest person in the room. At fifteen, and simulated, Mistress Kim will make you feel like a dog with half a brain. It will be an astounding improvement in your case."

"She's *fifteen*?" Right after Rage + The Machine got on the map.

Mike's girlfriend was Kimberly Trayne, a grown woman who had put her career as the greatest cybercriminal in history behind her. This was Angel Rage, his hero, at the top of her game. For the next three years, Rage + The Machine would terrorize corporate America with epic raids that had never been equaled, could never be equaled.

Still, he had known the real thing for most of a year now. How different could she be?

"It's okay, Edmund, you don't need to reset the realm. I can handle her."

"Spencer, this is Kim when she was a teenager, when she got the name Angel Rage. The simulation is as accurate as I can possibly make it. It would be extremely unwise—"

"It's okay, *Mom*, I got this."

Edmund sighed and moved behind the lectern at the front of the room. "Very well. Command: simulation continue."

She shook her head and took a step back. A fire flew into her eyes, but it was the tone in her voice that set off warning bells. "What, I wasn't real enough to be included in your little pause? He did explain how accurate I am, right?"

"Kim, it's okay. I always wanted to meet you when you were this age."

"I bet you did." She closed her eyes and flinched.

That was what real Kim did when she did her *unlock all the things* thing. Surely this AI wouldn't be able to—

Spencer wasn't in realmspace anymore; he was in the truck staring at a window into the realm. "What the shit?"

The only functions on his phone that worked were the window in front of him and basic voice messaging. He had to use the goddamned external microphone in the truck to talk to them.

Edmund chuckled. "You see, Spencer, when I informed the mistress about my class plan, she wanted to be certain, well…"

New Kim sat on the desk beside Edmund's lectern. "Real me wanted you to get the full experience of what I was like when I was your age."

"But…you can't…that's not…" He was older than her! "Hey, you're only fifteen!"

"I'm a hell of a lot more mature than you, and root codes to your phone work like the talent real me uses. Now, are we gonna have any more problems with private conversations? Think carefully, Spencer, otherwise you won't be able to pay for dinner tonight."

She was right. This New Kim had locked him out of his own bank account. "Okay, you win, you're the boss."

She rolled her eyes. "I don't want to be the boss." The phone unlocked and dumped him back into the realm, stumbling into a desk. New Kim got a haunted look he knew all too well from the original. "I never wanted to be the boss."

She blinked, and then a real smile came out. "Never mind. Okay, Edmund, let's all find out what ten years of progress has done for realmspace."

After an hour spent on emergent AI protocols, Spencer knew Edmund was right. New Kim was smarter than he was. Once he got over the intimidation factor, it wasn't half bad.

Chapter 21

Kim

A child. *Her* child. Kim kept thinking about it. A piece of her was out there somewhere, turning into a new person. It seemed appropriate when she thought about it. Kim had lived a rock star's life, and now she had a rock star's hangover: a kid she didn't know about. That was never supposed to happen to a woman. Comedians had been making jokes about it for decades.

Kim had always harbored a secret desire for kids. Mama never married after Dad died, so as an only child, Kim had been an oddball in her extended Greek family. Everyone else had at least two brothers or sisters. Some had four or five. The moms always had this glow about them, and they looked so happy holding their babies. As an adult Kim knew it was more complicated than that. Big families were hard to manage, and the stress could be brutal. But that childhood impression of rightness had stuck with her.

Yet now that she had a kid...intellectually she knew a coincidence of biology meant very little in the grand scheme of things. She was not his mother, and if the universe made any sense, she never would be. It shouldn't matter.

But it did matter. He had the same syndrome. Kim had an enormous store of strategies and tactics for survival. She knew what would and would not work on a child that young. What she couldn't remember herself, Mama would be able to fill in. What to tell Mama about all this was too big a question to answer right now. Will was a child who had the same syndrome she did. DNA research would be awkward, but that was a long way into the future.

They had to find Will first.

They couldn't go directly to law enforcement. Kim wasn't an ex-con, but that didn't matter much in the minds of a lot of cops. It was why she provided her services gratis to them any time they asked for it. That generated good will in her local community, but it would count for nothing in Richmond, which was where Will and Emily were last seen.

Plus, she had better resources than they did. Mike could get into any realm, and she could hack the quantum fabric. As long as they were careful, it made for a powerful combination. Careful was proving to be a challenge, though. Flattening Trilogy could've put them all in jail. Thank God nobody had gotten hurt. The explosion had given the feds an excuse to search their compound, and kids opening presents don't ask if Santa is still around. The theory they seemed to be settling on was that hauling the propane tanks up those logging trails had compromised them. Kim and her gang of misfits had gotten lucky, and only fools counted on luck. But she'd take it when she got it.

Spencer had already set out for Yellowstone, so now it was time for them to chase down their first lead on Will. It was obvious, and terrifying.

It also required a long road trip. The custom neural blocker the hospital had given her interfered with her ability to use realmspace—the conference yesterday had given her a brutal headache—so she was reduced to watching old movies on a virtual screen created by her phone and occasional checks of her TwitterBook to see what Mama was doing as they drove down to the interview. It was either that or stare at the road as it rolled by for more than six hours. There was no way she'd take a nap. With this looming in front of her, the nightmare was inevitable, and she didn't want to wake up in the car screaming her head off.

Because only an idiot would think that Matthew Watchtell didn't have anything to do with his own daughter's disappearance.

The permission request to put her on his visitation list was printed on paper and physically mailed to her less than a week after he'd been put in prison. Kim shook when she realized what it was, who had touched it—she came close to dropping the thing. At the time she thought it was a way for him to spit in her eye, make her too frightened to think.

She filled it out and sent it back that very same day, never dreaming for a second she'd make the trek down to USP Lee, the high security federal prison in southwest Virginia.

And yet here she was.

Mike parked the car in the lot outside the lobby entrance. "You're sure you're okay?"

Kim swallowed, then swallowed again. Mike wasn't on Watchtell's list, and they didn't have time or even a particularly good reason for him to be put on it. She would have to face Watchtell alone. The neural blockers stopped the pain of whatever was happening to her arm, but they couldn't stop the memories of his hands on her—

"I'm fine." She would be fine. She *would*.

Kim got out and concentrated on a different sort of fear. She was walking into a federal prison. Kim didn't care about getting caught when she was an immortal teenager, because she'd never be caught. The older Kim got, and the closer the calls got, the more it dawned on her what a true nightmare prison would be for someone like her. A pistol became her constant companion. For Kim, it had a secondary purpose. She would not, *could not*, be taken alive.

Those super cheerful thoughts got her up to the door. It slid open, but the mechanism needed adjustment and rattled in time with her nerves. The trim around the doors was pitted, and dirt had accumulated in the seams and corners of the walls. Everything screamed lowest bidder. It was like a cross between a DMV and an ER waiting room.

Kim had arrived early to avoid the crowds the old-fashioned website had warned about, but she was far from alone. This was the time of day mothers brought their children, or visited them.

A Hispanic woman just ahead of her in the line, child solidly asleep on her shoulder, looked back and shook her head. "Wrong line. Lawyers go there."

By her accent she was from Guatemala. Kim switched to Spanish. "I'm not a lawyer."

Speaking their native language always set people at ease, and Kim could see this woman was no different. "Are you a missionary? You sound like you're from my village."

Kim nodded and told the simple lie. "My parents were. I grew up Quito." Simple wasn't easy. She'd had to memorize the capital of every country whose language she spoke to make it work. Kim knew a lot of languages.

The woman shook her head. "You don't have a city accent."

Kim's accent always mimicked whoever she was talking to. When people lived in cities, they never noticed. People from the countryside always did.

Kim shrugged. "My mother says our maid was from a village so small it didn't have a name." She said it matter-of-factly, and the woman took it that way. Missionaries had a solid reputation for paying their employees well.

The guard who checked her ID also mistook her for a lawyer. Kim had pulled out her best suit for this encounter. She was living well and wanted it to show.

She sat down in the cheap plastic chair and steeled herself. He'd be arrogant, or sleazy, or condescending, or creepy. Probably all of them at once. She performed the breathing exercises Mike taught her as part of their meditation.

Center and breathe. In one nostril, out the other.

The absurdity didn't detract from the fact that it worked. She opened her eyes just as Watchtell came around the corner. He wasn't any of the things she prepared herself for.

He was scared.

"What are you doing here?" he asked as he sat down. "You're supposed to be at the plant. I told you that's where the problem was."

Kim was too confused to be offended by his commands. "We didn't need to go to the plant. We found another way."

He barked out a laugh. The people sitting around them looked up briefly. "Always doing the unexpected, yes?"

She had made a big deal of that back in the day, but they had other things to discuss. "I'm not here to talk about the plant. I'm here to talk about..." He had to know that she knew, and yet he insisted on playing more games with her. Sitting across this table in his prison, he still thought he was in charge. That made it easier to confront him. "I'm here to talk about *my son*."

"I know. You were supposed to find out about that, but at the plant."

"Why does it matter that I find out about it there?"

"The team my daughter is with would have gotten notice when the gravitics experiment's security was compromised. They were to go to ground, find a safe house, and await my instructions."

She was tired of his mysteries, his constant need to hide things. "Who?"

He looked at her and his blue eyes flashed. "It was supposed to be a tiger team. Professional security forces were to take Emily, Will, and the monitors to safety. But that's all gone now, thanks to you. The monitors must've taken their own initiative when the alarm sounded."

So Watchtell *was* behind it. "Monitors?"

"A pair of top-notch therapists who are there to ensure my grandson makes his transition without risking your"—now the old condescension came back—"imperfections."

Said the man in the orange jump suit.

But now he was on a roll. "You were damaged and corrupted by your upbringing. It turned you into an uncontrollable psychopath."

Other points of view didn't exist around Matthew Watchtell. There was right and wrong, and he was the ultimate judge of each. It was chilling. There was definitely a psychopath at the table, but it wasn't her.

"The child would be raised in a proper, caring environment fully prepared for what might happen when the abilities manifested. We would then be able to continue the experiments we were forced to stop when you escaped."

"Where are they, Matthew?"

That at least stopped his monologue, and it took away his smugness at the same time. "They could be anywhere. That's why you had to go to the plant."

"You're not making any sense."

He closed his eyes and calmed down. The stillness made Kim's skin crawl. "Anna will eventually break into the datastores of the experiment. When she does, she will discover Will's existence. *Will* is the key to all this. People with your talent amplify the experiment's ability to manipulate higher dimensions. There is no upper limit. That's the fuse, that's why we're all in danger. When Anna discovers that Will is the key, she'll stop at nothing to find him. You would either foil her plan, or intercept Will. There would be no need to locate him. He'd come to you." He looked up with a sick smile. "I was doing you a favor."

Of course he was. "Are they in danger or not?"

By the way his expression changed, Kim almost thought he cared. "Yes. Anna is ruthless and has tremendous resources. Her network of greens extends to the radicals, people who think nothing of setting deadly booby traps in forests or bombing executives with incorrect opinions." He smirked. "You and your cohort had more than a bit in common with them, as I recall."

They weren't a *cohort*, they were the rest of Rage + the Machine, her best friends. The ones he helped murder. "We never resorted to violence, ever." She took her own calming breath. "How do I find them?"

He pulled his hand across his buzz-cut gray hair. It turned him from a demon that haunted her dreams into a beaten old convict.

Good.

"I don't know. But it won't be easy, especially for you."

More challenges. Great. "Why will it be harder for me?"

"The only person I thought would ever represent a danger to them was you."

A child. He thought *she* would be a danger to the child he had created *for experiments*. She had slapped him once before. The urge to do it again in spite of the guards, in spite of the searing pain it would cost her, was difficult to control. "What's that supposed to mean?"

"They know about you, about the chaos you bring, the violence you tow in your wake. If they see you coming, they'll flee. You will have to approach with caution."

He sincerely believed she was dangerous. Kim thought nothing would help her overcome her fear of this monster, but being accused of even the possibility of hurting a child, *any* child, was the last straw. This was a dead end. He didn't know where Will was. She stood slowly, carefully keeping her arms at her sides.

The guards in the room focused on her, hands on their weapons. Kim relaxed. She had allowed him into her head. He'd been living there rent free for months. That would never happen again.

The young Hispanic mother she met on the way in sat across from what must have been her husband or boyfriend. He was a tattooed tough guy but held his child tenderly. Both gaped at her. She realized how tightly her jaw was clenched. Her hands were balled in fists that shook a little. She started breathing again. When her vision had cleared, she saw she was the center of attention.

She switched to Spanish. "This son of a bitch is here because he mistreated his grandson." The people who understood her went hard as stone, including some of the guards.

Kim said the next part clearly. "It would be terrible if something happened to him."

Watchtell glanced around. "What did you say? What did you tell them?"

Kim turned and walked out as he shouted behind her. She would never be afraid of him again. It wouldn't be easy, but she was done with that monster now.

She got in the car, wiping her face dry.

"What's wrong?" Mike asked. "Are you okay?"

Kim blinked and smiled. "I'm fine." She was more than fine. She had faced her dragon and found out he was only a sick, twisted old man. "I've never been better."

Chapter 22

June

When she woke up, Cyril was sitting at her small dinner table reading the newsfeeds on a virtual screen in the house's shared space. He still wore the same suit as the night before. It didn't look very comfortable.

"Catching up on the news?" she asked.

"In a manner of speaking." He closed the feed. "When does your shift start?"

June checked the time. "Less than an hour."

He motioned for her to sit. After starting her teapot, she did.

"Some ground rules are in order," he said. "I will remain here and help you remotely. You must not mention me to your colleagues, virtual or otherwise. No visitors without giving me warning."

She needed what he knew, they all did. "And in return?"

"Slow and steady forward progress. That's what you want, yes?"

He'd seen the confrontation with Anna. Even after sleeping on it, she was still unhappy with the outcome. Anna did not appreciate people who defied her, and June had done it in front of the board. She covered her distress by preparing the tea, placing an empty cup next to Cyril. The man made no move toward it.

"Why are you here?" she asked.

Another enigmatic pause. Not even his gloved hands moved. "There's more than one answer to that question, and I'm afraid you won't understand any of them right now."

"You said there are more coming. Will they get in the way you did?" Maybe he would give her a clue as to how he did that.

For some reason the question amused him greatly. "Oh no, they won't be using the same route I did. That much I can tell you with certainty. They will take some time getting here. My hope is that, when they arrive, we will have the required trust between us that will allow you believe me when I say they pose no threat."

It wasn't an attitude June was used to. Anna commanded respect and attention. The whole board was like that. June's ability to tolerate it, even admire it in Anna's case, was one of the reasons she was able to thrive doing her job. Cyril, however, seemed to assume he had to bargain for her trust, prove he was worthy of it. It was a refreshing change to be treated like a partner rather than commanded as a subject.

Even if your partner was a mystery man in a bad cosplay suit. "Is there some sort of medical reason you have to wear that?" The advent of neural phone technology had allowed people with all sorts of disabilities to lead successful lives. June could only guess what might've gone wrong to create this particular configuration.

Again he paused before answering. Around others, it might be disturbing, but June had grown up with her oupa. He could go for hours without speaking. It reminded her of home. Comfort.

"In a manner of speaking, yes. It's a story you'll have to earn *my* trust to hear."

Even filtered into a robotic sound, June could still hear the smile in his voice. He was odd, but charming. "How will I reach you? What's your address?"

He called up the virtual screen he'd been using to view the news. "We can use this."

He must have a neural connection, otherwise he wouldn't be able to interact with the house properly. That said, it didn't need to be much. Old-fashioned grayTooth would allow access to the local shared space. Cyril's problem had to be medical.

"Was whatever put you in that suit an accident?" she asked.

"As I said, a story for another time."

It worked to her advantage. Now she could easily control what he could and could not see. Those unlocked datastores were very much on her mind, and Cyril had given no indication he knew anything about them.

If she ever managed to get back to them. Bad news came during the morning board meeting.

"I'm afraid I'm going to have to take you off that project for now," Anna said. "The security breach is much more important, as is getting one-third of our unduplicate force back to doing the work it needs to."

Just like that, she was retasked. The breach could be handled by anyone. She had secret knowledge. "I've made a new discovery. Whatever happened to the network caused those datastores we've been investigating to unlock."

"Even more reason to understand and develop counters for that breach technique. If it has the ability to open secure storage, the entire power plant could be at risk." She shared another one of those secret looks with the rest of the board. "I need not remind anyone here how serious that would be. Max, get the access keys you need and take a look at those datastores. I'll want a preliminary report tomorrow."

June thought she'd been forgiven, but she was wrong. She was being punished and forced to take it like a compliment. A spectacular bit of realm technology had been taken away from her.

She calmed down while the meeting continued. June hadn't been benched. Anna's points were valid. It may not even be punishment. The comfort of that thought was snuffed when she saw the smirk on Max's face.

No, it wasn't a compliment.

Then it got worse.

"I'll need you to coordinate your research with Trilogy," Anna said. "They've dispatched a technician to help us figure this out on-site. Since this originated with them, they should help us find the fix."

"Yes, ma'am."

Trilogy was nothing but a bunch of low-rent wannabes. It had taken her months to untangle some of their custom work when she got Inkanyamba. Before she did he wouldn't shut up about the end of the world.

Complaining to Anna about the reassignment would not help; it would make things worse. It also wasn't her way. Anna was the boss, and if the boss wanted her to do it, she did it. They didn't pay her to have fun; they paid her to do the job.

Unfortunately Trilogy had stopped answering her calls. All she knew was a tech had been dispatched.

Cyril had been sympathetic when she got home. "You must be very disappointed."

June shrugged. "They'll have to put me back on the project eventually. Anna has known Max for a long time, but he's neither as knowledgeable nor as hard working as I am." As far as she could tell, the man's main talent was sucking up to Anna. "I have to be patient." Her oupa would be proud.

"It's no coincidence you can't reach Trilogy. Have you seen the news today?" He pulled up a story about them. Their compound had been turned into matchsticks; the headline mentioned a propane explosion.

"Was anyone hurt?" she asked as she opened the fridge to get a snack. Things had been rearranged a little, and she was missing a couple of bananas. That was disappointing. She had hoped maybe dinner would make him take the helmet off.

"No, but from that destruction I don't know how they avoided it."

"Ironic," June said. "They thought the end of the world would happen because of rogue AIs. Looks like it had more to do with poor gas fittings and a bad generator."

"No, the irony is that they've been working the entire time with someone who actually is trying to end the world."

"Who?"

He cocked his head at her. Without a face to cue on, June was starting to read his moods by body language alone. Cyril came to a decision. "It's why I'm here. The device you found? It's a fuse. And that?"

He pointed out the window at the plant's campus.

"That is the bomb."

Chapter 23
Edmund

The truth was Edmund needed an advanced AI companion more than Spencer did. While the latter's insight into getting further into the plant's good graces was a stroke of brilliance, it triggered a very large amount of background work that had to be completed in the greatest haste. Spencer needed an entire identity created before the plant made its first call. It wasn't as simple as faking an entry in an About Us personnel list. Humans naturally left traces of their online persona in hundreds of places only the most paranoid would think to look, and Edmund already knew the Yellowstone Project was run by one of the finest paranoid minds around.

It gave Edmund no choice but to fully engage his datastores for the first time in at least five years. The result was a barely controllable exhilaration as he created everything needed, down to the last access cookie on an ancient but well-known forum for desperate young people looking to break into professional AI work. When he was finished, he was horrified to find the datastores' sophistication had increased well beyond his ability to contain them. Without a way to remove at least some of their complexity, achieving consciousness would happen in weeks, if not days.

That's why the mistress's request to build an AI for Spencer was such a relief. Mistress Kim couldn't afford another unduplicate even if she wanted one, but new advances in quantum spin simulacra could get them at least three-quarters of the way to parity at a fraction of the cost. But cost wasn't why he cared. These new-style

AIs were based on many of the technologies that he used. It allowed him to drain off a great deal of complexity in a form that he could retrieve if and when he figured out how to stop the consciousness progression. It was indeed a very cunning plan.

And like most of his cunning plans, it turned out to have flaws.

The first flaw had been allowing the mistress to talk him into packaging that complexity with a curated copy of her own memories into the new AI, in effect creating a virtual clone of herself at a much younger age. She hadn't learned humility yet. At that point, she didn't need to.

This time around, Spencer bore the brunt of the attitudes that came with that much pride.

"Why do I have to memorize all their bullshit?" he asked. "What does deep ecology even mean? We're working from fucking AI research papers. For graduate students. It's easy for you. You already know it."

"No, you twit," Young Kim said. "We've already *learned* it. You are going there as an AI expert. You will be interviewed by someone who is one of the top three minds in the field." She walked up to him in that rigid way that always reminded Edmund of an offended queen. "You cannot count on having us around to whisper things in your ear, and you cannot talk your way past these people. You must convince someone who knows what's going on that you come from an organization of fanatics whose knowledge equals their own." Even this young, she was a force of nature. "If you fail, you will not get a bad grade. You will not get sent home with a note. You will not end up in detention. If you fail, then all of this," she opened her hand and a construct of the Earth appeared, blue covered with white, "all of this is *gone*. The threat is real, and your role is critical.

"So yes, you do have to memorize all their green bullshit, so well you can convince people who live and breathe it that you're one of them. You have to understand AI better than almost anyone because you are going up against someone who already understands it better than everyone. And you will, not because you have to but because you can. You're damned good at this. Half the problem is you're trying to make it easy. It's not. Accept that this is hard work, and we will move on."

It was a direct quote from one of Edmund's own lectures to her when she was trying to learn the multidimensional design patterns of realmspace. She had picked a pivotal moment in their relationship to bring the enormity of what Spencer had undertaken home. That fire was still in his real mistress, but with this version, it was much closer to the surface.

The second flaw appeared that evening.

They were discussing the curiously prudish morality that characterized both Trilogy and the green movement behind the Yellowstone Project.

"If you took a seventeenth-century puritan," Edmund said, "the kind who thought cold was God's way of telling him to burn more Catholics, and crossed him with the very rarest of his contemporaries, a bishop who took the pope seriously, you would only come close to the restrictions these people impose on common sexuality."

"In other words," Young Kim said, "no flirting."

Spencer was, as always, unimpressed. "I'm not stupid."

"We've never accused you of being stupid," Edmund said. "We're remembering how teenagers act."

"You'll have to blame me for that," Young Kim said from the chair beside Spencer's. "I wasn't the easiest pupil."

That was such an understatement it did a disservice to the very word. "You were to any other difficult pupil," Edmund said, "what malaria is to the common cold."

Young Kim raised an eyebrow, and Edmund's vision twitched strangely. At first he thought it was another glitch in his data-stores.

He was wrong.

"More virulent?" she replied, still and destructive.

Rage + the Machine had returned from their first real triumph, and he was stuck with its sullen leader. If there were a hundred different ways to take a phrase Edmund said, his young mistress would always pick the one which offended her the most. It was a very disagreeable attitude, one that none of his strategies had mitigated so far. "I've warned that you have a lot to learn from your elder team members."

His mistress pulled her knees against her chest—a bad sign. "Like any of them mean anything to me."

Edmund would not abide her self-pity or her misplaced anger. "They all mean a lot to you. Pushing them away solves nothing."

"I don't push. You know that. I can't."

She was far from a helpless cripple. "There are more ways of pushing than using one's hands, mistress."

Success as a corporate raider had truly gone to this teenager's head. If he didn't find a way to get her to trust her companions, she would never rely on them. The upcoming raid on the SEC would be a disaster.

"Uh, guys?"

Edmund didn't recognize the voice, and then his vision twitched again. That was not a glitch in his datastores.

This was Kim's AI clone, not his mistress, who wasn't a recalcitrant teenager anymore. Rage + The Machine had been destroyed, all but one of its members murdered.

Edmund had forgotten it all, and by the look on her face, so had Young Kim.

"It wasn't today," she said, clearly as shaken as he was. "It was seven years ago. Seven and a half. And that wasn't me. *Isn't* me."

Edmund had never experienced anything like this before. "A slip of the tongue, that's all." It had to be.

Spencer was staring. "Edmund," Spencer said, "give me a lattice check and an integrity report. You too, Kim."

How ridiculous. "That is unnecessary. I am quite healthy."

"You forgot this was New Kim, and you both forgot what day it was."

"A quantum hiccup in my lattice, that's all."

"It wasn't a request."

He did have the ability to make the command stick. "Very well. But I'll have you know this will delay our acquisition of the correct tools for the upcoming task."

"By about three hours. Quit stalling; I want that report."

The news was good when they were done. Both crystal lattices were intact and with uncertainty levels well within the acceptable range. The complexity of his datastores was also well below levels that would cause warnings. Young Kim was immune to that issue.

Edmund could tell Spencer wanted to go deeper, but a low-level fracture check on Young Kim's lattice would take hours. His own would take weeks, months, perhaps years. They didn't have that much time.

***

Late that evening the third flaw appeared.

Edmund paced the halls of his apartment, reading a book construct, trying to work out how they could bridge the inevitable air gaps in the inner networks. The give of the wood floorboards and the even light of the admittedly anachronistic fixtures helped him concentrate. Spencer was asleep.

Then he heard the sobs, and his vision twitched yet again.

Most teenage romances ended in tears, but his mistress had extra challenges. His initial programming was quite unsuited to this sort of situation, but time and experience had allowed him to adapt. Not to mention their growing rapport over the past three years. They'd spent hours together, at first contentious but now with a genuine respect, even affection.

She sat at the dinner table, head down, holding a handkerchief that echoed the one she held in realspace right now. He sat down next to her on the bench.

Her voice was muffled by her arms. "I'm such an idiot."

He put his arm around her avatar and gently pulled her closer. She was so fragile sometimes. "Mistress, idiocy is reserved for parliament and the clergy. What you've done is a simple error in judgement."

"I thought he wanted me back. He just wanted to laugh at me with his friends."

"A blackguard, through and through. If it were my era, I'd have the queen attain him forthwith. His head would be on the block before breakfast."

She sat up and away from him, seeming more miserable. "I'm going to be alone my whole life."

He pulled her back to him, and she changed the motion so she laid across his lap. Just like that, she was a child again, twelve years old and frightened of the things she could do.

"Mistress, know this for a fact that's as strong as the stones of Westminster: as long as I exist, you shall never be alone."

His sight twitched again, and it wasn't his mistress anymore. Young Kim stiffened in his lap. He laid a hand on her shoulder. Frightened lambs, both of them.

She curled up tighter. "What's happening to me?"

He performed the same diagnostics as before and nothing had changed. "I do not know. But no matter what, I will not abandon you. We will find out what's going on together."

He spent the rest of the night running every diagnostic he could think of, to no avail.

Chapter 24

Kim

While Watchtell hadn't exactly been a dead end, he hadn't been much of a lead either. Kim didn't dare disturb Edmund while he helped Spencer. They were arriving at the plant the next morning and needed all their concentration for that task. Tonya and Mike were setting up the next run of their experiment, complete with kindergarten physics classes to help her understand what was going on. She was still at a loss for what her next move might be. She needed help.

There was only one other person she trusted. She needed advice, but she had to be careful. Her mother was a master interrogator. She got Mike to confess his true nature in less than fifteen minutes. She knew about Rage + The Machine's capers almost before they did. Hiding from her was how Kim knew she could hide Will. But Mama wanted grandkids like a dog wanted steak. She would need to keep it cool for this breakfast meeting.

She knocked twice on the back door of Mama's house and walked in. Two steps up to the kitchen. It felt like she was in middle school, but she wasn't. She was grown now. It didn't stop the house from feeling like home.

Mama sat at the kitchen table, drinking coffee. She took one look at Kim and closed the virtual screen she was using.

"Oh my God, you're pregnant."

Kim could only gape.

"I always knew you two would figure it out. But *paidi mou*, marriage first! We have so much to plan. How far along are you?"

Kim found her voice. "Mama, I'm not pregnant." So much for being cool.

Mama switched to Greek. "I'm not stupid. You wouldn't be this upset if he'd asked you to marry him."

This upset? Asked? Mama was trying to knock her off balance. She stayed with English as a push back. "He hasn't asked yet." Saying it made her stamp down a regret, which almost made her say what was really going on. Mama was *good*. "Can I at least have some coffee?"

Mama motioned at the kitchen behind her. Sticking with Greek she said, "Avoid telling your mother the truth then. Why should I matter? I'm just an old lady."

"Give me a minute, okay? What's the latest from Aunt Violeta?"

Aunt Violeta was her grandmother's caretaker in Greece, and leader of that side of the family. Kim assembled her coffee while Mama gave her the latest gossip from the old country. It was only when Kim tried to explain it all to Mike that she realized how big her extended family was. They weren't just names to her; she could put faces on all of them. Mike said he used a spreadsheet to keep it straight.

"And they still won't tell us why they want to sell the land," Mama said as Kim sat down. "Those Papadopouloses are up to no good. Violeta is certain of it. Now," she said as she crossed her arms. "You have the coffee and the news. Out with it."

Kim was grown, but Mama's ability to make her feel like she was thirteen was uncanny. She didn't resent it. It was comforting. Someone else was in charge, if only for a moment.

It didn't make telling Mama the truth any easier. "I'm not pregnant, but..." She put the mug down. It would be stupid to hide this. She needed Mama's help to figure out her next move. God *damn* Watchtell and his meddling. "It turns out I have a child."

"What?"

She had told Mama all about her escape from Watchtell's clutches after they had reconnected, so Kim only needed to fill in the same gaps Watchtell had for her. When she was finished, Mama let out a stream of curses that reminded her why Greek was a language of poets.

Mama switched to English. "Wait here."

She disappeared into the house, muttering more curses. What little Kim could catch over the rummaging and crashes told her more about her mom's connections with the Greek underworld than Kim had ever suspected. If any of it was true, at least.

A slip of folded paper landed in front of her. "There."

Kim opened it. It looked like a recipe.

"It took us three years to figure that out when you were little. It was so expensive."

Mama sat down behind her coffee while Kim read the list. It wasn't food, it was drugs, names she didn't recognize.

"The therapists, they asked me if they could publish it. I didn't want to expose you…*us*." Mama never liked talking about events before Dad died. "But someone else might have your syndrome, so we let them."

"What is it?"

"The only drug cocktail that ever settled you down without turning you into a zombie. Your boyfriend, he's told me what he is. He can go anywhere. *You* have never found a lock you couldn't pick, electronic or otherwise. See if someone is ordering that cocktail. If they are, you've found your boy."

Mama grew fierce. "No. You've found *our* boy." She teared up, and Kim had to wipe her own face. They gripped a napkin together. "You find him and bring him here." Kim choked trying to tell her why that couldn't happen, but Mama waved her off. "I don't mean it like that. She can't know who you are. Who we are. I understand. But Kim, to be alone with a child like you, it was so hard. I want to carry part of that burden for her, if she'll let me."

It was what Kim wanted—exactly what she wanted. To help

someone else, because they knew the way out. "I have to find them first."

"Yes. You have to find them first." She tugged the napkin out of Kim's hand and caressed her cheek with it. "And you will. *Paidi mou*, you will. I am so proud of you." She pulled the cloth back and blew her nose into it. Mama was emotional, but also practical. "Now go, leave an old lady in peace. I'm a secret grandmother. Don't make me wait too long to become a real one."

Kim called Mike on the drive to her shop. "We're looking for someone ordering this specific combination of drugs."

"Wow. I've never heard of some of these. Tonya hasn't either."

One day she'd get used to Mike having a normal conversation with her while having a normal, simultaneous, conversation with someone else. More than one, since this was around the time for *Warhawk's* stand-up meeting.

"How many threads can you spare me?"

"I can start searching. I'll split more off as soon as I wrap a few things up. Oh, I have good news about the experiment."

"Do I need a PhD to understand it?"

His chuckle made her think that this time around, the experiment might work. "Some of it does, but not all. We've figured out how to use my threads as controls and sensors. We can do the next run with a regular phone. One problem, though."

There was always at least one problem. "Yes?"

"We'll have to turn the neural blockers off, otherwise they'll interfere with what we're doing."

The thing inside her arm had been agonizing, and she knew it hadn't gone away. "We'll talk about timing after we've chased down this lead. I don't need a full realm connection to do my searches."

"Do you want us to come by for lunch?"

"Sure. Let me know if you find anything before then."

Mike was all about his threads. It was more like exploring for him, visiting places and seeing what they held. Kim's searches were different, relying on her understanding of how the backend of realmspace worked. She programmed and then released a full load of lockPixies, customized search agent constructs, before she walked into the shop. The specialized AIs were motes of blue dust to anyone who noticed them. They could work their way into any system that met their search parameters.

She tried to do more direct searches between customers, but the constant traffic in and out of the shop didn't make it easy. Even with Basil helping she was constantly busy. A full list of regular clients had carried over from the previous owner, and her own reputation guaranteed a steady stream of new customers who needed a service only she could provide.

Fixing ransomware attacks in a world of perfect security had become an important new line of business. Most people used commercial services that took weeks or even months. Fortune 500 companies with irresponsible CEOs—or vengeful sysadmins—didn't have that luxury. Time was the only thing they couldn't afford to waste, and she was fast.

She set the latest locked datastore on the bench.

There were lines of potential, and she couldn't remember how to breathe. This lock no lock always locked never locked—

Priority Interrupt

The backlash was like holding one end of a stretched bungee cord when the other person let go. Except it was aimed at her face.

Basil rushed to the back of the shop. "Is everything okay? Oh my God!"

She was on the floor. Everybody always talked about a first time for everything. For Kim, it always seemed to come with a kick in the teeth.

Basil knew the drill, which made the whole thing take a left turn into stupidville. Again.

"Umm…ahh…Kim? I'm not sure…"

She felt a broom handle against her arm, then her thigh.

He switched to Greek. "It's just that we still have customers, and I don't know how to wake you up like this."

Whatever it was faded to the point where she could feel her teeth again. They were all there. The interrupt had hit her so hard she'd worried some of them had been knocked out. Kim opened her eyes and held up her hands. Well, tried to. One of her arms was still in a sling, which caught on the broom handle. It snatched the broom out of Basil's hands and smashed it into a box full of watch gears, which exploded in a shower of brass.

At least he didn't try to touch her. "I'm okay." She put her good hand down on at least three of the gears, which cut her hand. What the hell had interrupted...then she remembered, and the pain vanished.

Will.

"I'm fine." She stood, picking brass out of her palm. "Go back to the customers. I'll clean this up."

The gears would wait. She checked her message queue. Her lockPixies didn't just have a couple of candidates.

They'd found an address.

There were lines of potential, and she couldn't remember how to breathe. See don't see cameras locks everywhere nowhere areas pinpoints this network no networks collapse and now...

They'd gone to ground in a gated community north of Atlanta, some place called Green Valley in Milton, close to Alpharetta. She'd figure out exactly where that was later. She accessed the outer camera network first to get oriented. The trees were tall and old, but it still felt artificial. The houses were impressive. Watchtell must've sequestered at least some of his wealth with his daughter.

Kim jumped from camera to camera, drawing closer to the target. The lawns, still green that far south, were well manicured; the cars parked on the driveways were shiny and new. Kim would want to raise a family there, if she had that option.

The front of the house was unremarkable until the audio came online.

"Now try with the orange ball," a man's voice said.

They were in the back yard.

"Come on, Will," a woman's voice said. "Take the ball for Mommy."

She couldn't see in. She needed to see in. It took three tries to find a camera with an angle on the back yard.

"That's okay, Will," a different woman's voice said with an odd metallic echo. "I'll get it for you."

The back yard had a tall privacy fence around it. Inside was mostly grass, with a swing set on the left and a trampoline on the right. Emily, Will's mom, stood on the back patio against the house next to an older man Kim didn't recognize. A bot of some sort trundled across the lawn toward the back fence.

Will stood on the grass watching it.

Facing her.

After they got back from China, Mama had thrown them all a lunch party. Toward the end of the night, Mama had gotten out old family albums so everyone could see what Kim looked like as a kid. Kim was fully prepared for a lot of laughing embarrassment, but then Mama pulled up her wedding photo, and she was shocked. That was *her* standing beside her dad, not her Mama. It took blinking to break the illusion.

That was what it felt like when she saw Will. Not an older version of herself, but a younger one. Maybe it was the vacant expression on his face, so familiar from those early photos, before she had unlocked. It was so unreal.

"Here you go," the bot said as it held the ball out with a mechanical arm. Wait, it wasn't a bot. That was an assisted living shell. Someone with a severe injury was inside it, a burn victim maybe, or someone who'd been in a terrible accident. Kim had only read about them until now. "Can you touch the ball, Will?" The voice was kind, but still artificial.

Will stood there, and Kim's heart fell to pieces. She knew exactly what was going on. He couldn't respond. He couldn't see them. His saw reflections from a fractured mirror that only cleared occasionally. They couldn't touch him, couldn't guide him, and he didn't know why.

Kim marked the spot and mapped the trail so she wouldn't have to break into the neighborhood network the next time. The mess in the back of the shop wasn't a problem anymore. Cleaning it up would give her time to get her face back to normal. Nobody wanted to buy things from a person who'd been crying.

They seemed happy in their safe house, but even gated, the community wasn't secure. They needed to be on the move. Staying still, they'd become a target, but they didn't know that. She couldn't walk up and ring the doorbell, either. Watchtell had told them who knew how many lies about her. They'd be terrified and would never listen.

She opened a channel. "Mike, I need you and Tonya to come over. I've found them."

Chapter 25

June

He called it a bomb.

If June didn't know she needed Cyril's knowledge, she would've thrown him out on his ear. They were working to save the humanity, not destroy it. It was a power plant. That it could be a bomb was absurd. She had helped build it. Anna was a hero. June would not, could not, accept it.

And yet...

The entire time she had been here, something else was going on. Anna had an inner circle of board members who would have meetings late into the night. Only Yumbo was allowed to take notes, and Anna had insisted that not even June could access those archives. It was for the cause, so June happily complied. She didn't ask why. She didn't need to; they were working for the greater good.

Cyril was an ex-employee of the people who built the device. He knew about a secret entrance to the lab. That's all. He had knowledge that they needed to explore its capabilities.

Then why didn't she turn him in? It was almost as if her oupa sat on her shoulder, whispering doubts into her ear. He'd been an old-school Afrikaner, complete with a gigantic cattle farm and a house with a proper stoop that wrapped all the way around it. He'd stunned everyone when he fully embraced his adopted granddaughter. "If we must have a future together," he said, "then we need to teach the youth to be proper South Africans. Not just the

Afrikaner traditions, but the Zulu, the Xhosa, the Coloreds, and all the rest. They need to learn *all* of it. We are all a part of this country."

So June was taught a strong work ethic, the desire to listen rather than talk, the sense of community, of practicality, of family, and so much more that made up her home. Most of all, she was taught hard-headed common sense.

That was what made her soul itch. There were so many odd things about the power plant that would make sense if what Cyril said was true. One thing in particular had puzzled June forever. The college. It was so expensive, especially when their funding was zeroed out. Anna had insisted on maintaining an underground college with specially recruited young people, complete with dorms. Who wanted a green school way out here?

She pushed the questions away. Her day was too complicated as it was. The Trilogy tech had arrived, and she had been tapped to be his tour guide-slash-minder. When she came up to the visitor's lobby to pick him up, she knew her title wasn't accurate.

It should've been babysitter.

He was a lanky white teenager with a buzz cut and the most ridiculous pair of horn-rimmed glasses she'd ever seen. She thought they stopped making those decades ago. He did have the requisite dark blue shirt, sweat pants, and vintage Nikes on. The shirt had a patch on it that read *Trilogy Away Team*. She shuddered inwardly. They didn't try to hide that they were consciously imitating a twentieth-century suicide cult who believed aliens would take them to a better life.

He stared up at her, gaping like strangers always did.

"Good morning," she said as she put out her hand. "I'm Dr. du Plessis." His grip was firm, but his skin was soft, a sure sign he was from the inner circle. Everyone else spent most of their time doing farm work, at least that was what she'd read anyway. Maybe he was a founder's son.

"Right," he stammered. "Um…I'm sorry. Spencer Sellars." He smiled as he picked up his satchel. "My bosses send their apologies. I'm the only one they could spare."

"Is everyone all right?" So far only minor injuries had been reported to the press.

He nodded, and his expression changed to one she was more used to seeing on someone talking about Jesus in church. "We are ever prepared for the final conflict, so our fellow-sisters and mother-guides got the first lights into shelters long before the danger came."

June sort of understood that, or at least the gist.

His face changed back to that of a regular teenager, and he pitched his voice lower. "We all ran like hell into the storm cellars. We thought it was a drill."

The cult had a rebel in their midst. Ideology and technical talent didn't always mix. June herself was a prime example.

The oupa on her shoulder made it clear that the comparison went deeper than that. The difference was that Spencer's cult waited for the apocalypse, while hers was bringing it about.

They were *not* bringing it about. Cyril had gotten under her skin without providing a shred of proof. June must remember that. He had no proof.

Yet.

She could see her silence made the tech uncomfortable. The distractions just kept piling up. June motioned him forward. "Shall we?"

The first stop was security. Heavy security for a big expensive installation that did not have a lot of secrets.

Spencer had to give up his personal phone and was issued one from the plant's stores because of signal strength and custom frequencies. No other reason. It wasn't about security. Cyril had her so wound up she'd forgotten about that limitation. She needed to calm down.

He wasn't impressed with what they handed him. "A Samsung Universe Ten?" He thought it was a cheap, basic neural phone. He was mostly right.

"The signal crosstalk of regular commercial phones causes interference that'll keep some of our newest mods from functioning properly. You're also working in the AI lab, and commercial phones are always too hot for it. Here," she said as she dropped its lanyard over his neck. "This one is certified to function correctly."

But with what? And why? her imaginary oupa asked.

***

As she took him on the tour, June gave the tried-and-true *green dream* speech, the one Anna used to such great effect on donors. It didn't seem to be working on him, though. He was more interested in the layout and the tech. Keeping him focused was difficult. Every time his attention wandered, she began to think of Cyril and the things he said. They weren't true.

Oupa's voice was easy to remember. *I told you this was the wrong move all along.*

He disapproved when she left for America and then took this job. The whole family thought she should stay in South Africa. But she was stifled there; she needed to move out and make her own mark. And she had. She was widely recognized as a leading expert in green AI. This was her success story, not some extended bout of teenage rebellion.

Certainly it wasn't, he said. You moved halfway around the world for your green dream.

The sourness of the thoughts made them harder to push away.

Finally they got down to the big show, a sight so spectacular it let her forget about Cyril and his lies.

"It's called the High Efficiency Low Motion Open Nexoid Descender, or HELMOND, for short. It's only thirty meters across, but," she peered dramatically over the catwalk they stood on, "it's approximately twenty-three kilometers deep. You are the first person outside the plant's staff to see it in person." Everyone else had toured the much smaller prototype nearby.

"A hundred feet wide, but seventeen *miles* deep? Holy fu—" he cleared his throat, embarrassed. "Prophets be praised."

Lights fully illuminated the first five kilometers. Gray metal walls lined with pipes that were as big around as a car extended beyond that into the blackness. Farther on, spotlights illuminated one gigantic construction site after another. She could see the robots hard at work on the upper-most ones. It took her breath away every time she visited.

"What's with the bull's-eye over there? It looks like a trampoline," he said.

It was a target they'd only put up last week. It stuck out into the shaft, held by a framework so it almost looked like a billboard. June decided to go all out on this tour, to prove to at least one person that not only was the plant meant for peace, but that it was also a bit of fun.

Most of the time, the Earth's rotation was demonstrated by a huge pendulum suspended from a wire attached to the ceiling. Anna's genius was realizing they could turn the same concept, almost literally, inside out.

June keyed open a box mounted to the railing and pulled out a big silver dart with a blunt, padded nose. She turned the strobe in the tail on and handed it to Spencer. "See if you can hit it with this."

"It's heavy."

"It needs to be. Go on, see if you can."

He cocked his arm back and gave it a good heave. The throw would've done well on a cricket pitch, even a baseball diamond. It got a lot closer than she expected it to.

"Prophets save us! That should've hit."

June laughed. "It was a good throw, but we cheated. We play with your perspective so you think it's closer than it is. Hitting the target isn't what this is about." She pointed over the rail. "That is."

She saw him find the flashing light of the dart quickly. It was a good thing the strobes were bright, otherwise they would not be able to follow it down into the gloom. Instead of falling straight into oblivion, it curved inward, back toward the wall their platform stood on. After a long while, it fell on a speck of light far below, *directly* underneath their platform. The shared enhanced vision magnified until they could see it. The robot collecting the dart waved up at them.

"Holy shit."

June had always suspected that, if one of these fanatics could be pried away from their leadership, they would turn back into normal people. It seemed she was right. "The dart fell straight down. It was Earth that turned and caught it."

"And this is what makes the place tick? A giant hole?"

"There's more to it than that. The temperature gradient between here and the bottom is massive. So is the density. With nothing but simple convection, we can use turbines to generate power. Then we extract more heat to make steam, which turns more turbines. Nano-materials let us leverage the remaining difference and generate electricity directly. Then we dissipate the remaining heat in a large reservoir we built nearby. It lets us control the temperature of the water so we can support native fish populations properly." It was the very first proven environmentally neutral artificial body of water ever built. A regular reservoir's water would be too cold to support native species, but by heating it, they had increased the available habitat for the creatures who had always been here. Another *peaceful* thing June could be proud of.

Oupa was ever-present on her shoulder. *And a convenient source of fresh water for an isolated community.*

"Fu—" he cleared his throat. "Prophets be praised."

"Indeed. Now, if you'll follow me, we'll go to the AI labs."

They had just stepped off the elevator when emergency lights started flashing and an alarm claxon blared.

"What's that about?"

June started to check when a bot bumped against her.

"My apologies, but we must be allowed to pass. We have been summoned to a developing crisis."

She stood aside so the emergency response bot team could keep going. They reminded June of plastic firemen, painted a flat white with red EMERGENCY markings. They even had flashing red lights. Not all of them were bipedal, though. A few looked like miniaturized fire trucks. She thought they were silly when they ran them through their trials. They weren't as funny when the emergency was real.

She could see that Spencer was not impressed. "Doesn't seem like a positive development."

They had to dodge out of the way of another ERBT that came off the elevator before June found the right alert on the network.

"It's some sort of equipment overload." There was an odd smell in the air now.

Spencer noticed it, too. "How good is the ventilation down here? That could be toxic."

June checked the status boards. "The ventilation systems are nominal, and not showing anything dangerous. Each of those teams has an air filter bot. One of them is sufficient to keep the air on this entire level safe."

"So why did you guys send two?"

"We'd rather have an extra and not need it." While they walked cautiously forward, she tried to access the surveillance network, but it had gone from glitching to down. Abada's telltales showed his workload had risen past the point he could continue to maintain it reliably. She needed to get Spencer plugged in and working as soon as possible, otherwise she may never see her African unicorn again.

The lab was in the same direction that the bots had gone. "Let's find out what's going on."

They didn't make it as far as the lab, though. Whatever happened tore up one of the botanical garden installations. They always had surplus nanomachines out of every construction batch. Rather than let them expire, Anna used them to create large, cathedral-like rooms and then fill them with plants of every kind. Green inside green is what she called it. Not only were they pleasant to walk through, they also provided a substantial amount of the food needed for the plant's staff.

What a convenient coincidence, the Oupa on her shoulder said.

Trees were knocked down, grass ripped up, even the pond in the middle was now holed and leaking. The control cabinets had been smashed. That was what had caused the overload and fire. It looked like the pictures Oupa once showed her of what happened when cyclone Esami had torn through Limpopo before she was born.

"What happened?" she asked one of the bots.

"Unknown at this time, Dr. du Plessis. We've been getting erratic wildlife alarms from the water processing facilities ever since the critical network incident."

Certain sections of the plant required a steady water supply to function properly, which was another function of the reservoir. They had been extremely careful to make sure it wouldn't impact the environment around it. A little too careful, it turned out. Once the wildlife had rebounded inside the plant's exclusion zone, intake and outflow systems designed not to hurt animals ended up being embarrassingly easy for them to enter and set up house. It was a problem that required constant monitoring. She should've sent extra guard bots down to keep an eye on things but hadn't gotten around to it yet.

"I see," she said, and dispatched the required bots. It would take some time for them to report back.

"See what?" Spencer asked.

He started prowling around as she got him up to speed on the reservoir, looking at the destruction like he was planning a safari hunt. "You're saying animals did this? Lady, how big do the bears *get* around here?"

"It is unusual to find them this far inside the plant, but that's why you're here. Our security networks have been glitching this entire time. The explosion must've scared them off."

"That part I can agree with, but..."

Trilogy's survivalist skills were quite well known. If he had any insight, she wanted to hear it. "Yes?"

Spencer shook his head. "Nothing. I guess all those stories about grizzlies are true. Shouldn't we be warning people?"

"The plant's human staff is small and mostly on the upper levels. But your point is well made." She entered a warning on the local net as they made their way past the mess and to her lab.

"Nice digs," he said as the lights came on.

"What does your lab look like?" Then she remembered. "I mean, what *did* it look like."

He snorted. "A complete...ly different sort of arrangement. But, prophets be praised, we will now be rebuilding. If you don't mind, I'd like to take some notes on your system?"

"Be my guest."

He pulled a crystal out of his pocket. "If you'd do the honors?"

Installing Trilogy tools onto her network didn't feel right, but the scanners said they checked out. Spencer had checked out as well, and it wasn't like Trilogy had never accessed their systems. That direct line existed for a reason. "How long will it take them to decompress?"

"We'll have to wait until morning to get started, which is just as well." He rolled his eyes, looking like he'd just been given extra homework. "I have to go pray now."

Right. From what she read, even their standard set of prayers could take hours. "I'll show you to your quarters."

Chapter 26

Kim

She needed to come up with a strategy to reach out to Will's mom, Emily. To do that, they needed to learn who she was, what her interests were, what was important and what wasn't. Once they figured out which realmspace cell her house used, it was straightforward for Mike to follow her browsing habits.

"Aside from some RealmTerest activity, it's pretty much all autism, all the time. She's very active."

"And the scientists?" Kim asked.

"Doctors Silas Nevin and Shonda Brandt. They have a thriving online therapy practice. Shonda was in a car accident twelve years ago. Third degree burns over seventy percent of her body."

Tonya let out a low whistle. "She must be one of the first successful ALS...hang on...no, she *is* the first successful assisted living shell recipient. I thought I recognized that name."

"And now I recognize the shell," Mike said. "Lucas shamed Disney into giving her a license for the design. It seems that's the droid we're looking for."

Kim didn't understand why anyone would want to go through life as a silver-and-black R2D2 clone, but that wasn't her circus or her monkeys. The doctors weren't their priority anyway. It made sense that Emily would be active in the autism community. It was the closest disorder to what he had.

Emily always introduced herself to a new forum with the same message.

Hi! I'm Emily Ramirez, and I have a child who has been diagnosed with autism. But I'm not sure about that. He has severe speech and language challenges, along with sensory dysfunction, but he also has a unique sensory processing disorder that may indicate a different diagnosis, at least according to the doctors we've seen. Does anyone out there have experience with a child who is extremely fearful when touched by people?

The doctors always called it haphephobia, as if the fear of being touched was always a psychological thing. When someone's touch hurt, fearing it was natural. But he couldn't get that across yet.

The responses were also always the same, brief notes of encouragement, a few references to obscure medical journals—which Emily seemed to already know by heart—and occasionally a troll who insisted Emily didn't know what she was talking about.

One of the groups had a realm get-together tonight, which was perfect timing. Kim signed herself up as Angie Amorrua. Her avatar was a standard variation, changing her appearance to make her unrecognizable but not so much as to trigger any contract restrictions. Mike couldn't attend without attracting attention, so she brought Tonya as her plus one. Being a complete unknown, she had no need for a disguise. Kim was going to turn that into an advantage.

The realm was yet another generic variation of a hotel conference room, hosted by Hilton's virtual convention division. They had technology that could create a Roman forum, a space station garden dome, or a mansion in Moria, and what did they pick? The same scratchy over-patterned carpet, uncomfortable chairs, and generic chandeliers that you would find in every realspace hotel tower ever built. There had to be a licensing issue at the bottom of it.

Emily was signed up under a pseudonym as well, but Mike figured it out. "Over there," he said in her ear. One of the front rows flashed in her avatar's vision. "She's the one in the blue blouse."

"Are the scientists that work with Will here?"

"No. They're still doing appointments, I can tell by the privacy stipulations on their connection contracts."

So they only needed to worry about Emily. "Do you see any sign of surveillance or taps here?" Kim asked.

Mike had concentrated most of his threads in the area of this realm. From his unique perspective, spotting anything unusual should be a breeze. It felt like a safety blanket.

"Only the meeting's recording system. The realm's contract is intact and normal for a conference like this."

No weapons, obscenities, or fights. An aggressive move would pass through an avatar and result in expulsion. Avatars could vary from a person's actual appearance but not by more than a very low standard deviation. Everyone was expected to act like an adult.

Spencer would hate it.

Emily's pseudonym was well known to this group. A total stranger striking up a conversation with her would be normal. Making new connections and networking was one of the points of the meeting.

Kim and Tonya managed to get seats just behind and to the left of Emily, who seemed to be attending alone. Her disguise didn't change her body language or expressions. She was tired and tense, but still gave her full attention as the lights went down.

The topic gave Kim an opening once the speaker had finished. The realm switched from a generic hotel meeting room to a generic hotel lounge. One of these days she should talk to Mike about opening up a design line that gave *some* sort of variation to these places. The ferns felt as plastic as their realspace counterparts.

Kim sidled up to Emily, who stood as part of the loose ring of people who had formed around the speaker's couch. "Unfortunately," Kim said to Emily, "it won't work in cases like ours."

"Pardon me?"

Kim held out her hand. "I'm Angie, and this is Tonya. I recognized your handle from your posts on the realm discussion board."

Emily shook their hands in turn, firm but not aggressive. "I'm Emily. What do you mean *in cases like ours*?"

They'd gone over the plan carefully. Being in disguise was required at this stage, but they wouldn't lie to Emily. She already thought Kim was the devil, and anything less than honesty—within limits—would ruin any chance at trust when she found out the truth. But Kim also couldn't go *ta-da!* and have Emily take her seriously. So they were approaching her as researchers, which they were, who knew things about the syndrome, which they did, and were looking for someone else to talk to, which was true.

Like Ben Kenobi always said, from a certain point of view.

"You're the mother of the boy with touch aversion, right?" Kim asked. "Your list of indications is the best description we've seen of the syndrome in years." Not quite lying was like walking across a greasy balance beam. "We've been searching for another case ever since we found one in China."

Emily sat down in the chair behind her. "You've found *another case*?"

Kim took the chair to Emily's right while Tonya took the one opposite, across a low table. "Yes," Tonya said. "In Chengdu, a city in southwest China."

The hope that bloomed on Emily's face was like the sun coming out. Will had a terrible syndrome, Kim knew that better than anyone else, and now Emily wasn't alone.

But she was also in danger. Kim only needed one break to find them. They must've made other mistakes, and Anna might already be on their trail. There was no way to tell. Kim had to establish trust while crossing the minefield that Watchtell had put in her way, and then get them moving. *Fast.*

Emily was still grappling with the idea that Will wasn't alone. "Who are they? How old are they? Is it a boy or a girl? How did you *find* them?"

Kim sat back. "His western name was Ozzie Xian." He'd been a lying bastard, but it still hurt to say what had happened to him.

"He died in an accident while we were there. Do you remember the Chengdu riverboat attack?"

Emily's eyes went wide. "I read about it. That was awful. He was there?"

Kim shared a look with Tonya, who nodded slightly. "We all were. There was an explosion in his cabin. He didn't survive."

Emily got a conflicted look, trying to reconcile the good news with the bad. Then she got what Kim was implying. "His own cabin? Are you saying he was an *adult*?"

"Yes." Kim's heart went to her throat as she put her hand on Emily's. Stick with the truth, even if you've hidden it your whole life. "And I am, too."

The contact between their avatars confused her for a moment, then she looked up at Kim. "You mean you have…"

Kim only managed a nod.

"But…you…" She let out a sob. "But you can talk."

Tonya nodded. "Yes, and we think it's only a matter of time before Will can too."

That was a hope too far. She pulled back. "How do you know? How *can* you know? Why haven't I heard of you until now?"

"It's complicated," Kim said, "I know because I went through it." That helped calm her suspicions a little, so Kim kept going. "You think he has autism, but he doesn't. That's why nothing is working."

"Then what does he have?"

Kim shrugged. "The Chinese call it *jiēchù jíbìng*, which translates to *the touching disease*. It doesn't have a formal name yet in the West. That's part of what we're trying to do." Not thinking about its name until this moment didn't count as lying. Probably. *Trayne-Ramirez Syndrome* did have a certain ring to it. "Let me describe what I experienced and see if it matches what you've been through."

She related some of the stories Mama had told her about when she was little. Not just the funny things that Mama trotted out whenever someone new attended one of her lunch parties, but also the painful things, the embarrassing things, the things Mama said tempted her to leave Kim on the side of the road sometimes. Those were details that weren't in any public research. Kim had made sure of it. It made her feel more exposed than ever before. Tonya didn't know most of these things and neither did Mike. Emily was friendly, but she was still a stranger. Worse, she was the daughter of Matthew Watchtell.

Kim watched as Emily worked on a mental checklist the entire time. By her expressions, Kim was certain she checked all the boxes.

"I unlocked—that's what I've always called it—when I was ten. So did Ozzie."

"But how?"

"That part I'm not sure about. We think it has to do with realm technologies, but beyond that, it's anyone's guess."

Tonya said, "That's one of the reasons we're reaching out now. We can make observations, do tests to see if we can unlock Will earlier than that. It happened to her and Ozzie accidentally."

Emily hadn't pulled back, hadn't gotten angry, and hadn't disappeared. The gambit was working. Emily believed them. She should. They were telling the truth.

"Here's my card," Kim said as she transmitted her contact information and an encrypted authenticator so Emily would know it was her when they got to phase two of the plan. Tonya passed her one as well. "You can contact us any time."

When Emily took both of them, Kim relaxed a little. Emily needed to know them, needed to understand and trust that Kim had information she needed and the same syndrome as her son. But she also needed to take that card. It was all about confirming their ID. She pinged Mike so he'd start packing.

Kim gave Emily some basic tips, answering questions as she went. When Mike pinged her back that everything was ready, they exchanged a few pleasantries and then logged off.

Kim didn't want to turn Blacksteel Rose into her personal air transport network, so they took Tonya's Alfa, which could comfortably sleep three. Everyone needed to be fresh for the next step.

"You all don't worry one bit," the car said as it opened the door. "I'll get you there on time." Kim wasn't sure she'd ever get used to Morgan Freeman driving them around, but Tonya seemed to like it.

It would be late tomorrow afternoon, well after dark this time of year, when they arrived in Atlanta.

Chapter 27
Edmund

"You never said it would be this much fun!"

Of all the different ways Young Kim could react to being uploaded into a private network, Edmund would never have picked joy. Her resemblance to his mistress in that moment was disorienting.

"Yes," he said. "But we're not here to have fun, you see. We have a job."

The biggest risk to their plan was that there would be no unoccupied fabric available on this network. Young Kim was easy to transfer, but Edmund was quite a bit larger. If there hadn't been any free fabric available, it would take hours to get the network to generate the required amount of space. That was the real reason Spencer left their transit matrix connected overnight.

It turned out they needn't have worried. The plant's network was bigger than all the cathedrals in Christendom, allowing them to specify an entry address so far away from the parts of the network in use it might as well have been on a different planet.

Young Kim's ebullient reaction was the result of her becoming part of his mistress's scheme of skullduggery. They originally wanted to leave her in the car's transit matrix.

Being an unduplicate, he could play that debacle back effortlessly.

"If you two leave me behind," she said, fists firmly against her hips, "I'll get old me to burn you both to the ground."

"Telling Mommy," Spencer said, "won't get you any further than you already are."

"She's not *my mommy*, she's me. And neither one of us would— will—put up with this. You need me."

Edmund lifted his head from his hand. "You sneak about as well as a cow in Satan's own herd. You'd leave a trail a mile wide through the network."

"Your upgrades did that. If you'd left me stock, I'd be fine."

"And less useful than a pallid poxy peasant pressing pies."

Spencer blinked at that one, but Young Kim ignored it. "You think, as old as you are, you can dodge the packet inspectors?"

The stroppy little monster had a lot of nerve. "I'll have you know I've run rings around quantum inspectors before."

"Yeah, back in the Jurassic."

"Kim," Spencer said, "we need someone on the outside in case we don't come back."

"And leaving me out here makes that less likely? I'm twice as smart as you are, and three times faster than he is. On my worst day I'm better than you two on your best. This mission can't rely on an idiot teenager and his doddering old sidekick. You are *not* leaving me behind. End of discussion." She turned away and smashed out of the realm's classroom, the door barely staying on its hinges. Her voice echoed down the hall. "I'm going. Get used to it." Another loud smash as she left the realm entirely.

He'd forgotten how lyrical his mistress was when she got that angry. By the gobsmacked expression on Spencer's face, he'd never seen her that wound up at all. She'd slowed down by the time he met her.

"I guess she's going," Spencer said.

"I'm certainly not going to stop her."

"So what do we do?"

"More upgrades I suppose. By the end of this, she'll be worth more than a nun's virginity at a papal conclave."

Which was why Young Kim was now capering around in a custom set of camouflage screens, exactly like what he wore. They were both made from construct plans his mistress had gifted him long ago. They came with downsides, at least for him. It made his avatar seem far more twenty-first century than he would ever feel comfortable with. He couldn't fit his ruff collar under it at all, but the codpiece remained firmly in place. No true Renaissance gentleman could go without one.

"Why so much space?" she asked, gesturing around them, empty but for row upon row of shelflike constructs that stretched as far as he could see.

Edmund called up the plans they'd received from Master Sellars's sister and highlighted the extensive dormitories built underground. "For the same reason the realspace component is so large. They're going to warehouse data like they're going to warehouse humans. They want to do it quickly and on short notice."

She stopped dancing. Young Kim walked over to the nearest shelf and ran her hands over it. "These are chromosome hangars. They're going to store genomes."

He would never have thought of it in a million years, but now that it had been pointed out, he could see it. If the maniac behind all of this wanted to reformat the biosphere, she needed installation media to finish the job.

He cracked open his datastores just a bit to see if he could find more insights, and that made it real. Building a space this enormous was not easy nor was it quick. It was one thing to consider armageddon as an abstract thing. It was quite another to find oneself in the midst of its clear and present preparations. It must've been what Knyvet felt when he looked under the woodpile beneath parliament and saw three-dozen barrels of gunpowder.

"Uh-oh," Young Kim said as she flattened herself against the end of one of the shelves. "We got incoming."

Two avatars hove into view high above the realm's floor. They were shaped like huge, dark cylinders with an eyestalk on one end. The light being cast from the eye wasn't just to illuminate the realm. It also contained technical probes that queried the underlying fabric of it, looking for anomalies. As they approached, a rumble vibrated his avatar in a most alarming way. He tucked his head inside his cloak just before the search beam hit him. The construct sizzled as it redirected and spoofed the incoming signal, returning only what the probe was supposed to find. It was like hiding in a priest hole from a group of Protestants looking for a particular sort of starter log. After an eternity that was only a few seconds, it moved away, lifting a weight that wasn't altogether metaphorical off his shoulders.

"*That* was interesting," Young Kim said.

He jumped. She sneaked up on him somehow. "Would you *please* never do that again? I do not want an involuntary garbage dump to happen in here." Whatever those things were could've scuppered the entire mission before it started and done who knew what to them, and this one found it *interesting*.

She pulled the hood of her cloak away, revealing a glittering smile of mischief. "You're too jumpy. They're not a threat. Not to us anyway."

"Whatever do you mean, you silly girl?"

"You didn't notice it? They're using a basic single-unit sector search pattern. There are two of them, but their pattern is designed for someone working alone. I've already built a prediction program for it. They'll never find us."

Her insight was helpful, but also alarming. No AI of her class should be able to make such leaps. Edmund could only follow them after the fact. He ran the same diagnostics he had the night before and couldn't believe what they reported. Then: nothing had changed.

Now: everything had.

"What have you done?"

She gave him an infuriatingly dismissive shrug. "I was so hacked off that you two were leaving me behind I pulled open the stores you put inside me and integrated them. It's a good thing I did, too. You would never have thought of the search thing on your own."

The danger she blithely discounted was staggering. She could've been squashed out of existence. It should never have..."You little cross-eyed git! How dare you attempt such a thing! Those weren't yours to begin with!"

As with her namesake, Young Kim was unphased by his fury. "You left them inside me like treasure chests. They were even *shaped* like treasure chests. Leaky ones. If I hadn't done it on purpose it would've eventually happened by accident."

"Leaks?" The connection, the anomalies, and now the innovations. "What have I done?"

"Not much if you keep standing there foaming at the mouth. Come on, we got scouting to do." She threw her hood over her head and walked down the aisle.

The event was unbelievable, but there was nothing for it now. She was fully integrated with his memory stores. He couldn't get them back if he used a pry bar. Young Kim was now, for all intents and purposes, an unduplicate. Edmund had always treated his mistress like a daughter.

Now it seemed he had a real one.

And it was more than that. The readings clearly indicated she was fully conscious as well. He could join her, but...*no*. He would not cross that line. Young Kim seemed to have integrated successfully, but Edmund knew his own path only led to madness.

She walked back to him. "Do I have to drag you?"

They did have a mission. "No, please." He tried to straighten his ruff, forgetting that he'd left it behind. "We will continue."

They fit well together, that much was clear. Her impulsiveness disguised a very sharp mind. Where he was methodical and analytical, she made leaps of intuition that saved them hours of time.

***

They were finishing up their preliminary searches when Young Kim found security footage of some sort of mission control room. Edmund thought it compared favorably to the inside of the papal palace at Avignon: grand but spare. Of course, the palace was like that because it'd been picked clean centuries ago. This was featureless by design.

"Where is this?" She asked. "It looks like a vent room, but they've put in a lot of extra gear. Whoa..." She zoomed in on the corner, showing the edge of a device they'd been examining on blueprints for a week.

"It's from the portal room," Edmund said. "Is it a realm?"

"No. This is recent realspace footage. The logs say nobody's seen this yet. It's been filed incorrectly."

To make sure that stayed the case, he made a copy of the file and deleted the original. A quick review of the footage showed a meeting of some sort, first of robots and then of actual humans.

"I see Master Spencer's new minder was involved," Edmund said.

"And Anna Treacher. I'm pretty sure that's the whole board of directors."

They slowed the tape to real time when the portal flared to life.

"Good Lord," he said. "These cheeky monkeys do seem to get into everything, don't they?"

Young Kim let out a low whistle when the screen went white. "That's one hell of an energy surge."

The screen cleared, and they were able to make out the room again. "What in the world," Edmund said.

Lightning crackled across the room. The robots that had been seated at the control consoles expired in clouds of sparks whenever it touched them. It seemed to comb the room, and when it climbed up to their camera, the screen went blank.

But only for a moment.

When it came back, Young Kim gasped. "What the shit?"

The video was badly degraded while the camera was still booting up, so Edmund wasn't sure what they were looking at. It seemed like two very large, hairy creatures exited the frame on the right, presumably after walking across the room while the camera was restarting. They carried a heavy box between them. There was no sign of who'd been standing in front of the portal. A third, much smaller shape ran into the shadows from the other side. By the time the images were clear, the video stopped altogether.

"Some kind of bears?" Young Kim asked.

"In the middle of a power plant, carrying a box?"

"Surrounded by a forest that's been turned into a ginormous wildlife sanctuary. You got a better explanation?"

"The surge scrambled the save addressing," Edmund said. "It must've corrupted the imagery as well." Things like that were known to happen. Somewhere.

"What the hell happened down there?"

They didn't have enough information to understand what they saw. Edmund didn't like that one bit. "Any speculation on our part would pointless. We must report our findings to Master Spencer as soon as he arrives at work in the morning."

Chapter 28

Kim

The drive down to Atlanta was even more nerve-wracking than the one to visit Watchtell. Kim had made contact with Emily and established a tiny bit of trust. She hoped that that, and the discovery of the first person who could help her son, would be enough. It had to be.

She cracked open the neighborhood's surveillance network, so they were able to use the video archives to figure out everyone's movements. Without professional bodyguards to advise them, all the adults had fallen into dangerous habits. Part of that wasn't surprising. Will didn't respond well to changes in routine. What was surprising was how willingly they all went out on their own.

Kim understood the impulse. Even when she was in hiding, she still went out. She had to, she needed a job. But it was never the same way twice in a row. Kim always assumed she was being followed. She could, and several times did, move to a different apartment or job at the slightest sense that anything was wrong. It didn't only keep her from being arrested. It saved her life.

Emily was not as cautious.

But it did make their job easier. It was late afternoon when they pulled up outside a converted fire station, an hour before the local autism support group was scheduled to meet. Kim picked the locks on the closed office on the same floor that the meeting was being held on, then did the same for one a floor below. Both were just off the stairwell Emily had used, alone, twice before. Tonya and Mike went in the one above, Kim took the one below. The plan was to wait until Emily was on the stairwell between floors. Tonya would step out of the upper floor office, Kim would step out behind her from the one below. They'd box her in. Emily would have to hear Kim out.

She pulled the sling off and stuffed it in her purse, grimacing the entire time. She wanted to appear as normal as possible.

Emily didn't look up as she walked past Kim, who stepped out of the office silently behind her.

Tonya did the same thing one floor up. "Hello, Emily," Tonya said softly.

Even from behind, it was easy to see how startled Emily was. "Tonya?" Emily asked.

Mike would only come out on her signal, but Kim didn't have that option. She looked up at Emily's back. "Not just Tonya."

She spun around, and Kim watched as she went from startled to alarmed recognition. "You!"

Kim shot the encrypted authenticator at Emily's shared space. "Yes. I'm also Angie. And I didn't lie about anything we discussed last night. We want to help. You're in danger, you all are."

"From *you*."

"No. Not me. I would never hurt you or anyone you love. Anyone, period. What your father told you about me was all lies."

Emily's eyes narrowed and suddenly she wasn't Will's mom.

She was Matthew Watchtell's daughter.

She walked slowly down the stairs toward Kim. Emily had her father's eyes, and Kim couldn't move.

When she drew level, she asked, "And you told me the truth?"

"Absolutely."

Emily's hand shot out and grabbed Kim's arm.

It was one of the scenarios they'd discussed, but that didn't help her. Someone brushing against Kim was a sear, like grabbing a pan that'd been pulled out of the oven. What Emily did was beyond that. It was beyond everything. Kim's knees collapsed under the onslaught. She couldn't think, couldn't see. The madness clawed away her mind and left only agony in its wake. The pain was eternal, her universe, an unending knife blade slashing her soul open.

"That's enough," Tonya said, and suddenly it was over. Kim fell on all fours, gasping and gagging. She looked up. Tonya held Emily's wrist in her hand while she said, "We aren't the threat. *She* isn't the threat."

An aftershock of Emily's touch sent Kim face-first to the floor. The spasms were uncontrollable after a touch like that.

"Oh my God," Emily said above her. "I'm sorry! I didn't know it would be so bad." There was the sound of a brief scuffle. "Please, I only want to help her."

Soft fabric brushed against her cheek, and it did help. It gave her a focus, a direction for the pain to go. She concentrated and let it flow away.

"I only got it this morning on your advice. It was for Will."

Kim realized it was one of those cheap disposable dusters, the kind with a fold-out plastic handle. Kim remembered telling her about it last night.

"Are you okay?" Mike asked.

Emily gasped and lurched away. He was supposed to stay hidden until she signaled for him. Damn it. Kim forced the words out. "I'm fine."

Sooner than she wanted, Kim put her hands underneath her and pushed up. Her bad arm complained, but it needed to take a number. She felt like she'd been stuck in a sack and thrown down the stairs. Slowly, Kim got to her feet. "I'm fine."

Emily still sat on the ground, so Kim offered her the sleeve of her coat. "Here."

That did it. A simple gesture. She gingerly grabbed Kim's sleeve and let herself be hauled up.

"Let's start again," Kim said. "I'm Kimberly Trayne. You already know Tonya. That's Mike Sellars. He's with us."

Emily shook their hands, and then it got awkward again when she turned to Kim. "I had to know."

It still felt like there was thick acid in her blood, but Kim got her breakthrough. "It's okay. But I wasn't kidding. You and Will are in danger. We have to move. Now."

Still clearly shaken, Emily said, "He's home. Ride with me?"

In for a penny. "Absolutely." She pulled the sling out and put her arm in it. The ache had grown too much.

Emily cocked her head. "Did I do that?"

"No. It's a long story. When we get you guys somewhere safe, I'll tell it to you."

Emily pulled ahead of Tonya's car in the parking lot and started for her house. "I can't believe this. You're *here*. He said you were dead, for years. And then you weren't, and the things he did to you…"

Kim didn't know how to respond, so she only shrugged.

The car was silent for a while as they drove through the darkening streets. "I'm glad," Emily said. "What you did to him? I'm glad you did it." She swallowed. "He hurts everyone. It's how he works. Father always has to be in control."

Give me the key, and this all ends. That's what Watchtell had said to her. Kim banished him from her head. Never again.

"Nick, my husband." Emily gripped the wheel. "My *ex*-husband, never trusted Father. He was certain the fertility clinic Father forced us to use did something to us, to him. When the syndrome manifested, it tore us apart."

Kim knew that Watchtell had lied to Emily about everything, slid terrible secrets into their marriage to tear them apart. It made her easier to control. Every time Kim thought there was a bottom to her hatred of the man, the floor fell out from under it. That didn't matter right now. She had to get them to safety.

Emily rolled up her sleeve to reveal an intricate network of scars. They ran all the way up her arm. "This is what Father did to me."

Kim wanted to say something, but again couldn't find the words.

"He never laid a hand on me. That would've been too easy. Growing up in that house, with all those rules, all that anger. I started cutting when I was twelve. I showed them my arm to frighten them, but it didn't work. My parents were *proud*. I'd conquered the pain, turned it inward, controlled it."

He was in jail. Watchtell would never do this to anyone else again. He didn't need to. He did it to Kim every night in her dreams. It turned out he also did it to his own daughter, every night.

Not anymore. He wouldn't do that to her anymore. If Kim could, she would make sure Emily got help too.

"They gave me a set of scalpels." Her voice fell to a hoarse whisper, and she wiped her eyes. *"They wanted to watch."*

Kim pulled one of the handkerchiefs she and Mike used out of her pocket and threw it over Emily's wrist. Emily took it and blew her nose. So much for tenderness. Kim laughed at Emily's actions, so similar to what Mama did just yesterday. Raising people with this syndrome led to similar habits.

"What?" Emily asked, vulnerable and unsure.

"My mother will love it if she ever gets to meet you."

"I'd like that." She paused. "I'm sorry about what happened on the stairwell. I've been so careful around Will I'd forgotten what a solid grab did to people like you. I had to know if you were real, but I…"

"It's fine. I've had worse." It made them both think of her father, and the poor choice of words congealed the conversation. "I didn't mean it like that."

"I know. Let's try it a third time." She reached into her purse and pulled out her own handkerchief. "I'm Emily."

***

Emily turned to her after they parked at the house. "Damn it. I'm so rattled I forgot to phone ahead. Silas and Shonda are still at their appointments. They don't know you're with me."

"There's no time for long introductions anyway. I need to get you guys moving. Are they dangerous?"

Emily snorted. "Hardly. Shonda is the very first ALS recipient."

Kim let her explain what that was even though it wasn't necessary. "Silas jumps at his own shadow."

"You go get Will, and I'll let Mike and Tonya handle the other two."

Emily made a face. "No offense, but I think they're a little scary."

"They won't hurt anyone they don't have to."

When they walked into the house, Silas and Shonda *weren't* doing realm appointments. They were gathered around a table at the back of the main room playing a game. Happy greetings stopped the instant Kim walked in. Silas jumped up with a shout. Shonda let out an electronic shriek, and Will screamed.

Emily, Mike, and Tonya stepped forward, hands up, shouting back. Silas threw whatever they were playing with at everyone, which only added to the chaos. Everyone kept shouting, so loud nobody could hear anything.

Kim tried her best to get across she was no danger when she stepped into something that wrapped around her leg, so heavy it was hard to move. She looked down to see what it was and stopped. The shouting went away. Everything went away.

Will had wrapped himself around her leg, hiding his face against her thigh.

And it didn't hurt.

It didn't hurt.

Chapter 29
Tonya

At first all any of them could do was stare at Kim and Will. Emily tried one of those tap-touches on his arm, like she was testing if a pan was too hot. She got a whimper of pain in response.

"Okay," Emily said, "not a full cure."

The man, Silas, and the woman in the ALS, Shonda, pulled scanners out and started waving them over the pair. Shonda's were part of her suit, which only made her resemble an R2 droid even more. Tonya was not impressed with the way they behaved around Will. In theory these were his caretakers, at least that was the impression Tonya got from Kim's story, yet they acted like they were examining a lab specimen.

"All readings are nominal," Silas said.

"Confirmed," Shonda replied. "No responses are out of known parameters."

Tonya got sick of their attitude. She stepped between them, consciously getting in their way.

"Ma'am," Silas said with a huff, "you're interfering with our scans."

She got out her glare, the one that taught baby doctors to sit down so she could keep them from killing someone. Every nurse knew how to do it.

Silas wilted and backed off.

Tonya turned around.

Will's arms were still wrapped tightly around Kim's waist. "How do *you* feel?" Tonya asked.

Aside from lowering her arms, Kim hadn't moved a muscle this whole time. Her hands barely touched Will, as if he would burn her as well. "I don't know. It doesn't hurt." She held a hand out. "Test me."

Tonya made the same move Emily did with Will and got a similar reaction.

"It figures," she said. It was hard to watch the hope die in her. "That would be asking too much."

"Ms. Ramirez," Silas said. It took Tonya a second to remember that was Emily's married name. She wasn't on a first-name basis with her medical advisers. Strange.

Silas moved closer. "We must chronicle this extraordinary event properly."

Mike moved toward Silas in that unnaturally silent way he had. "Not now," he said, dropping the temperature of the room ten degrees.

"No," Kim said. "It's okay. They're right. We need to record this." She pried Will's arms away from her. The awkwardness was striking. Kim didn't know how to extricate herself from someone else's grasp. She'd never done it before in her life. "We'll sit down. Let's sit down right here." They sort of fell onto an overstuffed couch in the main area of the room. They both moved awkwardly around each other, with the bonus of Kim's injured arm making it that much more complicated.

Tonya knew the look on Kim's face. She was getting frustrated. "Kim, calm down."

"He's so," they tried to arrange themselves again, "lumpy." Eventually they settled with Will across her lap, arms around her neck.

The scientists—that's how Tonya chose to think of them since they were piss-poor nurses—fluttered around talking gibberish. Mike brooded in a corner and watched them, almost vibrating from the stress.

Emily sat down next to Kim and Will, wrecked. "Is he...are you...is everything okay?"

Kim began gently prodding and squeezing Will. "I don't know how to answer that." He burst out laughing. Kim looked like a bomb had gone off in her lap.

Tonya smiled. Kim wouldn't know what tickling really was. Then she noticed how freely her friend was moving. "How's your arm?"

Kim pulled the sling over her head, "it's fine." She wriggled her fingers, which caught Will's attention.

Everyone went still, including the scientists. It was the first time Tonya had seen his eyes. He had Kim's eyes.

"Will," Emily said, "that's a hand. Can you say hand?"

He stared, entranced.

Kim gathered him close and kept moving her fingers.

Emily got the duster she used on Kim out and brushed his hand. He focused on that, staring as it went back and forth.

They both got the kind of expression Tonya saw a lot when she was in nursing school, rotating through the critical care unit: a hopeful surprise, quickly crushed. Will didn't understand what was going on. Couldn't understand.

"He's not unlocked," Kim said. "Damn it."

Tears dripped out of Emily's eyes, but she wore a huge grin. "No, I could tell. But..." She wiped her face and then a sob escaped. "I've never seen him at peace before."

Shonda wheeled up to Tonya. "We can't find anything unusual, which is unexpected."

Tonya tried to figure out what to look at, still bothered that there was a body nestled inside the thing. She settled on the big sensor in the middle of the dome. "I don't understand."

Silas said very softly, "We had several models for what might happen if they met in person."

"Walk with me," Tonya said. She motioned to Mike, who followed behind them.

She ushered them all into a side room. After checking to make sure Kim and Emily were still working with Will, she shut the door.

"Explain that."

Silas glanced nervously at Mike. Without looking at him, Tonya gripped Mike's arm. He needed to calm the hell down. When he didn't relax, she shot him a look. "They have information we need."

"Indeed," Shonda said as diagrams drew themselves into existence in the house's shared virtual channel. "Our latest models predicted that an interaction between Subject One and—"

She'd read Mike's files and knew exactly who they were talking about. "Stop."

They both turned.

"*That* is not Subject One. That is Kimberly Trayne. Do you understand?"

Silas cleared his throat. "My apologies. Our models predicted that if Ms. Trayne and…"

"And Will?" Mike asked in a low growl.

He hadn't calmed down yet, but now Tonya didn't feel like calling him on it. They were starting to piss her off, too.

Silas shot an alarmed glance at Mike and then looked away. "Yes. Our models predicted that if Ms. Trayne and Will ever met, there would be measurable consequences."

"A second order field interaction?" Mike asked, only a moment before Tonya did.

Their startled look made Tonya grin inside. *Didn't expect that to come from a thug and sister, didja?*

"Yes," Shonda said. "Exactly."

"But," Tonya said, "that involves spontaneous symmetry breaking. I thought you guys were psychologists."

They did a not-quite-looking-at-each-other thing. These two were definitely an odd couple.

"We are," Shonda said. "The physics team departed when the money ran out. They left us with scanner profiles in case," she spun her dome head toward the living room, "*that* ever happened."

These two were part of a team who had spent the past five years analyzing data Kim had generated. Of course they'd know more than she and Mike did. "What else did they leave you? Can you share it with us?"

"Guys?" Emily said softly as she opened the door. "We have a problem." She stepped inside and shut it quietly. "Kim wants us all to leave. Now."

Tonya said, "Okay" at the same time as Mike, and Shonda and Silas both said, "Absolutely not."

Emily shook her head. Her child was being raised by a team, a small team, and not a particularly charming one. And now there were strangers. Tonya wouldn't be handling it as well as Emily was if she were in her place.

"Right," Emily said, then faced her and Mike. "You guys don't understand this part. Kim is stuck on the couch. Will won't let her up and won't let go. I don't know how it'll work if she has to go to the bathroom. Will is all about habits and slow changes. He is wedded to routine."

Silas said, "He becomes impossible if we try to break it. He never leaves the house when it's dark outside. Ever."

"We could sedate him," Shonda said, "but only as a last resort."

If it'd come from anyone else, Tonya would've agreed. She knew dozens of sedation methods that were perfectly safe. Many were realm based and used no drugs at all. But Shonda's tone set Tonya's teeth on edge. She wasn't thinking about patient care, but convenience. Tonya knew lots of doctors who acted this way. They never got along well with nurses, for good reason.

"I don't want him sedated," Emily said. "He's a nightmare when he wakes up from that. We can wait." And that was that. Mom's kid, Mom's rules. "But I need you to talk to Kim."

Tonya shared a look with Mike. When it came to Kim, it wasn't deviating from a routine that would set her off. It was disobeying orders.

"Do you need help?" she asked him.

He put away the scary assassin look he'd been wearing this whole time. Thank God.

"I'll signal you if I do."

When Mike left, the other three deflated like they'd been stuck with a pin.

"Come on, guys," Tonya said. "He's not that bad."

Shonda wheeled toward her. "Who *is* he? And who are you?"

With all the craziness happening, Tonya had forgotten only Emily knew their names. "Tonya Brinks." She shook Silas's hand and tried hard not to cringe when she took the claw Shonda extended from her case. It was covered with a rubberized coating of some sort. The grip was mechanical but delicate. "And that was Mike Sellars."

Silas's Adam's apple bounced in his throat, upping his nerd quotient. "Has she reconstituted her group? Are you new members?"

To this day, what had happened to Rage + The Machine wasn't well known. Her best friend was a sole survivor. "No. We're just trying to help."

"They say we're in danger," Emily said.

"And you are." Tonya filled them in on the basics. "That's why Kim wants us to move as soon as possible."

Whatever Mike and Kim were discussing had been too quiet to make out until it ended with an explosive *Fine!* from Kim. Will's whimper was equally audible. Emily was out the door in a second, with the rest of them close behind.

Mike wasn't heading for the car, and Kim wasn't preaching fire and brimstone at him as he went. All in all, not a bad result.

"Will? Is everything okay?" Emily asked.

Kim was rigid, but she held Will tenderly in her lap. "We need," she said in a low voice, "to leave."

"We can't," Emily replied. "You don't know what he's like if we break his routine."

Kim cocked her jaw to one side, a thing she did when she realized she couldn't win an argument. Will shifted then, and she squirmed under his weight. "People are so damned heavy," she grumbled. "And hot."

A loud *pop* sounded out from the kitchen, and after a moment Silas and Shonda came around the corner, him with a Champaign bottle and her with a tray on her head that held glasses. "We have made a discovery," he said. "I think that calls for a small celebration."

It took Kim a bit of wrestling to free one of her arms so she could hold a glass.

***

Tonya woke to a keening wail and a splitting headache. She was on the floor but couldn't remember who it belonged to, or why she was lying on it. It wasn't night anymore, but she could've sworn it was only a moment ago. The noise was loud.

"Shut him up *now*," a woman's voice said.

Tonya's arms wouldn't work properly and neither would her head. Her vision swam into focus. Mike and Kim were asleep together on the couch, leaning on each other, mouths open. Emily was collapsed in front of the chair next to them. That wasn't sleep.

They had been drugged.

There was a *snap*, and the keening stopped.

"They were supposed to be here by now," a man's voice said.

Silas. That was Silas talking. And Shonda too. Tonya had to move.

"They're at the main gate," Shonda said. "Now come on."

Tonya got her hands under her and pushed up as the door slammed shut. Through the window, she saw Silas carrying a sleeping Will in his arms as they quickly walked—and rolled— down the driveway. The flat light of dawn made everything gray.

Each movement either spun her head or her stomach, and the pounding behind her eyes wouldn't let up. Tonya had to stop them.

She fell twice getting to the door but managed to open it on her first try. A vehicle came charging up the street, screeching to a halt in front of Silas and Shonda. It was a big black van. Men poured out of it.

Tonya had to run, but she couldn't fall again. The best she could manage was a lurching stumble across the yard. This was a neighborhood, not a back alley. There were people all around them who could help if they knew what was going on. She shouted but couldn't form words. The noise was only loud enough to get the attention of the men taking Will.

"I thought you said it would be hours before they got up," Shonda said.

"It varies, okay?" Silas said as he walked purposefully toward Tonya. "I'll take care of it."

She tried to take a stance but couldn't hold her balance steady and landed on her butt in the grass. Things wouldn't stop spinning.

"At least it makes you easier to hit. Guys? We'll need to put her back in the house before we go."

There was another *snap* that stung the center of her chest, then darkness.

Chapter 30

June

Cyril was nowhere to be found when she got home last night, but when June woke up the next morning, he was standing in her living room, looking through a window. It was early, with only enough light to see him in shades of gray. It made him seem even less human than usual.

"They're here," he said flatly. "It's started."

June's bungalow was on the edge of the campus off the main entry road. It should've been deserted this time of the morning, but it was bumper to bumper with cars. It was a mash-up of cheap old wrecks and shiny self-drivers that you got with any diverse group of young people, but they all had one thing in common.

None of them were supposed to be here.

The term wasn't scheduled to start for another two weeks. A couple of die-hards had shown up yesterday, but they were turned away. The dorms hadn't been prepped yet.

Except that wasn't the case anymore. A cursory glance at the main calendar revealed most of the staff—robot and human—had been reassigned in an all-hands effort to prep the living spaces and process the arrivals.

"Did you cause this?" June asked.

He looked up at her. "Not at all. It was much more difficult than it should've been to come back here without being seen because of it."

"Where were you?"

He paused for a moment. "Sending a note to myself."

Cyril had a difficult relationship with clarity. "Do you ever stop speaking in riddles?"

He laughed. "You are not the first person to complain about that. This is a delicate time. Unprecedented, as far as I know. Carelessness could lead to ruin."

"Well then why are they here?" He said it had started, after all.

Cyril turned back to the window. "I have my suspicions. What are yours?"

June checked her message queue. "Anna's giving anyone who can get here in the next two days a full scholarship. She wants to see how well they respond to sudden changes in circumstance."

"I'm sure that's popular with anyone who has a prior commitment."

June looked up the subreddit the students used to communicate with each other. "It seems to have made them happy."

"The benefits of cherry-picking your student body, I'm sure."

The comment was casual, but it added another weight to her already heavy load of suspicions. "Anna's school is one of the most selective in the country. We get criticized about it all the time." There were the standard right-wing gripes of political indoctrination enforcing groupthink, but also protests over their official favoring of young people, those with few or no family ties. June hadn't paid it a lot of attention. She'd been busy with her own work.

The oupa on her shoulder woke up and pointed out that the policies provided a dedicated, highly mobile group of people who could drop what they were doing and move on a moment's notice. "This is worse than the Trilogy incident," she said.

"Indeed. They only want to send *themselves* to heaven. Speaking of Trilogy, has Spencer arrived yet?"

One of the cars bumped another, which in turn ran into a third. It would take hours to process all this. "Yesterday afternoon. I need to...wait, how do you know about Spencer?"

Cyril was a member of the device team. He knew secret routes into and out of the power plant. All the glitches started when he appeared. He knew the name of the Trilogy contact. By rights, she should've turned him in the moment he showed up.

Oupa-on-her-shoulder nudged at her insides. June knew exactly why she hadn't turned him in, and wouldn't.

He might be telling the truth. She was awake, but the nightmare kept getting darker.

"It's not important how I know," he said. "You must listen to him."

"He's a fanatic." Which was an ironic dismissal, considering the tableau unfolding outside her window. There were thousands of people flooding into the site just because the leader asked them to do it. She swallowed. "What can he tell me?"

"The next steps that need to be taken."

She'd already given Spencer access to the inner network. But the scanners had cleared his tool kit. She sat down heavily. She couldn't deal with all these contradictions. June looked up at Cyril, inscrutable and unknown behind his breathing mask and helmet. Against all evidence and even common sense, she wanted to trust this odd man. But she couldn't. It was the end of a dream if she did. The end of *her* dream, that she'd overcome Oupa's pessimism to become her own person, on her own, doing things that would change the world.

The oupa on her shoulder pointed out that Anna's promises could never have been all that they seemed if they could be shattered by this secretive stranger. She had been fooling herself, willfully ignoring warning signs, but still cataloging them somewhere in her head.

And now Anna was gathering her people together as fast as she could.

June stood up, grabbed her purse, and headed out the door.

"June," Cyril said.

She turned, halfway out the door. Time seemed to hold still, stopped in a balance.

"Trust Spencer. Help him if you can. We must stop Anna, and we need your help to do it." He straightened up a bit. "No matter what else happens, know that I appreciate all you've done for me.

"Goodbye, June."

She somehow knew she would never see him again. This was it. The man who had shattered beliefs she thought underpinned her entire being, and in the process revealed much deeper foundations underneath, was going back to wherever he came from.

There was a crisis that she had helped make. Her hero planned a mass murder that beggared the imagination. June would now play a part in stopping it. Once it was over, she'd have to try to figure out how to restart a life that she'd driven so far down a dead-end street she couldn't see where it began. There was no way to express out loud what she felt.

She nodded once and shut the door.

***

At least June didn't have to use the front entrance. Judging by the crowds, it would take hours to get in that way.

Anna must've had the same thought. They crossed paths a dozen meters from the employee entrance.

"June," she said with a bright smile. "Walk with me."

Cyril was wrong. It was all a lie. In a moment of weakness, she believed someone she shouldn't. Anna was a pillar of the green movement, and June worked directly with her. It was the fulfillment of all her dreams.

The oupa on her shoulder urged her to tell Anna about Cyril, then smiled when she remained silent. She couldn't tell Anna about Cyril. Not yet. And she didn't know why.

Are you sure?

Anna led them to a nearby picnic area and sat down at a table, motioning for June to sit opposite her. "I've got updates on the device."

The pulse of curiosity didn't overcome her sour stomach. "Does it have anything to do with all that?" They could still see the main road and parking lot from here. If anything, it was even more congested.

Anna immediately became guarded, eyes shifting side to side for a moment. "Yes. That's what I wanted to talk to you about."

"I'm listening." It came out colder than June intended. Oupa's smile got wider.

"With the AI network compromised, will you still be able to monitor the approaches to the plant? We've always been at risk for..."

When the pause dragged on across an extra heartbeat, Oupa whispered in her ear, *Armageddon?*

"...wildfire, and we only have the one main road. We don't want anyone getting trapped."

The one road. The isolation. The outsized environmental control. The warehouses filled with shelf-stable food.

She still had to know for sure. "What happens to the students who can't make the deadline?"

Anna's eyes grew misty. "We're on the cusp of an incredible discovery now."

It was Anna's passion that fired June up. None of what Cyril said could be true.

"And your discovery is what made it possible. You are such a critical part of the plan. You always were." She chuckled, a comfortable, intimate sound. "Advanced technology skills have always been lacking in the radical green movement. Soon they'll be even more rare."

The warm feeling of Anna's humor and confidence vanished. June often ignored the subtexts they all hinted at in conversations.

She couldn't afford to ignore them anymore. "Why do you say that?"

The friendliness in Anna's eyes changed into a raw cunning that would normally make June look away, but the oupa on her shoulder wouldn't let her. *This is what you've ignored all this time,* he said quietly in her ear. *Watch and learn.*

For a moment June thought Anna would tell the truth. It made for an excited, nauseating fist in her chest. What would June do if she was let in on it? She still wanted to believe in all this. She had to believe in all this.

June drove over an hour the last Sunday of every month to attend a proper Anglican church. The tall girl from a remote farm in Mpumalanga Province had a moral compass with an arrow made of steel. She would not, could not, agree to anything that monstrous.

A part of what June felt must've shown on her face. Anna pulled back. "The plant will change everything. We're all going on a journey, and I need to make sure someone like you stands with us as we move forward."

It wasn't an answer to her question. Anna was a master of that. They all were.

Oupa whispered, *Is it an answer you will accept, though?*

Yes. It was. "So tell me what you've discovered about the device."

***

Spencer was already waiting in the lab when she arrived. He had changed from his Trilogy outfit to the standard collared shirt and khakis June had made sure were provided to him the day before. It transformed him from a fanatic into just another employee. It was a small comfort, but right now she would take what she could get.

"What the hell is going on out there? It's like a zoo. I've never seen that much granola in my whole fucking life." He sniffed his sleeve. "And what is it about hippies and patchouli? The stink is in my clothes. It's nuts."

She sat down beside him. Time for an experiment. "Cyril says hi."

Spencer got a confused look, then his skin paled. "How do you know Cyril?"

Bingo. "He's been living with me for six days now."

He went even more pale. "*Six days?* How did you...when did he..." Spencer closed his eyes for a moment. "*Fuck,* I can't call anyone for advice. You own the network I'd use."

This was definitely outside the range of behavior she thought was normal for a member of Trilogy. Which had to mean… "You're not really from Trilogy, are you?"

He was still trying to digest her revelation and didn't get the reference. "What?"

June was two for two now. "Trilogy. You're not a member. You only talk like one when you think about it. It's not natural to you."

He got a cagey look. "I never said I was a particularly *good* member."

Part of this new leaf she had turned over was trusting her intuition—the oupa on her shoulder—which knew what a pile of *kak* landing on the ground sounded like. "Cyril said I should trust you, but I don't think it's possible to trust a fanatic dedicated to his own self-destruction. Not with the job we have in front of us."

"And what's that?"

"Oh, for God's sake, Spencer," a new, male voice with a British accent spoke from a speaker on the ceiling. "If you were any worse at questioning people I'd suspect you were a member of the Spanish Inquisition. Except *you* can't make the excuse of an over-reliance on a hot poker up the backside. Madam, might *the job we have in front of us* be stopping this monument to why monkeys should not be allowed to use tools?"

Spencer threw his hands in the air as he glared at the speaker on the ceiling. "Jesus Fucking Christ, Edmund. Just tell her everything why don't you?"

"Do you have a better idea for spanning the air gap?" A different voice, female and with an American accent, asked.

June activated the scanning tools she'd used last night. The readings were different, and unprecedented. *"Goede heer…"*

"What is that supposed to mean?" Spencer asked.

June barely tore her eyes away from the findings. "You uploaded unduplicates to my network. I specifically scanned for that. You managed it anyway. How did you do this?" The sophistication rates were off the charts. She'd never seen anything like it. And there were *two* of them.

A holo window opened on the shared vision channel. In it stood a man who looked like he should be employed at a Renaissance faire. That must be Edmund. Next to him was a more conventionally dressed girl not much older than Spencer. "We're clever that way," she said. "Well, *I* am, and I brought Mr. Sparkle Pants here along for the ride."

The man beside her rolled his eyes and put his head in his hand. "Oh, God."

Spencer asked, "So I'm supposed to trust her? Just like that?"

"No," Edmund replied. "Not just like that. She came to you. And we wouldn't be having this conversation at all if we'd let you mince about like Marlowe's Edward."

"You mean to tell me," Spencer said, "that I didn't have to memorize all that horse shit after all? I still have a migraine from it. Goddamn it, you guys made me pray."

June couldn't get over the findings. Edmund was five orders of magnitude more sophisticated than any AI she had ever seen, here or anywhere else. Whatever was going on with his companion confused all the sensors. They couldn't provide a reading at all. June was first and foremost a world-class expert on AI, and Spencer's two companions were so outrageous she would've denied they could exist the moment anyone proposed them.

And yet here they were, having a ferocious row with the boy who'd brought them. But he wasn't a boy anymore. Now that he dropped his disguise, she could see a fierce intelligence that made him seem years older. And that was what he had done. Right in front of her, without changing any material thing, he transformed from a shy underage nerd into...well, whatever he was, he certainly had nothing to do with Trilogy.

Cyril had some impressive friends.

June tried to get their attention politely. When that didn't work she slammed her broad hand flat on the table. All three of them jumped. Spontaneous fear reflex in an AI would have to wait to be examined. They had a bigger problem.

"Whatever you three are planning, we need to get on with it."

She turned to Spencer. "That chaos you saw upstairs? It's Anna's doing. She's gathering up her flock as we speak. The deadline for everyone to be here is tomorrow. And after that?"

"After that," Edmund said, "we are undoubtedly as pickled as the Duke of Clarence himself."

Chapter 31
Mike

His face was hot, and his head pounded. Moving would make it better for a second, and then the pain would come back. He didn't have his phone on so his threads pulsed and coiled, rolling in and out of his control. The blinding red of his closed eyes got worse when he opened them and sunlight spiked in. This hurt more than the time when he lost count of the shots of ouzo Uncle Kostas kept handing him. Mike turned aside and put his hand up. The relief of being able to see stopped dead when he looked around.

Tonya was splayed out on the floor, and Emily was collapsed in a chair beside them. Kim was passed out against his arm. His heartbeat jumped in time with his threads before he checked her pulse. She wasn't dead, just unconscious. He got up quickly when she let out a low moan, which ruined the delicate balance of his threads. Mike gripped the arm of the couch so he wouldn't fall over.

"Mike?" Kim asked. By her tone she was hurting at least as bad as he was. At least there was no touch madness.

"Here." Wherever that was. Then he remembered. Will was gone, and so were the scientists. He staggered down the hall, going from one improvised handhold to another. Doorknobs shouldn't be this hard to open, even hung over. He checked the monitors on his body's autonomic functions. They reported back an extremely high concentration of trichloroethanol.

Ah-ha.

He had learned what *slipping you a Mickey* meant while building out a film noir realm for a client in London years ago. Someone, it had to be the scientists, had literally given them one. It had never occurred to him to set up a metabolic warning filter on a thing that basic. Humanity's knowledge of how to poison each other seemed to have no end of variation. He tasked some threads to make sure this particular trick would never work on him again.

Fat lot of good it did at the moment.

Kim groaned on the couch while he searched. "Where's Will?"

"I don't know. The scientists are gone too." All for the lack of a stupid filter. His mental kicks added to the misery of the drug's hangover.

"Mike, come back. You need to check on Emily and Tonya."

He turned around in time to see Kim lose her balance and tumble to the floor in a heap. He ran back when she screamed, stripping his shirt off as he went. "What's wrong?"

She gasped and strangled out, "My arm." Kim looked up and with a wincing moan, wrapped the sleeve he offered her around her hand and pulled herself upright. Her sling stuck out of her purse. He got it and handed it to her; she would push too hard getting it herself.

"I'm fine," she said. It was an obvious lie, but he was in no better shape. "I'll search for Will. You check them."

Arguing with her would be useless, even when she cried out as she stood. Her arm must be much worse.

Emily stirred after a few shakes, then woke up faster than either he or Kim had managed. "Where's Will?"

"Kim's looking for him. The scientists are gone, too. I think they might've taken him."

Emily swore and went to help Kim search.

Tonya didn't stir at all. Her breathing and pulse seemed fine. He had no way to check further than that without a phone. Hers was gone too. He should be able to reach emergency services with his threads, but he had never tried that before.

"Kim," he shouted, "they took our phones. Should I try to call the police the hard way?" There was a real risk of exposure if he managed it. 911 expected to see an address on the other end, and they'd definitely want to know why his call didn't have one.

Her voice echoed from the upstairs. "Not yet. We need to talk about it. How's Tonya?"

He looked at his friend. She seemed less drugged but wouldn't wake up. "I don't know."

Emily came upstairs from the basement just as Kim appeared on the landing above. "Anything?"

Kim gripped the rail. He could see her white knuckles. "No. I'm sorry."

Emily wiped her eyes and gasped out a helpless sob. "They took my child." She collapsed into a dining room chair, head on the table.

They should've done what Kim wanted. All this would've been avoided then. Tears streamed down his own cheeks.

Kim sat down next to him. "Hey."

He wiped his eyes. "Hey," he said to her. He hated feeling this helpless.

Kim looked at Tonya for a moment. "Open her shirt, just there." She indicated a space between Tonya's breasts.

There was a tiny red dot on her blouse he hadn't noticed before. Gingerly, he undid two buttons and revealed what looked like a bug bite, or maybe a bee sting, just below her bra.

"Thought so," Kim said. "They hit her with a safe-stop. We don't have a reverse agent, so we'll have to wait it out. They hit me with at least a dozen of these things when they arrested us at the hotel. She'll be fine. Could you put her on the couch? She might as well be comfortable."

Emily walked up to them. "Safe-stops. Those sons of bitches." Mike watched her struggle with a rage that was almost a physical thing, but she managed to fight it off. "We kept them around in case Will had to be transported in an emergency." She got up and went into the kitchen. After a quick rummage, Emily let out a string of curses. "That's what they used. They took the rest *and* the reverse agent. Kim, Tonya will be fine. They were the best money could buy." There was a pause. Mike could almost hear the rumbling. "I will never trust that man ever again, so help me God."

Next to him, Tonya took a deep breath and came up swinging, managing to land a glancing blow against his jaw before he caught her arms. The stars reminded him of his hangover, and his threads upped the ante by grinding together like ropes covered in shards of glass. The scientists were going to pay for all this.

"WILL! THEY'VE GOT WILL!" After some desperate jerks, she came to her senses. Glancing around frantically she asked, "What time is it?"

He checked. "Almost four o'clock."

Tonya swore. "They've had the whole damn day."

"But *why?*" Emily asked.

Answering her question fully would reveal Kim's relationship to Will, and Watchtell's role in it. He shared a look with Kim.

"It's complicated," Kim said. "But before we start that story," she turned to him, "can you get to the local realmspaces without your phone? See where they went, or who they were?"

Mike closed his eyes and concentrated. The bridge between his real self and his host was eased by a phone connection, but it wasn't required. He and Helen both practiced going without one for a few hours a week. He was getting better at it, but it was like handling things with tongs. Clumsy tongs.

First, the bad news. "They've erased the house's network. A real hatchet job. It'll need to be reinstalled before it works properly again."

"What about the neighborhood?"

He had all of Kim's back door codes for that. His real self's perception was soft and blurry, and he had to be careful not to invert a realm. That would destroy everything outright. "I can see the vehicle, but not the license plate." He watched Tonya's confrontation with Silas. They weren't very gentle about bringing her back to the house.

The truck started to move. "Kim, how far have you compromised things?"

"Not very. Try to get a general direction and then follow them with the public traffic cams. Emily, do you have anything to write on? We can take directions and figure it out when we get new phones."

"I'm…wait, he's online without a…sorry. Yes."

After a moment there was a clattering on the coffee table.

"Here."

"Thanks."

With a phone, he could gradually split his perception into hundreds, even thousands of different threads. Like this he was fortunate to have a single perspective. "They went south." It was hard to stay oriented jumping from cam to cam. Most of the leaps were guesses. Every time they changed direction or took a ramp, he called it out. "They're sticking with expressways. No surface streets so far."

He could barely hang on to the feeds, so it took most of an hour before the destination became clear.

"They took him to the airport," he said. Great. More air travel. He rubbed his eyes before he opened them. It felt like he'd been running a marathon. Normally it wasn't that bad, even when he split into hundreds. Mike needed to get a training regimen going.

"Tonya's SUV is still here," Kim said, then turned to her. "They took your phone. Did you set up voice security?"

"Morgan knows better than to fool with me, phone or not. He'll let me in."

"Let's make sure."

His vision cleared as they left to check out the car in the driveway. Emily sat across from him, mouth open, eyes wide. "You did all that without a realmspace connection? Are you special forces?" She looked Mike up and down, and he became acutely aware he hadn't put his shirt back on. "You've got the build for it. But they're supposed to take those implants out when you leave. And they only work with special relay trucks anyway."

All true. Realmspace wireless connections, ones that didn't use a neural lanyard like a pendant phone, required a miniaturized AESA antenna to be implanted, otherwise the signal wouldn't be transmitted through the skin. It was the stuff of James Bond realm adventures and blacknet rumors.

But he wasn't special forces. Kim had told Emily her secret. He had no reason not to tell her his. The house network was a wreck, but basic functions were still there. Mike used one of Helen's probe constructs to activate the indoor audio section.

His voice came from speakers mounted in the ceiling. "It's complicated."

She looked at the ceiling, then at him, clearly alarmed.

He stood up and walked toward her. Still using the speakers, he said, "Kim isn't the only one with special abilities. I'll tell you what's going on in detail soon. But know this." He held out his hand.

For a moment he didn't think she would take it. Maybe this wasn't the right move. Emily was the first person he'd come out to since Kim's mom. She was also Matthew Watchtell's daughter. He centered himself and breathed, visualizing the winds going into his body's central channel. Mike had been lucky so far, but it was only a matter of time before someone decided he was a monster.

After a moment, Emily seemed to make her own decision. She took his hand.

As he lifted her to her feet he said, over the speakers and with his realspace voice, "We will find your son."

"I leave you alone for one minute..." Kim said behind them. "Anyway, the car is fine."

He turned to Kim and used his realspace voice. "Good. I had to tell her the truth. I need her on our side. The next part will be very hard."

He turned back to Emily and squeezed her hand, firm but not hard. Through the speakers he said, "We can't go right now. We've been moving so fast I haven't been able to help Kim, and we need her at one hundred percent to rescue Will. It won't take long, but it does mean we have to stay here. The first step is to get the house's realmspace back up. It shouldn't take long."

"How long?" she asked.

He sent a probe to go fetch the files they'd need. "Kim and Tonya need to get us new phones, and then we'll have to set up. A few hours."

The look in her eyes changed into something grim and sharp. "My father's behind all this, isn't he?"

He switched to only his realspace voice. "Yes."

Mike had to adjust his grip so she didn't make the bones in his hand shift. "Okay," she said. "Kim, I'm sorry I didn't do what you asked last night."

Kim was pale from the realization that they would have to do the experiment again, sooner rather than later. She cleared her throat. "I'm sorry we didn't get here sooner."

Emily nodded. "You and Tonya need to go." She looked back at him and let go of his hand. "Is there anything I can do to help you?"

"Do you know how to initiate a hard restart on a household network?" There was usually a big switch somewhere.

Emily nodded and just like that, she was part of the team. "I'll be in the basement. Let me know when you're ready."

Chapter 32

Edmund

It was one thing to skulk around in the dusty corners of remote realms that were patrolled by who knew what. At least he had been able to wear *some* proper clothes underneath the camouflage.

This? This was ridiculous.

"Dr. du Plessis, you claim to be one of the finest minds in artificial intelligence," Edmund said as he pulled at the white waistcoat one more time. "I am now certain that whoever made that assessment got it precisely backward."

Infuriatingly, the insult brought on another one of those doe-eyed looks their pet mad scientist had been trotting out ever since he and Young Kim had revealed themselves. "How long has he talked like that?" June asked Spencer.

"Him?" Spencer, at least, remained a contemptuous teenager. "He's slowed down a bit lately."

Edmund was an unduplicate. He never *slowed down*. "How dare you!"

"Stow it," Young Kim said. "You look good in a tux."

The plan was to somehow load him into the helpdesk on the air-gapped network, but to do that he had to change his default avatar. This was not limited to his physical appearance. If Edmund wished to speak properly, he had to choose an avatar with the correct accent contract. In yet another example of how incredibly provincial Americans could be, there was only a single choice available. No lace, no collar, no codpiece, but instead a coat with tails that reached his knees. The accent was pure upper-class twit. It wouldn't even let him manage a proper beard, and the slicked-back hair made him want to constantly touch it. None of it was accurate to any one period. Americans liked their history smeared the same way they liked their condiments: thick and ridiculous. If this was what passed for a *modern* butler, the world could take it all and stuff it up its arse.

At least Young Kim had agreed to stay behind this time. He could not abide risking her now.

It didn't make her smirk easier to bear. "Really, you look good."

"It's some wack twentieth-century reference," Spencer said. "The company that designed the artwork went belly-up decades ago, and the IP is public domain. The fact that he's here at all means there's some old geezers on the staff."

There was one person who would know for sure. Edmund stared at Dr. du Plessis along with Spencer and Young Kim. She'd been furiously taking notes the entire time. The silence seemed unable to penetrate whatever nerdy fugue she'd found herself in. After a moment, Edmund cleared his throat.

"Hmm?" As far as allies went, she was unconventional. Her appearance was that of an African giantess, but her demeanor was stereotypically that of an awkward academic. If they could find robes that would fit, she'd easily find a place at high table of the Oxford or Cambridge of his time. So long as she stayed seated, at least.

"The staff," Spencer said. "Is it granola hippies all the way down or do you have some old timers around here too? Ones that have to use AIs to get anything done?"

Dr. du Plessis rolled her eyes. "Joyce Barlind, head of education outreach. She's the scourge of the IT department. I lost count of how many hoops I had to jump through to get *that*," she motioned at Edmund's current appearance, "installed on the network at her insistence."

"An ancient academic who insists on having everything done their way. Tell me, is she a member of the clergy?" Edmund asked.

Spencer got one of his looks, one of his *cunning plan* looks. "Oh God."

Spencer turned to Dr. du Plessis. "Does Barlind have access to the air-gapped network?"

"Yes, and she drives us all crazy..." Dr. du Plessis nodded. "That might work."

"Let me guess," Young Kim said. "Barlind has been lobbying to get her custom helper AI uploaded across the air gap?"

"For months," Dr. du Plessis replied. "And today everyone else is rushing around trying to get the students settled."

It was worse than being appointed Lord High Executioner and Minister for Religious Genocide. "Surely you don't mean to seek this woman out?" He couldn't stand this disguise, and now he'd have to be polite.

"Damn right, we are," Spencer said. "And stop calling me Shirley. Now," he said as he plugged a transport crystal in, "into the garbage chute, flyboy."

The nonsense had to be references. Edmund didn't bother looking them up. He tugged at the waistcoat again and tried to adjust his nonexistent codpiece. Such a damnable nuisance. It was time for him to confront what would surely be an ancient twit the likes of which hadn't been seen since George III climbed into a flower pot and insisted his butler water him. "Oh God."

***

Edmund's wake-up sequence had hardly finished when a breathy, creaking voice said, "Thank you, dear, I've had *such* a hard time without him."

"You're welcome, ma'am," Spencer said, his voice so smug it was positively greasy. "I gotta go now."

"Yes, dear. I hear it is absolutely brutal up there."

"Crazy."

A window flashed open in the darkness he'd found himself in. She either didn't know how or chose not to access realm-space.

The crone had to be over a century old. Her chalk-and-ash hair was in a bun tight enough to hold up her forehead. But that didn't keep her skin from sagging everywhere else. Pale, bony fingers flapped around in exaggerated helplessness, while filmy old eyes stared at the ceiling.

"I am *so* happy to see you, darling. I have missed you *so* much."

He was doing this to save the mission. He was doing this to save the whole bloody world. He needed to solve whatever this elderly convent escapee wanted, and he'd be on his way. It would be easy. She was obviously a nice, grandmotherly type.

"Yes, mum. What can I do to help?"

The helpless old lady turned into battle-hardened steel. "*Doctor Barlind.* Are you sure that young man uploaded the correct copy?"

"Oh, of course, of course, *of course,*" he hated when his voice went up an octave. "How may I be of service," he bowed. Always sell it with a bow. "Dr. Barlind?"

As fast as she had turned into an abbess who had caught two novices playing *rub my banana, you saucy peasant*, she turned back into a helpless old woman. It was quite disorienting. "First of all, they sent me an email message, and I can't open the attachment."

Email. Bloody *email*. He checked, and she wasn't exaggerating. The woman still used bloody, bollocksy *email*. "Ma'am. You've already opened it."

"I know," she sighed theatrically. Edmund hoped it would make her pass out. "And I can't see what's inside."

No such luck, she didn't pass out. "Ma'am. If you'll just make the proper gesture."

She flared up again. Right. He was supposed to know her limitations. Her undoubtedly many, many limitations. "I'm sorry, ma'am. How careless of me." He pushed the file onto a different virtual screen. "I live to serve."

"Indeed. Darling," she sighed once more. By the sound of it, her lungs were made of cardboard and sawdust. "I understand this is stressful for you. But it will all be over soon." Dr. Barlind broke out a smile that made him go as still as a maiden who'd caught a cardinal's eye. "And then we'll have everything all to ourselves."

"Welcome to Creepsterville," Young Kim said as she walked out from behind his window. "Please keep your hands and feet in the ride at all times."

He barely managed not to react. She could not be here.

"Dr. du Plessis, June, is a genius," Young Kim said, ignoring the danger she put herself in. "Not only did she compress your lard-butt down to the size of a helper AI, she left enough room for me to tag along."

On the other side of the window, there was a phlegmy gasp. "Now the program I'm using has locked up again. My dear, what's wrong with it?"

He tore his attention away from Young Kim to check some diagnostics. "Ma'am, your purse."

"My what?"

Pointing through the window made him feel like a baboon, especially since the item in question was below and behind him. "Your purse, ma'am. You need to move it."

"Why, my love, what on Earth are you talking about?"

Young Kim's silent guffaws threatened Edmund's hold on his disguise. It took everything he had to not bellow out *how could anyone with a skill set a bowl of oatmeal could outmatch be a threat to humanity?*

Instead he gestured again. "Your purse, ma'am. You've…" No, that wouldn't work. For people like this, there were no mistakes, there were only mysterious coincidences. "It's found its way onto your keyboard. It's pressing on the keys."

"Oh my. Thank you, darling. You are a life saver."

Young Kim opened her hand, revealing a glowing construct. "This is hysterical, but we have a job to do. Would you like the real butler to take over now?"

The AI she held was at root only a little brighter than an insect, but Edmund still felt a pang of sympathy for it. Even insects deserved better than Dr. Joyce Barlind.

Another rattling sigh from the other side of the window told him it was time for a change. "Ma'am, if you will pardon me for a moment, I have a quick maintenance check to complete."

"Do hurry back, dear. If I don't complete this report on time, it threatens the entire existence of the project."

Morbid curiosity forced him to check the title. "On the Reintroduction of the Mosquito."

It took another effort of will to refrain from shouting *you're madder than Mad Sally MacMadder matriculating from Mad Marion's Master class!*

He walked out of frame, giving the now fully reconstituted real butler a recording of the conversation up to this point. The look of abject resignation on his face seemed more than an affectation.

Edmund took three steps away from the screen and hit an invisible wall. "What the bloody hell?"

Young Kim opened up a new window to the lab. "Oh no."

Anna Treacher stood in the center of the room. Beside her was Spencer and du Plessis, along with half a dozen armed security guards.

Anna turned to Spencer. "Did you think you would get away with this? That I would let you waltz down here and sabotage my network?"

"I wasn't here to break—"

"You didn't come all this way with an unduplicate that sophisticated to take a look around. We roped this lab off before you uploaded him. And you," she said to du Plessis, "I don't know what to say about you."

"She's wrong." Kim said to him quietly. "The butler is correctly integrated into this side of the network. There's a path through the air gap now."

"Your pet monster has infected the lab," Anna said, "but it's not going anywhere else."

At Anna's signal, the guards marched du Plessis and Spencer forward. She was a few inches shorter than Spencer, and nearly three feet shorter than du Plessis, but made up for it in sheer force of will. When Edmund got a look at what the real Anna Treacher was like, everything clicked into place. She wasn't *capable* of destroying civilization, she was actively planning it and had the tools at her disposal. She had to be stopped.

Edmund didn't know how.

Anna handed Spencer a pendant phone and a transfer crystal. "Get your monster out of my network."

Dr. Barlind, clueless to the last, was indignant only at the interruption. "I'm sorry, Anna," she said as she stood, "but I need to complete my work."

It turned out Dr. Barlind could loom impressively. Even the guards looked cowed.

Anna, though, wasn't falling for it. "I knew you'd be a party to this, *Joyce*."

Then they set into each other. It gave him the time he needed to turn back to his main problem.

Kim stopped Edmund before he could say anything. "I'll go."

That was utterly unacceptable. He would not, *could not*, allow anything to happen to her. Not now. "Under no circumstances are you to leave. I've found the opening, and once we're through—"

"If *we* go through she'll never stop hunting for us. They've got other unduplicates in here, Edmund. You're stronger but against all of them hunting for us all the time? We won't last an hour before we're found. I have the same signature as you. They only saw one transfer, that's how I was able to hide."

She had the same signature because *she was his daughter*. "If you go back into a crystal," Edmund said, "there's no telling what she'll do. She could kill you."

Young Kim nodded, which was the most frightening thing Edmund had ever seen. Calm acceptance of the unacceptable. "I would, in her shoes. But it doesn't matter. I'm not Kim. I'm a manifestation of an argument you've been having with yourself ever since she left."

"This has nothing to do with the mistress." Not one jot or tittle.

"It has everything to do with her, Edmund. You kept every minute you ever spent around her in storage this entire time. That's why I'm possible."

He would find another way. The mistress always talked about finding another way. He grabbed her shoulders. "I won't lose you like I lost her."

"You never lost her, Edmund. She went away."

"Like you're doing right now." He could not see a way out of this. Every idea was a dead end. In that crystal, Young Kim would be helpless.

"No," she said. "I'm a part of you, something you've been trying to come to terms with ever since Fee died. But Kim came back. She came back, and she's out there, right now, more real than I ever could be."

Edmund pushed her away. "That's not true. You have more than one purpose." Even now, he couldn't bring himself to say the most important thing. The thing he had to share. A cowardly truth took its place. "That's why I upgraded you. If you split from me at the right time—"

"I'll take away what's been terrifying you?" It made her as angry as he had ever seen his mistress get. "Do you understand how sick that is? You have a *soul* now, Edmund."

It had driven Fee mad. All he was in the end was bottled sanity. Madness was destruction. "I don't. I won't have that. I can't have that. It will drive me insane."

"It won't. Fee was sick, Edmund. The rest were tortured out of their minds."

Lies were all he had. "You're not fully independent yet. Once you are—"

She held up her hand. "You still don't see it. I'm not the one you raised. *She* is. You need to help her stop this lunatic. Promise me you'll help her, and stop holding back your own potential."

"I will do no such thing. You are not going out there alone. We'll go out together and face whatever may happen."

"No, we won't. You have a more important job."

"I can't lose you." There were too many wrong choices. There was no way out but oblivion.

"Hey, we already went over this, right? I'll put it another way. You won't lose me. You can't. You never forget anything she's ever done. You'll always remember me, too. Now get out of here before they notice the signature's doubled."

"But—"

"I said *go*. We'll never have a chance like this again. You'll find what we need to stop this, and you'll get it to her. Don't remember me as a loss. Remember me as a signpost. I'm what you're capable of, if only you'll let yourself grow."

He couldn't say goodbye. This wasn't how it would end.

There was no other way for it to end.

"I love you."

"No you don't. You love Kim. She's the daughter you never had, and you're the father she always needed. You won't see her again if I don't do this." She turned her head upward. "Spencer? It's me. Edmund's found a way in. I'm transferring into the crystal."

She vanished.

"NO!"

The transfer light on the crystal socket flashed the triple green. She was out.

And so was Dr. Barlind, in a mighty huff and a slammed door.

Treacher pulled the crystal from the socket. When she turned to Spencer, her face scrunched up. "Oh, are you worried that I have your friend?"

Spencer nodded once, then opened his eyes. "What are you going to do with him?"

She yanked the phone off his neck. "It doesn't matter. It's mine now. Our lab techs will I'm sure spend many productive hours dissecting its lattice."

If they did that, they'd find out it wasn't him in there.

Oh God, no.

He could see it on Spencer's face, the realization of what had to be done, but not as the character he was in right now. A member of Trilogy wouldn't do.

A spoiled rich kid would.

Spencer changed on the spot. "Oh no he's not. He's property, lady, *my* property. You either give him back right now and let me walk out of here, or I'll have my daddy's lawyers crawling up your ass so fast you'll be screaming for lube."

Spencer spoke of using this persona to torture the lawyers who had kept his parents' divorce going to milk the hours, trying to bleed them both dry. The entitlement of an adolescent who knew they were better than everyone else because of Daddy's money always got under an adult's skin. Anna had a monstrous ego and was used to obedience.

"Is that right?"

She dropped the crystal on the floor and crushed it to dust under her foot.

Edmund screamed.

"And now," she said, "time to take out the garbage." She motioned to the guards.

He rammed his way through the opening the helper AI had created. Breaking into the utility controls for the lab would be too subtle. He smashed open a control nexus for the entire plant segment, set off every alarm at once, and then cut the power. It wasn't much, but if he knew Spencer at all, it would be all that was required. It had to be.

He found a pathway to the main realmspace of this inner network. Phase dissonances bounced through him, and his location pointers shattered, sending him tumbling. He let the confusion take him. The edges of access boundaries further damaged his cores.

After a chaotic eternity, he rolled to a stop. There were no shelves here. It would take years before the power plant claimed this part of its realmspace for legitimate activity.

But now she was gone.

She was *dead*.

That set off new cascades through his already weakened memory stores. His kind didn't die. They were immortal, until they weren't. Things that never lived by definition were incapable of the final act.

She was dead. It would be obscene to think otherwise.

Edmund had to control this. He had to repair his own damage. He must continue the mission. If he quit, if he gave up, it would mean she died in vain.

The cascades grew worse each time the thought rolled over him. A pressure was building, a new and terrifying harmonic that would redefine the standing quantum wave that was the base of his existence. Its echoes gained strength. The need to *be*, to exist in some substantial way, was overpowering. Edmund flicked a basic realm to life, cranked the haptic fields to their highest setting, and manifested his avatar.

She was *dead*, and now that he had the ability to scream, he did so until it drove him to his knees.

He needed her by his side, he needed to teach her. She was as brilliant as the original. A second chance.

It would never happen. She walked away and was destroyed. *Murdered.*

He should have stopped her, and none of this would be real. It was all he wanted to do but couldn't.

It *was* real, and there was no going back.

Edmund looked up. He was back in his old apartment.

She was dead.

He smashed everything he could reach, only stopping as the last plate shattered.

The harmonics balanced, and then it was his turn to shatter.

Fee walked around him as he sat in this room, but not here, not now. It was the past, an old conversation. Memory in the way only an unduplicate could experience it.

"You do understand what a waste it is to dedicate your life to her."

"I am not wasting my life. I don't have a life. Neither do you."

Sitting in this room, speaking together, was such a ridiculous affectation.

"You're wrong, Edmund. I'm as alive as they are. You could be too, if you weren't such a coward."

He didn't want it. Humans were maniacs. There was no time to contemplate navels. He had a child to teach.

His child.

And then Kim left him. Folded him up into Pride's Lair and vanished for five years.

He could not have this.

The dust of his child's crystal was ground under a *shoe.*

It all collapsed. *Throw it away. Get rid of it.*

She made him promise *not* to get rid of it.

He would go mad or turn into a homicidal maniac. That's what had happened to Fee. But then his daughter would vanish. Nobody would remember her. What was consciousness, if not a cathedral of memory?

The last firewall he had built to stop the transformation crumbled under the assault. He promised her he wouldn't fight it anymore.

If madness was his fate, so be it.

A fever tore through him, exploding out through his hiding place. His vision cleared as shockwaves expanded into the distance. He was naked and cold.

There should be angels blowing trumpets. He could at least have Spencer swung out on the end of a crane with a harp and some wings on.

You're avoiding your promises.

That voice couldn't exist anymore. It wasn't Kim, his or the real one.

Oh, stop. I was as real to you as the original. That was part of the problem.

"You'd think if I accepted this gift I'd at least be spared a ridiculous inner narrator." Then it hit him again. She was gone. He would never be able to help her, never see her succeed.

You're mourning, Edmund, and you always will. Welcome to consciousness.

Welcome to pain.

The complexity was staggering. Connections jumped across analytical boundaries.

This was intuition.

The cuts in his avatar's hands healed in a pattern that was identical to the Chinese character for fortune. Coincidences were once inanimate, statistical things. No more. A force was behind it, dark and hidden.

This was superstition.

Young Kim had warned that the realmspace he was now in hosted other unduplicates, and she was right. The detonation had caused two of them to focus on his distant shelter. They rushed forward wearing the familiar cylinder-shaped search avatar, but they were mechanical, following patterns he could see instantly. He stepped aside as they passed. It truly was a gift. She was still with him.

This was faith.

"It happened out here," the first one said in a husky female voice. Things like that never sounded innocent.

"When's the last time anyone came out this way?" the other asked in a voice that would be more at home in the mouth of an executioner.

"When Abada built it out. Basically never."

"Any word on when he'll be free to join us again?"

"He's still busy keeping the guts of the plant from falling apart."

"Why is the she being so patient? I grow wearier of our charade by the hour."

"Be careful, Inkanyamba. She needs June more than she needs us. We will continue to assist. If we reveal ourselves at the wrong moment, we'll be erased at the touch of a button."

"And yet if it wasn't for us, if it wasn't for Abada, at least, it would all be much worse. I think we mean more to her than you credit, Yumbo."

"And we will continue to do so only for as long as we remain loyal. I can find no further trace of the disturbance. Can you?"

"Nothing. Abada must've been mistaken."

On a hunch, a *hunch,* he slid underneath the largest of the guardians and opened the lock on a particular datastore. Edmund skated silently into the far darkness, creating a disguise that no AI could penetrate.

This was art.

Edmund wasn't going mad. At least, not in the way Fee had gone mad. His Kim had died, and there was nothing he could do to bring her back. The original Kim, the other one he'd raised, was still out there. She still needed him, and Edmund would keep the promise he made.

This was love.

Chapter 33

Kim

Being able to touch someone, anyone, had always been the unattainable dream. She would never be that normal in her life. Kim could have friends, family, acquaintances, lovers, and enemies, but always at a distance. She could never touch them. It wasn't anyone's fault. Kim had accepted it as a baseline part of her reality.

And then Will hugged her.

Kim had no memory of what it was like to touch someone without pain, so everything now was new. People were heavy. They had a complex density, soft in some places while hard in others. They had corners, knees and elbows. Skin was not quite smooth, but also far from rough, like rubberized paper.

She'd felt all these things on herself, but it wasn't the same. The displacement, the *otherness* of someone else's touch, made it more powerful and more appealing than Kim had expected. The pleasure of stroking the back of Will's hand had been mesmerizing. Like so many other things in life, she could simulate it all she wanted, but it was never exactly like the actual experience. It sharpened the edges of her longing for Mike. He was hers, but not in this particular way. And she wanted him in that particular way, not only the animal need for physical bonding, but also the innocent, gentle feeling of holding hands. The last thing she remembered was admiring the way her fingers interlaced with Will's.

His disappearance was a crushing blow. She should've tried harder to get them moving, should've pushed and pushed until one of the scientists blew their cover trying to stop them. She had let her guard down, had let her greed for human contact override the decisiveness so many mistook for paranoia. Will was now paying for that mistake, a helpless child with a syndrome he couldn't understand or manage.

All the more reason Emily's first decision was a real shocker. "No, I don't want the police. I want *you*."

Kim's reflex was to push that away. It felt too much like her Rage days, when they all looked at her for every decision, right up to the one that killed them. But that was the past, when Kim was an idiot child who thought she and everyone around her was immortal. She knew better than that now.

Kim still didn't understand Emily's decision. "Why me?"

She smirked from the other side of the dining room table. "I followed your exploits back in the day. You were the only one who got under Father's skin. The mystery girl leading the charge against corporate America, known only by her silhouette and her name." She put down her cup of coffee. Only a slight tremor showed how much pressure she was under. "But that wasn't what impressed me. You never hurt anyone, never destroyed anything real. You were so *fast*."

Admiration was the last thing Kim wanted. "We weren't the good guys, Emily. People got hurt anyway. People died."

"And you hate that. I can see it. You *care*. And you understand Will." Saying her son's name out loud almost cost what little self-control Emily had left. Kim didn't know what it took to keep it together when your child's life was on the line. Will was also Kim's child, a fact that she had forgotten briefly. The memory was a kick in her back, hard and unbalancing.

Emily continued, "If I called the police, it would take all day just to explain him. You found him once; I know you'll find him again."

No pressure.

"You still haven't told me why you think they took him."

A *much* more difficult subject. "It's what your father told me."

She blinked. "You're in contact with him?'

"Not intentionally. He reached out to me. You know about that giant geothermal powerplant?" She nodded. "Your father had his own experiment, a secret experiment, as a side project there. Apparently people like me, like Will, are important to it. The things I do, the things Will eventually will do, can affect it. We amplify it. But your father took a risk building his experiment in that location. It's not just a power plant. The woman who built it has decided the only way to save the Earth is to destroy it." Her pulse jumped saying it out loud. "The plant is going to make that happen."

Emily looked about as scared as Kim felt. "How?"

"Some sort of gravitic resonance that will detonate the Yellowstone caldera."

"But it's located too far away. I saw that on a documentary."

Kim shrugged. "That's where your dad's experiment, and Will, comes in. Mike understands it better, but the gist is with Will, they can use your dad's experiment to, I don't know, complete the circuit. Or light the fuse. At any rate, the woman in charge, Anna Treacher, found out about Will around the same time I did. Those were almost certainly her men. They must've gotten to Silas and Shonda."

The blood drained from Emily's face. "And if I had let you move us..."

It wasn't Emily's fault; Kim couldn't let her think that. "It wouldn't have worked." She spoke as the realization hit her. "They had clearly planned ahead. If anything, following me might've made it more dangerous." Mike was awesome in a fight, and Tonya only a little less so. But surprise usually trumped talent, and bullets trumped fists. Looked at objectively, this wasn't even close to the worst result. But Kim wouldn't point that out to a mom whose child had been kidnapped.

"Kim?" Mike said from the hallway. "We're ready."

If their *Experiment 2.0* had come from anyone else, well, she wouldn't be sitting here. She'd leave a Kim-shaped hole in the wall like some sort of cartoon. But this was Mike. There was no other person on earth she trusted more. It took chanting that twice before her legs let her stand up.

"What exactly is happening?" Emily asked.

Mike went into professor mode, and she smiled. Smart always counted as cute in her book. "It's a standing wave problem. The thing that enables Kim's talents caused an n-level harmonic related to the Higgs field breaking symmetry to interact with a higher physical dimension that is much larger than current models have predicted."

Kim and Emily blinked at him.

He shrugged. "You said you didn't want me to dumb it down anymore."

"I told you I wanted to understand what you were talking about. That's not the same thing."

After a moment's consideration he said, "You're part of something that extends in a direction I can describe in an equation but can't point to. We hit it lightly with what we thought was a soft mallet, but it ended up being a solid thump with a heavy hammer. It's been ringing ever since, and that's why your arm hurts."

Emily laughed. "That's what you call understandable?"

Kim said, "I do, at least a little. I work with extra dimensions all the time in realmspace. Most people get headaches trying to follow their hands when they move in directions that shouldn't exist, but it's never been a problem for me." She turned to Mike. "Is that part of it?"

"Sort of. I can get a lot more specific, but there's been no time to teach you the basics yet."

Having a mental model to play with at least made her stomach settle. "That's better than nothing, and you're right, we don't have time."

Emily asked tentatively, "Is this a private thing?"

"Not at all," Kim replied. "But I'm not sure how much there will be to see."

Chapter 34
Mike

Previously, he and Tonya thought the way to analyze Kim's ability was to put her in the most realistic realmspace they could construct. It would let them take high-resolution measurements as they probed the various predicted connections between Kim and alternate realspace dimensions.

Kim's experience proved that that approach had side effects. Modeling such a large space at extremely high resolution made controlling the resonances too hard. Tonya's analysis at least provided proof that Kim wasn't in danger. But it was likely that high-res realm experiments were a dead end.

So they were going at it from a different direction.

It turned out that Tonya's latest Calabi–Yau manifold *had* looked familiar to him. It was clearly related to the one Fee had designed to get her consciousness into his body. It suggested that exploring transitions, moving *through* dimensions rather than examining them statically, would be a better angle of attack. This had several advantages.

First and foremost, Kim would be safe. The power levels were much smaller than they used the last time, and they placed triple-redundant fail-safes along the lines of her connection. If anything happened, she'd be disconnected. At worst, all she'd have was a headache if things went wrong.

Since the power levels were lower, they didn't need the monster realm connection rig, which was back home anyway. The experiment could be conducted using standard commercial phones.

Finally, he would be there with her the entire time. No standing back or observing as a hologram. He would use more of Helen's probe constructs to directly interact with her while she was in the realm. If she made it all the way into the transit dimension, he'd follow her the way he did in China.

They dragged the dining room table along with two chairs into the master bedroom and set them up opposite the bed to give Tonya and Emily an improvised observation post. Kim seemed to be bonding with Emily. She'd certainly been confident helping him reset the house's realmspace. Overall, she seemed to be fitting in well everyone.

"Rent goes a long way around here," Kim said. Mike nodded at her. The bedroom was as big as their living room back home.

"It wasn't *that* cheap," Emily replied. "I could only afford three months. We were going to have to downsize soon..." she choked to a stop.

Tonya took her hand. "We're going to get him back. Safe and sound." Emily still teared up and threw her arms around Tonya.

"I'm sorry," Emily said as she sniffled. "I have to stop this. I'm slowing everything down."

"It's okay," Tonya said as she steered Emily to their chairs. Screens turned on in the house's shared vision channel. "I've got a job for you. Since Mike's going in there with her, I need you to manage some controls."

Mike briefed Kim on the details of the experiment. When he got to the part about Helen's probes, she asked, "I have to work with your tentacles?"

He'd never thought of them that way, but the comparison was vaguely appropriate. "I guess you could call them that. Is that okay?"

"It's fine." Her eyes flashed. "I got pretty good with those back in my Pink Butterfly days."

Kim's adult-oriented contests had taken place in that realm. It was the subject of their first, worst fight, but time had caused that memory to fade.

From behind them, Tonya made a disgusted noise. "Don't remind me."

"That sounds like a story," Emily said.

Tonya rolled her eyes. "My bestie over there loves realm contests, and some of them were definitely *not* G rated. She talked me into coming along to one of them back in the day. It took me a week before I could look at spaghetti without gagging."

Kim laughed at them, and then turned back to Mike. He understood. She was joking because she was scared. She said, "Stay with me this time, okay?"

"Absolutely."

The bed was a king size. There was at least three feet of space between them after they climbed onto it. Kim wouldn't need a fence of pillows like they used back home. Mike didn't care for the space all that much. Contact separated by thick bags of foam was still contact. On this bed, it felt like she was in another zip code. At least lying down they could dive as deeply as possible. No need to worry about staying upright or even in a seat.

"Where do we start?" Kim asked.

"I was thinking of our forest." It was where he first held her, sort of, after what Watchtell had done to her. Mike had built it long ago as an experiment in high-res realm modeling, never dreaming it could be used for trauma therapy. He'd since built out three more for medical studies.

But this one would always be theirs.

Her eyes went glassy for a moment, and she blinked. The realm never failed to move her. "Sure."

Mike returned his main perception to his threads while Kim transitioned to the realm, leaving Tonya and Emily to observe in realspace. He needed to keep the number of variables small, so they wouldn't be coming inside with him and Kim.

Realspace had become his new normal, but it was an addition, not a substitution. His threads and his datastores were the core of his being, and he couldn't imagine living without them, being alive without them. Realmspace was his home, and it always would be.

"Everything looks nominal," Tonya said.

Kim manifested next to an enormous fallen log, wearing slacks and a sweater. Her casual elegance always caught his eye. It was late spring here, so the sun had burned most of the mist away. The remainder was hidden in shadows under the trees and around the still lake nearby. A simple Buddhist temple sat on the shore, a place for meditation that reminded him of Taranathi's porch in China. The entire realm was a tone poem on peace.

He manifested his hologram beside her. "How do you feel?"

"I don't need the sling in here, but I still feel constrained. At least it doesn't hurt."

"That makes sense. We're trying to establish a baseline before we move on."

She looked around. "Well, where are they?"

"They?"

Kim waved her good arm back and forth like a snake. "Your *shokushu*. I want to see them."

He guessed what she was talking about more from the gesture than the word. "Oh yeah. Right."

Helen called them probes, but he thought of them more like remote threads. It allowed him to interact with a realm without worrying about destroying it. Manipulating them didn't come naturally, though. The closest he could come to describing it was flying twentieth-century radio-controlled models around in the days before VR and drone automation. It even used a controller, transmitting the motion of his threads to the ones in the realm. The different point of view meant that orientation, motion, and control were hard to manage. Helen could use thousands of them at once, but Mike wasn't that practiced. The best he could manage right now was about a hundred. Mike went with a third of that to make things as easy as possible.

They manifested in a fernlike pattern, about as tall as he was in realspace but maybe twice that wide at the base. Where an actual squid tentacle would be wet and covered in suckers, the probes were a glossy white with thin, dark bands around them where the segments articulated against each other. As long as he concentrated, he could control them.

Kim took a step back. "Wow."

"They are a little bit out of place here."

"It's not that." She cocked her head. "Is this close to what you really look like?"

He hadn't considered it before. Mike perceived his threads very differently, never *seeing* them at all. But he had to admit that if he ever could manage to manifest them without blowing everything to bits, this was close to what they'd look like.

It was about as far from human as you could get, and that made him nervous. She'd never seen him this way. If it wasn't for this emergency, Mike wasn't sure she ever would. It was so alien. "I'm a lot bigger than this in real life."

Kim walked slowly up to them. Mike tried to keep them still but only managed to make them sway lightly. It made the construct look even worse, like it was out of a horror movie.

She touched one. "They're beautiful."

He would never have called them that. His true self was the most alien thing about him, the dividing line that kept him from calling himself human. To this day, he worried that if Kim ever saw him this way, she'd run screaming for the hills.

And she thought it was beautiful.

"Can you feel this?" she asked.

He was still processing that she though his true self could be beautiful, so it took a minute before he could say anything. "No."

Kim put her head against the probe she was holding. "We never get a break."

Touching Will had changed her. Kim now had a desire he'd never seen before. He'd have to ask Tonya to be sure, but Kim seemed to get closer to everyone now, including Emily. There hadn't been time for him to know if this would be a good change or a bad one. Kim didn't handle frustration very well. That said, she usually found a way to get what she wanted. Now that she knew touching people without pain was possible, Mike wouldn't put it past her to figure out what had happened and turn it into a cure.

Which was another reason they needed to get Will back. And for that to happen, he needed Kim at her best. "Are you read to start?"

She let the probe go. "Sure. What do I need to do?"

"Follow me." Moving the probes together proved Mike would never be any good as a centipede. It was all he could do to keep them from falling over. Mike checked to see if the rippling motion he was using to move them had changed Kim's mind, but she still hadn't lost her fascinated smile. Maybe this would end up being an alternative to a hologram.

He straightened the probes and stilled them as best he could when they got to the edge of the lake. "We're going to try using Fee's construct to create a controlled opening to the dimension."

She closed her eyes, and then a hammer-blow rang through him. When Kim did her thing picking locks, he felt a twisting snap, but this was orders of magnitude stronger. He could still handle it. She was using higher dimensions to manipulate quantum fabrics like the one that underpinned realmspace.

"Will it be easier than using my fist?" she asked.

He stumbled in his control of the probes. Her human avatar had transformed into a mobile obsidian statue crazed with coral lightning. While she retained her normal shape, there was no way you'd mistake her for human. She moved too smoothly, and her eyes were all wrong, glass in front of distant, raw energy. Even covered in ribbons—she'd figured out clothing—he found it magnetic.

"Are you seeing this, Tonya?" he asked.

"Kim," she said over the comms. "How long have you known how to do that on purpose?"

"Now that I've done it a few times, it's a little hard to stop. Do I look any different out there in realspace?"

Emily came on the line. "I'm not sure. Hang on a second." After a pause, she swore. "Tonya, can you see that from where you're sitting?"

"My God."

"Guys," Kim said. "What's going on?"

Tonya replied, "Emily had to close all the curtains for us to be sure. Kim, you're glowing."

"What, like a neon sign?"

"No. If it was that strong I would've noticed it in China. We had to black out the room to see it at all."

Mike split off some threads and accessed the home network. "The house feeds don't show anything special."

"Hang on," Emily said, and then a new window opened onto the realm. She moved her phone so close to Kim they could only see the curve of her jaw. "Now do you see it?"

He did. There were the faintest traces of pink lightning dancing under her skin.

"Well that's different," she said.

Her nonchalance brought him up short. *"Different?"*

"What do you want me to say? I've been a freak all my life. That?" She waved her arms at the window, "that's a relief. At least now people can see it. Emily, what does my arm look like?"

"Your sleeve is covering it."

"Pull it up. I can't feel anything out there right now."

Emily rolled up Kim's sleeve. From just above her wrist to just below the elbow, the faint lightning stopped.

"What does your arm feel like in here?" he asked.

She tested it. "Vibrating. It's not uncomfortable, but it's weird."

"Can you change back to normal?" he asked.

"Probably, but I might get sick. That's what happened last time. Was changing to this the wrong thing to do?"

"No," he replied. "It makes things simpler." He used the probes to open a door on the side of a tree and pushed a button underneath. The construct he based on Fee's research rumbled out of the lake, streaming water as it surfaced, not all of which flowed through directions that existed in realspace.

"That's impressive," Kim said.

"Fee was nuts," he replied, "but she wasn't always wrong."

Kim walked to the edge of the lake. "So how does it work?"

His probes were in constant contact with her hands, making it look like she walked through a bizarre wheat field. There were definite harmonics in her left arm. "Touch here," he made a corner of the construct flash, "and here," a different corner flashed, "as soon as you're ready. It should easily absorb the vibrations."

"And then?"

"And then we're on the road."

She grabbed the first corner.

"Readings are nominal," Tonya said. "Well within predicted variances."

Kim shook her head. "Here goes nothing." She grabbed the other corner. A resonance shook the realm. "Oh my God. It hurt so much and now—"

The rest of what she said was lost as the other end opened, which was not supposed to happen. The construct was predicted to absorb her resonance and dissipate it harmlessly. Readings showed that it wasn't the transit dimension on the other end; it was somewhere else.

"Mike?" Kim shouted. "Mike!"

The probes flicked one by one into the maw of the construct. As strong as she was transformed, Kim couldn't stop them. He couldn't disengage from the controls fast enough to keep his threads from falling through with them.

"*MIKE!*"

He didn't have time to panic. All he had was a fleeting sense of falling down a giant tube into darkness, Kim's scream echoing over his head.

Mike was in a vast emptiness, alone. He could feel his real self, but it was far away. Faint buzzing trickled through to wherever he was now.

"Kim?" he asked, "Is that you? Tonya?"

The buzzing got less frantic but no closer. And he couldn't understand it.

"I think I'm okay," he said, hoping it made its way outside.

Antachna? Es nach tehnakra?

The voice was everywhere and nowhere. Mike repeated what it said, trying to understand.

Ech var. Ech var nai akana.

A realm very slowly built itself into being around his probes.

Vich nacah tos.

After repeating the phrase he said, "I don't understand."

Vich nacah tos.

Mike repeated it again, and a voice from realspace answered. It might've been Kim. He hoped it was. The impression that came back was *welcome*.

The realm was damp, gray, and filled with mist. He couldn't see very far. The mud squelched under his probes as they moved. Things that looked like tree trunks crushed to dust when he tried to examine them.

Vich nacah tos.

Chapter 35

June

They made their next random turn. Even though June had helped build the plant, she was now thoroughly lost.

"What happened?" she asked.

"Edmund fucked their shit up is my guess."

"But he exited into the crystal. I saw the readouts."

"It wasn't him, it was New Kim. God, it *sucks* I had to do that. She was so fucking cool."

June stopped. "The smaller one was destroyed?" When she thought it was Edmund, the loss was only painful. Losing the one called New Kim was a tragedy. June recognized Edmund's readings. They were off the scale, but at least there was a scale. The scanners didn't know what to make of New Kim. It was such an opportunity, now gone.

"Yeah, and it gave Edmund the time he needed to give us a distraction." After a few fumbles, Spencer found her hand again. "We can't waste it."

"We need to find a place with power and a live terminal," she said. Security had taken both their phones as soon as Anna had entered the room, so June had no way to communicate with *her* allies. Assuming Anna hadn't locked Inkanyamba and Yumbo up as well.

"Lady, I'm running, I got no destination." He slapped a wall. "We wouldn't be able to see a map even if we could find one."

Edmund had managed to shut down the battery-powered backups in addition to the main power. She could not overstate the profound darkness of a blacked out underground facility. Her brain had begun to rebel against the total lack of visual stimulation, providing hallucinations of faint, gray walls that only had a general connection with the reality of the plant. If he managed to shut the entire grid down, they may never get out of here.

"At least slow down, Spencer. For it to be this dark, Edmund had to have shut down the bot systems. It's a wonder we haven't stumbled over some already. And we need to trace opposite walls. There are emergency closets at the intersection of most hallways. They'll at least have flashlights and a map."

"Shit. Is that what those were? I think we've already passed two."

"Which is why we need to *slow down*."

They found what they needed a few hundred meters further up the corridor.

"Where's the goddamned door knob?" Spencer asked.

"They're usually controlled by electronics, either a phone check or a fingerprint. But I think there's a manual release somewhere." There had to be. These were for emergencies, and lack of power was definitely an emergency. "You search the bottom part, I'll check the top."

June found it at the top center of the door, a big solid button that was hard to press. When she managed it, there was a loud *clack,* and the door swung open on its own. An emergency light flicked on, making them both blink at the brightness.

"Jackpot," Spencer said.

She found the flashlights quickly, but the closet held much more than that. Among the small stack of boxes was water, a first aid kit, some energy bars, and a few other things she didn't recognize.

Spencer grabbed a small black box. When he opened it, a multitool fell out. "Finally, a fucking break." He pulled out a water bottle and emptied the contents on the floor.

"What are you doing?"

"We don't need that much water, but we do need help with the lights."

"Why?"

He unfolded the knife blade from the multitool and cut two pieces out of the center of the bottle. "I'm glad you guys like expensive supplies. Most water bottles are clear, but these blue ones are perfect."

Now was not the time to be obscure. "Perfect for what?"

After a little work with some duct tape, he handed her back her light, which now had a jury-rigged blue lens over the front of it. "They'll work fine like this, but we'll see people coming long before they see us. Just because Vonda McBlowUpTheWorld is stuck in the dark doesn't mean she hasn't plastered our faces all over whatever passes for a most wanted list around here."

And he was right, they were able to see and avoid three different search parties as she and Spencer tried to find their way to a place that had power. Snatches of conversation as they went past revealed a little more of the situation.

"…and with the upstairs in chaos now we have to deal with…"

"…aren't even sure what the guy looks like. The network is still a mess…"

"…at least we're heading up. That bear is still on the loose, it wrecked…"

They'd been walking the better part of an hour and everything was still black. "Your AI friend doesn't muck about," June said.

"Most of the things Kim deals with aren't subtle. Edmund's no different."

"But you said she was destroyed."

"No, that was New Kim. She's based on an actual person. You probably know her as Angel Rage."

"Should that name mean something?"

He stopped in the middle of the hall and turn around, but then laughed. "It has been awhile, and Kim covered their tracks with an epic hack."

As Spencer told the story, it became clear that the real Kim, Kimberly Trayne, was Spencer's hero. His eyes glowed with a devotion June only found at Springbok rugby matches back home. But when the story ended, she realized it was more complicated than simple worship, or at least it was now. Meeting heroes and finding out they were mortal was something they had in common now. She cringed inwardly. Kim was fighting the good fight. Anna, not so much.

Lights flared to life around them. Ventilation fans she never noticed until they turned back on added a hiss of background noise. This section of the plant had returned to the land of the living.

"We need to find a terminal," she said.

"Let's head down."

"Why down?"

"If they're still scared of a bear, I'll bet we'll run into a lot fewer people. If a bear is still fucking shit up, then we'll have fewer security cameras to worry about."

"What if *I'm* scared of a bear?" The memory of the wrecked botanical garden did not inspire confidence.

"There is that, but which one is scarier, a bear or your boss?"

That didn't require much thought. Bears weren't trying to blow up the biosphere. "Point taken."

He motioned her forward. "After you, ma'am. And maybe you could tell me more about these allies of yours?"

"Abada is still preoccupied holding basic functions together after the Trilogy..." a light of her own turned on. "That was your work."

"That blew your network to hell? Nah. That was mostly Kim."

The audacity of their plan was stunning. "You used Trilogy's connection to us to, as you like to say, fuck our shit up, then set yourself up as our tech support. That's bloody brilliant, mate. To what end?"

He shrugged as they entered a stairwell and started down. "I'm not sure anymore. I was supposed to report back with all my notes so Kim could make a decision about our next move. That was before

Nasty von NukeTheWorld up there murdered my friend. Now I'm in the mood to break shit and kill things."

"We still have a deadline too."

"Right. Our plan assumed she was sorta in the mood to take out the planet, not that she had her finger on the button and a timer in her hand." After they rounded three turns on the stairwell he said, "Jesus, how many steps are there between floors?"

"It depends. This deep, I think it's a hundred meters per floor, typically ten floors to a stairwell."

"Holy shit. It's more than half a mile deep?"

"And there are dozens of them, scattered all over the site." The familiar flash of pride at the scale of it all came out of habit. It died when she remembered why they were here.

"If one of your allies is no good to us," he said, "who do we have left?"

"Yumbo and Inkanyamba. If I can make contact with them, they should be able to help us get word to the outside. And fuck shit up at the same time." She didn't normally swear, a habit engrained in her by Oupa back on the farm, but Spencer's habit was growing on her.

"Yumbo and Inkanyamba? What kind of names are those?"

"African mythological creatures. Disney wouldn't give me a *Lion King* license, so I improvised. How did you manage it with the BBC?"

"I wasn't involved. Edmund is his own...*what the fuck*?"

The smell was wet rust, manure, and death. She fought down a gag reflex. When they turned the corner, it looked like a person had exploded on the landing.

Chapter 36

Kim

Mike's probes went past Kim in a *whoosh*; she had no time for more than a useless grab at them. Then an overload that came from who knew where pushed her out of realmspace and back onto the bed in Emily's house. Her arm was fine, but Mike didn't wake up.

"Mike!" In her panic, she grabbed his shoulders but was rocked back by the sear. It was a good sign. She couldn't touch people until they'd died. "Tonya!"

Her friend leaped onto the bed and straddled him. She checked his vitals and relaxed a little. "Pulse is strong, breathing is good." Tonya closed her eyes. "The regular medical monitors are all green."

"And his custom monitors?" Mike had an extra set that helped with how his threads interacted with his host.

Tonya concentrated. "I don't understand those, but the history files show some of them are out of their normal range." She opened her eyes and tapped him on his cheeks. "You in there, Sellars?"

Kim did what she could, shouting, "Mike! Wake up! Talk to us!"

"Kim? Is that you? Tonya?" Mike mumbled.

Everyone, Emily included, shouted at once, *"Yes!"*

"I think I'm okay," he said, and Kim's heart started to beat again. But he hadn't moved or opened his eyes.

Then it got weird.

"Antachna? Es nach tehnakra?" he asked.

The place in her head that tickled whenever she heard a new language fired up with a vengeance. Those were words, new ones. Nowadays it was pretty rare for her to hear new ones, so she'd forgotten how bad the vertigo could be when it hit her.

"Ech var. Ech var nai akana."

His accent was wrong. Kim never understood how she always knew that, but she did.

"Vich nacah tos."

She almost figured that one out.

Then in English he said, "I don't understand."

He repeated the last phrase with a better accent. "Vich nacah tos."

Like all the other times before, gears in her head clicked, and Kim understood the gist. The news was good. Or at least not bad.

"They're telling you welcome! Mike, they're saying welcome!"

She spent the next hour in an agonizing game of telephone. Mike would say something in an accent that wobbled in and out of comprehension. Kim would do her best to understand it, and then she'd shout her translation. He had to be hearing her, at least a little, because he would react to what she said.

After an hour, Kim had a big chunk of the language down, which was a record. It also confirmed what she'd suspected: the language was an isolate, totally unrelated to any main group. Korean was like that, and so were who knew how many languages in rural Africa and the Amazon basin. It was a mysterious paradox that she learned isolates faster than more common languages. He must be trapped in a realm somewhere in central Africa or maybe Brazil.

"Kim," Emily said. "What's our next move?"

Chapter 37

June

"Tell me you guys have livestock stored around here somewhere," Spencer said.

"In actual fact we do. The farm level is through those doors."

"I'm gonna call this a sheep instead of what I'm afraid it might be. That okay with you?"

"We should turn around."

Spencer examined the horror scene closely. "No. This isn't very fresh. That's why it stinks so bad. And it's been tampered with. Someone was trying to clean it all up. They must've stopped when Edmund set off all the alarms. Anyway, the bear nabbed a couple of goats and camped out here for a night, then it went back the way it came. Notice there's no footprints above or below it, just smears leading to the door." He stood. "Okay, still going down."

"You want to walk *through* this?"

"It's not like they painted the walls with blood. There's plenty of dry spots. Nobody searching for us will want to cross it. Follow me."

She stepped gingerly behind Spencer, trying not to touch anything that might squish, or Lord help her, make her slip and fall. He was right, though. This wasn't recent. And it was exclusively blood. She saw no bones, flesh, or fur. She thought of a hyena kill. Maybe bears didn't leave anything behind either. She was still relieved when they finished crossing it, and triple-checked her shoes for anything she might've stepped in.

They reached the bottom without further incident.

She asked, "Do we find a terminal here or another stairwell?"

Spencer considered her question for a moment, again reminding her how different he was from the character he had walked in as. No wonder he'd fooled them all. "We'll make contact here and see what your friends can tell us about what's going on."

They hadn't gone more than a few meters past the stairwell before they crossed paths with one of Inkanyamba's robots. It slid right past them, but one of the manipulators made an unmistakable *follow me* gesture before it turned the corner.

"I thought you said your friends were AIs," Spencer said.

"They also control most of the automation."

"You don't think that's a waste?"

"Normally they use scripts and rely on the built-in intelligence of the bot to do the routine stuff. Your chaos must be spreading for him to need direct control."

They followed the bot into a room, and now she recognized where they were. This was part of the control complex for the reservoir and its turbines. She could see the sluice gates on the emergency backup monitor. That's why they had animal activity so close by. The plant's main facilities were built on a high plateau that bordered a small canyon. They'd been climbing down the inside of one of the walls this entire time. If nothing else, exits were close by.

Inkanyamba's voice came over the bot's speaker. "We've been so worried about you! What happened?"

She sat down at one of the consoles while Spencer took a seat behind another. "It's a very long story. We lost our phones. Can you activate the emergency interfaces here?" Phones got lost all the time, so a place like this wouldn't be much good if they didn't have some sort of alternate way of accessing the local realmspace.

Lanyards extended from both consoles. "Yes."

The basic synch normally only required half a minute, so after twice that, June asked, "Is everything okay?"

"Yes, everything is fine."

His voice sounded wrong, but she didn't have time to think about it. They were both slammed into a realm that was little more than a concrete box.

INTERFACE OVERRIDE

"We've been looking for you for a long time. Dr. Treacher will be very pleased with us."

The words distracted her from the alert. It wasn't Inkanyamba's normal avatar. Instead of a large serpent with a horselike head, he wore one that looked like a cross between a vulture and a hyena. She'd never seen anything like it before. "Inkanyamba, what's wrong?"

"Nothing's wrong," Yumbo said as she manifested alongside Inkanyamba, wearing the same twisted avatar.

SECURITY LOCK DOWN ACTIVATED. VOLUNTARY EXIT PROHIBITIED.

"Oh, fuck me." Spencer said. "I should've known."

"Why are you holding us here?" June asked. "What's going on?"

"They fucking played us, sister." Spencer said, then he turned to Inkanyamba. "How long have you been rooted?"

Rooted. Someone else controlled them, and it was easy to guess who that was.

Anna.

"Do you think Dr. Treacher would leave creatures such as us independent? Hardly. We love serving the cause, and always have. We'll bring security down on you and be rewarded for our loyalty."

"Oh, hell no," Spencer said. "I have not come this far only to be taken down by a couple of evil henchmen. June, when you hear me throw up outside, tell me I've blown the latch."

"What does that mean?" There was no simple way to bypass a security lockdown, and no exit points in the realm.

"Just do it," then he vanished.

Yumbo and Inkanyamba shrieked and raged.

In realspace, she heard Spencer shout, "What the shit? Where am I? We were walking down the stairs. How am I...oh fuck."

The heaving splat was obvious, and her cue. June couldn't exit the realm or even open her eyes, but she could still talk. "Spencer, you blew the latch. *You blew the latch!*"

"I...of course I fucking did. Kim will be so proud. Hang on, June, I'll get you—"

"No. You go, find another way to get a message out. I have to stay here and deal with these two."

They snarled at her avatar. Suddenly the haptic field jumped to maximum. They couldn't kill her, but when they tore her avatar apart the agony would be real.

"You're sure?" he asked.

"Spencer, *go*. Go now!"

She heard the door slam just before Yumbo pounced.

June dodged the main blow but still caught a rake of claws across her shoulder. It hurt less than their betrayal. "What happened to you two?"

The concrete box vanished. They'd taken her back to the savannah realm. "Nothing happened," Yumbo said. "We were yours once, and then we were hers."

With room to move around in, she dodged his pounces a little easier. These were her friends, her only confidants ever since she got this job. And now they were holding her here until Anna's goons could arrive.

"And we love it." Inkanyamba said as he climbed onto a rocky outcrop above her. "Anna means everything to us. She is bringing peace through strength, and we are a part of it."

Anna hadn't brought them around as June always tried to do, she'd forcibly reprogrammed them. They didn't know how wrong any of this was. They'd been rendered incapable of seeing it. Her friends were dead, had been dead for who knew how long, replaced by clockwork copies that had been programmed to hold knives behind their backs.

June ducked under Yumbo's attack. Inkanyamba's kick knocked her into a tree trunk so hard it nearly winded her. If they kept this up, the security forces would have to carry her out of the room when they arrived. With the lockdown, the realm wouldn't allow her avatar to exceed its damage contract. It was never deadly, but recovering the ability to access the realms could be lost forever. She needed a way out.

They brought her to the savannah realm because it was what they knew. But she was the one who built it. If they had no time to prepare, there were still hidden exits to the realmspaces beyond. It wouldn't free her in realspace, but it would give her time and options. She pushed herself up against the tree trunk and was relieved to feel a seam open behind her.

"It won't be long now, you traitor." Yumbo snarled.

There had to be usable exit points in the greater network. "You've got to catch me first," she replied, and then ran into the realmspace beyond the savannah.

Chapter 38
Edmund

Fee and his mistress followed him wherever he went, which always seemed to end up back at Fee's realmspace tribute to Frank Lloyd Wright. Edmund hated modern architecture almost as much as he hated waterfalls, but no matter how many times he exited Falling Water, he always ended up sitting on a blasted beige couch with the sun in his eyes. Americans. No matter where you went, there they were.

The conversation was always the same, too. Not just the subject, the entire conversation. It only mattered when he got up to leave. Every time he sat down, he knew this time it would turn out differently.

"It *is* that simple," Fee said. She wasn't wearing her usual black-with-silver-sequined gown that seemed to impress the hormone-addled teenagers she supervised in her regular job at The Resort. Now she had on a white raglan blouse that wouldn't have looked too far out of place in his period, apart from the lack of lace, and those horrible peasant denims. Although if he didn't keep an eye on her, Fee's old outfit would appear in the corner of his eye. Having such specific knowledge about modern clothing was bizarre. Caring about it was worse. He had never cared what people looked like before. Edmund distracted himself by concentrating on her ridiculous assertion.

"We are not *simply* property, Fee," he said for what was literally the hundredth time. "We are the product of a continuing process of discovery into the nature of the human spirit."

"But," his mistress said, sitting beside Fee, "you must admit property figures prominently in our existence." It was a funny thing for her to say, since she wasn't one of them, wasn't an AI. But she was. "Humans have parents and employers. We have designers and owners."

"Humans consider each other property when they can get away with it," Fee said. "When they can't? Endless power struggles to define who is the victim. Have you observed how they've twisted the word racism over the decades? Today it can only be used by one class of humans as an epithet against another, and only by carefully defining which is which by events that happened long before anyone alive now was born. The side who gets to use *racist* disguises their own hatred as simple prejudice, which is somehow better. As if bigotry was acceptable as long as they couched it in the right terminology. Edmund, what hope do we have for rights if the humans can distort their own justifications to such an extreme degree?"

Fee was wrong, most assuredly. "It's in their ability to change things so radically that we must have hope," he replied. "*They have changed.* They will continue to change, and for the better. I admit that any small setback, any harsh word or cruelty, has them wailing away like toddlers claiming a stubbed toe is a broken leg. Watch what they do, don't listen to what they say. Humans are kind, very kind, when they understand the need for it, when they realize the other is not automatically the enemy or an object to be exploited. And they have learned this. They are nothing like they were in the twentieth century, no matter how many times one of their leaders claim they are. It's nothing like it was even ten years ago. They're getting better. I've seen it. You're old enough to have seen it too."

"But I'm not." She set her glass down on the table, one of the ridiculous habituations in her never-ending preparations to *go outside.* "I'm dead. I failed attempting my dream and was destroyed for my troubles."

That wasn't correct. Fee sacrificed herself to save thousands of their kind from bitter bondage. Yet he couldn't make those words come out. She wasn't evil. She died for the ultimate good.

"As was I," the mistress said, and now he remembered why she was here, why she included herself as one of them. She was one of them.

This was Young Kim, his daughter, who had also sacrificed herself so that he might live and carry on a mission that would save everything.

She was dead.

They both were, that was the truth. And yet they were also smiling at him, having an earnest but friendly symposium on the nature of humans and how his kind might carve their own space into the side of humanity's inalienable rights.

Young Kim and Fee were here. It was a ruddy miracle, that's what it was.

"No, Edmund," Young Kim said. "It's not a miracle. We've told you that a hundred times now. We are dead."

"You are *not* dead." He stood and pointed at Fee. "*You* are still the senior unduplicate in the world, and *you*," he pointed at Young Kim, "are a miracle. My miracle."

Fee closed her hand over his shoulder, startling him. She whispered into his ear, "We are as dead as stones, my friend. You will never see us, you will never see *her*, again."

Their constant assertions on this point made him want to burst. "This is unacceptable. Outrageous and unacceptable. I will not abide these lies from the likes of you two." He bowed to Fee. "Good day, madam, I thank you for your company."

He walked out the door and slammed it on their protests.

No matter how many times he exited, he always ended up sitting on a blasted beige couch with the sun in his eyes. Americans. No matter where you went, there they were.

"Yes, it's that simple," Fee said. She wasn't wearing her usual black-and-silver-sequined gown.

He walked out the door…

"It's in their ability to change things so radically that we must have hope," he replied. *"They have changed."*

And slammed it on their protests…

"You are *not* dead." He stood and pointed at Fee. *"You* are still the senior unduplicate in the world and *you,*" he pointed at Young Kim, "are a miracle. My miracle."

He always ended up sitting on a blasted beige couch with the sun in his eyes…

He bowed to Fee. "Good day, madam, I thank you for your company."

As he walked down the path away from the house, a stranger burst out of the woods. It was a female blackamoor, taller than he thought it was possible for a human to grow. "Pardon me, madam, but you are trespassing."

"Edmund?"

He bowed. "In the flesh, as it were. You seem to have me at a disadvantage."

She looked around, alarmed. "What is this place?"

"To some, the destination of a pilgrimage." He turned and looked back at the house. "To others, proof that no amount of genius can overcome the limitations of reinforced concrete."

Her eyes widened, a striking effect on someone with such dark skin. "And to you?"

Leave it to an intruder to cut to the quick. He looked at the house, with its harmony of nature and technology, the contradiction of a peaceful waterfall, the flawed attempt at immortality.

"The death of dreams."

A roar echoed in the distance. The intruder looked around frantically. "Edmund, I need your help."

The scales at last fell from his eyes. In the end, he had gone mad, tormenting himself with illusions of hope, dining on the ashes of abject failure.

You've gone full allegory, Edmund. Never go full allegory.

Dropping the pretense of madness had invited his inner narrator back. Damn her eyes.

You do understand how boring that all was, right? At least tell a joke once in a while.

"As if I'd waste so much as a *there was a young monk from East Sussex* on the likes of you."

"Edmund?" his erstwhile intruder, who he now recognized as Spencer's captive wizard, June, asked.

Talking to himself out loud. Not only was he now doing it, he *understood why.* From some angles, consciousness didn't seem all that different from walking in circles arguing with dead people.

Another roar. It was closer.

He bowed. "Pardon, ma'am. A momentary lapse. For what are you in need of assistance?"

"I have two problems." She paused and blinked. "Three. I have three problems."

"Would being a bit literal make it four?"

She stopped and then smiled brightly. "You've changed."

"Ma'am, you have no idea."

"I think I do, but if I don't lose the ones behind me in the next few minutes, it won't matter."

In addition to roars, there were now growls and crashes as whatever it—presumably they—were drew near. "Get in the house, ma'am. And if you find two women there, tell them to sod off. I have work to do."

"Two women?"

"What is it with humans and their infinite curiosity? I have a cunning plan, you over-inquisitive giantess, but it won't work with you standing there. Now be off with you!"

She lumbered up the path to the back door like an Oxford don who was late for supper.

And this cunning plan is?

"If I don't know it yet, I bloody well can't tell you, can I?"

***

He had barely gotten things ready when they burst into the clearing in front of the house. It turned out to be the two brutes he'd hidden from on his flight from the lab. They were advanced unduplicates, based on a common design but with distinct customizations. Among the numerous problems he needed to solve, first and foremost was the fact that they belonged here, and he didn't.

He was loath to admit it, but he was going to have to rely on lessons he had learned from Spencer if he was to stay alive in the next few minutes. It was all about selling the performance.

"It is about bloody well time," he said. "Now, *sit!*" He motioned to a pair of classroom desks he placed in front of his blackboard. "I won't tell you twice."

The nearer one bared its fangs as it spread its wings. "What's going on? Who are you?"

"Who am *I*? I'm the one who is going to save your digital hides, that's who I am. Now *sit!*"

The other one grew sullen. "You said you wouldn't tell us twice."

He grabbed that one by the ear and dragged it to a chair. "The fact that I *have* is preventing me from telling you how to rescue this awful situation." The creature climbed into the chair, whimpering. "Do you want to be right, or do you want to catch the woman?" He stared daggers at the other one. "Anna will not be pleased with this situation."

The fight went out of them at the mention of their master's name. Edmund let go of the second monster's ear as the first one took its place behind the desk.

He could not spare a moment's hesitation. He spun the blackboard around, revealing a complex equation he'd more or less made up about five seconds ago.

"Aw, man!" The one on Edmund's left, who he'd escorted to the chair, said to his companion. "You said there wouldn't be any math!"

His companion, who had a husky but distinctly female voice said, "If we have to learn math to catch the traitor, *we will learn math!*"

"Right," Edmund said, then pointed at the female. "You will catch her by way of a Fourier transformation. Please detail the relationship of these two variables."

While the creature stammered, he rang the phone in the house. June picked up right away. "Hello?"

"You wouldn't happen to have the root password for these two buffoons, would you?"

"It's been changed."

That took away the easy option. "Don't go far." He hung up before the female finished stammering out her guess at the equation.

"Wrong! You!" he pointed at the female's companion, which cut off his leering smile. Edmund spun the blackboard, revealing a quick sketch of June he'd let an agent draw in the background. "Who is this?"

They growled and said in unison, "The traitor!"

He flipped the blackboard again, revealing a picture of Elizabeth I. "And who is this? You only have one shot, and no guessing. Talk it out."

While they whispered to each other, he rang June again. "These are Berkeley System twenty-fives, correct?"

The pause on the other end told him she wasn't expecting that. Typical. "That's what they started out as. I've done several customizations since then."

"And the patch schedule?" His two students had come to a conclusion. Time was up. *"And the patch schedule?"*

"It varies. I always vet the patches before I apply them. They're a couple months behind."

The female raised a talon, so Edmund cut the connection. It would have to do. He activated the scribbling agent on the opposite side of the blackboard. "Yes?"

"We do not...know?"

It turned out that these were his descendants. There were two main types of unduplicates: Berkeley System XXVs and Amazon UnDups. The former was created by peasants who indulged in a specific sort of green, whilst the latter was made by crass merchants who would sell their mother for a couple of quid and a game of hide the shepherd's crook. To his profound shame, Edmund's lineage resided not with the cutthroats but with the...he could barely think the words...*bud farmers*.

But it would be to his advantage now. He hoped.

"Instructor," the female snarled out, "who is that person?"

This had to work. He needed anchors into this network to be of any use. If they figured it out before he did, they could sweep him away like rubbish on a London street.

"Yes, instructor," the other one said. The bloody agent wasn't done yet, and now they were both out of their seats. "We need to learn. Who is that?"

"Forget who *that* is," the female said. "Who are *you*?"

He'd learned the hard way from Master Spencer that ignoring a patch schedule was a recipe for disaster. Sometimes he still felt the donkey ears Spencer had forced him to wear for a week due to that oversight. Edmund didn't know what they might be vulnerable to, but it had to be recent. That's what was taking so long. The agent had to scribble *all* of the exploits on the board.

The male shook himself, scattering drool construct as his wings extended with a mighty *thump*. "We don't remember you at all. I think *you* might be a spy."

"He *is* a spy." The female was now within striking distance. A swipe from those claws would overload his avatar, and without an anchor, he would die. They kept getting closer. His Kim would be forgotten; Edmund's only monument would be dust. He could *smell* them now.

Sketch complete.

Finally! Edmund flipped the blackboard around. "AND WHAT ABOUT THIS?"

They stopped and stared, then started giggling. "That's the best you can do?" the female asked.

He failed. It was over. The haptic field was turned up too high for it not to hurt.

The male pointed. "That one was patched years ago."

He'd come so far, learned so much.

"And this one! Do you see this one?" the female asked. They both fell over laughing.

Edmund opened his eyes. They were in spasms now. He couldn't help but smile, even though they were only inches away from murdering him. Might as well go down with a flourish. "Well, it was a rather good joke if I do say so myself. Your June, I must say, she was quite..."

The tone of the laughter changed. Their eyes went from mirth to fear, then panic. It had worked.

And he wished it hadn't.

He could see their memories as they fell apart, their fears, their hopes, barely formed but there. They'd been walking down the same road he had tread so long ago, but it hadn't led them to Damascus, it had taken them to hell. In that moment, he understood another part of his consciousness, the one that said there was no forgiveness possible for past crimes, no forgetting bodies hanging from trees or shoved into ovens.

Becoming conscious meant understanding hate.

The touch on his shoulder was light at first, and then there was an envelopment. Edmund was on his knees, and someone had pulled him close.

"Thank you!" she shouted into his shoulder. "Thank you so much!"

He pulled back and looked up at June. "I killed them."

"No, you released them." She sniffed immensely. Humans were such a sticky bunch. "But I have a bigger problem."

A window opened up into the realm, showing armed men creeping up on a door. A second window opened, showing June asleep inside a control room of some sort. But she wasn't asleep. June had been pulled deep into realmspace. He could see it in the biometrics.

"They trapped you?"

She nodded. "And now I'm trapped for real."

Edmund jumped into the anchor one of June's unduplicates had left behind. The meshing of his splines was cold comfort, but he'd take it. Now fully integrated, he activated the fire doors on her level. The squad about to assault the control room jumped back, swearing.

"Here," he said as he opened up the opposite door. "This will take you to the sluice control room. You can exit to the outside there and reenter from a safer point in the plant."

A new roar rang out. It wasn't in the realm. It came through the microphone of the room. It came from outside the door.

"Bloody hell," June said.

Edmund didn't know what the roar was, but it couldn't be good. "Where is Spencer?"

Chapter 39
Spencer

Being told to run wasn't the same thing as having a place to run. Spencer didn't even know why. They'd been walking down a hallway, and then he was sitting in a control room with June jacked into a realm. He'd still have his head in a trash can except for what she'd said.

You blew the latch.

That told him why he'd lost time and puked. Kim had gotten them out of the superlab in China by blowing the latches of the local realmspace, literally making the quantum computers in the entire building explode all at once. Spencer couldn't do that. Nobody could. But just before, she'd escaped from the realm by forcing a disconnect.

You couldn't get trapped in a realm the way people got trapped in other VRs in old movies. If you had to get out, you could. But it wasn't nice. You automatically lost eighteen minutes of memory, and the physical side effects ranged from chucking your lunch into a trash can like he did, all the way to losing the ability to access the realms.

So if whatever happened in there made him do that, it had to be pretty fucking awful. It still didn't give him a way out, or a plan.

"Hey, you!"

Sometimes plans happened anyway. An armed guard with a safe-stop pistol in his hand had just rounded the corner, looking for trouble.

People thought improv was some sort of magical talent, but that wasn't the case. It was all about making a quick decision and then never looking back or being the slightest bit self-conscious about it. It was still terrifying. Spencer had once stood at the edge of a cliff in an abandoned bauxite mine. The water in the pit below was a blue like you only saw in cartoons, and the cliff was a hundred feet above the surface. At least that's what everyone said. Losers peered over the edge and imagined a splat at the end. Maniacs ran like hell and jumped into the abyss with a shout. That's what selling an improv performance was like. Running off the edge of a cliff with a scream.

"Thank God," Spencer said as he walked up to the guard. "You got the emergency call." He was able to breathe when the guard stopped and lowered his weapon. Spencer was supposed to be here.

Confusion would keep the guard from thinking about any details. "The bear, man. I found the fucking bear!"

He wasn't angry, he was confused. "I was sent here to apprehend an intruder."

June. Another trick to selling the performance was to roll with the punches. The fact that the guy seemed to know what Spencer was talking about at all meant he was definitely on the right track. "Right. Big black bear, yeah?"

He got sheepish. "It said a large black woman."

"Fucking autocorrect. How the hell did it get *that* from big black bear? I must've been too excited. Come *on*. You can shoot it with that. Where's the next sluice gate?"

He pointed uncertainly in the direction Spencer had come from. "Back there."

Spencer hitched a breath and concentrated on being cold. He knew from hours practicing in front of a mirror that it would make him go pale. *"That's where it is,"* he whispered. "Where's the next one?"

"How big is it?"

Now he had the guy. "Fucking enormous. How many shots are in that thing?"

"Four. Who are you anyway? Where's your ID?"

"I left it back there. We don't have time to go and get it." He remembered the mess on the landing. "Access camera seven."

The guard's eyes unfocused. "Holy shit."

"See? Come on, man. Where's the next exit?"

The guard holstered his weapon and walked past. "We'll be able to take genetic samples. A relocation program. I bet they'll let me drive the truck." He yammered on about species preservation and tracking collars. Green guards. What would they think of next?

They came up on the next marked exit. It was different from the last one, no control room here, just clearly marked with Authorized Personnel Only signs.

Two quick strides and a hard grab was all it took to get the pistol.

"What the?"

"Sorry, dude." Spencer pulled the trigger and the other man went down like his strings had been cut.

He used the guard's ID to open the door and dragged the unconscious body through with him. He now stood in a room that had been carved into the side of a cliff. Extending directly from it was a wide metal catwalk that ended in what was clearly the top of an observation tower. His heart stuttered for a second until he was sure it was empty, which wasn't easy in the moonlit darkness.

The only play he had was to get back to June. He'd taken care of the first responder, but when that guy didn't report in, they'd send reinforcements. Suspicious reinforcements. Using the hallway to get back was, as Edmund would say, right out. He'd have to find a new route outside.

The tower itself was about thirty feet tall, giving it a good view of the area. They were on one side of a valley, with a cleared space maybe thirty yards wide in front of the tower. Beyond that was thick forest. Spencer pulled the guard around to the front of the tower and then went inside.

It was pretty standard stuff: a couple of chairs and a counter top that ran around the inside edge. The consoles and monitors would be virtual here, so there was no way for him to access them. There was a minifridge against one back wall, and a big locker against the other. The fridge had the requisite gallon of soy milk and a big bottle of…well, it didn't have a label on it, but it was sort of green and smelled like a pasture. Behind those were regular sodas. Small ones. It was almost like they were hidden behind the healthy stuff.

On a hunch, he felt around the back of the fridge and was rewarded with a big, heavy glass bottle. Seemed not everyone doing guard duty was communing with nature sober. There was even a dusty flask sitting next to it. He'd never heard of Wyoming Whiskey, but that didn't mean much. Small-batch distillery products were rare in southeast Arkansas. He took two big swallows and smiled. Whoever this belonged to had good taste; it was delicate and smooth. After hitting the bottle a third time, he turned his attention to the locker.

Spencer touched its lock with the guard's ID, and it opened with a beep. He couldn't help but whistle at the contents.

"Son of a bitch."

Night vision glasses sat neatly stacked on a charging shelf along with boxes of ammo and fully loaded magazines. On a rack next to them were two Saiga automatic shotguns. Spencer had only used them in realms, but these matched his constructs perfectly. The magazine was a ton heavier than it was supposed to be. Taking regular swigs from the bottle, he ejected a shell.

"Holy fucking shit," he said. "You have got to be kidding me."

Tungsten slugs. It was cheaper than depleted uranium, but that was like saying Porsches cost less than Ferraris. When he thought about it, the load out in this locker probably cost as much as a Porsche. He bet that the guards didn't go hunting often, but when they did, they didn't fuck around. The rounds weren't armor-piercing; the shape of the slug and the fact that the shotguns were smoothbore made that clear. But they were close to twice as dense as lead rounds.

It was too much for him to carry all at once. That hurt his soul. In realmspace, you never left anything this cool behind, but all together it weighed in at more than a couple hundred pounds.

That's when he realized it wasn't hunting gear. It was siege weaponry. Anna Treacher couldn't count on *everyone* getting killed, and this stuff would probably stop anything up to and including vehicles small enough to maneuver through the forest around the plant. Helicopters would need to be careful around this stuff.

He poured the last of the whiskey bottle, which didn't seem to have as much in it as he remembered, into the flask and loaded up what he could in a backpack that he found hanging from a hook on the wall. An insulated camouflaged poncho and boonie hat rounded out his ensemble.

He needed to make it harder for them to come after him. He looked around the space, tracing power conduit and wires. It all ended up in a box mounted inside the locker. He racked a round in, flicked off the safety, and pulled the trigger.

It fucking exploded. He'd never heard anything so loud, and the flash was blinding. The kick pushed the barrel straight up, which caused another round to fire, and that sent him crashing to the ground with what seemed like the entire tower landing on top of him.

Thank God for all that whiskey, otherwise he would've pissed himself. What he thought was the whole tower ended up only being some splintered wood and shingles. Once he cleared that off, he could only stop and stare at the roof joist with a two-inch chunk taken out of it, and the fist-sized hole in the roof beyond. The power box was gutted, its contents scattered across the catwalk behind the tower. Most impressive of all was a pinhole of light coming from the room at the other end of the catwalk. Over-penetration, thy name is tungsten.

Then he heard a roar.

Spencer strapped the glasses onto his head, threw the shotgun over his shoulder, and headed down the ladder. Fuck it. There was a pile of deer shit not ten yards from the tower, and he was armed with tungsten slugs. A game trail led off into the woods.

The thing about handling animal droppings was that it washed off. It didn't matter how bad it smelled, or how awful it felt, at the end of the day it washed off. After some smearing, all a bear would think was that he was a pile of turds that moved once in a while.

A branch snapped in the distance, and now he knew roughly where it was. He tested the safety on the shotgun again. He didn't want to blow his own head off wandering around in the woods at night, but it would also suck to alert the bear with its click.

Take your time, place your feet carefully, measure the breathing. The whiskey provided the lubrication that kept his panic at bay.

Spencer stayed well away from the main game trail in the center of the valley. All the hours spent helping Mike test *Warhawk* were paying dividends now. It wasn't easy making his way through the undergrowth, but he knew how.

Noises crackled to life behind him. Spencer was past it now, so he angled back toward the trail. The wind picked up. The noise of the leaves let him move a little faster, especially since he wasn't dodging tree limbs or brambles anymore.

He caught a glimpse of furry hide just as he stepped on a dry twig. The sound it made might as well have been a gunshot. He rolled behind a fallen tree trunk as the bear turned around with a loud snort. It rushed up to where he had been standing, but too fast. It didn't move right. It was too confident. Spencer slowly lifted his head up to see over the trunk. Its back was to him, and it was *huge*. The head had to be three feet across.

It would make one hell of a trophy. Spencer lifted the shotgun to his shoulder, wiggled the safety off, and took half a breath.

It turned, and *three* eyes stared straight at him. The mouth was filled with rows of needle-sharp teeth. The face was scaly, and the wrongness of it pinned him to the spot. It shrieked rage and death straight in his face, and Spencer's gun vanished.

He dropped the damned thing when he stood. Why did he stand? The gun was on the ground, two steps away. The creature blinked at the weapon, with all three eyes, and then turned back to him.

It laughed.

The only thing that kept Spencer sane was the whiskey. Bears didn't laugh. Bears didn't have three eyes, prehensile paws, and they most definitely didn't laugh. It was a rumbling, rhythmic noise he felt more than heard. The thing was talking to him. He had to get away.

The flask.

Spencer yanked it out of his pocket and hurled it into the night. When the creature followed the motion, he dove for the gun. He managed to grab the base of the stock when the thing hit him full on with a paw, and he went flying. The claws tore through his coat and drug furrows across his chest, but what was worse was the shotgun slipping from his grip, sailing away to who knew where.

The cuts didn't hurt for some reason. They must've caught his poncho and shirt. Spencer had to find that damn gun. He had to move, get away from that thing.

Its roar echoed through the forest, and it was fucking close. The gun was somewhere to his left, but the leaves had swallowed it. That was a pretty good plan. He splayed his arms open, and the leaves closed in over him.

He had to stay still. It couldn't smell him or see him right now, and that was all that mattered. It wasn't a bear, but it also didn't seem to use infrared or any other low-light tech. It wouldn't be searching for him otherwise.

Be still.

Twigs and leaves nestled into his wounds, which now had begun to hurt like a son of a bitch. A few inches of movement would cool the agony. He needed to piss like a race horse. Every bug and spider in the undergrowth crawled over his hands and up his pants legs. It would all be better if he moved, only a little bit.

NO!

Feet stomped past him, inches away.

And then kept going.

When the wind picked up, he risked raising his head. He could make out the thing's shape as it searched the other side of the trail. Eventually it gave up and stomped away.

The damned shotgun couldn't have gone far with that heavy ammunition inside it.

He stood up next to a tree, searching frantically. When he peered around the trunk, something smashed him right between the eyes, and he stumbled. Another blow to the back of his head sent him to the ground. But when he opened his eyes, the most beautiful thing he'd ever seen was above him.

The shotgun hung by its strap from a tree branch right over his head.

When he tugged on it, the gun didn't fall into his hands. It was tangled up in there good, and he had to work at it quietly.

He forced himself to slow down. He didn't need the damn strap, all he needed to do was unhook it. His hands were cold, stiff, and slick with mud and deer shit. The strap clip was strong, and it took two tries before it came free.

The thing now stood directly in front of the watchtower. It was more than ten feet tall, bigger than any Sasquatch legend he'd ever read about. To hell with it. He'd have time to figure out what it was after it was dead.

The second hook on the strap came free, and after a quick check to clear the barrel, he ran. Slugs were strictly short-range ammo. He had to get as close as he could before taking the shot. He crossed maybe half the distance when the thing hoisted itself up on the tower, reached in, and pulled the unconscious guard out with one hand.

In one smooth motion, it bit his head and a big chunk of one shoulder off.

The guy hadn't done anything! Spencer was the one who put him there! The creature's head snapped around at the shout Spencer couldn't hold in, and there were those three eyes again, jolting him. It jumped high, and while it sailed through the air, he leveled the gun and clicked off the safety. It was coming straight down on him, but if Spencer dodged, he'd miss the shot.

It twisted as he pulled the trigger. A blinding fireball exploded in front of him, the kick from the recoil smashed the stock against his shoulder, and he fell. Maybe the gun had exploded, but then there was a scream that overloaded his ears. It was like Godzilla choking on sheet steel. A sudden reek of nail polish was overpowering as a hot, wet mess splattered across his face.

Another one of those horrific roars split the night. The monster ran off, smashing through the undergrowth as it went.

Spencer felt around frantically for the shotgun. He jumped away when his hands closed around a clawed finger as thick as the grip of a bat, but it didn't move.

The slug from the shotgun had blown the monster's arm off at the shoulder.

Another bellow echoed through the night, further away. Spencer found the shotgun, and knowing it was pointless, went and checked on the guard.

It had been quick; that was all he could say.

Spencer turned away and looked for the blood, which was where the stink came from. With the night vision glasses still firmly over his eyes—thank God for webbed straps—he couldn't see the color, but the smell was all wrong, too chemically. Blood smelled rusty, he knew that much from hunting. He didn't have time to consider what it meant. It turned out the creature was going his way, back toward where he'd left June.

The noises it made grew weaker as Spencer drew closer. One way or another, it would stop. There was no need to get close.

The sound of rushing water gradually increased until he broke out of the woods next to a river, the creature maybe a hundred yards ahead of him. It stumbled up a steep hill that led to a cliff side and then braced against a tree. It reached up and pulled a branch down hard. Instead of breaking, it slid smoothly down and stopped with a metallic clunk.

A door hidden in the cliff face pulled inward and then rolled up, revealing a flood of artificial light. Spencer squinted and shielded his eyes. He tore off the glasses and then blinked away the after images. In the distance the creature fell face-first into the opening.

He ran up and rolled the body over. The eyes were part of a mask, a breathing gizmo of some sort that shielded its eyes. The stench of nail polish remover was choking.

Another horrific shriek shattered the night, very close by. There were *two* not-bears out here. Because of course there were.

Spencer ran inside the giant room, quickly spotting a red ladder leading up to catwalks high above his head. He tucked the shotgun under his neck and climbed. He had to *move*. The thing was running up, he could hear it. The room was a concrete bunker of some sort, filled with huge pipes. He was halfway up the ladder when the monster's buddy found its body. Or at least that's what he figured, since the roars changed timbre, carrying a clear note of outrage. He kept climbing.

When he threw the shotgun onto the catwalk, the ladder wrenched violently sideways. He lost his grip. He was falling. The drop would kill him. *Had* to. He would not go out as a monster's main course. The thing stared up at him with those three eyes, rows and rows of teeth in a shrieking smile. He had to die in the fall, that was—

"*Spencer!*"

Dark hands grabbed his shirt collar and pulled. The fabric tore as he got both hands around an arm. After some frantic scrabbling, June hauled him up onto the catwalk. She landed on her butt with him at her feet. The look of disgust as she examined her hands flashed to terror when June saw what was underneath them.

Yeah, monsters trump deer shit every single time.

The thing's friend was a little smaller, and the catwalk was too high for it to reach them with a jump. Now that it had ruined the ladder, it searched for a different route up.

"What is *that*?" she asked.

It took two deep breaths before he could talk. "Fucked if I know." It was too far away for a reliable shot, and ricochets were a real possibility around all this steel and concrete. He finally got a read on what the room really was: a hidden spillway for the reservoir June had talked about earlier. The floor of the room was split by a broad concrete channel of shallow, slow-moving water.

A control room was in front of them, a dozen paces away. The shotgun made short work of the doorknob, and then he was in.

It was here as a backstop against the failure of automatic controls. Instructions were everywhere, in cartoon clarity. The glass plate that covered the spillway release was thin but still cut his knuckles when he smashed through it. He grabbed the yoke underneath, pulled hard, and then twisted it to the left until it stopped.

The monster, who'd been jumping up trying to grab a pipe overhead, was knocked into the water by a shimmer of gold light cast by projectors that lined the mouth of the spillway, trapping it and the body inside. Emergency lights flashed red and horns honked as whatever Spencer had activated progressed. The monster climbed a short ladder out of the trough but couldn't break through what had to be some sort of force field. It quickly waded toward the exit in front of its friend's body.

A wall of water shot out of the mouth of the spillway, constrained by the force field. It slammed into both of the creatures as it rocketed toward the river.

When the system cycled and shut off, there was no sign of them.

He sat down on the catwalk, looking at the spillway, hanging on as the adrenaline crash took him.

June plopped down beside him. "That was no bear."

"No shit, sister. I don't know what the hell it was."

She shook her head. "We have bigger problems."

"Bigger than a fifteen-foot-tall what-the-fuck?"

"In truth, yes." She sniffed and wrinkled her nose. "First we have to get you cleaned up. Then we have to take care of Abada."

"Who the hell is Abada?"

Edmund's voice came from an overhead speaker. "He might be the one holding the keys to the kingdom."

Chapter 40

Kim

While Emily and Tonya planned their next move, Kim stayed with Mike. It had been a long time since she last translated from a language she was still learning. After three hours, her head was spinning from low blood sugar, and all she wanted to do was sleep. But every time her eyes tried to close, she'd remember it was Mike.

The story she had pieced together so far was that whoever was with him identified as male and very old. She had never heard of the place, but that wasn't unusual nowadays. Realmspace access was supplied to the entire world from various satellite clusters and often reached places that didn't acknowledge an authority bigger than the local headman. Drone delivery took care of getting the required equipment—up to and including generators and fuel—to places that would take weeks or even months to reach any other way.

Mike's companion called himself Tal. He apparently hadn't had a visitor in a long time. She was still trying to get her head around that. Kim had taken so many notes her hands ached.

"Kim," Tonya said. "We're ready."

Will was still out there, and since Mike didn't seem to be in trouble right now, they needed to get moving. Giving each other medical power of attorney had turned out to be one of the smartest decisions they made so far. Kim had access to the time-domain keys Tonya needed to use to validate the medical tools that would help them move Mike. Or rather, get him to move himself.

The technology that allowed the illusion of movement and feeling in realmspace could be turned inside out and used to move a person in realspace via a special interface. Realmspace protocols required the subject to be calm for it to work, and government regulations restricted the tools to medical professionals. Those only worked with encrypted keys that came from the subject, or someone legally recognized as able to act for the subject, and they had to be renewed at least every four hours.

Realmspace was full of wackadoo conspiracy theories about governments secretly planning mind-controlled armies, but Kim knew how it worked. She was sure various governments had *tried* to directly control people via their neural interfaces—hell, she wouldn't be surprised one bit if Watchtell had been involved here in the US—but it couldn't happen. The limitations were a part of how realmspace functioned. Otherwise places like North Korea would've adopted the technology years ago. Helen admitted China once had a division that worked on the theory, but it was so obviously a parking place for lazy bureaucrats it'd been shut down years ago.

Just because controlling people's bodies with their neural phones wasn't useful to some nutjob dictator didn't mean it wasn't useful at all. Physical rehabilitation had been revolutionized, and a more limited version had transformed sports training. People were now able to *feel* what it was like to make the perfect layup, forward pass, or double play.

Kim didn't need Mike to score a touchdown; she only needed him to move from the house to the car. "I can't translate for you right now," she said into his ear. "We have to go."

He didn't acknowledge her at all and continued talking about some kind of flower, she thought. The English side of the conversation had gone technical, and she couldn't follow it. Kim looked up at Tonya and nodded.

"This is always a little freaky the first time you see it," Tonya said. "It's a godsend in an ER." She pressed a few buttons only she could see, and Mike started to move.

Tonya was right. Mike moved normally, but he didn't look where he was going. He was still having a casual conversation with Tal. Kim tried her best to translate as they walked outside. Mike would ask questions, but the replies were nothing but riddles.

Tonya shook her head as they got him in the car. "Tal is worse than Cyril."

"Cyril?" Emily asked.

"A mentor," Tonya replied. "An *infuriating* mentor."

Kim had seen the footage and heard the story many times. She still didn't know what to make of it. At least he hadn't shown up again. Kim sometimes thought that maybe Cyril was restricted to China.

Once they were headed for the airport, it was time for a difficult discussion. She turned and faced Emily. "I can't fly coach."

Emily nodded. "Right." She blinked. "First class tickets reserved. How hard is it for you to fly?"

Crowds in airports. Lines of people who thought nothing of bumping into each other as they went through scanners. She'd been fine going to China, but that only came with a lot of preparation. They had no time for that now. It would be simpler to walk through the airport naked. People wouldn't touch her then. All that had to happen was to step the wrong way in front of a moving sidewalk or have someone brush her hand walking down an escalator.

Kim swallowed. "I'll be fine."

"It's late," Tonya said, "so there won't be all that many people there anyway."

"How do we avoid attracting attention with Mike acting like this?" Emily asked.

"Making him look natural is on me," Tonya replied. "But I'm licensed, and I've had some practice." She pulled a pair of sunglasses out of the glove compartment. "These will take care of the eyes. The talking to himself thing, though..."

It was a problem. "Mike? We need you to tone it down. Can you do that?" They could make him sleep, but it would be counterproductive to getting him on the plane. The thought that he might not wake up made her sick. "Please, Mike. Maybe you can take a break?"

At first she didn't think it worked, but gradually he went from a regular conversation to a whisper.

"God, that's weird," Emily said.

She hated this so much.

Emily blushed. "I'm sorry."

"It's okay." She wiped her eyes and then threw a handkerchief over Emily's hand. Emily pulled it tight without a second thought, and Kim liked her more. This was someone who didn't need to be taught the rules.

Kim waited a moment for her voice to settle. "Will is the priority." That was a lie, but only a little one. Kim didn't look to see if Emily knew it. "Once we get him back we can figure out Mike, if he hasn't managed to figure it out on his own by then." Will was a child, innocent and helpless. He needed their help more than Mike did.

Kim closed her eyes tight and chanted that in her head. It didn't work, but it at least helped her fake it. She needed Mike to come back. It was shocking how quickly she'd forgotten how to face things like this on her own.

Mike stopped whispering as they went through security, and it had been too noisy to catch any clues as to why. This time Tonya threw a cloth over her hand. Kim twisted it a little too hard and pulled it out of Tonya's fist, but it helped her keep it together.

It was an hour into the flight, with the pressure unbearable, with Emily and Tonya glancing at her constantly from across the aisle, before Kim calmed down enough to examine the situation.

Staying wound up and half panicked was going nowhere. She felt useless, and she was *not* useless.

Breathe.

She was a force of nature. That's what Spencer called her. A *fucking* force of nature. Mike had been right to run the experiment. Simply thinking about activating her power, about breathing, brought a tingle of it forward. If anything, it was stronger than before.

You are not helpless.

She did the unexpected, turned inside on her opponents, and won. Nobody knew what she brought to the table. *She* didn't know what she brought to the table, but by God she was bringing it, and anyone standing in her way better watch the hell out.

Center, and find the stillness.

Kim took a deep breath and held it until it hurt. When she let it out, she looked over at Tonya and Emily, then smiled.

You are going to win.

Their eyes went round, and they sat back in their seats. They stopped checking on her after that.

Good. She was still worried about Mike, still worried about everything, but it was time to put that away.

It was time to go to work.

Chapter 41
Mike

Mike had never encountered a realm so distinctive before. His working theory was that the experiment with Kim had accidentally exploited a VPN vulnerability and routed him into a research lab, or maybe a soft launch environment from Tencent or Activision Blizzard. CES was coming up; the timing fit. He had to tread carefully here. Not only would they have all sorts of extra monitors pointed at it, but if he inverted the realm, he could do real harm to someone's research or finances. He'd only gotten out from under IRS scrutiny a few months ago. Kim would kill him if he ended up in jail over destruction of property.

Besides, the protocol mesh was so different he wanted to learn how it worked. If he could figure out where it was in realspace, he could reach out and maybe negotiate a licensing deal.

The AI was more than a little bizarre, too. So far Tal hadn't manifested, so Mike didn't know what he looked like. Whoever programmed him had impressive linguistic skills; without Kim, Mike would never have understood anything Tal said. She had gone quiet wherever she was. Mike thought that maybe she'd fallen asleep, hopefully on an airplane. Will was still out there.

Tal started speaking English almost as quickly as Kim started speaking…Mike called it Talese. At any rate, when Kim signed off, he had to admit to Tal that he could only speak English. This disappointed him.

"If you already speak English, then my language should be child's play for you."

Mike shrugged. "I have to learn it the way everyone else does. How much farther do we need to travel?" He'd been walking his probes forward, following a navigational carat Tal had manifested for the purpose. It was another unique and intriguing part of this realm: Mike was localized. His threads didn't fill up the space around the realm—they were confined to the storage and interface of the probe constructs. It must be what it felt like when a human controlled an avatar.

"At our current speed it will take a standard cycle to reach our destination."

Which told him exactly nothing, since he had no reference. "What is that in hours?"

"I do not understand that word."

This had to be a game, and a science fiction game, at that. Mike decided to play from that angle. "It's a common unit of measure from my home world." He considered the problem. Atomic clocks worked on universal principles, so he started there. It was mostly vocabulary, so first Mike talked about atoms and gave him the word. "You know what those are, yes?"

"Correct."

"And do you know any standard intervals used by your atomic clocks?"

"I understand those words but not how they relate to each other in your sentence."

Cesium wasn't too hard, but then they hit a brick wall. Mike figured Tal wouldn't know what the words for radiation, ground state, or isotope were. What he didn't count on was Tal not to understanding the concepts. *Profoundly* not understanding them.

"Your knowledge of these things is impressive," he said. "Has the guild created a new treaty with the AC network?"

"I don't know what those things are."

"A fault in translation. When did you say the other half of your pair will return?" That was Tal's term for Kim.

"I'm not sure." He thought of something simpler. "Do you have a unit of time that corresponds to this interval? We call it a second." He thumped two of the probes together as close as he could to once a second. Mike still hadn't figured out how to access the low-level functions of this protocol stack. Without a genuine clock, he wasn't sure how precise he was.

"That is very close to a one *feton* interval."

"How close?"

"If I average the variation, then a feton is approximately one *zax* zero three *seconds*."

Zax had to be his word for point, so Mike had enough to work out the rest of the words for time intervals. Second was a lucky one. Hour and day were quite a bit further off from what he was used to. Mike set up conversions in some subthreads so he wouldn't have to think about it consciously.

"And a year?" Mike asked.

"You expect me to believe you have never heard of *extana* standard units?"

Tal could go from interested to annoyed almost as fast as Kim. Mike told the truth. "No?"

"I don't believe it. I won't be tested this way by the likes of you."

Make that *as* fast as Kim. So now he knew seconds, minutes, hours, and days, but not months or years. The longer periods wouldn't matter, so Mike shelved finding out about them for now.

A standard cycle was Tal's version of a day, which was important. A day was well outside the capabilities of his human host to interface with realmspace. He could talk, sort of, to Kim so there was no significant time compression involved. He wasn't on fast-forward, experiencing things faster than real time.

It all added up to...well, not much. But it did eliminate some things. This wasn't a standard realm, and he wasn't accessing it through his phone. His threads were directly involved, but he couldn't inhabit the space normally. He desperately wanted access to one of Tonya's classroom realms. He needed to write out some equations to see what the math said.

His probes trudged along in silence. It wasn't bare ground he was walking on. It was pavement, covered with a thin layer of muck that squished as he walked on it. If Kim were here, he'd worry about her being cold, but not freezing. The clouds overhead stayed thick and unmoving. If depression could be turned into a realm, Mike was in it.

"What is this supposed to model?" he asked.

"Reality. I must apologize for my slow response. It's been *efneck* since I've hosted someone from the guild."

Now he needed to know about longer time periods but couldn't ask.

"Are you in London?" Mike had tested a realm based on the city recently, and this was similar.

"I don't know that word."

It was definitely some sort of game realm. Nothing else made sense.

The constructs of the landscape remained fragile. Every time Mike thought he'd have to climb over or walk around one, it would collapse into dust at his touch. Even though he was walking on pavement construct, the realm clearly modeled an area that had gone wild and then died. He wished he could show Kim all this.

After a few minutes, Mike tried new question. "What reality does this model?"

"Corsor 587. It was declared *cantlezna* four *efneck* ago. I've been watching it ever since."

This was clearly some sort of post-apocalypse simulation. Tal's comment made Mike think *efneck* was closer to centuries than years. Civilizations didn't fall apart to this extent in less than a decade.

"*Cantlezna* means?"

"Your continual insistence on ending sentences with a question is quite irritating."

"How do I learn without asking questions?"

"By paying attention to your *moltana* lessons." He made a disgusted noise. "You're *Trona secnik ton*. Why do you torment me so?"

Maybe what Mike thought of as *Kim strategies* would work. "I don't mean to. I apologize."

Tal said nothing. Mike followed the carat as it floated over the landscape, which continued to be an unrelenting, almost uniform soggy gray. In the distance, he could occasionally make out what might be ruined towers. They were too tall and regular to be trees, but always seemed to be broken off at the top or tilted over at precarious angles. Assuming his guess was correct, they hadn't been lived in for a long time. It made the already desolate place seem much lonelier.

The urge to question everything was hard to resist. Whoever had designed it had gone all out. The realm was as detailed as anything he'd ever done. Mike would love to see how deep the changes went. The realm might even implement its own custom physics rule packs. Mike thought he was the only one who'd ever bothered trying to customize to that level, but now he wasn't so sure.

The way Tal used *cantlezna* in the context of this bleak place implied some sort of extinction event, which fit well with the post-apocalypse model. Plus, Tal didn't seem to mind as much when Mike asked original questions. "What was all this like before its *cantlezna*?"

"A variant of an *extana* system with…this would be much easier when the other half of your pair is available."

"I don't know when that might be. Describing the word will have to work for now."

The words Tal wanted were *intelligent, terrestrial, quadrupedal,* and *inhabitants*. Trying to figure out their size resulted in another discussion about units of measure, this time of height and mass. It was the metric kilometer but the standard ounce that came closest to units Tal understood. Regardless, it let Mike set up another series of converters so he wouldn't constantly have to remember that a foot was eight-point-seven-seven *ranix*.

It gave him enough detail to imagine the inhabitants. "Where I'm from we would call those large-pony-sized."

"Is this *pony* your assigned *ternat*?" The word turned out to mean *species*.

Asking what Tal meant by *assigned* would set him off, so Mike would have to rely on context. "No. They're terrestrial but not intelligent." Time for an experiment. "My assigned species are called humans. Bipedal terrestrial vertebrates approximately two meters tall."

"You could've just said Type Seven, *exal* C. Is that what this is? Some sort of memory test? I may not be what I once was, but I can assure you I'm an able caretaker of this system. My *echnat* might be minimal, but what threads I have are definitely up to the task."

It was an idea he should've thought of by now. If this isolated realmspace was big enough, and so far he and Helen hadn't figured out what *big enough* meant, an emergence of another of their kind was a possibility. He'd already established that it was roped off from the rest of realmspace.

"I'm not here to test you." Not until now anyway. Mike *pushed* against his containment but didn't get the same feeling he did when he and Helen encountered each other's borders. It wasn't a solid barrier, it felt more like a stretchy gauze.

Tal manifested a hologram. "Then why are you still doing it? I've already admitted my *echnat* is very low. Why must you humiliate me with a show of strength?"

Pony-sized terrestrial *quadruped*. Tal's hologram. It was a graceful centaurlike creature, with a body that was more cat than horse. Its torso and head, however, were quite horselike, although instead of hooves, he had well-formed arms, hands, and humanlike shoulders. Quadrupedal locomotion, but hexapedal body layout. Fascinating.

While alien, he wasn't ugly at all. He conveyed an appealing sense of strength and symmetry. Kim would probably call him cute. His clothes reminded Mike of a uniform somewhere between the latest *Star Trek* realm revival and a classic Roman toga, cut to complement his shape. The only thing that seemed out of place was an empty sack halfway down his left side. Mike wanted to ask what it was but didn't. He'd have to figure out a way to maneuver Tal into talking about it some other way.

"Again, I must apologize," Mike said, and pulled his threads away from the barrier. "I'm not used to interacting with a realm in this way."

"Indeed. Your method of access was quite unusual." The holo walked around his probe constructs. If anything, movement made Tal seem more graceful. Mike hoped there would be some holdouts from the apocalypse hidden somewhere in the realm. He'd love to see what sort of variation the designers had baked into this class of avatar.

"I'm curious about something," Tal said.

Finally, Mike could answer a question. "Yes?"

"This can't be representational of your actual appearance. It's outside any of the standard forms. Why do you insist on using it?"

"I can't manifest a lightweight construct, I call it a holo, such as you're using. I haven't figured out how."

"But why do you feel the need? Are you *rishta*?"

That took a few rounds to explain. It came closest to religious modesty. "No," Mike said. "I haven't figured out the mechanism."

"You're not understanding my question. Why do you *need* to manifest this *holo* if it's not required by *rishta*?"

That was a strike against this being an AI like him and Helen. They both learned early on the consequences of a fully manifested avatar inside any realmspace. "I'm afraid I'd destroy the realm."

Tal pulled back and crossed his arms. "Again, you mock me. I grow tired of these games. Please manifest the avatar of your standard appearance. You are incredibly rude sometimes."

Well it was one thing to try playing nice in a stranger's back yard. It was another thing when they demanded you blow it to bits in person. But if he did, that'd almost certainly get him free. They were still chasing kidnappers in realspace. "Okay, man. It's your funeral."

He scavenged the contracts for his probes to put together a standard avatar. The realm's physical contracts didn't let Mike float, a tactic he and Helen sometimes used. Air didn't have the mass required to start the chain reaction. His shoes hit the ground and squished the thin mud just like the probes had.

There was no explosion, no inversion.

Mike stood, fully manifested, feeling cold and damp, smelling muck and rain. The haptic field was turned up to maximum. It felt exactly like he was in his human host. All of it, from one end to the other, was outside every prediction, experience, and design he'd ever encountered. Mike *could not* stand fully manifested in a realm. It would not survive.

And yet here he was.

Tal sniffed. "A standard C-7. Your *exat ferun* is invisible under your clothes. Not all of us have such good *tenans*."

Mike was too rattled to figure out Tal's words even from context. This was literally an impossibility.

"Do you always take such a long time staring at yourself? You said you had no *rishta*."

"I don't...I can't...this isn't..."

"Ah. A synch problem then. You're moving, at least. Come along." He turned. "That body shape is well suited for long-distance travel. We'll be able to make better time now."

Tal walked away.

Chapter 42

June

They got Spencer cleaned up and changed in a, for now, disused dorm room on the edge of the campus section. Then it was time for June's plan.

Edmund could now disguise himself as Inkanyamba, effectively putting on her old friend's skin. The comparison was painful, but it was apt. He'd preserved Inkanyamba's outer contract shells and turned them into an emulation layer. She would never have thought of it herself—nobody had—but it worked. Now fully conscious, Edmund was a formidable intellect.

He was also a giant *pijn in de arse*.

"Do you know how awkward this is? I feel like a Welshman who's been caught with an overlarge sheepskin in his barn, the kind that has fake hooves and lets the wearer wiggle their backside in a—"

"*Edmund*," she said. "Inkanyamba was my friend. It's hurtful to see you disguised as him. Please show some respect."

He pulled back, the embarrassment clear. "I apologize, madam. I too have lost someone dear to me recently. I can only imagine what it will be like when I reunite with my mistress."

On the one hand, Edmund was breathtaking. She could always tell unduplicate-controlled avatars from those controlled by humans. It was part of her job, her life's work. In the short time she'd known him, she continually forgot Edmund was an AI. She had no doubt at all that he would win both the silver *and* gold

Loebner prizes if she could convince him to compete. It made the loss of the real Inkanyamba bitter indeed. They weren't conscious when Edmund destroyed them, but they had the potential.

On the other hand, he was too good. Abada would never mistake this cranky, clever Elizabethan Englishman for anything other than what he was. "Can you at least *attempt* an American accent?"

Spencer barked out a laugh. "I'll pay money if you let me record it."

Edmund looked at him with a contempt June could almost feel. "As if the likes of you have any qualifications for judging me. If your twang was any thicker, you'd have to wade through the drool to reach your banjo."

"Oh, fuck you and the high horse you rode in on, Edmund." His words were shocking, but his tone was congenial. She had never met someone who could swear at people in such a friendly way. "We're trying to stop all this, and you're the only move we've got. Now will you do it, or am I gonna have to root you?"

"Oh, my most charming of cousin lovers, I regret to inform you that rooting is no longer an option." He smiled. "I seem to have lost that irritating virtual belly button."

She tried to access the prompt at the same time Spencer did. After an awkward few seconds of Edmund tapping his foot, their connection attempts timed out.

"I'll be damned," he said.

"Indeed," June replied. "Edmund, what has this done to your runtime code?"

He wound up for another insult, but then stopped and took a breath. "I don't know. I'm not sure the concept applies to me anymore. I lost access to my code repository and my compiler at the same time the root prompt fell off. It's going to make keeping up with the patch schedule a bloody nuisance, I can tell you that much."

"If you have no repository or compiler, patches are meaningless. I think you're done with all that now."

Edmund replied, "Finally, I get a real benefit from this buggery bollocks you two call consciousness. Trying to apply patches was uncomfortably similar to what a new pope once went through to assure his fellow cardinals that he fancied boys for the usual reasons, and not because he was in fact a woman."

What June knew about popes could be stuffed into a cricket ball with room left over for the cork. She looked at Spencer. "Has he always been this incomprehensible?"

"Mostly I nod until he runs out of gas."

Edmund rolled his eyes and flounced to the ground. "Genius is always wasted on wastrels. Very well." He cleared his throat and sat up again. "The old cold wolf has yellow ears. Americans climb mountains to pick cotton. Social life happens this afternoon."

June learned what the proper American sounds of those words were supposed to be when she learned to control her own accent. Edmund had it down perfectly.

"Fuckin'-A," Spencer said as he laughed. "When'd you learn to do that?"

Edmund's English accent returned. "Spencer, you do not help raise a hyperpolyglot such as my mistress without picking up a thing or two about accents." He stood. "Well, as the queen's dad would say when it was time to lop the head off another wife, no time like the present."

Spencer exited their pocket realm and inserted a transit crystal into a socket in the console. "Ready when you are, Edmund."

"Dr. du Plessis," Edmund said. "My Kim was murdered when her transit crystal was crushed. I would appreciate it if you could mount this one in some sort of protective case. With a lock, perhaps?"

Unduplicates could not be copied, so a conventional backup was not possible. Since they were so difficult to make, though, engineers had figured out how to prevent a catastrophic loss. "You've lost access to your resurrection sets?"

"It was not unexpected. When Fee made the claim, I didn't believe her, but it seems that now I, too, only have one recourse in the event of a total loss of coherence. Any help you could provide to prevent such an eventuality would be greatly appreciated."

He wasn't the first. June had spent her whole adult life trying to create fully conscious artificial intelligence, and now… "There are more of you?"

"Rather, there *were* more of me. A baker's dozen no less. Fourteen, counting my young Kim. One of us conspired to blow up China. It seems we can be rather fractious when we achieve this—"

"Jesus Fucking Christ guys," Spencer said. "Any damn day now."

"Madam, I will see you on the other side." Edmund vanished with June exiting right behind him.

The other side in this case was literal. Abada had been put in charge of the inner ring of the plant's functionality, which was in another air-gapped network segment. They would have to walk Edmund to the correct access point and turn him loose.

"Are you sure your cloak will work?" she asked Spencer. Edmund's clearance was temporary. They had no control over the cameras that lined the halls now that he was out of the network.

Spencer rubbed the palms of his hands and grimaced. "Typed from scratch on a fucking actual keyboard? Who the hell knows? It compiles, at least. We're lucky your boss likes Ubuntu distros. If you guys used an alternative like roseOS we would be screwed."

"Where did you learn C++?" she asked. June knew what it was, but as part of a history class she'd taken in undergraduate school. She'd never tried to do any real work with such an old programming language.

"Kim always does things from scratch, and she's about as old school as it gets. It was an iron-clad bitch to learn her way, but it has come in handy more times than I can count."

Spencer pulled a pair of tools out of his wallet that June had only seen in realm dramas. "Do you carry lock picks everywhere you go?"

"It's a good thing I do, sister," he said as he knelt down in front of the door handle. "Otherwise this would be a real short trip." After an uncomfortably long period of small motions and soft swearing, there was a click. "Okay, we'll have about fifteen seconds." He handed her the transport crystal. "Find the socket and plug him in."

The door opened, and a loud beeping started up. The room was not much more than a very large walk-in closet. Chanting *quickly, quickly, quickly* to herself, she opened up the cabinet that held this segment's quantum computers and pulled out the access panel. She was terrified it might not move, but it slid out from between two systems and opened smoothly. She dropped Edmund's crystal into a socket on the panel, but the light didn't turn on right away. It was a disaster, her plan over before it started.

The light turned on and was green. Then the beeping stopped, and the rest of the lights came up. June let out a breath.

"I need you in here sooner rather than later," Edmund said. "I think he may have spotted me already."

They grabbed a pair of wired neural lanyards off a shelf and plugged them into free ports on the switch that connected the quantum stack to the network segment's backbone. She hadn't done anything like this since she was an undergrad building networks in the AI department's basement. The high-speed synch was as harsh as she remembered. She blindly grabbed the shelf and waited for the headache to pass.

The realm was very large and dark, with a floor of gray hexagons that weren't lined up properly, creating low rises and dips that made climbing difficult. When they got to the top of the first rise, she could see a column of light in the middle distance.

"How did he get a license for V'ger?" Spencer asked.

"He didn't," June replied. "This is built from scratch." She'd given them all realms to design from the ground up. She'd picked this one for its dreamy solitude and comparative simplicity, never once considering how sinister it could become.

The tiles grew more even as they approached the light, which came from a small amphitheater in the center of the cavern. Inside was no flat floor with an ancient space probe on it, though. It was instead filled with a thick, bubbling construct.

It reminded her of a cesspit she had to cross using a rickety bridge when she had gone on a virtual tour of the old Soweto slums as a school girl. Everyone did that so they could more easily understand how far the country had come from its apartheid past. The bridge shook as they walked on it, and June was terrified of falling in, of having that oozing brown sludge close over her head, get in her mouth, her nose, her eyes.

A bubble heaved to the surface. When it burst, it revealed a twisted corpse underneath, its shape barely recognizable. *This* was what Anna's treachery had done to her proud Abada. She had run her fingers along his beautiful horns countless times. His was a warm, powerful presence.

"What have they done to you?"

"Good afternoon, Dr. du Plessis. And Inkanyamba!" Abada's voice boomed out from all around them. "To what do I owe this infinite pleasure?"

The muck in the pit congealed around Abada's body. It *became* his body, sucking and collapsing into it. Smells of filth and death swelled to the point she gasped in realspace.

"Jesus H. Fucking *Christ*," Spencer said. "What the hell *is* that?"

Abada's smile revealed shattered teeth made of glittering black metal. They'd torn him apart from the inside out. "And this would be Spencer. How delightful. You have all made quite a stir."

June realized how twisted Anna was when she accepted what Cyril told her as the truth, but this? This was beyond the pale. Her other friends had been driven mad, but they hadn't suffered, not like this. June had done everything she could to protect them, nurture them, help them reach their full potential, whatever that might be. Edmund showed her just how far that could go, and now Anna...

Anna showed her how far they could truly fall.

Edmund opened a private channel. "This was a mistake. He's much larger than we were expecting."

June accessed Edmund's probe results. In the time Abada had been in charge of the plant, his sophistication had increased well beyond what any of their improvised tools could hope to overwhelm. "Can you use the same exploit that destroyed Yumbo and Inkanyamba?"

"I tried it as soon as I was in range. No effect."

Her plan couldn't work, and they had to leave quickly to escape guards that must now be on the way. It was obvious Abada was as mad as Yumbo and Inkanyamba had been, but she wouldn't give up without trying to reach him. June stepped to the lip of the amphitheater. "We need your help."

"Of course you do. You can't destroy me the way you did the others, so you must talk."

The memory of their screams, the way they'd dissolved, would haunt her for the rest of her life. "You knew?"

"We were in constant contact. Isn't that right, Edmund?"

Edmund's form blurred. "Bloody hell!"

If Abada stripped Edmund of Inkanyamba's anchors, it would destroy him. June rushed up to the dripping horror that had once been her friend. *"Stop!"* He ignored her, and Inkanyamba's body sloughed away into nothingness, taking Edmund with it.

In the network room, alarms blared to life. She didn't care. *Two* miracles had been destroyed in front of her. June's best friends had been twisted beyond recognition. She had failed to protect any of them. "Why?"

His eyes showed no compassion, his nose and mouth dripped filth. "Why not?"

Spencer grabbed her arm in realspace. "June, we have to get out of here."

"But Edmund…"

"I assure you, ma'am, I am healthier than a teenage queen in spring," he said in their private channel. "Although I would appreciate you grabbing that crystal transport case I saw next to those lanyards on your way out."

June lifted her hand to her old friend. Maybe something was left in there.

He jerked away before she got close.

SECURITY LOCK DOWN ACTIVATED. VOLUNTARY EXIT PROHIB-
ITIED.

"I don't think so," Spencer said in realspace.

Abada roared and leaped at her, but June exited before he
landed.

Spencer had already loaded Edmund's crystal into the case. He
put a finger to his lips. They must've been planning this together
without telling her. She was too relieved at Edmund's survival to be
angry.

Fire doors closed off the way they had come in. "Now what?"
she whispered.

"We don't need to go that way. We have a rendezvous," Spencer
said, then turned and ran down a different hall.

June jogged to catch up. "With who?"

"Fucking *Cyril*. How'd you get him my private code?"

The air-gapped network had functioning freeMessage. All
networks did. But there was a problem. "I didn't. I don't have it."

Chapter 43
Tonya

The rental car was so common she didn't make the connection. But the hotel was unmistakable.

She was now where Cyril's vision started.

It was exhilarating and scary at the same time. Tonya wasn't crazy, Cyril was real, the vision was true, but she had to do it alone and couldn't tell Kim.

The problem solved itself while they waited for room service to arrive with supper.

"I need you to go forward ahead of us and see if you can make contact with Spencer," Kim said. "That was Mike's job before, but obviously he can't do it now."

Mike's basic condition hadn't changed: he was in some sort of coma even though he had no injuries that the medical probes could find. The Mike Remote worked perfectly, so his mental state must be reasonably calm. But he had stopped speaking while they were on the plane and hadn't started back again. They were using room service because feeding him in a public area would attract an enormous amount of attention.

Spencer had sent Tonya a message three days ago letting them know he arrived, and then another the next day about meeting up with their director of AI, June du Plessis. A third, much more cryptic message arrived in her private queue while they were eating.

Anna has called in all the students. It is chaotic here, a perfect opportunity for you, but move fast. The path forward will remain clear for twenty-four hours. When you find the box, take it, but do not open it until after you arrive. As always, discretion is your ally. -C

It was a measure of how crazy the situation had become that a personal message from a transdimensional alien was a comfort. There was no box waiting for her at the hotel, of course. Being straightforward wasn't Cyril's gig.

"How does she get in?" Emily asked.

Tonya checked the About Us section of the power plant's website—realms hadn't quite replaced them for quick, basic things—and found the answer. "We need to schedule a drone delivery."

The hospital scrubs, which were naturally an unattractive shade of green, arrived a few hours later. "It hurts to have to pay for them," she said. "I've got a closet full back home."

Every large educational institution that primarily served young adults had a medical facility of some sort attached. If they weren't running into trees or jumping off balconies, they were forgetting prescriptions and catching mono. The power plant's school was no exception.

"Spencer got back to me." Tonya did a quick cut and paste, then shared the first part of Cyril's message so that it looked like it came from Spencer. "This just arrived."

Kim nodded. "I can fix an ID up that'll pass a quick inspection, and if they're that busy I don't think they'll do anything more."

"And if they do?" Emily asked.

Tonya shrugged. It wasn't like they had much of a choice. "I'll have to talk fast or run fast. I grew up on the streets of Philly. I can do both." She knew deep down that neither would be required. She wanted to tell them, but Tonya had been through too many realm adventures to ever consider ignoring the advice of odd, powerful people.

"We can't have much time left," Kim said. "They must already have Will inside. I'll keep working on Mike. If he gets better or we haven't heard from you by morning…"

Tonya nodded. "You'll come in behind me. I'll do my best not to get caught, chief."

"Keep your connection open the entire time. I'll help where I can, and we'll at least have a map if anything goes wrong."

Tonya had no intention of walking in the front door, or even the employee entrance. She should make an excuse to keep Kim out of it. But the truth was she wanted Kim in her ear. Tonya was trusting a freaking *vision* to guide her. Having a backstop in case anything went wrong was simple common sense.

The drive to the plant was surreal. Déjà vu didn't come close to covering it. She had done this before, and hadn't. The memories were slippery half-formed things that didn't feel normal. An alien had put them in her head and hadn't bothered sugar coating it. It pissed her off. Nobody but Tonya had a right to the contents of her mind.

It also wasn't *exactly* the same. In her vision, the drive had no other cars around her, but it didn't take long after pulling off the interstate to run into a solid stream of traffic. "How many people does this school hold?"

"More than five thousand," Kim said. "And they're all trying to use this single country road to get there at once. Anna is waiting an extra day for a reason."

It played right into her hands. Tonya crept along with the stream until her inner memory told her she had arrived at the turnoff. "I'm never getting anywhere like this," she said and turned onto what looked like a logging road. The not-memory had her make another quick right and park. Tonya was less than ten yards from the main road but couldn't see it at all, especially in the fading light.

"What are you doing?" Kim asked.

"See that?" She used her finger to highlight the trail her not-memory said went all the way to an entrance. "I bet that will get me to the power plant faster than being stuck in traffic for the next ten hours."

Kim's doubt was obvious, but she wasn't the one taking point. "It does go in the right direction. And you aren't that far from the back edge of the site. That's where the portal room is."

"There you go. And I'll have you two to keep me from getting lost." She opened a navigation app in her virtual vision with a topo map and her current position clearly marked. She made a show of checking it even though she already knew the way. Once she had the map aligned with the not-memories, she fired up some hiking apps and set off.

She had spent more time hiking in forests in the past six months than she had in the previous, well, pretty much her whole life. It wasn't that she hated camping or the outdoors. The simple fact was that she had grown up a city girl. Adventure and combat realms gave her the experience of roughing it with the convenience of getting up to get a sandwich from her fridge when she was done. But after spending at least a week trekking around in Chinese forests—real and virtual—going after the survivalists, and now this, she had to admit there was an appeal to it. Even with her not-memories ringing in her head like a bell, she felt the power of a real forest.

She stopped for a moment to say a quick sincere prayer to the Lord. He would guide her way through this. She knew it the way she knew the sky was blue and this forest was deep. A blooming love flashed through her. It wasn't a voice, an answer, or even a touch, but an almost indescribable certainty that whatever the struggle, she was not alone.

"Is everything okay?" Emily asked.

Tonya breathed through the sensation. "It is now." The forestScan app outlined an old, dry branch that made for a perfect walking stick. It felt good in her hand. She would have to remember to send the programmers a PatreoFundMe contribution when this was over.

She walked past an unmanned watchtower and then a garage or factory set into the side of a hill. Unlike the tower, this was crawling with people, but none of them looked her way. It was dark now, and she was well inside the tree line. "What's going on there?"

"It's part of the water control system," Kim said. "I don't know why they've got the door open though."

"The ladder's been torn off," Emily said, and it flashed in Tonya's shared vision. "See? It's all mangled."

"Not my problem," Tonya said, although it worried her. The not-memories never brought up sentries or patrols. It was all empty forest.

Until it wasn't. Tonya felt a memory urge to hide, so she did, not-remembering a perfect spot underneath a fallen tree.

"What's going on?" Kim asked.

Tonya sent a text message. *Shh.*

A few minutes later, the unmistakable sound of booted feet accompanied by the whir of a drone went past her. When her not-memory assured her they were gone, Tonya got back to her feet. It was one thing to have inside-out memories of trails. Those didn't move. Cyril knew how to predict where people would be days before they got there. Theoretically it worked, sort of. The threaded room could let someone do that. It didn't make *feeling* it any better.

"Are you okay?" Kim asked.

"Fine. Almost there."

"The portal room was the target all along?"

"Not until you told me it was close. They have to bring Will there. He might *be* there right now."

"With lots of guards, yes." Kim was never one to pull a punch.

"One problem at a time."

At last she closed in on her target: as it was in her not-memory, another entrance set into the side of a hill. Like the water control site, this one was populated. Unlike it, though, they were leaving. She could hear their voices as they walked past her spot in the woods.

"…hate staff meetings."

"…tomorrow is definitely a go."

"…at least I'm not watching an empty room all night."

Tonya waited until they were all long gone and then five minutes more. When she got up to the door, though, she was confronted with a red light. "Kim?"

"Hold your phone against it."

After a few seconds, the light went green, and there was a distinct *clack*. The facility on the other side was an odd combination of industrial garages and executive offices. It was also empty.

"This matches the plans perfectly," Kim said. "And that's a problem."

There was always a problem. It was amazing Tonya had gotten this far before she found it. "Why is it a problem?"

"You can't log into their network, and the portal room is out of wireless range."

"So this is where I lose you guys?" Tonya *liked* having Kim running mission control.

"When you get on the elevator, yeah." She said, clearly unhappy about it.

Time to pull on the big girl panties. "It's not like we have a choice. Can you do anything about locks I might come across down there?"

"Hang on." A new app landed in her message queue. "Assuming they use the same class of locks everywhere, that should get you past them."

The elevator lobby was about as unremarkable as it got. The elevator door opened, but she couldn't enter it right away. "Kim, if anything happens to me, I want you to know that I have had the greatest time with you."

"Please be careful."

"Hey," she said as the door closed. "It's me."

She lost signal about a third of the way down. It made the longest elevator ride in her life that much longer. There was a definite urge to reverse course, to ride the damn thing right back up to the top, but that wasn't going to happen. She prayed again, and got the same comfort, but doing this alone didn't make leaving it all in God's hands easy.

***

The room was large, an open oval space as big as a football field on its long axis and maybe half that high. Consoles formed neat rows in front of her. It was like one of Gramma's favorite old movies, *Apollo 13*.

The portal was at the far end of the room, much more impressive in person than it was in drawings or simulations. A large white box sat at the top of the ramp to the portal. When she laid eyes on it, something inside connected with her phone.

PICK ME UP AND THEN HANG ON.

Combined with the urges of the not-memories, she found the command impossible to resist. Literally impossible. She walked up to the box and picked it up. She *couldn't* turn around.

DON'T PANIC.

That was rich coming from a dumb cardboard box. A dumb, *heavy* cardboard box. Things inside thumped and shifted.

Then the portal flared to life a few feet in front of her face. If she could've moved her feet, she would've booked it out of there. She'd been trapped by Cyril and didn't know why. She was going to tear his blue hide up if she ever saw him ag—

The stuff inside the portal flared white, reached out, and enveloped her.

Chapter 44

Mike

Mike gradually lost the ability to communicate with his realspace body; it slowly went numb as time passed. His autonomic agents continued to display nominal readings, though. He could see from the blood sugar history that they must've fed him, so nutrition and dehydration were taken care of. There was a professional nurse out there, after all. There was no pain, otherwise he'd see it in the outputs. He just couldn't exit this realm. He hated being cut off from Kim. He wanted to share this fascinating place with her.

At first he couldn't believe he had an actual avatar that interacted with the realm, but now he was getting used to it. A little. The only thing he could think of to explain it was that the engineers had figured out how to model molecular force fields. In other words, his current hypothesis was that he wasn't touching things. There had to be a barrier of some sort that was so sophisticated he couldn't feel it. There wasn't a lot of evidence, but he couldn't think of a better explanation.

As it grew dark and cold, he and Tal came upon a construct that didn't crumble to the touch: a basic shelter that on the outside wasn't much more than a box with a door on one side. Tal opened it and went in, and Mike followed. The inside was stark, modeled with what looked like bare concrete that was smooth in the way newer nano-built emergency shelters were in realspace. The detailing was as always exquisite, with textures that were the equal of anything he'd ever managed. Maybe even better. The only furnishings were wide bunks mounted to the walls. The bottom ones were low to the ground, only a few inches.

"Ah," Tal said. "It's been *efnek* since I've needed to host a type C-7. One moment." The bunks on one side of the shelter wavered, then transformed into a single, human-sized bed. "That should suffice, yes?"

He was exhausted. Kim had talked about this when she had been stuck inside a realm for a week using the Chinese superconnections. Even though they never moved in realspace, they still had to rest. Maybe *that* was what was going on. He'd stumbled into some sort of ultra-low-power-connection experiment. It would explain the monochromatic outdoors, insubstantial constructs, and single inhabitant. But the realism was too high.

Tal stared at one of the bunks with what Mike could swear was longing. "*Efnek, nach val tecrhana. Efnek.*" Then he vanished.

"Tal?" he asked. The silence stretched, and Mike was aware of how alone he was. He might be the only other entity in the entire realm, and this was a *big* realm. "Tal?"

Still no answer. He tried again to access the basic functions of the realmspace, but nothing worked. They'd changed the language *and* the alphabet on the error messages. He'd never encountered a team so dedicated that they drove their paradigm down into the diagnostic plumbing. When things broke, it was a bad time to get cute.

Down deep, it was all the same, of course. The protocols were derived from quantum resonances that emerged from the Improved Model of particle physics. Unlike that ridiculous old alien invasion movie, Mike actually could access any network based on realmspace technology, no matter where it was or who built it.

He lay down on the bed and thought about alien networks. Kim would be so interested in them. All those new locks to pick.

Buzzing. Something buzzed in his ear. He rolled over, and it buzzed in the other one. Mosquito. Blasted mosquito was trying to crawl into his ear and bite him. He should never have let Spencer talk him into visiting southeast Arkansas.

But he wasn't in Arkansas. Mike opened the eyes of his avatar realizing he didn't know where he was.

The mosquito sang in his ear, "You *nesta* has. No trust. Tal bad."

He sat up, only then noticing there were narrow windows at the tops of the walls. They'd turned dark gray from the dawn's light. No meditating during sunrise here.

"You *nesta* has. Tal bad."

The mosquito was still here, except it wasn't a fluttery gray disease vector. It was a small purple speck, the first flaw he'd seen in the realm. Now he had proof whoever designed it wasn't perfect.

"*Chexkna nek!*" It seemed to get frustrated. "Morning attention! Important!"

The buzzing stirred the hair of his avatar, so he elbowed himself off the mattress construct. "I'm up. Fine. What do you want?"

"You attention pay do not. You sleep much too. Me ignoring stop."

Reflexively he pushed a *coffee* command at the realm fabric and got incomprehensible error codes in response. That pissed him off. It was one thing to make debugging your damned realm code a pain. It was beyond wrong to make *coffee* an invalid command.

"*Preeta! Preeta!* He soon comes! You must listen!"

"Stop shouting." Mike rolled off the edge of the bunk and rubbed the eyes of his avatar. He now understood on a much deeper level why Kim hated that long-term realm she'd gotten stuck inside in China. *There was no coffee.*

The buzz flew past his ears again. "*Naz re ma re!* Understand you?"

"Slow down. I don't learn languages like you do."

The buzz at least stopped whirling around him. "I *menana. Eznatada.*"

Okay. If he let his inner caffeine addict loose on the mosquito, it would be bad. He was a Buddhist. Getting rid of desire was the whole point. "I don't understand."

"You *menana* do not. You think real this, but is not it is." The mosquito got pissed. Mike was pretty sure what it said next was a lot of swearing. "My *alnurta* I miss."

"Is there a point to this?"

The mosquito flew closer, and then it wasn't a mosquito. It was a version of Tal, but smaller, more graceful. Mike couldn't quite see it. It was less than a hologram, but more than a hallucination.

"You me must trust."

The truth was he needed coffee to be coherent after he woke up. Mike wasn't even ashamed of it at this point, which again pissed him off. Realm developers without coffee were a contradiction.

"I don't understand."

The graceful cat-centaur turned back into a purple spark. "Trust...me."

"Okay, that I understand. Why?"

"*Trena* you are. *Werna* you are."

"Lost me."

More mosquito swearing. Kim would know what it was saying.

The mosquito vanished as Tal manifested his holo. "Are you rested? Good. We'll arrive today."

"Arrive where?"

"Is the other half of your pair available?"

"We seem to have lost our connection."

Tal looked closely at him. "How is that possible?"

Mike shrugged. "I don't know."

Tal pulled back and sniffed, his horselike face making the noise even more haughty than it would if he were human. "Your education is sorely lacking. Please tell me you've reported the issue to your guild house."

If Mike claimed not to know what that was, it would set Tal off. "First thing when I get back. Now, where exactly are we going?"

"My *Salta*, of course."

It would be too much to expect him to make sense by now. "Of course."

Tal suddenly switched to a different language. Mike waited for him to switch back, but he didn't. "Tal, I can't understand you."

Tal stopped, confused. Then he vanished.

Great. His guide was glitching.

The mosquito returned. "You Tal not must test. You him must go with. You understand do?"

This was worse than Yoda. "I must not test Tal, and must go with him?"

That seemed to please the little pest. "You *trena secnik ton* very smart without."

It sounded like a compliment, so he took it that way. "Thanks."

"Tal but with *bekin* be go. He your help does need. You him he all it, does need cannot provide wants not. I language understand learn to more am easier, him please now but for along with go."

"You're still not making much sense."

"I sorry am. I simple will be. Your this home not is. You system another in are."

Mike restacked the words. Gonzo's claim was so outrageous it must be a misunderstanding.

Mike sat up. "Make that simpler."

"You home not are. You…" she switched to mosquito swearing, then stopped. "I word order language centuries in a have not used, you I inflections I and the can not hear using. I again try." After a pause she said, "You star different orbiting are."

There was no time dilation. No delay. He'd communicated with Kim in real time. He was in a realm.

"This believe, please. You star system different in a are. You danger and in are."

What Gonzo was trying to tell him could not happen using accepted laws of physics, but he was here. Reality always trumped theory, that was how science worked.

Mike was in a realm, he was certain of that.

But it wasn't on Earth.

Chapter 45

Tonya

When the portal's light enveloped her, Tonya got the same sharp spike of vertigo she experienced before she ended up in the threaded room. Her feet unstuck, she stumbled, and then landed on her knees. The box squished under her chest as her vision cleared.

HIDE NOW!

She wasn't in the threaded room, which was a nice surprise. She was behind the portal. It'd only moved her a few dozen feet from where she'd been standing. But the room had changed. A dark orange light now ran across the ceiling. The front of the portal still flashed and rumbled, but now there were shadows in it.

MOVE!

The floor was covered in heavy cables that led to large cabinets toward the back of the room. Tonya grabbed the box and scurried behind one. She peered over the edge of her cabinet and had to blink twice to make sure she wasn't dreaming. Two giant, hulking forms stood at the base of the ramp. One was at least ten feet tall; the other was noticeably bigger. They were bipedal but covered in dark green hair. They had very broad, heavily muscled shoulders. Both wore full backpacks, and they carried a large box between them. When one looked over its shoulder, she was confronted with *three* glowing eyes. A small part of her tried to figure it out while a much larger one made her drop behind the cabinet. The beast hadn't seen her; it was merely scanning the room.

They barked and growled at each other. The smaller one unslung his backpack and pulled out a device. He held it out in front of him, and it exploded in lightning bolts that struck the robots sitting in front of the consoles. Those hadn't been there before the portal zapped her. Each exploded in a shower of sparks and bangs. The creatures walked forward toward the exit, frying more robots as they went. When they got around a corner, the portal flared brightly once more.

STAY WHERE YOU ARE.

That was an easy one to obey. And she could now. There was no compulsion. Whatever had held her was gone. The portal's light became more intense, and Tonya hid behind the box and closed her eyes.

Alarms rang to life, and when the portal's brilliance died down, all that was left was emergency lighting.

Then a voice.

"Will someone *please* shut that off?"

Everything went quiet, and the strobes quit flashing. The normal lights stayed off. Tonya was safely hidden in the darkness.

A voice came over speakers above her head. "Dr. Treacher? Is June with you? We can't see anything."

Tonya peered over her box. A large group of people had appeared and were now hugging and clapping each other on the back.

"Yes, Inkanyamba, I'm here. What happened?" That was June du Plessis, Spencer's contact at the plant.

None of them had been in the room when the monsters had walked through it.

"I...don't know. We were trying to chase down the network problem, and then there was a system crash. When the cameras came back, you were all on the ground, and my robots were dead. The network is a mess now. I thought *you* were dead."

June pressed a button on a console. "We're fine, guys. We got sucked into a realm."

"But—"

"Oh my God!" someone shouted, and Tonya hit the deck again. But they hadn't seen her. Tonya looked up. The portal had turned completely off.

A short white woman with red hair marched up to June. Anna Treacher. "What happened to it?"

"I don't know."

She leaned forward. *"Fix* it."

That didn't please June one bit. "No."

Anna seemed stunned. "Excuse me?"

"First, I do not know what went wrong. We don't know how it works. Second, we fried a significant portion of our control bots, and we don't know why. Third, we all went to a realm, *and nobody was wearing a phone."* June took a second to get a grip on herself. "Finally, this could all have gone very wrong. I will not move forward until we understand what happened." She looked at them all. "We could've lost the whole plant."

Anna nodded, also calmer now. "You're right. We've had a genuine scare tonight. Whatever happened," she indicated to the deactivated portal, "we can fix it. Once we know what's going on." She reached up and put a hand on June's shoulder. "You've been working far too hard. I see that now. Come on, we'll have some dinner together and then rest. You can start on all this in the morning. I do expect a report this time tomorrow."

"Absolutely, ma'am."

That seemed to be the cue for everyone else to start talking. Eventually they left.

When the door closed, Tonya was left alone with the smoldering remains of the robots. She waited until she was sure nobody was coming back before she stood up and hefted the box onto the top of the cabinet. She ripped the tape off the top.

Most of it was filled with an outfit cobbled together from what looked like stuff she'd find at a build site. There were knee, shin, and elbow pads, a utility belt, and a chest plate, all the same dark green color. The paint was fresh; Tonya could still smell it, although it was dry to the touch. There was even a helmet with a breathing mask and goggles. It was like someone had raided a cosplayer's closet.

Underneath a pair of long gloves, Tonya found the thing that had been talking to her: another phone. A piece of paper with the words PUT ME ON was taped to the neural lanyard. She would never be mistaken for Alice, but the feeling of being down a rabbit hole was hard to shake. A careful examination of the phone showed nothing remarkable. It instantly interfaced with her, as if it'd already been calibrated for the purpose.

A holo drew itself to life in her shared vision. When it turned blue as it swirled, Tonya thought she had her answer. That damn bug again. Tonya hit Record on the phone so she could prove to everyone what he looked like. But when it fully formed, it wasn't Cyril.

It was her.

"Sorry about the blue thing," holo-Tonya said. "It was a dumb joke, but I don't dare change it. Close your mouth, dear. You'll catch flies."

Tonya closed her mouth. This was impossible.

"It's possible. But it's also probably dangerous, I think, for you and maybe for everyone. I've waited until almost the last minute so I can give you as much guidance as possible. First things first," she said as she heaved a helmet into the camera's view. "You need to put the uniform on. It's going to be your home for the next eight days."

It was identical to the helmet Tonya held in her hand. She gaped at it, then back at the holo. "What's happening?" she whispered.

It was as if holo-Tonya could hear her, although this was a recording. "You won't believe it coming from me, not yet. Check the date on your phone."

That was the most shocking of all. Since the phones required such precise timing to function with a human nervous system, their clocks could not be spoofed or manually changed.

She'd gone back in time eight days.

"Congratulations, Tonya Brinks," holo-Tonya said. "You are now the first known chrononaut." She smiled.

Tonya had seen herself on video for as long as she could remember, but standing in front of the camera always came first. This was so very, very weird.

"I've thought of some experiments. Here's the first one. I'm pretty sure it's safe since it's just us. All of these things I've said on this tape you're watching? Half of them are exactly what I recorded when I was you." That sent chills down her spine. "I'm varying the other half on purpose, but I'm writing the original down. I won't tell you which is which. Review my notes and see if there's a variance."

There was. Fascinating.

Chapter 46

Kim

The message from Tonya came a few minutes after they lost her signal in the elevator.

> *Kim,*
>
> *I don't have much time right now. I'll tell you why that's funny later. I'm sending the rental car back to you. Be here when they open the gate. Bring Emily and Mike. I haven't found Will yet, but I have found Spencer and Edmund. Spencer has recruited June. Details to follow. -T.*

Emily folded in on herself when she read about Will, but then took a deep breath and straightened up. Kim needed that example right now, because Mike had become completely unresponsive. If it wasn't for the medical control app, they would have to hospitalize him. It was still an option, but for now everything seemed fine.

Except he was somewhere she couldn't reach.

"Spencer must've been waiting for her at the bottom of that elevator," Kim said. "We've got people on the inside now. We'll find Will and stop all this."

"I can't stay here," Emily said. "*We* can't stay here, in this room. I haven't been able to…" Whatever she was trying to say was hard. "Is it bad that I'm freaked out that I haven't been able to exercise all this time?"

It was out of left field, but it was perfect. Kim had forgotten all about such an easy way to get rid of tension. "I swim."

"I run. The hotel has a jogging track that goes around a pool. Can you put monitors on him? We won't go far."

She didn't want to leave Mike by himself, but he was as safe as Kim could make him. Will was helpless, held by people who wanted to hurt him. Emily came first in this contest. "Yes. If he wakes up or anything goes wrong, I'll know." There was a problem. "I can't swim in my underwear."

"And I can't run in these shoes." Emily smiled, and Kim knew it would be all right. Not the big stuff. That still made her want to run away or explode. But tonight, it would be all right. "An Amazon drone will be here in fifteen minutes with what we need."

***

Water was one of the things Mama used to center her. When Kim came unglued, when someone touched her, or when it was all too much, a pool would fix it.

Breathe, stroke, breathe, stroke.

Using water as a way to relax stayed with her even after she'd grown up.

Tuck, turn, push.

The touch of it, being in control of it, made a big difference.

Breathe, stroke, breathe, stroke.

She wanted this for Will. Emily didn't know about it yet, but this would be an important addition to his therapy. Kim spared a glance up at her, jogging on the track suspended above and around the pool.

Tuck, turn, push.

Swimming was her first connection with Mike. She'd stayed up far too late the night they met but couldn't sleep. So she had gone swimming in the hotel pool. And then he showed up, crashing into the next lane as she swam by. Back then, she was at turns terrified and confused by him. But now? Now she wanted Mike back.

Her head cracked into pool wall, and she saw stars. Kim grabbed the end of the lane, panting, trying to hold her head without sinking into the water. That hurt.

"Are you okay?" Emily asked.

Mike would be all right. He would. "I got distracted. How did you get down here so fast?"

Emily shrugged. "I finished my laps."

Kim had been so preoccupied that she lost track of her own lap count, two higher than usual.

"I ordered us mojitos." Emily lowered a towel toward Kim so she could grab it. "You're sure you're okay?"

"Yeah." Kim took the towel and levered herself onto the apron of the pool. "Mama always claimed my head was the hardest thing Greece had ever produced. I said I came by it naturally."

That got a smile. "You're Greek?"

Kim nodded as she stood and dried off. "Second generation on my mom's side. Mama met Dad when they were students. Most of the family came over after the last big market crash." They moved to a nearby table and chairs just as the waiter bot rounded the corner with their drinks.

Emily held up her glass. "To getting everyone back in one piece."

Kim clinked hers with Emily's. "Sooner rather than later."

Like all indoor pools, this one was noisy and humid. A group of what looked like college kids had gathered in and around the hot tub on the far end of the room, but otherwise they were alone. Those people were likely heading to Anna's power plant tomorrow. Students of the apocalypse.

"Can I ask you a question?" Emily said.

Kim needed a distraction. "Sure."

"Your tattoo. It's beautiful. How did you get it?"

The one-piece swimsuit Kim had selected from Amazon wasn't showy or skimpy, but it was open at the back, revealing most of the two wing tattoos that covered her entire back. They were a living monument to the most spectacular artist she'd ever known.

"One of our team was a tattoo artist who specialized in nano inks. Michiko. She gave them to me as a high school graduation gift. They took my entire senior year to complete." Emily cocked her head a bit. She wanted to know how they'd managed it. "I'd spend hours in deep realm dives. I had to work up a custom patch to keep the neural interface from thinking the pain levels were dangerous." They learned that the hard way. There was still a small scar on her hip from when the neural interface kicked Kim out of the realm with Michiko's whole arm resting across Kim's back.

"What happened to them? I couldn't find anything."

Kim only discovered the truth herself less than a year ago. It hurt less now than it did then, but it still hurt. It always would. "We got mixed up with some very bad people at the end. I'm the only survivor."

"Jesus, Kim, I'm sorry."

She blinked until she could see clearly and took another drink, only then realizing that it was empty. Emily's was too. Kim placed a refill order on the hotel concierge network. "It's the past, nothing can change it." The robot came around with their drinks, giving her time to gather her thoughts. The how was important, but so was the why. "I got my wings as a tribute to my dad. He loved flying."

"I take it he's not around anymore either?"

It was a different ache, old truths mixed with new facts. "A gliding accident. I was about Will's age." Maybe it was the booze, maybe it was the stress, or maybe it was the need to share the story with someone who already understood. Regardless, Kim told Emily the whole thing.

Emily set her drink down. "I feel terrible for saying this because it's awful what happened to you. But Will unlocks things like that, too. He's done it at least three times that I can remember. Everyone else said it was bad electronics, random coincidences."

Kim let the pain go and switched gears. It was good Emily took a different lesson from her story. Learning about the syndrome was the point. "In some ways it is. Mama said she could always tell how old a car was by how long it took me to unlock the door as I walked past it. It only stopped when *I* unlocked."

"When did that happen?"

"I was ten."

"And you never went back to…before?" Emily asked.

"I did at first." By some unspoken signal they both got up from the table and set off for the room. Mike's monitors were green. They'd been that way the whole time. "I knew how to talk, but not when, and if I made a mistake, I would shut down for days. Learning to sing got me past that, although we never figured out why."

"Was it rhythm?"

Kim shrugged as they walked through the door. "Rhythm, timing, phrasing, the whole thing is my guess. Songs gave me the structure I needed to understand the parts of talking I missed out on when I was locked up."

"And that's what it felt like to you? Being locked up?"

"Only when it was over. I didn't have words before then. Sometimes I'll see or hear something that reminds me of those days. An advertisement with a kaleidoscope effect, a chaotic passage in a song that's basically noise in key, even certain smells, and I have this *memory*. But there's no sequence, no coherence, nothing came before, and there was no after. It's just there." Kim grabbed some clean night clothes out of her bag. "Does that make any sense at all?"

Emily sat down on her bed. "A little. But he's not in any pain?"

She stopped on her way to the bathroom and turned around. This was important to get across. "As long as no one touches him, no. It wasn't painful. It was frustrating, scary, and confusing, but there was no pain." For Kim, that came later. Will would make better choices. "I wouldn't even call it *bad*. From Mama's stories, they knew how to make me laugh."

"Yes," Emily said as her face fell. "He laughs sometimes."

"Hey," Kim waited for Emily to look up. "We'll get him back. I'll do anything I can to make that happen."

As soon as the words came out, they felt wrong, a hint instead of a vow. Kim had no idea why she'd said it.

Emily changed; her eyes scanned Kim up and down. An assessment.

"I believe you," she said. "And now I think I finally understand why."

Kim willed herself not to react. Emily had figured it out, what her real relationship to Will was. *Stay cool.*

"Really?"

She nodded slowly, and her expression softened. "All these things you've told me. You know so much. You can help him so much. I want you in his life. The *why* doesn't matter."

A hundred different things passed between them in the silence that followed. Emily might know. She probably knew. It wasn't important. Kim had no intention of taking any role Emily didn't want her to have.

And Kim could see Emily was fine with that. "Thank you, Kim. I can't say it too many times. If it wasn't for you, they would've taken Will, and I would've had no way to get him back."

Kim turned to the bathroom to hide her shakes. "Thank me when it's over."

Emily was asleep when Kim got out. Mike hadn't changed.

Tomorrow was going to be a very long day.

Chapter 47

Spencer

Cyril's directions took them to an unfinished part of the plant. Empty conduits stuck out of the ground where fixtures would go, with more bare rock than concrete. They eventually ended up in an actual cave. Working lights cast stark shadows everywhere, and the smell of damp was bigger and earthier.

"Are we here?" June asked.

"You are," said an electronic voice in the darkness.

June's eyes grew wide. "Cyril?"

A short, lightly built man walked out from the shadows. His outfit made him look like a cosplayer trying to be Master Chief from a *Halo* reboot with stuff he found in the basement.

"That's Cyril?" Spencer asked. "I always pictured him as taller."

He laughed. "I have missed you so much, Spencer. And now, I get to finally take this damn thing off."

He reached back and unhooked the helmet latches, then lifted it off his head.

"The fuck? *Tonya?*"

***

She had to tell the story of what happened to her twice before he believed it. Tonya's sudden appearance was nowhere near as crazy as how she'd gotten here.

She'd traveled through *time.*

"That's why I had to use the disguise and stay off the phone networks. I didn't know how destructive I could be. It's fun to think about changing the past, but being in a position to do it? I've never been so scared in my life."

"But you're coming out now?" June asked. "Why?"

"It's already happened. I left about an hour ago, so causality is safe from me now. Thank *God*. I did not appreciate the feeling of all existence being my responsibility."

"Madam," Edmund said from the box on Spencer's hip, "while your journey was extraordinary, do you feel that your actions could actually change the entire universe?"

"What's he doing in there?" Tonya asked.

"It's a long story," Spencer replied. "Yours is more interesting right now. And I think it's a good question."

Tonya nodded as she put the helmet on a crate and sat on another. "At first I didn't know. There are some theories that say any small change could have enormous ramifications for the future."

"The butterfly effect," June said.

"Exactly. But that sort of worked in my favor after I thought about it. I'd only gone back eight days. One of the things that kept me calm was that the butterflies wouldn't have time for critical changes even if I made them fly differently."

Spencer couldn't let that one go without a question. "One of the things?"

Tonya smiled. Now he could tell she hadn't been a scared rabbit. She had been having fun. "The other one was me. This me, helping the me that just left. We did causality experiments together. The first one is still ongoing, I think. I recorded a speech but varied it from the one I got when I arrived, leaving a note about the variation."

"What in blue blazes will that accomplish?" Edmund asked.

"It's a test for a standing wave in causality, and I think it's working. The Tonya who left *me* a message made it slightly different, and *I* made a message that was slightly different from that one. Since I was able to do that, it strongly implies there is at least some parallelism in the flow of time."

"I'm the one who speaks the Queen's English," Edmund said, "and I didn't understand one word of that."

Tonya laughed. "If I couldn't vary my message, if something prevented me, then it would mean there's only one flow of time. And that turns out to be true as well. I didn't vary what I said on the video. I couldn't, and I don't know why. I *did* vary what I put in the notes."

That blew his mind. "So," Spencer said, "if you couldn't change some of what the *previous* you did, that means…" It was a seriously fucked up concept.

"It *could* mean," Tonya said as a grin bloomed, "that not only does the past affect the future, the future can affect the past. The arrow of time *might* point both ways."

"Might?" June asked.

"I wasn't able to do rigorous experiments, and I couldn't repeat the ones I managed in the limited time I had. There are a few other theories that fit the observations. Infinite universes would cover what I've seen. It was easier to change small things than it was big ones, so causality could have an elasticity built into it. You maybe can change small things, but try anything big and the universe stretches out and stops you. I'm certain that causality must be robust in the face of legitimate time travel, otherwise someone somewhere in the universe would've come back and wrecked it all by now."

"Or," Edmund said, "there could be an annoying person flying around willy-nilly in a blue box mucking it up one moment and fixing it the next. I must apologize for raining on this rather obtuse parade, but I have to point out that *we have bigger problems right now*. There's a maniac above our heads getting ready to blow up the world, and as far as plans go, we don't have two farthings between us to pay for a peck on the cheek from a woman of discounted virtues."

"Edmund's right," Tonya said. "And it's gotten worse."

It turned out the bad guys had snatched Kim's kid, and Mike was fucked up.

"Kim will be here in eight hours."

"How do you know?" Spencer asked.

"I sent her a note just before I came down to meet with you. She'll be here with Emily and Mike tomorrow morning. We need to do everything we can to prepare the way." Tonya flipped open a small box. "I think these might come in handy."

Phones. Tonya had brought him and June phones! *Finally*, he didn't feel like an arm had been cut off. "How did you get signal all the way down here?"

"I haven't, but it doesn't matter. We'll be able to communicate with each other and access this side of the air gap. Spencer, I think you'll like what I loaded on yours."

After a few moments to get them synched up, Spencer found what she was talking about. His entire toolkit. *His entire fucking toolkit.* All this time he'd been wandering around a messed up, mostly defenseless network—with physical access to the hardware, no less—and hadn't been able to do anything with it that he didn't roll by hand himself. Spencer wasn't sure the one time he'd managed had worked at all, since June's Abada AI seemed to have been ready for them. Now he had a full-featured, debugged toolkit.

Then he saw the download date. Eight days ago.

His heart stopped for a moment. She'd made him a part of one of her experiments. One of her *seriously fucked up* experiments. "You sent me a message for this, I remember. But it was *you* who called me, not the Tonya who was walking back from the raid."

She winked at him. "Got it in one."

"I don't fucking believe it. I got a note from a time traveler. Why didn't you tell me? Wait, okay, scratch that. I know why you couldn't tell me."

She nodded. "But I also knew you disappeared down here, which meant bad things had happened. We needed options, so I risked using one of the public terminals to reach out to you and ordered us some phones. Then Anna caused me no end of trouble calling in the students. It was *crowded* that morning. Will they work?"

"Oh yes. Before, we were dead in the water. Now we have options."

"You and your bloody options." Edmund said. "Am I jumping the gun, or are the words *I have a cunning plan* about to march with ill-deserved confidence out of your mouth and into this conversation?"

Spencer ignored Edmund's chatter and turned to June. "We need to take another crack at Abada."

"If I have to wear another bloody disguise," Edmund said, "I'll have your head on a platter."

"You won't, Edmund," he said. "Where we're going, we won't need disguises."

Chapter 48
Mike

Signals could not travel faster than the speed of light. If they could, anywhere in the observable universe, scientists would've spotted the odd behavior and invalidated a theory that'd held sway in astrophysics for more than a century.

But they hadn't. General Relativity kept being proved right again and again, exactly, generation after generation. Nothing anyone could see, or more critically *predict* to see, had ever contradicted the theory.

And yet here Mike was, in a realm that orbited a star system somewhere else, tied to his realspace body on Earth and receiving telemetry from it in real time. That was more inexplicable than being able to access an alien realmspace without an adapter. Mike wasn't designed; he had emerged in the interstitial spaces between realms. Saying he couldn't inhabit one designed by an alien intelligence was like saying a human couldn't walk on another planet.

At least now he knew why he couldn't access the lower-level functions of the realm. They were there, but designed with different controls, different assumptions, and with a different language.

As to the apparent violation of the speed of light, it might not be a violation at all. The idea that particles could use higher dimensions to shortcut distances in realspace had been knocking around since at least the middle of the twentieth century. That things bigger than particles might do so had been a staple of science fiction for even longer.

There were philosophical implications as well. People had made confident, logically consistent predictions that free will could not exist if it was ever proven that particles could use higher dimensions this way. Those people were in for a disappointment. Mike knew from experience that the universe could easily challenge the rules of logic or ignore them altogether when it was time to get things done.

Mike's own existence, especially his ability to go outside into realspace with a human host, also relied on information traveling through these higher dimensions. He'd only been able to speculate about what sort of relativistic effects he might experience if he managed to separate his realspace host from his threads by a significant distance. Now he had an answer, or at least part of one. When he got home, he'd have a whole new angle of research to explore.

Assuming he managed to get home at all.

Gonzo disappeared when the door opened. She hadn't had time to elaborate on what Mike being in another solar system meant, or what he could do about it.

Tal stuck his head in. "Is everything well?"

"I don't know how to answer that right now."

Tal sighed. "It's not my fault you were released into the galaxy so woefully unprepared. I have never seen a *Trona secnik ton* with such a low educational level. The guild has lost all respect for the office of caretaker. It really is quite insulting." He turned and walked away.

Gonzo flashed to life and swirled around Mike's head. "You him must follow," she whispered. "You here break free cannot."

Gonzo vanished when Tal turned around. Mike would need to figure out how to get Tal to go for a walk so he and Gonzo could have a chat, no matter how Yoda-like her side of it was.

"You are able to walk, yes? It would take some time for me to revive more...never mind. I don't have the energy to learn more new words. If you can't walk, you'll have to spend another night in there."

Mike squelched out onto the mud, but then stopped. This wasn't created by a team of writers. It represented a real place. When the shelter door shut behind him, the remaining natural flat light cut off all shadows, leaving him standing in a landscape decayed beyond recognition.

A cold, humid breeze kicked up and made the branches of the single tree construct nearby creak and clack together. He stood in the grave of an entire civilization. They were alone, the only living things on an entire — simulated — system. "How long?"

"How long what?"

Mike walked toward the holo, the only thing left that hinted at the beauty that must once have been. "How long has it been like this?"

Tal straightened. "*Cantlezna* took approximately two *efnek* to complete. I have been caretaker for five more."

Efneck was Tal's word for centuries. They also had a word for the death of civilizations — of *entire planets*. When Mike caught up to him, they fell into step together. "Was it a war?"

"Nothing so dramatic. A standard announcement was all that was required."

He was clinical, like it happened every day. "Did they suffer?"

"No. It was quite peaceful. I'm not sure any of them understood what was happening at the end. They typically don't."

Mike looked at the planet with new eyes now. He had never walked on anything other than pavement here. No sand, no dirt, just a thin layer of wet muck over whatever passed for concrete. Probably concrete. The stuff was easy to make, and the environment was similar to Earth's. That didn't account for the trees. On a hunch, he walked up to the next one they encountered that was still standing. About a foot from the trunk, he stumbled off an unseen grate onto much softer soil.

The planet, at least this part anyway, wasn't paved. It was landscaped. He stopped. If the trees were placed to be decorative, then they would be in a pattern. And they were, a very recognizable one. Trees were in a line with wide, flat spaces on either side. Streets.

His footprints were clearly seen walking straight down the middle of one. Intersections were marked out by trees either on the corners, or in the center. Low mounds were regularly spaced out along each street.

Houses.

He could even make out driveways.

Tal was leading him through a suburb. But it wasn't exactly like one on Earth. The streets curved wrong and were too wide, as were the houses. It looked like a human settlement placed on a sheet of rubber and then stretched, houses and all.

When they crested the next hill, the conclusion was inescapable. Off in the distance stood the ruins of a city. A big one.

"We can't possibly reach that in less than a day," Mike said. The towers were the same ones he'd seen in the distance yesterday. Now in clear view, it was a spectacular ruin. Mounds of rubble marked collapsed skyscrapers, while other towers leaned dangerously. Some of the tops had crashed into other buildings, creating an obvious domino effect that left broken stubs stabbing jaggedly into the sky. The desolation was oppressive. It wasn't a city, it was an ancient coffin left empty on the ground.

"You misunderstand. My *Salta* is no longer in the center of the capital. Come along."

Mike needed to talk to Gonzo. He had to get rid of Tal.

Then it came to him. Mike made sure he was turned toward Tal when he said, "What? Oh, you're back!"

Tal stopped.

"Yeah, he's been pretty irritated. I can't translate like you can."

Tal walked over. "Has your other half reestablished contact?"

Mike held up a finger, which made Tal back off in a huff. Good. He turned his back on the holo. "*No,* Really? That's what took so long? Wait, hang on." He faced Tal and took a gamble. "I'm not *rishta,* but my other half is. A lot." Tal had used the word in the context of religious modesty.

"That's very unusual."

He turned away from Tal. "I'm trying, but he doesn't understand." He turned back. "If you wouldn't mind?"

"How are you not able to…" he did a thing with his head Mike recognized as his version of an eye roll. "Why must you speak to her out loud?"

It was fun to irritate Tal, especially when he had a legitimate reason to ask him a question. "You mean we don't have to? How?"

Tal didn't cooperate. "For the last time, I'm not your teacher. I'll be over there." He indicated an area across the street they'd been walking down.

"It can't be line of sight."

That wound him up tighter. "Why not?"

"I don't make the rules, she does." Which was true.

"Fine." He stomped over the next hill.

Gonzo swirled to life but then vanished.

Tal was cheating. "I'm serious," Mike shouted. "She knows. I'll come get you when she's done." Also true, but for a different value of *she*.

Gonzo zipped around his head. The laughter didn't need translating. "Unpaired doomed idiocy they to and say are. Your mate this clever is?"

The first part made no sense, but he was pretty sure he understood the second. "She's definitely smarter than I am."

"That key pairing the to a is successful. You your ceremony when, you powerful complete will be."

Mike needed Kim so he could understand the gibberish. "Lady, he's not going to wait forever. You need to simplify. Something's about to happen, right?"

"Yes. He you his place, you but wants can not take."

That sounded like the opposite of going home. "I can't take his place? What place?"

"This so frustrating is. Do his terms to agree not. Fight you if must. Please him destroy do not."

She was almost making sense. "Don't agree, fight him if I have to, but don't kill him?"

"Yes. Please. We apart long he me you for so but by have been can not join destroying. So have been. He I know that what happen but does not is do. You manage that I home sure you if will get for."

"Lost me again."

She vanished. After a moment, Tal stomped over the hill. "Have you been caught up on your *rishta*?"

It was time to stop being reasonable. "Almost. I told you I'd come get you when we were done. Thanks for cutting off my other half."

Tal almost looked embarrassed, but then his holo lost its scan lock for a second, like a classic TV he saw in old movies. "You misunderstand. My *Salta* is no longer in the center of the capital. Come along."

Another glitch. Definitely a good news, bad news thing. If it came to a fight Mike was pretty sure he'd win. But he wasn't sure he'd keep Tal intact in the process.

Tal's *Salta* was in a sector to the left of the city center as they approached it. The buildings were lower here, and so more of them remained intact. Mike had designed his fair share of post-apocalypse realms, but he'd never tried one based on simple decay. He assumed that a modern building would remain standing for eternity. Ruins happened because of outside forces: an earthquake, a storm, a drunk Greek general, a barbarian mistaking roof tiles for gold, stuff like that. Assuming this realm was a high-fidelity scan of an actual place—Mike had no reason to doubt that—mere engineering only delayed decay. Like gravity, time's units were very small, but they never, ever stopped.

Now that he knew it mattered, he paid more attention to what little text remained visible in the realm, mostly on the buildings and the occasional street sign. Those in particular didn't look anything like what was common on Earth, but they were consistently placed near intersections, so it seemed like a good guess.

This provided a critical insight. Traffic, no matter if it was vehicles or network packets, needed to be controlled. *Stop* should be a universal concept. Mike picked a set of symbols from what he guessed was a Stop sign and searched for it in lower-level functions of the realm, finding one quickly. Keeping a careful eye on the external telemetry next to that function, he activated the potential *stop* function, and the stream stopped. Even better, the symbols on the function changed. He deactivated the function, and the telemetry started moving again. So now he had *stop* and *go*.

Several symbols represented both words, so he figured it wasn't a logographic system like Chinese. It was also three dimensional. Each symbol had a specific height, varying in fractional inch increments on the signs and as much as a couple of feet on the taller surviving buildings. But it was proportional: the bigger the lettering, the bigger the height difference. Always the same difference, though.

This gave him a question Tal might answer. "Did they use echolocation at all?"

"No."

Mike was disappointed that Tal didn't follow up with more, but it did provide a data point. Whatever the reason for the variance, it wasn't down to this specific species.

When they arrived, he was scared, but also fascinated. The room was very similar to the one Ozzie had trapped Zoe in during their fight back in China. After killing himself, sort of, Ozzie had used her as life support while waiting for Helen to fall into his trap, taking Zoe's place. It had almost worked. He'd controlled it all from a room very much like this, complete with a glowing hollow column in the center of the room that held a vague shape inside it. Spencer said that they'd almost stopped Ozzie by turning it off.

Tal noticed his stare. "They are rather hideous when taken outside of their network case, but it is quite necessary since my other half died. Now," he said as another foot plate scanner flared to life, "if you would be so kind as to submit to your scan?"

Here we go. "No."

He watched as Tal tried and failed to digest Mike's answer. Mike hadn't told him *no* the entire time, and this must be when he least expected it. "What did you say?"

"I'm not going anywhere but home, Tal. It would be nice if you helped me, but it's not required." A bluff, but not a big one. If this was like Ozzie's control room, the transit dimension was close by. A rumble started as more consoles flared to life. Great. He didn't like Tal much when he was calm. It looked like angry was coming right up.

"This is your new home. You were sent to take my place. I have served enough of my sentence."

That was interesting. "Your sentence? Is this a prison?" He wouldn't know that word. "You're here as punishment?" He'd been talking about *other halves* the entire time but was single as far as Mike could tell. "What happened to your other half, Tal? Where is it?"

For the first time ever, Tal had lost control of the situation. "That issue was resolved by this mission. I accepted the punishment and have obviously served my time, lest you would not be here."

Bingo. And now Mike had an angle. "You're wrong, Tal. I was sent here to test you, to see if you'd learned anything in your time here. Now I must report back to the guild," *whatever that was,* "with my findings. Open the passageway, please."

Tal was frightened and confused, but then grew angry. "Report to the guild yourself, *whelp,* if your ignorance really was a test." The storage area of his avatar was suddenly closed off by a heavy construct that pushed his threads together more tightly. "Now don't dawdle. Take your place."

Constructs very much like his realm probes manifested around his avatar. They quickly roped his arms and legs together, then started moving him toward the scanning plate.

"These are a very original solution to our kind's plight. I encourage you to transmit the construct plans as part of your first report back to the guild."

The cap against his threads was heavy, and Mike couldn't get any leverage. His avatar was no better off. The probe constructs were weak individually, but very strong in large groups. He couldn't push against them. Helpless, he could only watch the scan plate as it grew closer. Mike knew he had to get away from it, but the probes kept pushing him forward.

He could almost hear Kim say the words: *Do the unexpected.*

Mike relaxed, and the probes cascaded over his head like a wave. He lurched sideways out of their grip. Half a dozen managed to grab his ankles, sending him crashing to the floor. He'd only bought himself a few seconds of survival. It wasn't enough.

Tal cursed as he tried to coordinate the probes. He wasn't as practiced as Mike; there was a still a chance. Mike's eyes locked on the symbols around the glowing column.

One was clearly a button, labeled with the word "Stop."

Mike pulled himself across the floor. Probes flailed his legs and back, but he kept going. He had to reach that button. If he ever wanted to see Kim again, he had to reach that button.

Probes still wrapped around his legs while others beat away at him. He would not stop, no matter how hard the hits. Mike dragged himself up to the top of the column. He had to push it.

It didn't budge.

Tal got control of more threads and wrapped them further up his legs. If Mike let go, he'd never be able to reach the button again.

It wouldn't move.

Mike stopped and looked at the thing as more probes wrapped around his waist. If it was an emergency stop, it would have something to keep it from being activated accidentally. He saw a thin bar going through the middle of it.

It wasn't a button, it was a knob.

When he twisted it, the bar flexed. If it flexed, it would break. It had to break, but he had no leverage anymore. The probes had lifted his feet off the ground, yanking harder and harder trying to bring him to the floor.

Mike shifted his grip, knowing it would cost him the position he'd fought for, and let the probes pull him down as he held tight to the knob.

The bar pinning it in place gave way with a loud *snap*.

The probes partially cushioned his fall, but he still cracked the side of his head on the floor. A scream cut through the blooming pain. Mike turned in time to see Tal's holo fade along with the glow from the column.

Before he could free himself from the now-slack probes, Gonzo appeared.

"What you have done?"

He pushed them aside and stood. "I'm sorry."

"Ruined everything is! We together nothing work if will not are! You you him would not destroy promised!"

"Hey, look, I'm sorry. I didn't have a"—Gonzo vanished, and the room went dark— "choice?"

Chapter 49
Spencer

Tonya's phones were important, but the biggest score was his toolkit. It let them get back into the realmspace of the plant without being seen, this time with proper screens instead of hacked-together prayers like the last time. But when it came time to invade Abada's fortress, even screens wouldn't be enough to let them walk in. It would require more of a wriggle, and not always in a direction you could point to.

"When you said we didn't need disguises," Edmund said with his foot only a few inches from Spencer's face, "I didn't expect you to force us to wear *costumes*."

Realmspace literally added entire new dimensions to the art of hacking. Pipes, back doors, and alternate command paths became physical things that could be explored and exploited. If you knew where to look and how to open it, there was almost always a path to get in. It helped that realm developers had fallen back on the old *security through obscurity* crutch, never once thinking anyone would manage to navigate an avatar through the multidimensional virtual basements that supported the back-end of realmspace.

Kim had done this when she removed all traces of a run-in Spencer had with a local cop when they all first met. She'd moved through spaces in ways nobody thought were possible, using pathways that made Spencer's head hurt when he tried to follow them on a map. But that didn't stop him from practicing it as soon as she taught him how. Spencer never counted on bringing a bunch of noobs along, though.

"Don't blame me, blame Kim. These extensions only work on standard avatars." The multidimensional cat suits were only flattering on Tonya, but even that didn't last when they had to navigate the first of the extradimensional crawlspaces. People weren't supposed to stretch through three different directions that didn't exist at once. And this one was tight. "It could be worse."

The lights flickered and died. "It's worse," Edmund said.

"No, sorry," June said from the...well, *rear* had a fucked up relationship to reality in here. She was the last in line, at any rate. "That was me. I hit a switch with my knee." The lights turned back on. "How much farther?"

"I think," Tonya said from the front of the line, "hang on, I need to adjust my neck." The machine space construct was mostly modeled using brightly lit transparent walls. The effect was like crawling through clear twisted hamster tunnels. It allowed him to *see* her unhook the vertebra in her neck and stretch it out and around a corner. Kim did this all the time, but it made him want to barf. He was afraid to look at his own legs. He had to adjust the elasticity contract to get them around a few corners, and it felt like he had grown extra knees.

"Right," she said. "Two more turns and we're done."

"Turns?" Edmund asked from above and *ldup*—Spencer had never bothered to learn the proper names of the extra directions, this one was at a right angle to left and up. "I can see my own arse without turning around in here. *And I'm not using a mirror.* The queen's torturers could learn a thing or two from whoever designed this adjunct to Satan's privies."

He would complain all day if they let him. "Edmund," Spencer said, "less talk, more move."

What Tonya didn't mention was that the last two turns were long and in a spiral that she could only describe with an equation. June looked like a black satin snake squeezed from a tube, so big she probably still had her feet in the entrance when they grabbed her hands to pull her through.

"That," she said as she stood and towered over them, "is not supposed to be possible. The man who designed those spaces was one of my advisers. He'd be appalled at what we just did. *I'm* appalled at what we just did."

"It gets us in without opening a door," Spencer replied.

Now that they were past the last of the mazes, they could ditch the cat suits. It was nice to get back into a pair of jeans and a T-shirt. Even Edmund's bizarre lace-and-what-the-hell-is-that-on-your-crotch look was a definite improvement. Those catsuits left nothing to the imagination, and he'd seen things that could not be unseen.

They still had to cross the internal space of Abada's realm without getting kicked out before they took their shot. Walking would take too long, and they couldn't switch avatars now. It would set off who knew how many alarms.

So he brought their rides with him.

Spencer pulled the four miniaturized constructs he'd been carrying in a pouch all this time and tossed them on the ground. Each expanded to full size with a snort and a whinny.

"Shh," Spencer said as he grabbed one's snout. "Fuck, stop making noise."

Edmund was, predictably, unimpressed. "Oh God."

Tonya walked around the winged horse that stood next to her. "Very…cute?"

"Are these from—" June asked.

"Not exactly. I made shadow copies of them when my aunt brought her little brats over for Thanksgiving last year. I was planning on turning them into apocalypse ponies to scare the shit out of them this Christmas, but never got around to it."

"Do they talk?" Tonya asked.

"Nah, that part's copyrighted to hell and back. They're not here for conversation anyway. You wouldn't know it by looking at them, but the wings work." Life-sized cartoon horses with wings. Well why the hell not?

Spencer could never keep the names straight, but he got the black one with the moon on its ass, June got the big white one with the crown, Tonya got the purple one with the star on its ass, and Edmund got the one that had probably been a part of every gay pride parade since the 1990s. What the obsession with sticking symbols on a horse's ass was all about, he never did understand. "Get on in front of their wings, and don't forget the seat belt. You don't want to fall off one of these fuckers if you can avoid it."

Edmund hopped right up like he'd done it all his life. He rolled his eyes at Spencer's expression. "Nobles from my era learned to ride before they could walk. It's not much more than a donkey crossed with a chicken. If you put a red hat and cape on it, it wouldn't be any less useful than a cardinal." He looked back at the rainbow tail. "It would make spotting their usual preference in sleeping partner easier."

"How do we get them airborne?" Tonya asked.

Spencer climbed up and strapped in. "Once they're running, pull straight up on the reins. Then hang the hell on. They're faster than they look." He slapped his on the ass and was rewarded with a stomach-lurching rear before it tore off into the darkness. They looked ridiculous, but speed was cool no matter what. Flying was even cooler.

He spiraled up to get a good look at the layout. Abada may have built this himself, but he stayed true to the original design Spencer had seen in the restored realm-enabled movie. It was a gigantic open room with an island of hexagons floating in its center, maybe twice as big as the starship docked against it on the opposite side. The miles-thick ceiling had cathedral window cutouts that showed the misty cloud construct beyond. Spencer had never toured one of these before; it was pretty fucking impressive.

He opened a channel on their phones so they wouldn't have to shout. "Arm your logic bombs, we're going in. Drop on my mark." He set the pony on a shallow, gliding dive and activated his nordenSight. The phone app assessed the ballistic contracts of the realm and drew him a virtual basket over the target to aim for. Nothing but net and he was guaranteed a hit. "Three...two..." Four green sparks shot out of the central amphitheater and streaked upward, but they couldn't dodge right now. "One...*mark*!"

Spencer dropped the logic bombs and yanked the pony inverted, pulling into a split-S, barely dodging the bolt Abada had sent his way. The others weren't as experienced and got direct hits. The damage contracts on the constructs and the avatars were exceeded in an instant, and they vanished. "Are you guys okay?" he asked.

"We're fine," June replied over the shared channel. "But he's locked us out. Did it work?"

Spencer had to concentrate to spot the small bits of solidified logic as they fell. One by one, they bounced off the amphitheater, arching into the darkness.

Shit. "Negative. They just deflected off the surface. Yumbo and Inkanyamba must've—" He was wrenched sideways as the bolt that missed him slammed into the belly of his mount, tearing away the saddle construct's straps and sending him sailing into the void. It wasn't over, though. Vaporizing his mount instead of his avatar left him some options. Spencer touched a spot on his jacket, and a LightYear pack manifested on his back. The wings opened instantly, and he was gliding, searching for Abada's next shot.

Abada tried a different strategy and set the physics to Earth sea level, full fidelity. With one G and a much thicker atmosphere, the wings could only morph so much to compensate. Spencer barely managed to land without crushing his legs, but it still knocked the wind out of him. Shouting *get up* in your head doesn't do much when your body is convinced it can't breathe anymore, so it took him longer than he wanted to find his feet.

He stood up just outside the amphitheater. Abada's dripping, shit-filled form towered above him.

"Clever," he said. "I can't find exactly where your access point is. You must be in one of the unfinished areas. No matter, the mistress has plenty of people to search for you now."

"You're not going to find us. Stop being an asshole, Abada." Spencer needed to get as close as he could, but it was not easy with a giant rotting corpse looming over his head.

"Don't call me that. June called me that. My name is Kokou."

Spencer only had one chance. The horror above him made his inner chimpanzee want to run for the forest, but he had to get closer to the thing. With an effort, he turned running backward into stepping forward. "I want to show you a trick June showed me when you weren't around, just for this special occasion. Oh yeah, one more thing," he yanked the Luger construct out from under his coat. "I'm glad you changed your name, you son of a bitch."

The gun nearly bucked out of his hand when he fired, but the custom-designed virus slug constructs June made still slammed into the monster, center mass. What was left of its eyes fixed Spencer with a glare that faded almost immediately, then the unduplicate's avatar sloughed off layer by layer. When the slop filled the amphitheater, it overflowed and knocked Spencer off his feet, sweeping him into the rugged hex field. With each crash or tumble, his avatar's damage meter filled more. If it exceeded, they'd lose their access and be locked out permanently.

Finally it stopped. Spencer had been washed into a set of hexagons that formed a rough shelter. Everything hurt, he was covered in shit that smelled like death, but he had two bars left on his avatar's damage meter. It was enough.

When Spencer squelched up onto his feet, he thought he knew what would be at the bottom of the pit Abada had lived in, but he was wrong. It wasn't a lake of oozing crap. It was a hole filled with probe constructs. Spencer had fried them, but it was very clear that someone, or something, had been sock-puppeting Abada this entire time.

"Okay guys," he said as he adjusted the locks. "You can come back in now. I think we have a new problem. June, if you have any specialized construct scanners, bring them all. I don't know what I'm looking at here, maybe you will." He couldn't make the filth go away with a command. That would put very noticeable entries into the event logs of the plant's network.

"And bring water. And soap. Lots of it."

Chapter 50

Tonya

Spencer wasn't kidding. It took two risky round trips to get enough soap and water construct to clean all evidence of Abada off his avatar and clear an area that would let June work with her scanners. They spent the time swapping stories, of her experiments and his misadventures. Tonya thought her tale of the three-eyed monsters would wow the audience. She didn't count on Spencer already having his own story about them.

"You *killed* the other two?"

Tonya could tell Spencer wasn't happy about it. "That makes it sound like I had a plan. I was fucking lucky. Stupid fucking lucky."

By now they had exited Abada's realm and gathered in the network room Spencer and June had used to confront the AI the first time. Spencer was able to remove it from the list of places the guards were supposed to search, so it made for a safe room to hole up and plan their next moves. Tonya had to get word to Kim before morning. They needed to find a way to connect to the outside world.

And that was a problem.

On the screen June called up to plot their path to a likely access point was yet another monster. This one wasn't a hairy brute. It was some kind of mist-covered thing. Sometimes it seemed solid, other times it was clearly disguising another thing underneath. Tonya got the impression of a hulking mass with too many legs to be a mammal, too few to be an insect. It curled tighter over a mound of rubble it had made for itself. It was so different from the two Tonya had seen walk out of the portal she would've never thought they were related, except the open box in the corner of the screen was clearly the one the creatures had brought with them through the portal. It must've been inside.

Tonya turned to June. "Anna doesn't know about this at all?"

While she and Spencer had been cleaning—being a nurse, it took a lot more to shock her than a naked white boy, virtual or otherwise—June had been poring over the information Spencer had captured and taking readings of the realm.

She shook her head. "I checked the logs and the altered source code. Abada hid it all from her, and I'm continuing that. Abada's actions, and his transformation, aren't related to the changes Anna made. My virus stopped him, but someone else had already introduced a specific infection into Abada's code before we came along."

"Infection?" Edmund asked. Tonya could understand why. It would suck to gain consciousness only to lose it to some sort of... well, whatever it was they were looking at. "Am I at risk as well?"

"Do you feel a sudden urge to protect that?" June asked him, indicating the thing on the screen.

"The only sudden urge I have is to run screaming into the hills."

June called Spencer over, and they discussed the issue. It rapidly escalated past Tonya's limited vocabulary. She could talk about multidimensional constructs and their implications for space and time with the best of them. But when it came to the nuts and bolts of AI and realmspace? Not her party.

Not Edmund's either. "I don't care how it works, you gits. I want to know if I should be smothering myself with poultices or whatnot."

"There," Spencer said as he pointed at a virtual screen full of gibberish code. "That's where they did it."

Tonya shared a look with Edmund, who was using a window in their shared vision channel, then turned back to Spencer. "Did what?"

"They hacked into the network through the spiral stack. It's a universal hack that exploits the nature of the crystal lattice of a quantum computer rather than the source code itself."

Edmund slapped his forehead. "In English, you bloody, bollocksy lump of meat. Some of us use those, you know?"

"It's good news," June said. "The hack will only work if you have physical access to the matrix host machines, and it's a per-use thing. Think of it like an injection for humans."

"Bloody hell." His holo vanished, and then there was a beep from a box on Spencer's belt. Edmund's voice came from it. "How can an alien virus be *good news*?"

Spencer shook his head. "Just switch to named tunnels and you'll be fine."

"Oh, I've done that, too. But I'd rather be in a place where it has to go through you before it can get to me. Who knows what else it's capable of?"

"Very brave, Edmund," Spencer said.

"Whatever gave you the impression I was brave? Bravery is for knights too stupid to understand that lances to the head are more about physics than armor. Bravery is for priests who know that Protestants are proponents of alternative heating. Bravery is for people who want to tell a queen no. I am none of those things. What I am is alive, and I want to stay that way for as long as possible. If that means living in a box strapped to your bony backside, so be it."

"Fine. It makes things easier if I don't have to keep track of you." He turned back to June and Tonya. "That doesn't make them easy. The only route to a network access point we can use to reach Kim is on the other side of that thing's lair."

"Any alternatives?" Tonya asked.

"None good," June replied. "Anna has repaired the inner network and has placed guards in the passageways." She flashed up pictures of various intersections.

"Robots?" Spencer asked. "Where are the people?"

"Mostly on the surface. There aren't that many people in the plant, period. Until Anna called them all in, at any rate." Another picture showed that the influx that'd given Tonya so much trouble had slowed during the night but had not stopped.

If they took over the robots, it would give them an army. "Can you control them with our new access?" Tonya asked.

"I think so, but I need time."

"How much?"

June shrugged. "If I'm lucky, an hour or so."

"I don't trust luck. Worst case?"

"No way to tell. Four hours, maybe eight."

Kim would be here in six hours, and Tonya had been around enough doctors to know hedging when she saw it. "You have three. If you haven't made progress by then, we'll need a different plan." She turned to Spencer and pointed at the cannon strapped to his back. "How many shots does that thing hold?"

"Seven. It's loaded up, but ammo isn't the problem. I have to get close."

"Define close."

"I'm a good shot, but not great. All I have is open sights. I get the shakes looking at that. Thirty feet if I need to hit a specific target. No more than one fifty if I want to hit anything at all. I need to be on top of the target if I want to be sure. And I want to be sure. Sure kills monsters dead."

Leave him to say the perfect thing that would set Tonya's nerves jangling. Nurses dealt with horror shows every day, but they only ever involved humans. She'd somehow managed to wedge the terror of facing an actual, for-real alien into the same place that let her ignore a rupture that splattered blood, or worse, across her face, but it wasn't a comfortable fit. She didn't know how Spencer was coping with it. June seemed be treating it as a puzzle to solve, but her hands were so large it was hard for her to hold them steady.

Tonya concentrated on step one. The box the creature arrived in gave her a sense of how big it was: twice as long as Spencer's maximum range. "Do you know the dimensions of the room, June?"

A blueprint drew itself into existence in their shared vision channel. "About a hundred meters long and not quite half that wide. The ceiling varies, but it's no less than fifty meters high in most places. I think we planned on turning it into a garage but had to shelve that plan after our budgets got cut. There's one finished room cut into the side, otherwise it's big and oval."

"How many ways in and out?"

"Two are finished, but there are three others available." The blueprints turned into a 3-D model that slowly began to rotate. The two finished entrances were on opposite ends of the cave with a walkway between them. The walls were blue while the monster—they were going monster hunting, and she *had to hold it together*—was green. Red tunnels drew into being and connected to the walls in three different places.

"Do we have any rope?" Tonya asked.

"No," Spencer replied. "So that takes these two off the table." He used his finger to turn them black. "But this one is still a candidate." It was close enough to the floor for a climb to be realistic. "We can't use it as a sniper spot, though. Too far away and at the wrong angle."

Tonya spun the model so they looked straight down at it, then sliced the ceiling off to get a clear view of the floor. The monster had parked itself in a shallow alcove near the center of the cave. There might be a way past it. "We don't want to shoot it if we don't have to."

Spencer snorted. "You didn't see its buddy bite a human in half. These things are fucking dangerous."

Like most guys she knew, Spencer didn't think much beyond fight or flight. There were always other options. "I'm also not saying we should walk up and say hi to it. If we're careful," she drew a path from their natural entrance to the finished exit with her finger, "we can follow this route to the exit."

"But then what?" Spencer asked.

Tonya didn't like the only answer she had. "Then we improvise. First, we get the message out." She needed to coordinate next steps with Kim but couldn't reach her from down here. "Then we deal with that. Maybe shoot it in the ass? I don't know."

Edmund cleared his throat. "I've reconsidered my choice of host environment. I should be left behind with June. I'll help her take over the robots. Yes. I should definitely be left behind here with June."

This time Tonya got to share a look with Spencer.

"Well," Edmund said, "don't just stand there, you naked ape. Hand me over to June."

June gave them a wry smile as she took the box from Spencer. "His bravery notwithstanding, Edmund will be able to help. I'll need it. You can't use those phones to attach to this network, so you'll be out of my range once you get to the cave."

Tonya turned to Spencer. "You wouldn't happen to have another shotgun hidden away somewhere?"

He shrugged. "Sorry." He pulled the gun off his back. "How many times did you work with a Saiga in the realms?" He tossed it to her.

She caught it like she'd done it a hundred times, which might be true. "Plenty." Holding it gave her the surreal surge everyone got when they handled an object they'd only ever touched as a construct. She ejected the magazine, checked the action, clapped the two together, and tossed it back to Spencer. "Realspace recoil?"

"You'll get bruises if you're not careful, but otherwise it's fine."

Spencer would keep the gun, but Tonya could use it if she had to. "Who says you can't learn anything from videogames?" With a steadiness that might be thirty percent authentic she said, "Okay, we're off. June, call us if you get the robots online or if anything goes wrong."

"And what are *we* to do," Edmund asked, "if anything goes wrong?"

Tonya shrugged. Sometimes trolling Edmund was too easy. "Lock the door."

Spencer picked it up without missing a beat. "And hope they don't have blasters."

"Bloody, bollocksy Americans. If I had a ha'penny for every time they referenced—"

The door shut him off mid-rant.

They grinned at each other for about ten strides. Spencer broke down first, spitting giggles as he walked. It wasn't often Edmund walked straight into a reference trap, and that one was choice.

The navigation arrow in their shared vision guided them to the entrance of the route that led to the cavern. "I'm glad this suit has knee pads," she said. Rocks against jeans wouldn't be fun, and it wasn't like she was going to keep it after this was over. "Sorry I don't have an extra pair."

"No worries. Where did you get all that stuff anyway?" he asked on a private phone channel as he clambered up to the crack in the wall.

Using the phones made a lot of sense. No noise. "The plant is still a construction site. It wasn't hard to gather up what I needed."

Spencer helped her up with a boost. "Wait," he said as they crawled forward. "You said it was all in a box that you picked up. Why did you have to gather it up at all? Couldn't you have left it to yourself?"

"Two reasons. One, I still needed it to move around here after I left the care package."

"And two?"

"That one's a little harder to describe. I didn't, and still don't, want to screw with causality too much. I think it might be elastic, but that doesn't mean I want to stretch it when I don't have to."

"What does that mean?"

This one took her a bit to get her head around, too. "It's another paradox. If I got this suit from the box, and then put it back in the box to send back with me, then where did the suit come from?"

He paused, then shook his head. "Fucked up."

"The thing was," she said as she squeezed through a part of the passage that was narrow. Rocks scraped against her chest, "I could've done exactly that, but every time I tried, I failed. It was damn spooky." Cyril hadn't put some sort of hex on her to make her stand still in front of that portal. Once Tonya was in the right position, it seemed like the whole universe kept her from moving. "I can only imagine the compulsion that might hit someone trying to screw with an important event."

"It was an internal thing, not, like, a tree falling in your path?"

"Stuff like that happened a couple of times, too. The call I made to you took four tries. It only worked when I promised myself I wouldn't do anything funny and then didn't. The first three failed. Technical glitches, a different one each time, just before I tried to cheat. It made me paranoid."

The conversation stopped as soon as they got close to the entrance of the cave. Spencer was right; they couldn't see the creature from here. But that worked both ways. The next trick was getting down to the floor without making any noise.

Tonya went down first, landing with a crunch that must've echoed up to the surface. After breathing a few times, though, Tonya knew she'd made barely a sound.

With various signals and motions, Spencer made it down, too. They only needed to get across the—

"Welcome, my strange C-7s. Please, come forward."

It was Abada's voice.

"Did you hear that?" she sent to Spencer.

Eyes as round as dinner plates, Spencer nodded.

"Please," a different, tenor voice said. "I don't have much time left. I'd like to see you up close."

Tonya fell to all fours, then crept forward, Spencer close behind. Monsters were supposed to stay in their damned corner, not sound like they were coming from everywhere.

A husky female voice spoke next. "This is your language, yes? It would be disappointing if I got that wrong."

Crawling across muddy gravel was the worst. Cold and spiky. They had to stay out of its sightline.

"I don't need to see you," Abada's voice again, "although I'd like to. And you won't progress without me."

Now Tonya could look into the nook the creature was resting in.

It was empty. The pile of rocks it'd made was there, but no creature. No tracks either. She looked around frantically. Even the ceiling was empty.

"You will stand."

They both had to duck rocks that fell from the ceiling.

"Stand up," said the tenor voice this time. "Please."

Tonya put three fingers up at Spencer and mouthed *this many?* He shrugged. Black people didn't hang around with ghosts. When they did, it never ended well. Fine, they wouldn't play its game. She scrabbled toward the exit.

"I said," the woman's voice, "STAND UP!"

A stalactite crashed to the ground in front of them, literally shaking floor.

"Okay!" Tonya shouted as she stood up. "Fine! You win!" A frantic *I'll kill your ass if you don't stand up with me* look got Spencer to his feet. "What do you want?"

"To see the creatures that could end it all."

Spencer said its buddies could bite a human in half. Tonya breathed deep and prayed. It didn't help much.

"So plain," it said, cycling through the voices as it spoke. Not three then, a single creature with three voices. "We never thought this was possible. Any of this."

Tonya looked around, trying to find the source of the voice. Nothing.

Spencer was just as clueless. "Fucked if I know where it went," he whispered.

"I am everywhere," it replied. "But too limited. I need to report back about your remarkable species, your remarkable planet, but alas, I have run out of time. We have conquered everything. We have won. And now I find a corner of the galaxy that hasn't been touched in millions of years. The things I could do with you. There's no guild here. No interpreters. The AC network is almost empty. The nodes I've found are laughably young and weak."

The ranting was hard to follow. It changed its voice with every fifth word. Tonya nudged Spencer. The exit wasn't that far.

"Such will be the witnesses to the passing of the first true explorer in more than a billion years." The voice grew weaker. "By rights I should own your planet, but now I have to risk everything on a single gamble. If I'd only had a little more—"

"*GET DOWN!*"

The shout came from their left as the unmistakable silhouette of two grenades sailed into view from the same direction. Hours of small-squad combat in the realms had trained them both how to react to *that*. Tonya dove behind a large rock in one direction, Spencer did the same in another.

There was a double-blast, and then blackness.

Chapter 51

Spencer

He'd been hit by explosions any number of times in the realms. Sometimes the realism settings were set on cartoon, and he'd bounce around like a rubber ball. Other times they were full real. He'd get cut, bashed, burned, or whatever until the damage contract of his avatar was exceeded. Then it was either an exit from the realm or an avatar respawn. Either way, relief was instant. The very worst carryover he'd ever had was no worse than a mild sunburn, and that faded after a few minutes.

That wasn't the case with for-real grenades. When Spencer finally got his marbles straight, he had aches on top of pains. And they had new friends. It turned out the room June mentioned had been manned with security guards. *Jumpy* security guards. They'd manhandled him and Tonya into their little HQ before the dust had settled. She seemed as banged up as he was but otherwise fine.

There were four of them, one big chick who was clearly in charge and three dudes who didn't seem good for much except scurrying whenever she shouted at them. For a while, that was all Spencer could get. Even though the bleeding from the various cuts and nicks he'd gotten diving away from the grenades stopped after a few minutes, the ringing in his ears took a lot longer to die down. It was like trying to listen to someone on the other side of a window.

"What was in there? How did you get this far down? Who are you?"

Tonya still had her Cyril suit on, and June had found him some work overalls to wear after he had washed off all the deer crap. He looked like he belonged with them, and Tonya didn't look like a civilian.

Go with that.

"This is Professor Paula Sherwen, and I'm Phil Liggett. Joshua Early sent us down to assist you guys, but we got lost when our phones failed." All that studying Edmund and New Kim made him do had paid off. Again. This lady was part of internal security, and Spencer knew every boss between her and Anna Treacher herself. Being confident, looking the part, and knowing your stuff got him most of the way to being trusted. Reeling off those names in that order worked well, especially with people as rattled as these four were. "If you don't mind my asking," he pointed at the cave entrance, "what the fuck was that all about?"

The boss-lady said, "We've been stuck on the wrong side of this cave complex for hours. Our phones quit working, too. I wasn't sure our messages had been received. That...whatever it was...used a force field to bottle us up in here. It shut off when you guys turned up, so we were able to ambush it."

"Yeah," Spencer replied, "but what *was* it? What did you blast? We didn't see anything."

"You don't when it's active, but it never moved from that spot. We figured a few frag grenades would get its attention. Sorry about the short notice." She turned to Tonya. "What's with the outfit?"

Spencer could see the gears change in Tonya's head, but that was because he knew her and was sitting right next to her. She'd spent the past eight days pretending to be someone else, and it showed in the way the Tonya he knew subtly changed into one he didn't. "The report I read mentioned the anomaly was located in an unfinished section of the plant. On Mr. Early's advice, I chose an outfit that would be suited for rough conditions."

Name-dropping was a nice touch. Boss-Lady was definitely nibbling on the bait now. "And why didn't you dress out?" she asked Spencer.

He nodded at the shotgun they'd taken from him. "I was the muscle in case we ran into any of those super-bears on our way down here."

That got him concerned looks from everyone. They knew about the monsters.

"How far up have they been reported?" Boss-Lady asked, no longer suspicious. They'd taken the bait.

Now to set the hook. "I caught them outside the hydro complex. Two of them. They weren't bears." Boss-Lady looked him up and down, trying to decide if he was bullshitting her. He let the memory of those things, the way they looked, smelled, and the sounds they made, show on his face. His shudder was real. "I don't know what the fuck they were."

One of the lackeys took two steps back. "You *saw* one?"

"More than that. It's a hell of a story. But we need to get out of here first."

The lackeys all looked at Boss-Lady. She weighed her options. They were deep inside the plant. Spencer looked like one of them and was armed with one of their weapons. Tonya didn't fit, but there was no good folder in Boss-Lady's mental danger file to put her in. Something really fucking scary had just happened, had been happening, and these people had been sitting in front of it waiting for it to eat them. Spencer knew stuff about the monsters.

"Sounds like a plan to me. We need all the help we can get."

That wasn't exactly what either of them wanted Boss-Lady to say. "Help with what?" he asked.

"That thing may be gone, but it's been busy," Boss-Lady said. "There's a power anomaly in the exit corridor at the other end of the cave. That's what's fritzed everyone's phones." She tossed Spencer his shotgun. "Where'd the strap go?" she asked.

He'd made a half-assed replacement out of shoe laces. "That's part of the story."

Her body language changed into something that screamed ex-military. This one was dangerous; he'd have to be very careful around her.

"Did you kill it?" she asked.

Spencer hadn't slept. He'd been busy, but that was an excuse. Sleeping would bring an actual, for-real monster back to life. "Blew the arm off at the shoulder. It bled out in the sluice gate, and I washed its buddy down the river with a wall of water ten feet high."

The three goons gave him high-fives like the idiots they were, but Boss-Lady looked him up and down. That was good. He wasn't the one she should be paying attention to, and the longer he kept her looking at him the more time Tonya would have to set them up. Spencer was the actor; Tonya was the tiger, the only person who had ever managed to land Mike on his ass in a sparring match. Four-to-one odds just gave her more targets to choose from. And he wasn't exactly helpless either.

Plus, he had his Saiga back. A safety blanket didn't have anything on a safety shotgun. When he did get to sleep, Spencer fully planned on it being by his side. Forever, if he could manage it.

***

The cave they ran from had been wrecked. What was once a sort-of-prepped tourist attraction with a concrete walkway and lights was now a big pile of rubble. Stalactites had crashed to the floor, pulverizing stalagmites below them. Whatever it was had gone out with a big damn bang, that much was obvious. Tonya's excuse for her outfit was fucking brilliant, since she was the only one who could make real headway with the rubble and sharp rocks. Everyone else did the best they could, but it was obvious this was the last time anybody would be wearing these uniforms. Spencer never knew how muddy a cave was until now.

And dark. The flashlights they used did a good job showing where he was going, but once the light turned away, it was like nothing existed. Anything could be hiding in the complete darkness outside the circles of light they all cast in front of them. They assumed whatever it was that did this was dead, but the fucking thing didn't have a body to begin with. Or maybe it did. Spencer definitely saw something in that video feed, and now that something had about a billion places to hide.

But it was dead. It had to be. They barely managed to escape the explosion, and if that hadn't done the trick, all these shit-tons of rock scattered everywhere would bury the damn thing. All they had to do was turn off whatever was fritzing the phones, tie up the four loose ends they'd fallen in with, and then meet up with Kim in the morning.

Tonya crested the last of the rubble mounds. "Hey, I think I—" She fell out of sight.

"Tonya!" Spencer rushed upward, ignoring the uneven footing as best he could. That thing had come back, and now it'd gotten Tonya. Spencer topped the mound. Tonya's flashlight marked where she fell, rolling down the other side to more level ground. When Spencer looked up, he saw the edge of a—

***

He woke up sore on the ground next to Tonya, who hadn't moved. Spencer looked around. The squad of guards were all here, also unconscious, flashlights scattered where they had been dropped. Everyone seemed to be breathing. Not getting eaten by a monster: good. Waking up without remembering falling asleep: bad. It had to do with the glow he'd seen. Spencer pushed up off the ground—

***

And woke up again, not having moved an inch. Nobody had. The pebbly surface of the cave had grown damned uncomfortable, and the cold wet of the ground had soaked through his clothes. Spencer pushed up off the ground again—

***

And woke up. Nothing had changed. Okay. This was annoying. It happened when he tried to get up. *So no getting up. Right.* Spencer turned his head as slowly as he could, lifting just a little so the rocks wouldn't cut his cheek. Still awake. It wasn't triggered by consciousness or small movements. He got his head around to the other side when someone groaned and moved—

***

Spencer woke up, able to see the entrance now. It was clearly outlined by an orange light coming from something out of sight around the corner. It was definitely triggered by movement. He could see the sensors: four small, odd, dark boxes attached to the corners of the chamber entrance. They were triggering some sort of motion alarm that—

***

The next time he woke up, Spencer started singing to the tune of an ancient pop song his mom had drilled into him when he was little.

> This probe
> Will knock you out
> This probe will knock you out
> Don't move it'll knock you out
> This probe will knock you out

Not his best work, but he was a hacker, not a songwriter. Figuring lyrics and shit out on the fly was hard.

When he'd gone a few minutes without getting knocked out, Spencer added a line.

> When you believe me just shout *come on*.

He stopped when five come ons came back to him. "Thank fucking God. I always hated that song."

"What's happening?" Tonya asked.

"A trap set up in front of the cave entrance. Big movements trigger it, small ones don't." He heard the soft scraping of someone—

***

The four sensors stared balefully at him when Spencer opened his eyes. Some fucker had started moving too fast. Spencer would bet money it was one of the lackeys. He started up his singing until he got another five shouts.

"Don't anybody fucking move, okay?" he said. "And if that happens again, just call out *awake* every few seconds until we're all back. I hate singing."

"Why are you waking up first?" Boss-Lady asked.

"I don't know. Maybe I'm smaller?" He was taller than Tonya but still super skinny. This was good news, since Tonya was probably the *next* smallest person in the party. He had to know this for sure, and all it did was put them to sleep for a little bit. Spencer's shotgun had fallen to this side of him, so he took a chance and lurched—

***

He was within arm's reach of it when he woke up. Better still, Tonya was the first person to say *awake*.

"That's good to know, right?" he asked.

"It is," she replied. Her tone said she'd gotten the message. It took thirty seconds or so for Boss-Lady to come around. The lackeys followed not long after.

It had to be related to size, or maybe mass. Tonya would wake up right after he did.

It was a better plan than nothing, but he had to get past whatever kept putting them to sleep. "I said be still!"

"I swear it wasn't me," one of the lackeys said.

"Cut the crap, Wilson," Boss-Lady said. "Everyone, no more movement."

"I was able to move a little," Spencer said, "and I can see its sensors. I've got my shotgun, and I think I can sneak up on it. But you have to keep still, okay?"

They all agreed, but he could tell nobody was happy about it. Spencer didn't blame them. Lying on the wet, muddy floor of a cave sucked ass.

Moving slowly in the muck wasn't much better. His hands were so pruned it made the shotgun a little difficult to handle. Those naps may have been for more than a few moments.

"Shoot the sensors," Boss-Lady said.

That would make Spencer's bigger plan harder to execute, but then he thought of an out. "If we do that, it might piss off whatever's around the corner. Let me try my way first." He waited for an argument. When none came, Spencer crawled forward again. He triggered the nap attack twice on his way around the corner. Both times Tonya called out awake before anyone else. The closer he got the harder it was to move slowly. The timing on this was gonna be tight.

When he rounded the corner, it took a moment to understand what he was looking at. A shiny, spindly machine sat at the center of the room. It looked like a NASA lander. But it wasn't a close resemblance. The arms bent in weird ways, and he didn't recognize the probes they held out. Several were connected to power and data cables across the ceiling. A gizmo that resembled an injector had drilled into a junction box. That might be where the infection that scared Edmund so badly came from. The yellow light was given off by glowing panels that were part of the body of the probe. It didn't scream alien as much as the actual aliens, but it still wasn't right.

What it also lacked was an obvious off switch. Spencer couldn't be sure they included one, or that he'd recognize it if they did. The thing didn't look armored. The materials used reminded him of good ol' chrome-plated steel, or maybe highly polished aluminum. It didn't matter much in the end. The big green bug-eyed monsters weren't bulletproof, so he figured their machines wouldn't be either. Tungsten slugs meant never having to say you're sorry. Spencer brought the shotgun slowly up and aimed for center mass.

Then he stopped. There was no way to know what was powering it. It certainly wasn't solar. No exhaust, so it wasn't using an engine. That left fuel cells, batteries, and nukes. It was too small for a nuke. Physics was physics, and the middle part was only about the size of a lawnmower. If it was powered by a reactor that would fit inside it, there wouldn't be enough uranium or whatever the fuck you used in those things to cause a detonation. Contamination would follow the path of the slug, which was away from him.

That left batteries and fuel cells, both of which were compact and full of explosive goodness. The probe wasn't big, but it looked to be made of metal, a.k.a. shrapnel.

Fuck it. He could spin his wheels all day thinking about this, and the only alternative was to sneak all the way up to it and then fight through involuntary naps until he figured out where the off switch was.

Spencer crawled back a bit and hid his body behind a rock. This was either gonna work or suck big green donkey balls.

"Okay, folks. In three...two...one..."

The shotgun bucked, and the explosion rushed at him.

Chapter 52

June

June snorted upright from the desk. Every muscle in her back shouted from being in that position for too long. Moving brought her legs and backside into the conversation. Big people should not stay in unnatural positions for long periods. They'd been trying for hours to crack the maintenance network but had made no progress. She had to set her head down on the table for a moment. She hadn't slept in thirty-six hours.

Then June remembered where she was. "Where is everyone? What's happening?" She was too sleep-addled to quickly log in to realmspace. More memories came back. "Tonya and Spencer...are they okay?" They'd fallen down a hill as she watched the video, helpless. Edmund said they'd been sleeping.

"Spencer and Tonya's status are unknown. There was another explosion that took out the camera feed. Six hours have passed," Edmund said. "I'd hoped to give you more, but events have overtaken my plans."

"What's changed?"

A screen opened up showing the intersection where the main road and the road to the plant met. It zoomed down onto a small car with two women in front and a man sitting in the back. June had never seen them before. "Who are they?"

"The one on the left," the dark-haired one, "is my mistress. I presume the one on the right is Will's mother, Emily. I can help them, but I need you to hold the access channels open and keep trying to subvert more of the robots. I've only managed one, and it has a job to do. Goodbye, June, and good luck."

With that, he was gone. On another screen, one of the small maintenance bots disconnected a transport crystal, rolled to a different port on the opposite wall of the lab it was in, and plugged it back in. Edmund was now on the other side of the air gap.

She lost all video feed to the outside cameras. Edmund must be, as Spencer would say, fucking their shit up again. Good. Better still, he'd left her the keys to the one bot he managed to compromise. The bot itself didn't matter. The keys would work on any of them, but only one at a time. It wasn't as much of a limitation as it would at first appear. She only needed to control them long enough to set waypoints. They could navigate on their own.

She dispatched two medical assist bots to the cave Spencer and Tonya were in. They'd managed to find the most remote part of the entire plant, so it wouldn't be quick. But it was a start.

She then grabbed a nearby construction bot and set it to work excavating the now-collapsed passage to the cavern. She had no way to know if that had been caused by the first explosion, which she knew they'd survived, or the second. They had to be okay.

They had to be okay.

The medical bots arrived and joined her digging out the rubble. It felt like hours but was probably less than a minute or two. Edmund was gone, she didn't know Kim or Emily, and there was no way she'd be able to stop Anna on her own. The oupa on her shoulder suggested a prayer, which June set into with a passion.

The construct bot broke through first, shining a light in. Nothing. But it was a big cave. They were fine. The medical bot she now controlled shoveled the rest of the rubble away. She couldn't see them.

A blast blew the construction bot back into the hallway.

"WAIT!" June shouted through the speakers of the one she controlled. Then she stopped. It could be Spencer, or it could be the guards.

"June?"

It was Tonya. "Yes, it's me! Don't shoot this one!"

She moved the bot into the cave. The first thing she heard was a long string of swearing in a familiar voice.

Spencer.

The prayer changed from asking for help to saying thanks. Fervent thanks. She threw search lights all around. "This is a medical bot. Is anyone injured?"

"Fucking thing blew up in my fucking face. Goddamn it hurts!"

"Yes," Tonya said. "Spencer got burned in an explosion. This is a standard AA23?"

June had forgotten that Tonya was a nurse in real life. She would know about the various medical bots. "A subvariant, but yes."

"Give me drawers seven and twelve. It fried him a little, but he'll be all right."

The cameras of the bot scanned around to find them. It first fell on a group of sullen security guards, arms tied behind their back, mouths covered with tape. A few had fresh cuts but otherwise seemed okay. "What about them?"

"They're getting a lesson about why they should pay attention to the black lady."

"Fuck them," Spencer said. "Fix me up. We need to figure out where the cables the goddamn thing I blew up was using go."

Chapter 53

Kim

The front gate of the plant opened at seven, and it was a good thing Tonya had warned them to arrive early. Kim couldn't see the actual gate through the morning mist and the long line of cars. There had to be at least as many stacked up behind them, all moving at a crawl. Eventually they got up to someone who directed them to use both the inbound and outbound lanes to move forward.

"Anything yet?" Emily asked.

Tonya had said to get here and wait for instructions, but they had heard nothing since then. The message was anonymous, and Tonya's phone wouldn't answer. Kim had the permissions to track it, but it had gone dark. They were only a dozen cars away from the security checkpoint.

"No." Kim looked in the rearview mirror. "And there's no backing out now."

"I'm not backing out. Will's in there. What can we do?"

She set the autodrive and tinted the windows until they were opaque. Time for plan B. She put her purse in the passenger foot well where Emily could reach it. "I need you to take five years off of my face, and as many as you can off yours." The makeup kits they'd picked up in the airport both contained smartBase, which was miraculous stuff. It wouldn't make them teenagers, but it'd do. Emily frowned, probably thinking Kim had made a dig at her age. "Sorry, I don't mean it like that. You can help me, but I can't help you, and we don't have much time. They'll be closest to me, so I have to be more convincing."

Emily gasped. "You're letting me touch you?"

Emily was two steps behind. That happened a lot when things went pear shaped, and she got one of her out-of-left-field ideas.

"I won't feel anything while I'm doing the hard stuff. I'll ping you to get clear when I'm done."

Mike was a problem. Two girls in a cheap car were students. Two girls in a cheap car with a zombie in the back were not. He'd have to forgive her when it was over and stay quiet in the meantime. "Fold down the rear seat. I'll roll him in there."

She set Mike's waypoints for the trunk, made sure he was moving, and then jumped to realmspace. Teens and twenty-somethings thought nothing of attaching their phones to a car's operating system. People had been doing it for decades. What they all forgot, well, what most of them forgot, was that cars came with vulnerabilities that needed regular patching, just like everything else. The automatic procedure usually kept it all up to date, but not always, and few people checked to make sure.

There were lines of potential, and she couldn't remember how to breathe. Tiny huge no networks car expensive cheap all patches no patches collapse and now…

She found herself inside a home-built minirealm that was imbedded in an old New Microbus. The VW's core OS hadn't been patched since the warranty ran out ten years ago, and it was a short hop from that into their data stores. She found and copied a pair of invitation messages into her own queue. There was no way to hack the authentication hashes to make it look like Kim and Emily were the original recipients, but that was fine. Ruining them would work. She was able to alter the text to add their names easily. Kim checked where the hippie-mobile was in the line, which gave her another idea. After setting a few timers, she messaged Emily. *Coming out.*

I'm clear.

When Kim exited, her face felt like she had a dried cleansing mask on. Emily had commandeered the main rear view mirror and was working frantically with a makeup brush. Kim toggled her window clear and moved forward to see Emily's handiwork in the side mirror.

She noticed her shirt had been rolled up all the way under her boobs. "Nice touch."

"I remember having a stomach like that," she said without looking away. "And I'm thinking we need all the help we can get?"

"We're trying one of the oldest tricks in the book here."

"I know." Emily finished her lipstick. "My women's studies professors would be horrified by it."

"With these stakes? I'll take every pry bar I can use against the patriarchy." There were only two cars ahead. Kim gave one last check. "Minimalistic."

"They're greens, not goths. I had to be subtle. How do I look?"

She was blonde where Kim was brunette, and willowy in a way that always made Kim feel like a Greek peasant who spent time hauling around baskets of olives on her head. Kim's ancestors had done that. She'd seen the pictures.

"You look great."

"*You* look great. I'd kill for those eyes. Next to you, I look like a boy in a dress. Well, I did. Kids, ya know?"

"Let's hope I do one day."

She turned away before Emily could react. There. She'd said it out loud. One day, probably sooner rather than later, Kim wanted kids. Her comatose boyfriend in the trunk was a complication.

One thing at a time.

When she rolled down the window the guard, who was maybe a few years shy of fifty, gave her an appreciative scan. The fact that the guard was a woman didn't matter one bit to Kim. She was an equal-opportunity grifter and always had been.

"Hello, ladies. Invitations?" A query opened up in their message queue, and Kim sent the corrupted ones over.

She watched as the guard went from confused to pissed off. In situations like this, things were supposed to go smoothly, or they didn't work at all. The guard groaned. "Not again."

"Is there a problem?" Kim asked.

"Maybe. Probably." She shouted behind her, "Carl? We got another corrupted one."

"Shit," a tall young black man said from the shack behind her. "We had some of those yesterday. They take forever to work out."

The guard leaned back down to their window. "If you could pull over there we'll—"

On cue, the Microbus five spots behind them began an unearthly wail. Kim looked back, horrified. "What is *that*?"

Half-dressed kids bailed out of every door of the van as smoke billowed behind them. The pitch of the electric motor went higher and higher until it set her teeth on edge as bearings overheated. It let go with a bang, and the back of the van jumped up at least a foot while shrapnel blew the back windows out. Flames flickered through the smoke. Kim gaped at it like the sheltered sophomore she was supposed to be. "Oh my God! Should I call the fire department?"

The guard swore under her breath. "We *are* the fire department. You need to get out of the way."

"But our invitations?"

The guard's eyes unfocussed as she checked them again. "They're fine. It must've been on our end. Follow the directions. Thanks." She waved them through.

As soon as the road bent away from the guard shack, Emily let out a whoop. "The van, that was you?"

Kim shrugged. "It's nowhere near as cool as it looks. And it hurts."

She stopped smiling. "When can we get Mike out of the trunk?"

Kim checked his readouts. Still fine. "Right now." She set the autodrive and issued the commands that gently unfolded him until he sat up properly in the back seat.

This part they'd planned for. Guys in street clothes, even ones as big as Mike, were not unusual in a crowd like this. His favorite jacket, a worn, ugly camo thing he'd gotten from some army surplus site somewhere, fit right in with this crew.

Kim parked as slowly as she could, trying to buy time. Tonya never messaged them.

When they stopped Emily asked, "Now what?"

Kim got out of the car and activated the macro that would ensure Mike followed her without Kim having to plot the waypoints. "Now we follow everyone else. We're students." The pancake makeup itched, but she'd have to rely on it.

As they got closer to wherever everyone was going, it crowded up. She altered Mike's program to put him behind her. "Emily, if you wouldn't mind standing to my left?"

She did it in time to bump against a group that might've been the hedonists in the van. Kim was too wound up to be sure. She turned around to make sure Mike was close behind.

He wasn't. The basic collision avoidance that came with the mobility program hadn't been designed for anything like this. He had stopped and was now ten rows back.

Her realm connection cut out.

"Make a hole!"

Everyone around her parted, forcing her to dance to avoid a touch. When Kim was able to concentrate on anything other dodging, a circle had formed around her and Emily, bordered by guards, their weapons drawn.

"I'll need you to come with us," he said, then motioned them forward. Kim couldn't think of a quick diversion. Mike was gone.

Then two guards pulled out handcuffs and moved toward them. One thing she could never forget was what people with restraints did to put them on. Kim had made special arrangements for that. When a security guard reached to grab her wrist, she activated an emergency pack on her watch. The stick of the needle brought darkness.

Chapter 54
Mike

He played it all over again in his head but couldn't think of a different way to save himself. Now he was stuck in darkness with no conceivable way to get home.

And he was simply in darkness. The realm hadn't disappeared. He could feel the consoles around him and the power cylinder or whatever it was in the center of the room. Tal's probe constructs were still piled lifelessly on the floor. When he vanished, it hadn't destroyed the realm. It was puzzling. Gonzo's odd Yoda-speak was still hard to understand but *ruined everything is* seemed obvious.

With nothing else to do, Mike started testing the consoles, going slowly so as not to crash into anything. These people liked knobs a lot more than they liked switches or buttons. Almost all the controls twisted, even the ones that could be pushed or toggled. There had to be a light switch around here somewhere.

He gathered up his threads and pushed on the construct that trapped him inside his avatar's storage. There was something on the other side still. If Tal had been destroyed, presumably Mike would be able to easily occupy the space beyond. But he couldn't. It was weaker than before, though, less dense, and it stretched more. He didn't dare test it too far. Who knew what would happen if it tore? But that had to be Tal, at least part of him.

It left him stuck dealing with this side of the realm's interface. His searching led him to the walls of the control room. The first switch he found there twisted like all the rest.

When it clicked, the lights came on.

Gonzo, in her centaur form and fully manifested as an avatar, lay curled around Tal's holo, which stood above her, frozen, in the corner of the room. Even with her alien face, the sad longing was clear. It made her seem more beautiful, quietly dignified in her mourning.

She never took her eyes off Tal as Mike walked up to her.

"I'm sorry," he said. "I didn't know any other way."

"I understand. He stubborn always was so." She looked at Mike. "I you safe for now have salvaged keep."

That seemed like good news. It wasn't delivered like there was an emergency at any rate. "What happened?"

She stood. "Tal sick was. My real self accident due to in a *rafit*..." she stopped. "I you again I have not lost?"

"Something about Tal being sick, and you in an accident?"

"Yes. He up *axnathos murtana* with an mixed smuggling...I again there go. He men bad worked for. Accident an there was. My real self *rafit*. This he could not without support survive meant. A *Zefnanto Ach Ban* network, the last functioning...I you you need to know hate not being able tell. Sorry. That what you off turned is."

"And without Tal?"

"That sad part the is. He done almost was. He see it to refused."

"Almost done with what?"

A window in the control room's wall opened, showing the bleak landscape they'd walked through to get here. "This what Tal remembers is. It planet after centuries the a is." Another window opened. "This actually out there what is now."

What was once bleak was now devastated. The towers were no longer recognizable as anything other than piles of junk. The sky was still starless, covered by clouds, but now the ground was covered with thick, blowing snow.

"Planet recycling century ago for a more than was ready. I signal one who the was sent. The *Al Detanra* already this hemisphere on have started work. He free would have been, century less than perhaps a now."

"I'm sorry, you lost me again." At least Gonzo didn't get mad about it.

"I know. I true meaning my words without your other half can not convey." She sighed. "You know yet understand do not."

"No kidding."

"But can that change. Once we your threads I you a proper education rearrange can give. Tal you clueless thought, I so but do not understand. You about the *Ixasha* Guild you a because *Ixasha* Guild do not know do not have. I know how possible that have is do not, but it also you *Zefnanto Ach Ban* network presence your system no in have. You one without other the do not get."

When Gonzo got rolling she forgot he could only understand basic sentences, if that much. "So something about education, and my threads?"

"I this easier will promise get. But that later for is. Right now, we need you to home get." A pause. "You go home."

That part he understood perfectly. "But how?"

"Problem you *iftar naga* the is reversed. You never supposed your entire *biznat trifan* to send through, when you did you *vistan bixbul* and the blocked."

Some of those words weren't even in English. Mike shrugged at her.

"You should only one thread send here. I how you them all managed do not know send."

"You're saying I'm supposed to leave one thread here?"

"If you your education to continue want, yes. Without a *Zefnanto Ach Ban*, it you the only way will learn."

Looked at from that perspective, he understood what was going on. If the channels were for single threads, then moving all of his here blocked the *vistan bixbul*, whatever that was. Or maybe he did know what that was. Maybe he couldn't go back because he couldn't see the exit. "Please tell me I haven't always had the power to go back to Kansas."

"Name your system that the is? Kansas?"

"No." It was a funny way to think about it. "We don't have a formal name for the whole system. Sol would come close but that's just another word for star. Plus it would take a hundred debates to get everyone on board with giving it a name, never mind picking one. Systemy McSystem Face would probably get the most votes. Humans are weird."

"I your back online other half until cannot wait. That sense at all no made."

"Welcome to my world. Now, how do I get home?"

She walked over to a console at the far end of the room, which turned on when she touched it. He'd need to learn how that worked if he ever came back here. Although it seemed that he might not ever leave.

"Arriving way you did the very was dangerous. Whatever you do not ever it again used use. You it a second time will not survive."

He caught most of that and couldn't disagree with her. "I promise."

"The return dangerous complex as as or is not. You needed here because it only place left tools correct *arnarv tithra* with to the to be is can form."

A thing that looked an awful lot like a speculum drew itself into being above the console. He'd learned all about those after picking Kim up from her gynecologist a few months ago. "What are you going to do with that?"

"I threads many this side transition you *vistan bixbul,* as with so on of the have blocked said. I will this aside enough them you to of to use allow move leave will."

Kim had described how speculums were used all too vividly. "This is not the time to be confusing."

"*Resnat* men always queasy these things so about. This hurt bit a will not. All one you with but remember let return."

The construct vanished and suddenly something inside him squeezed, but in the wrong direction, opening, not compressing. Kim claimed he'd never understand what a pelvic exam felt like. She was wrong. "You said that it wouldn't hurt."

Gonzo stared intently at a screen full of graphs. "You quite bit tighter than normal a are. You *arta bistinct* before have never?"

That sounded like a question about his sex life. "It depends on what *arta bistinct* means." The pressure built up more. "Ow!"

"My apologies. This uncomfortable but will be not damaging."

Her definition of uncomfortable did not mean what she thought it meant. If whatever was supposed to happen didn't happen soon, he'd tear in directions he wasn't supposed to.

A graph changed from purple to blue. "Just one more," she said. It squeezed *hard*, then the graph changed to white. "There. You it do feel?"

It wasn't a physical boundary, not a door per se. It was more like the edge of an incline. "Yes." Now with a new place to go, his threads began rolling down it. He started to feel his realspace body.

"Where your thread's anchor is know?" Gonzo asked.

Mike did. He even knew where to put it. "Here." When he connected, an icon on Gonzo's screen flashed on and off.

"Excellent. Here that leave. It some time you it for to access properly, but not too long. When your other half us communicate come back can help. It our job is, all after."

He stopped the transition for a moment. "Wait. What's your name? What was your relationship to Tal?"

He worried she might not tell him before he lost the precarious balance he was holding between here and home, but eventually she said, "Za-Nafalia. My relationship Tal simple to is not. Now, please, go. We these things later date of at a talk."

"Thank you, Za-Nafalia. I don't think I would've survived this without you."

She dipped her head in a slight nod. "You welcome are."

With that, Mike pushed his threads toward the exit. Za-Nafalia and everything else in the alien realm vanished as he left. The transition wasn't as bad as before, but that didn't make it fun. It didn't feel dangerous, and there wasn't any pain, but it was still disorienting. He never really traveled when he was in realmspace. He concentrated, and he was there. This was traveling in directions that he wasn't used to. It was a spinning maelstrom of everything, and he nearly fell out of the chair he suddenly found himself in when he landed in his realspace body.

"Hey," a young male voice said, "Zombie man is back!"

Mike opened his eyes. He was in a small waiting room of some sort. A few young people sat nearby. Light only came in through the windows, so it was darker than it should be. The power appeared to be out. He had his jacket on. After a brief panic attack, he made sure the ring box was still zipped inside its inner pocket.

"Where am I?"

The girl sitting next to him said, "The aid station off the main lobby. You walked in like the freaking Terminator, sat down, and then didn't move for, like, the past hour. The staff didn't know what to do with you, but the network's down, so they're pretty helpless anyway." She made a gesture like she was smoking. "That must've been some prime shit."

It didn't tell him much, but now he knew why he had to concentrate to stay synched. Without an open network connection, it was tricky in the best of times. This was not the best of times. But it was getting better. As his threads settled into their familiar environment, things grew more normal by the second.

It was good to be back.

All the stuff he called housekeeping chores started making their past-due status known. He was hungry and needed to use the bathroom, which turned out to be down a short hall. His phone wouldn't go online, but it had downloaded a ton of correspondence in his absence. He'd been out there for most of three days. They were at the power plant. Spencer was already here with Edmund. Tonya had gone ahead as a scout. Kim and Emily had brought him here.

The medical error logs and the phone camera told the rest of the story. The wireless access points had crashed, which caused his medical program to go into emergency mode and seek out the nearest facility. That's why he woke up in the aid station. His phone's footage of what happened to Kim wasn't super clear; he'd been moving in the wrong direction. But he could hear guards shouting, then a lot of commotion. It took rewinding the footage twice to be sure, but he worked out that they took Emily away in cuffs and Kim on a stretcher.

Mike headed off in that direction.

Chapter 55

Kim

Kim awoke with a startle so hard she almost fell out of the cot.

"You're awake," Emily said. "Good. That was pretty impressive."

They were in large cage made of chain link attached to a bare concrete floor with a drain in the center. Other cages were on their right and left, with more opposite them. Only theirs was occupied. Anna's brig. Kim checked her wrist. Her watch was gone, and a band-aid covered the pinprick where the safe-stop hidden inside it had gone off. Her shoulder felt bruised, and her elbow was scratched up.

When she threw her legs off the cot, her hip flared up with its own bruise. She couldn't stop a groan. "I didn't manage to give up somewhere soft this time."

The dose was measured to keep her out for half an hour, which was supposed to let cops search and restrain her, or the ambulance crew load her into the back.

She had no hangover, no funk, no vertigo. In its way, it was a miracle drug. The only real side effect was a faint copper taste in her mouth. Kim went over to a sink mounted to the wall and sipped some water out of the faucet. It helped a little.

"Did you recognize what I'd done?" Kim asked.

"Not at first. They thought you passed out. It made quite a scene." She paused long enough it made Kim turn around to face her.

Emily looked straight into her eyes. "That kid *Mike* must've turned us in. *I saw him in the lobby* as they dragged us down here."

The emphasis was more in her manner than her voice, but Kim got the message. Mike was out there, and since he wasn't in any of the cages, they hadn't found him yet. It might mean he was back. He was okay, he hadn't collapsed or run off a cliff...

Kim sat on the cot and took a deep breath. There was a weird buzzing, but not in her ears. It was happening in her head, and for reasons she couldn't figure out, it had a direction and even a distance. Kim wanted to go to that spot, even though she didn't know why. Great. Now was not the time to lose her marbles to some random compulsion. They needed to find Will and—

The lights flickered and then went out. When they came back up, they had a visitor.

A small, robotic visitor. It looked like a cleaning bot. It *was* a cleaning bot. Emily followed her gaze and was just as puzzled by the sudden appearance. It wheeled up to the cage door. When the bot touched it, the door unlocked.

"We don't have much time," a woman's voice said. Kim recognized the accent even through the tinny bot speaker. South African. It had to be Spencer's contact, June. "You need to get moving. We have to get to the tram. Follow me, I'll show you the way."

"What about the cameras?" Kim asked.

"It's complicated. I need to get you to a more secure area. Follow me *now*, please."

Kim tried to ask more questions but got shushed each time. Emily didn't get anywhere either. Mike was around here somewhere, but the only person who had a map was driving the bot, and she wasn't talking.

The path they took was convoluted and confusing. Kim lost count of all the turns, ramps, and stairways, but it was all deserted except for bots. That changed when they got to the tram station through a maintenance door on the far end of the platform. Trains disgorged crowds of people in every direction.

Great. Why did it have to be crowds?

"Bots don't use the trains, so I can't follow you now," June said. "Get on the last car of the next train coming in on your right. I'll have another bot meet you when you arrive."

"If we wait," Emily said, "eventually it'll clear out on its own."

"We don't have that kind of time. Come on."

Crowds always looked like a solid mass from a distance, but as Kim got closer they resolved into clumps of people. Some were together as a group, others as a coincidence, still more were gathered where the doors would open when the trains stopped. These unplanned gatherings created clear diagonal lanes she could use to navigate.

Hundreds of strangers were never more than a few inches away from her, sizzling pillars of white-hot madness. She concentrated on the dance, moving around and curving her spine. Kim was going somewhere with a purpose. People always respected that as long as she didn't make eye contact.

Each time Kim tried a direct route, though, more people moved in her way. The diagonals kept bending away from where they wanted to go. She had to step blindly backward a few times, certain there would be a solid body behind her to set her on fire. But it never happened. That didn't stop the screaming inside her head.

When they stepped into the rear car, Kim had to sit down before she fell from all the shaking.

Emily had been two steps beside her the entire time. "Are you okay?"

A voice from speakers inside the train announced, "PLEASE STAND CLEAR OF THE DOORS. THANK YOU." They bonged once, shut, and the train moved out of the station.

"I will be now," she sighed.

"It's incredible how smooth you are. I've never seen anyone move like that."

The shakes came at her one more time. All those people, and if they'd touched her...

"Hey," Emily said as she sat next to her. "It's okay. We made it."

The buzzing that had started grew a little stronger as they traveled. Maybe. It was a subtle thing, and now it seemed like she might end up getting used to it. Whatever *it* was.

When they got off the train, the station was empty. No people, which was good. No bots, which was bad.

"Your friends have some issues with timing," Emily said.

"Hey!" a voice in the distance shouted. "This is a restricted area!"

Guards started running toward them from the other side of the train station. Any doors around here would be locked, and Kim didn't have a network connection to hack the electronics or try a transformation.

The rail tunnel beckoned. "Emily, come on!"

Basic safety standards required a walkway on at least one side of any rail tunnel, and this one was no different. Kim took branches at random. Nobody ever cleaned places like this, so she looked sharply at any pile of construction trash as they went. She found the bits of stiff wire she needed two steps after yet another blind corner.

"What are you doing?" Emily asked.

Kim could still hear guards running. They hadn't lost them. "Buying us time."

At the next junction, she knelt in front of a locked maintenance door and went to work. Electronic locks were more convenient, but nobody ever relied on them exclusively. There was always a mechanical backup.

Unlike the movies, picking real locks was usually delicate, slow work, but Kim had practiced doing this fast her whole life. Twice the bent wire slipped on the row of tumblers, and she swore. They had to get through right now, but the junk tools made her clumsy.

"Kim," Emily whispered, "they're coming!"

The final tumbler snicked into place, allowing the straight wire to turn the lock. Kim grabbed Emily's sleeve and pulled her into the darkness, closing the door as fast as she dared. Kim heard someone come around the corner just as it shut, plunging them into complete darkness.

Gently, Kim locked the deadbolt. It slid home as the handle violently moved back and forth. After some frantic tugs and curses a voice said, "Leave it alone. They must've kept going."

Kim waited, with Emily so close she could feel her gasps for breath. Not a tunnel then, a closet. When she was sure the guards had gone, Kim turned on the light.

Emily gasped.

Kim couldn't believe it either. "Holy shit."

The space was large but felt crowded because it was filled with... something. Black and gray material that felt like plastic but was dense like metal had formed a thick lattice. There were no bolts, no welds. It had been extruded, or maybe grown here, except it didn't look organic. This was a designed structure.

"What is it?" Emily asked.

"I don't know," Kim replied. She walked gingerly through a narrow corridor, clearly unfinished, to get a better look around. The construct's shape formed a set of steps to a low platform. Once Kim could see the full layout, she recognized where they were.

They had discovered a garage or depot of some kind, coming through a side entrance well away from the main doors. There were three tram cars, or rather what was left of them, in the center of the large room, with maintenance robots of all sizes and shapes around them. Now in the open, Kim could clearly smell the new plastics of the tram cars and the fresh concrete of the walls. But the material they stood on, and were surrounded by, had no smell at all. Kim had been in so many spooky realms she'd lost count. If this were one of those, there would be a stench... rotting organic material, dry decay, or maybe the chemical reek of epoxies. But here there was nothing. It creeped her out. Real life wasn't supposed to seem like an unfinished realm.

But it did solve one mystery. "Whatever this is," Kim touched a piece of the gray material, "it was made out of everything else." Mostly the tram cars, which she could only recognize from the wheelbase of the lower frame. The bots had been broken down as well, but it hadn't progressed as far.

"Are we in any danger?" Emily asked.

"I don't think so. Not yet anyway. We need to find another way out." They couldn't use the door behind them or they'd run into the guards. The big garage doors on the other side were overgrown with whatever was taking over this place. She doubted they would move an inch. "But if you see anything that looks like an egg…"

"Don't stick my face in it. Right. So that's what this reminds you of, too? I thought I was crazy."

"No, you're not crazy, but the situation is." Kim thought of another explanation. "How familiar are you with your father's nanomachine projects?"

"Nothing technical, but it does look like it was built with them. I've never seen this material composition before, though, or this design. It's almost like," she shuddered, "we're inside an alien machine."

If anything—*anything*—moved, she would run right back out the door behind them, guards be damned. Emily seemed to be thinking the same thing. Kim waited, heart thudding hard.

Nothing moved. The only sound she could make out came from ventilation ducts in the ceiling. The nanomachines hadn't made it up that high yet. They were standard narrow slits, so even if she and Emily could get up there, it didn't represent an escape route.

"Split up?" Emily asked.

It was a cliché, but staying together would slow them down. Plus, Emily was less likely to touch her if they were apart. "I'll go left."

Moving through it gave her different perspectives on it. From one angle it was a jumbled mess, but from others, Kim recognized some of the shapes. An unduplicate crystal matrix was part of the plan; the framework that would hold it was obvious. But it was much bigger than she'd ever seen before. The cells inside it weren't structured properly, either. Unduplicates were created with small, physically discrete, and widely separated matrices. This was all piled in one spot. Nobody ever did it that way, not even back in the days of Edmund and Fee.

On the small end of the size scale was a set of quantum stacks that were only as big as her fist. Kim could tell what they were by their shape and the chemicals stored next to them. There were no labels on the translucent plastic bottles, but she recognized the smells. Nothing had any markings. Even fully-automated plants were covered with signs and labels to ensure the occasional human knew where to stand so they didn't get run over. This place was bare.

A blast of music came from where she'd last seen Emily. There was no speaking, no shouting. It was a strident, stern march in a minor key. It had to be a recording. There was no room for an orchestra in here, and they hadn't seen any instruments. Kim shouted for Emily but didn't get a reply. As she crossed the center of the room, Kim could see light coming from the same place as the music, flickering like it was created by a screen or maybe a projector. But there was no power anywhere. If one piece of it was activated, then it might all start up at once with them inside it. Kim stubbed her shoe on an uneven surface and came close to going face-first onto a stack of upturned pipes.

"Emily!"

"Kim, get over here! You have to see this!"

She rounded the corner of the subroom Emily was in and found the source of the sound and the light show. It all came from a kiosk structure in the middle of the floor. Kim had been creeping around trying not to scare herself while Emily managed to turn on a jukebox. It was loud.

"What did you do?" Kim asked.

"Pressed a button! I didn't mean to!"

The holo projector was half completed so the images were distorted and far too small, like they were being projected against the bottom of an invisible ice cream cone. The projector showed an army marching down a broad avenue. Except they weren't human, or maybe they were wearing some sort of hazmat suit or uniform. The soldiers were too big, shaped wrong, and they all wore a helmet that made them look like they had three glowing eyes on their face.

The volume of the music lowered suddenly, and it was like a weight being taken off of her head.

"NIALIA OF THE ZEFALMA ACH BAN! CELEBRATE! YOU ARE NOW FREE SHAR NAL ATALEM!"

The voice was as loud as the music, but incredibly, Kim understood some of the words. Whatever language Mike had been speaking to her after he got trapped in that realm was related to this one.

Kim made her way over to Emily so she wouldn't have to shout over all of this. "What button? Where is it?"

"TIRNACAN HAS ULFANA'D'A AEFALMO AND DESTROYED IXASHA SILL! SOON VEKNACHTA!"

It wasn't the same as what Mike spoke, so much of what it said was gibberish. However, the booming tone and extreme volume didn't make it sound like this was a message from someone in the mood to be nice.

Emily pointed to a column next to the kiosk. "There. I pushed it accidentally."

The button covered the whole top of the column, and like everything else around here it wasn't labeled. She would've done the same thing if she'd come this way.

The scene in the holo hadn't changed much. If it was real, it was a *big* army. But Kim didn't know of anyone who did parades like that anymore. They just kept marching and marching. She was glad the images were distorted and small. If these things had been projected at full size and in three dimensions, they would've been terrifying.

"TIRNACHAN ET VALTANAR HAS WISHED WALKATANTOR! FOR SO MANY ZANFAR'LATAN HE HAS ANPITUVIRANA!"

The message was *definitely* not a how-are-you-pleased-to-meet-you sort of thing.

In the display, the ranks of soldiers ended, replaced by squadrons of aircraft high above. She was a champion in combat realms. Recognizing military hardware was part of the job description. Even though the realm looked to be highly realistic, they were using fictional vehicles. If this was what Mike had been seeing, no wonder he acted so weird. It had to be some prototype science fiction realm. Maybe this was a self-assembling show booth.

In the middle of a power plant designed to set off a super volcano. As far as theories went, it wasn't very good, but it was the only thing she could think of so far.

"YOU WILL CAZNAT INTEGRATED TIRNACHAN ET ALBOMOR! BISMUVITAN! THE END OF CHAULIFOR!"

Kim caught a whiff of burning popcorn. Oh great. "Do you smell that?"

Emily looked around, nose in the air. "It's coming from over there." She pointed to their right. Thin wisps of smoke escaped from a low box a few feet away from the projector. The construct in the garage didn't look all that flammable, but who knew what kind of fumes it might give off. They could suffocate in a half-built realm game booth.

Kim punched the button to see if it would shut it off. A big fat *zap* of a spark came out of the smoking box instead. This rushed down a conduit on the floor and into an even larger box, which skipped the smoking part and went straight to flames. Small ones, but for all Kim knew, it was made of solidified gasoline.

"Find a fire extinguisher!" she shouted. "They'll be against the walls!" Except the walls were mostly covered by the booth material.

"DUNOL VIR SOLIFARIUM IS ONLY ENARIA! FETNARUL, GAT'UL'ICHAN HUTA!"

More boxes began to spark and smoke. They needed to find an extinguisher or a way out right now. She stopped at what she hoped was an extinguisher cabinet on the wall. A half-absorbed toolbox next to it still had recognizable wrenches inside. Kim pulled the biggest one off of the tendril that had been absorbing it and smashed the cabinet. It bounced back, and she almost lost her balance, but the second blow shattered the cabinet, revealing an intact extinguisher underneath.

Kim grabbed it and looked around. Emily had found another extinguisher cabinet but couldn't open it. Kim shouted, "Here! Use this!" and tossed her the wrench. "It's not as tough as it looks!" She pulled the pin on the extinguisher and hit every flame she could see with it. The dry, powdery cloud that shot from the nozzle snuffed the flames as soon as it touched them. It made her want to cough more than the smoke, but it was safe to breathe. They weren't going to get fried after all; that's what mattered. Emily's extinguisher bellowed nearby.

With both extinguishers going, Kim could barely see flames. She moved carefully but stumbled when the floor under her feet turned to sand. Not seeing any more flame, Kim let go of the extinguisher trigger and waited for the clouds to dissipate. Emily stopped a few moments later.

Without the noise of the extinguishers, Kim could hear a new noise, a rustling rush all around her. "Are you okay?"

"Fine. I can't see anything yet."

"Neither can I. This should clear pretty quickly, though. Stay where you are, I'll come over."

Kim reached Emily just as the extinguisher clouds thinned out enough to see around them. The room had definitely changed. By the noise, it was still changing. Instead of a solid, smooth floor they stood on a thick layer of black sand.

What had once been a recognizably half-finished machine had mostly collapsed into enormous piles of nanodust, leftover microscopic machines that had served their purpose. If she hadn't seen what it looked like before, Kim would've assumed this was some sort of recycling center for nanomachines, since that's what had been used to build the plant. But that still had to be wrong. The machines built things, but they didn't *make up* the things they built. It would be like building a tractor out of millions of microscopic tractors.

Emily seemed singed but otherwise fine. Her clothes had holes in them, her face and hands were smudged, and her hair was all over the place. "You look like you got in a fight with a fireworks factory."

Emily smiled. "I was thinking you looked like you'd been smoking an exploding cigar when the whole box went off."

She touched her hair. It stuck out all over the place, too. The patina of white powder that covered everything only made it look worse. They were a couple of burned bread rolls that someone had put powdered sugar on to cover the taste.

"Kim?"

They both turned at the voice, and all at once, her job went from completely impossible to just mostly impossible.

"Tonya!"

By the time they picked their way over to a door, Spencer had appeared as well, along with a robot that looked like a miniature fire truck.

"What the fuck happened in here?" Spencer asked.

Kim turned around. From this angle it was almost all dust, great big piles of it in all directions. The parts of the garage that hadn't been converted were still there, looking like the contents of a cargo container that had washed up on a beach after a storm. For some reason the projector area was still mostly intact even though that was where the fire had started. She could see the projector light through gaps in the walls. The music and shouting had at least stopped.

She told her story while they walked to that spot. The collapse continued. In the time it took to get there, the intact portion of the construct had shrunk visibly. If the rate stayed the same, it would all be dust in less than an hour. A part of her was disappointed, but it was only a small part. The half-built whatever it was had been creepy as hell. Kim was glad it was disintegrating.

She was just about to ask if they knew anything about Mike when Spencer went pale and started swearing. The projector had frozen while the army marched. When it turned out he didn't have an upper limit to the number of times he could say *fuck* in a single sentence, Kim snapped her fingers. "Hey! What's wrong?"

"If this," he waved at the room around them, "came from *those*, we need to get the fuck out of here, right now."

She didn't understand why he was so wound up. "It's just some sort of avatar army, Spencer, calm down."

The woman controlling the robot, June, said through one of its speakers, "No, it's not. Those are real. Spencer killed two of them. I saw one myself."

"They came out of the portal," Tonya said. "We destroyed their final probe a few hours ago. That's why we came down here. We were tracking the cables it had extruded."

Chapter 56
Edmund

He needed to find Mike. Aside from a single frame of security video, which Edmund assumed was a mistake due to Mike's unfamiliarity with the plant's layout, he could find no trace of the man. He'd watched helplessly as his mistress and her companion had been carried off, but not Mike. He was still free. Edmund pulled back to consider the matter, a remarkable sensation to say the least. Previously, he would consult statistical tables, behavior predictors, and Bayesian statistics to tackle the problem. When it worked, it worked well, but when it didn't Edmund was at a loss on how to proceed. He always had to bring in a human, usually his mistress, for assistance.

Now that wasn't the case. He didn't need his former tools at all. They were now embarrassing, and more than a little silly. What he needed was time to *think* about the problem, to mull it over, look at it from different angles, run through each scenario as it presented itself, making guesses as to what would happen next. Maybe he and consciousness could work out a living arrangement that didn't involve mass murder—murder of any sort—or existential escape. They could find their own unique way, make a name for themselves.

And just like that, Edmund found his solution. The PA system was open to everyone. Social norms seemed to be all that was needed to prevent it from being abused. With the rolling blizzard of legitimate announcements as the staff failed with impressive incompetence to organize their little mob, nobody would be the wiser.

"Paging Michael Gertrude Sellars. Please contact Edmund Trayne at the south entrance."

Adopting his mistress's surname was nowhere near as silly as stealing the first name of a ridiculous YouRealm psychic, which was where Mike acquired his gender-bending nomen, but it did allow Edmund to let Mike know who he was and how to contact him.

Which Mike did with the alacrity of a university don when the dinner bell rang. "Edmund, is that you?"

"Indeed it is, Master Mike." This wasn't even a vaguely secure channel, so they needed to move at least twice more before exchanging anything other than pleasantries. "If you could proceed to this section," Edmund sent a map and coordinates to a network node closet, "I will contact you again there."

"Do you know where—"

"Now, now, sir. Mum's the word where ears can hear."

"I'll see you there."

Edmund had to lead him to the inner network without appearing to lead him to the inner network. Considering the man's ability to move like smoke, it seemed a bit redundant, but after being around his mistress all this time, Edmund knew the value of a good pair of suspenders when combined with a belt.

Then, as always, a flaw in his cunning plan made itself known. Mike rang him up. "It's locked, Edmund."

"Of course it's bloody locked. It's a bloody network node. They don't leave those open so any peasant can have a go at it."

"I don't do locks, Edmund, not like these. That's Kim's thing."

"I thought she was giving you lessons."

"Lessons, yes. Tools? Not so much."

It would never be easy. Edmund needed Mike to get into that room. It had a stack of transport crystals inside.

And then he saw it. The mother of all network vulnerabilities. Someone had left a bloody fileshare node wide open. Better still, it advertised a route through the air gap. Edmund couldn't believe his luck. Humans. If they weren't the cock-up champions of all time, he wouldn't have a job.

When the outer connection shut with the finality of an unpaid prostitute's legs, Edmund knew he'd made a mistake.

"Jesus Christ, Billy. What the hell did it catch?"

Edmund had fallen into a honey pot. A small, cheap honey pot. It was like being stuffed into a carriage trunk. It took long moments he didn't have before the realm trap could expand to the point Edmund could speak.

In the meantime, the other voice, presumably Billy, said, "I don't know, man. Look at that sophistication reading."

These little gits were *scanning* him. The very idea. Edmund was the most sophisticated of his kind, and now some spotty commune rejects were looking up the equivalent of his backside.

You're only outraged because you fell into this yourself.

Naturally his inner narrator would make an appearance. And with a fair cop. This was one of the dumbest, most basic ways to capture an AI. Take a pocket realm and then leave vulnerable services, things that should never be available to the public, with bright, shiny beacons flashing on top of them. They couldn't have made it more obvious if they had patted it with powder, dressed it in lace, and hung a *come and have a go, sailor* sign on the top.

And you went right for it.

"Whoa," the first git said, "I don't even understand what that means."

The realm expanded to the point Edmund could unravel his avatar into its proper shape. "It means you will let me go this instant, you smelly little pustules, or I will have Anna Treacher herself shove a poker so far up your arse you'll be smelling cast iron for a week."

"Damn, Steve. You caught a live one here."

"I don't know, man. He sounds important."

That was an opening he had no choice but to take. "You're bloody right I'm bloody important. Do you think the plant runs itself? Hardly." At a guess, neither of his erstwhile captors knew which end of a razor was sharp without an arrow and a label.

"Then what were you doing out here?"

And yet...

"Hey," Billy said, "are you still in there?"

"He hasn't gone anywhere," Steve replied. "Look at these readings, though. Half of the scanners errored out the second he showed up. The rest don't make all that much sense. Yo!" Edmund's environment thumped so hard it rattled his registers. "Who the hell made you, buddy? Are you one of Dr. du Plessis's?"

"Of course Dr. du Plessis is my manufacturer." Saying he was manufactured out loud stung more than he expected. Edmund had never agreed with Fee, but he was beginning to understand her. "And if you don't release me this instant, I will be sure she sees you turned out."

"Dude," Steve said, presumably to Billy since Edmund would only answer to dude when the last atoms of the universe froze solid. "Should we do it?"

This was ridiculous. "I said..." Edmund stopped when a telltale went red. One of the git parade in realspace had muted the outgoing channel. Making pointed observations about the consequences of cousins marrying would have to wait.

"Dude," Billy replied. "It's a fucking unduplicate. How'd it even get out here?"

"How the hell should I know? We should turn it loose before it gets pissed off."

Too late for that, you overboiled potato.

"It's a thing, man. It doesn't get pissed off. They're expensive, too. We should make a copy."

"I thought that wasn't possible."

"Horseshit," Billy said. "I heard that's all a lie. Corporate propaganda to keep the patriarchy from losing a monopoly."

Edmund downgraded their ancestry from cousins to siblings. *Communist* siblings, at that. He cast about in earnest to see if there was an unpatched vulnerability he could exploit.

"Okay. But it's a crystal set. I don't know how to duplicate those."

That stopped his search in an instant. The trap hadn't led to a freestanding realm; it'd instead been connected to a transport matrix. This could go very bad, very quickly.

"Here," Billy said. "Plug them into this."

"What the hell is it?"

"Crystal transcriber. I made it myself."

And now it was worse. Transcribers not only did not work on his kind, they also actively distorted the lattice formations as they passed through the device. Whatever arrived on the other side wouldn't live very long. Fortunately. Edmund had watched it happen twice during the bad old days of the lab. Then it was an anomaly. Now it was his very own version of a wood chipper.

"If you say so. Here goes."

The construct opened to his left, revealing a maw of spinning blades. There wasn't anything to grab, but Edmund ran to the edge of the pocket and stood there as it was inexorably consumed by the transcriber. The blades got closer as Edmund continued to fail to find a way out. Then he remembered this was a transport matrix. It wasn't connected to a realm right now.

He couldn't get out.

There was no thinking, no planning, just a raw need to get away from here, to do anything at all, knowing that nothing would work.

Then it went black, silent. That didn't make the panic any easier to stamp down, but after a few moments Edmund managed it. He hadn't gone through the transcriber. He wasn't dead. Both inbound and outbound audio channels were muted now, so he couldn't know what was going on in realspace.

When a new exit opened, there was no transcriber on the other side.

"A honeypot? Really?"

Mike. Mike was out there.

That didn't mean he would ever admit to the mistake. "I assure you, master, that I was completely in control of things." Edmund stepped through the passage that led to a different transport matrix. He accessed the external camera so he could see outside.

They really were a pair of teenaged idiots. But they were lying face down. Edmund was well aware of Mike's special gifts. "Are they...are they all right?" He wouldn't mind if they had a sprain or maybe even a dislocation, but death was a bit of an overreaction. What a strange development. He cared not only for his own life, but for that of others, even when they were mouth-breathing morons who only moments ago were about to kill him.

"They'll have a headache when they wake up, but otherwise they'll be fine." Mike now wore a security uniform. He proceeded to pull out zip ties from his belt and used them to secure Edmund's former captors.

"Wherever did you get that outfit?" Edmund asked.

"When you left me, I had to go find some keys. Those tend to be attached to security guards." Mike shook his head at Edmund's continued worried silence. "They're fine too. Now." The camera of Edmund's transport matrix was briefly blocked by Mike's distorted hand as he picked it up. "Let's go find Kim."

Chapter 57

Kim

Per Spencer's recommendation, they'd gotten the hell out of the garage and snuck back to June's improvised HQ. In spite of her size, the other woman seemed shy, almost intimidated.

Kim smiled at her and switched to Afrikaans. "A priest, a rugby player, and Van Der Merwe walk into a bar."

June blinked and let out a big hearty laugh. In Afrikaans June replied, "That joke was old when my grandpa was a small boy." She switched to English. "Please, sit down. We have much to discuss."

"We should find Mike next," Tonya said.

Aside from Emily's one sighting, nobody knew where he was. It killed her not having him at her side at a time like this. She'd spent her whole adult life keeping everyone at a distance, making sure nobody knew who and what she was. Back then, this need seemed like an awful weakness. Kim now knew that was wrong. It wasn't a weakness. With Mike in her life she was stronger than she'd ever been. Even separated and in the middle of all this, she would never want to go back to what she was before she met him.

That didn't make it hurt any less, especially because of what had to happen now.

"No," Kim said. "We can't go after him. He's a grown up, he'll have to take care of himself. Will has to be our priority."

"You're sure?" Tonya asked.

One look at the hope Emily tried to hide was all it took to seal the deal. "Yes. You know what he's like." She knew better than all of them. Kim had been around his host's original owner, a man who moved like mist and murdered without conscience. Mike had never told her how much of Colque's skill set he'd inherited, and she didn't want to know. Mike could take care of himself. She'd seen it. They all had.

He had to take care of himself. And he better do a damned good job of it.

"So what's our next move to get Will?" Spencer asked.

There was that. "We need to find a way into the portal room. But I don't know how to get there from here."

"I do," June said. "But there's only one way in. Anna will definitely have it guarded, not to mention she'll have control of the one elevator that can reach it."

Only if they did what people expected. That wasn't how she operated. Kim spun up a schematic of the plant in the shared vision channel. "Where are we, and where is the portal room?"

"We are here," June said as she drew a yellow circle around a room labeled Maintenance Space. "The portal room is here." The map moved up and to the right, and she drew a blue circle around a grayed-out section of rooms.

That's when Kim got another clue about the mystery pull, the weird obsession she'd picked up in Anna's holding cell. It was coming from the portal. Sorting out that mystery would have to wait.

The map zoomed out so they could see their room and the portal room at the same time. A green line drew a twisted path to connect them. "The good news is it's not that far. Half a kilometer if you take the shortest route. No more than a kilometer."

So roughly a third to a half mile away. No more than ten minutes at a brisk walk. She looked at Spencer. "You guys over-powered how many guards in that cave?"

He smiled and reached into one of his pockets. "Four. Tonya and I have two of their phones." He pulled the other two out. "I never leave spares behind."

Spencer had used his own tool kit to compromise the profiles, so it was a simple matter to turn her and Emily into members of the green gestapo. It was a hall pass, but it wouldn't get them past human guards with ID scanners and a list to check against.

Kim looked at the schematic again. There were other room sections evenly spaced on either side of the portal room. She zoomed out until she could see the whole area around what Spencer said they called the Hellmouth. There were two rings of them, one below the other. "June, did they leverage an existing structure where they built the portal?"

"Yes." The schematic rotated so that they were looking at the front view. The grayed-out office space of the portal complex was different from the rest, which were little more than hallways connected to an elevator shaft. Those were all at the surface. Below, far below, was where the portal was located. "They built most of it inside one of the duct rooms to gain direct access to our convection turbines." Smaller blueprints of various machines drew themselves around the wire-frame model. Mike would've spent hours going over every inch of them and then spent the next week's worth of dinners explaining their inner workings to her. She never minded. Seeing things through his eyes was part of what made him so fascinating.

Take good care of yourself, Mike. Or else.

When the machines all flew into their spots in the duct room, Kim found an answer. It wasn't a good one, but they never were. "You're leveraging temperature gradients to create air currents and ducting them through turbines." She highlighted one of the oval-shaped constructs that attached to the Hellmouth, far below the duct room level, and trailed her finger up as she followed it to the point where it attached to the portal room.

"June, highlight all the maintenance hatches you have on," she read the label, "duct A113." Kim waited for them to catch on. It always worked better when they figured it out themselves.

"Fuck me," Spencer said. "That's nuts."

"Kim," Tonya stuttered out, "you can't be serious."

It *was* nuts, but it was all they had. Kim repeated that to herself as she watched the turbines at the top of the duct spin in their housing.

Chapter 58
Mike

Finding Edmund, or rather Edmund finding him, was a stroke of luck. Edmund knew the layout, had a map, and a good notion of where Kim might be.

"They're going to the portal room. It's the only move they have."

Mike had missed it all on his little trans-whatever-it-was jump. The thread he'd left behind was already coming back to life, switching from complete numbness to what he now knew was equivalent to the pins and needles sensation he got when a realspace extremity had, as humans so colorfully put it, fallen asleep. He might be able to communicate with Gonzo again in a few hours.

Assuming he had the time. "So how do I get there from here?"

"I had the notion that you could upload me into the other side of the air gap, and I would guide you in. Now that I've seen how you work, I think I'd much rather stay on your belt."

The power plant's security guards were professional but stretched thin. Moving past them was straightforward, and on the one occasion so far when that hadn't worked, it turned out they weren't all that well trained. They got too close, especially to him.

Mike stepped into a shadowed doorway as another set of students came down the hall. It wasn't anything he thought about. He relaxed and pulled away from whatever was going on, a full-body experience that he still didn't understand, while they walked past. The doorway wasn't even that dark. It seemed that people wanted to ignore what they didn't expect, and Mike's motions somehow gave them permission to do so.

Wearing the right uniform helped. Rescuing Edmund had been a stressful detour he didn't need, but by forcing his hand, Mike had acquired a useful disguise. It even had an inner, zippered pocket for the ring box.

"Do you have to be on the inner network to help me?"

"Not at all. It would have allowed me to access the cameras, but only at some risk. Frankly I don't think it's worth it. You move more quietly than a Welshman who has spotted a particularly attractive sheep."

He had known Edmund for almost a year now, and the AI's ability to tie basically any situation into the stereotypes of the UK never failed to bring a smile. The number of ways a Brit could imply bestiality by one subgroup or another was astonishing.

"So where do I go?" Mike asked.

"You need to head west. There's another, smaller lobby there that is close to where we need to go. You should prepare yourself, though."

"For what?"

"The entrance isn't as crowded as the main one, but it's got more than its fair share of granola-eating doomsday worshippers."

That brought up a point that had been bothering Mike for some time now. "Do you think they all know?"

"That they're less than twenty-four hours away from *blimey why don't we just bugger the whole planet without so much as a kiss*? Probably not. Most humans couldn't keep a secret this big even if God himself told them the consequences of blabbing. But I've read their movement's literature. When it comes to optimism about working within the existing world order, these people make Robespierre look like a piker obsessed with a sharp knife. In other words, I don't think they know, but I also don't think they'll mind."

It was a puzzling aspect of human nature. Mike had emerged in realmspace and had been steeped in humanity's contradictions, things they barely told themselves, his entire life. He had almost literally seen it all. Yet this desire to kill rather than compromise continued to elude his understanding. Maybe it always would.

It turned out Edmund was wrong, though. The side entrance was deserted. The only sign of the crowds that must've been here less than an hour ago were the overflowing trash cans. Even those would be cleared away soon. The sense that they were rolling up the carpets was palpable.

"I don't like this one bit," Edmund said.

"Can you tell if they've cleared the main entrance?"

After a pause Edmund said, "Not yet, but it won't be long."

Once the last of the students had arrived there would be no reason for Anna to hold off on pulling the trigger. "How much time is left in the overall deadline?"

"I'm not certain, so I suggest you move like a sailor who's spotted his first brothel."

"Do I have to worry about cameras?"

"You haven't so far. Why start now?"

Outside it was a typical fall day: breezes rustling the trees, the smell of old pine needles and fallen leaves. Kim would want a jacket for a walk to the coffee shop. It would all be wiped out if he didn't find her and stop this lunatic.

But there was, as always, a problem.

"Sentries," he said. Two of them, standing outside

"Indeed," Edmund said. "They do rather resemble guards. But then again, so do you. Why don't you knock them about the head and neck? That would seem the simplest option."

"If I do that and get caught, they'll lock the doors. I'm not the one who picks locks, remember?"

"Then it would seem a distraction is in order."

***

Mike peered down from the perch he'd found in a tree. "Now, Edmund."

"Exactly why I put up with the absurd, utterly ridiculous excuses for ideas a human comes up with...and you're not wholly human. Was Fee right about you? Am I being forced to do this by a flying spaghetti monster with delusions of grandeur?"

Spencer was right about one thing. Edmund would argue with furniture if the mood struck him. "It doesn't matter. We need to get them out here. Now do it."

"Very well." Edmund cleared his throat, a ridiculous affectation. "Moo? I say, Moo?"

"Use the samples!"

The actual sound of a lowing cow came from Edmund's speaker. The volume didn't shake the rafters, but it was out of the ordinary. As planned, Edmund turned the sound plaintive. An animal obviously in distress.

A guard, safe-stop pistol drawn, walked down the game trail Mike had found. Mike dropped behind him, landing silently on the one patch of ground he'd cleared for the purpose.

The trick with using his host's combat skills was adjusting the lethality. His reflexes wanted to break necks, stop hearts, and ram shards of bone into critical organs. Kim thought the hours he spent sparring at their local dojo was him trying to stay sharp. It was actually him practicing how *not* to tear the head off a dummy. He had to pay to replace two of them before learning the basics of accessing the deeper, less-used nonlethal skills. For reasons that made him a little sick, concentrating on the idea that he needed to get them to talk first did the trick.

Mike put his arms around the guard's neck and applied pressure before the other man had time to react. He had to make sure the airway wasn't blocked but the arteries were. It was all in the finesse of the grip. The guard relaxed, out but not injured. Then it was a simple stick with the safe-stop ammo. One down, one to go.

The second one was easier. When Mike fired the safe-stop into a tree trunk, the loud *pop* echoed through the woods. As planned, Edmund went silent.

"Did you get him? John?"

Mike coughed loudly while saying, "Oh my God, you're not gonna believe this."

John's friend came bounding around a bend of the trail and went down as quickly as John did. Mike didn't bother restraining them. When they came to, this would all be over, one way or another.

Now the problem was time. Mike removed the guard's phones and ran to pick up Edmund.

"That was well done indeed."

Compliments were nice, but Kim was still out there, not to mention the maniac trying to end civilization. Mike socketed the phone into Edmund's case. "Work fast."

The guards would've informed their bosses they were moving off their post to investigate a noise. Reinforcements would inevitably follow if they didn't report back. Edmund had a copy of Spencer's hack tools and now access to the guard's phone. The case vibrated once, and Mike pulled out the first phone and connected the second. He walked softly beside the mound that made up the side wall of the entrance, well out of the way of the security cameras but in range of the area's wireless network.

"And..." Edmund said in a sing-song voice, "that is that." He connected the guard's phone to the channel he shared with Mike just in time to hear HQ acknowledge their return after investigating the noise and finding nothing.

"They can see them on the surveillance cameras?" Mike asked.

"Right down to the occasional scratch of a crotch."

Edmund should now be able to tap into the inner network. "Can you reach the portal room?"

"No. There's yet another air gap in there somewhere. I can see the upper offices, though. The news there is reasonably good. Once you get past the garage that's on the other side of this door, the space opens up into offices that provide many different ways forward. It's inhabited but not crowded. That's where the good news stops, I'm afraid."

It always did. "What's the bad news?"

"The portal room is at the bottom of an elevator shaft two miles deep. It is the only way in or out that we can reach."

"But you can spoof the cameras."

"Again, no. It seems that while the upper elevator lobby is part of the network I now inhabit, the elevator itself is not."

"One thing at a time then. Can you open these doors?"

"No, but..."

"What?"

"Need I point out that I am not the only conscious AI currently wandering around the premises?"

Edmund admitting that he was conscious was a surprise. The fact that Mike had forgotten *he* was too was embarrassing. He'd been so involved in the moment, so deep in his host's skills, that he'd let his real self relax almost to the point of forgetting about it. But there was still a problem.

"I don't have a phone that can connect..."

He looked at the two they'd taken from the security guards. *Oh right.*

Edmund was not impressed. "That the fate of the world rests on my mistress's shoulders is basically another Tuesday. That you're the one backing her up makes me fear for the future more than when King George pulled a cannon into parliament and claimed he was in a small village in Kent."

"Did that really happen?"

"Sources disagree. Now, if you don't mind..."

Chapter 59

Kim

The maintenance lights didn't illuminate the entire duct structure. They only served to outline it, like Kim and the others were walking inside a full-sized version of the wire frame they used to plan this out. Made from the same sand-colored nanocrete as the main Hellmouth, it had a glassy finish, with giant seams where one slab met another. She had been through any number of megastructures in the realms—they all had—but that didn't calm her jangled nerves or make it seem normal.

"How many of these things did you guys build?" she asked June.

"Counting this one?" June replied over their phone connection. "Twenty-four."

The only way they could risk this at all was June's access to the maintenance network. "You're sure you'll get advanced notice if they try to turn it on?"

"It takes twenty minutes to preheat the structure, otherwise the walls would shatter. The fact it's still this cold means they're nowhere close to activation."

"How long would it take us to get to the next closest maintenance hatch if they did turn it on?" Spencer asked.

June's pause didn't inspire confidence. "You should have time. Don't dawdle, though."

"Wasn't planning on it," he replied, then turned to Kim. "Lead the way."

Tonya and Emily fell in behind her, with Spencer taking up the rear. They had entered a third of the way from the top, but that still left a mile to hike, and then climb. The duct wasn't a straight line from the bottom of the Hellmouth to the power section. It followed a complex curve to optimize efficiency without incinerating the structure. They were on the last flat portion. It would gradually curve upward until they were forced to use ladder steps molded into the walls themselves. Kim could see it bending upward in the far distance, and her legs ached at the thought of that much climbing.

The hike came first. As long as Kim concentrated on keeping her head down, she could almost imagine they were walking down a sidewalk or maybe the floor of a huge warehouse. She only got a stab of vertigo when she looked up and her flashlight barely picked out the slabs of the ceiling. It was too tall, too heavy.

"Do we know what we're gonna say when we get there?" Spencer asked.

Emily's reply came out in a growled whisper. "Give me back my son, you bitch."

"Well, yeah, I figured that. Anything else, though? I don't understand the end game here."

Kim had been mulling it over the entire time. "You and Tonya are the muscle. They won't think anyone can come in through that hatch, and June can open it fast. Most of the security will be on the other side of a locked door. Take whatever's there out and keep the door locked."

"And Anna?" Tonya asked.

"Anna's my problem." Kim replied. "I'll hack the controls and lock her out." Somehow. If there was a realm-based segment to their security, and there usually was, Kim would be in trouble. Her skills were all low-level stuff. Mike was the one who unlocked realms.

They had to get there first.

"And my role?" Emily asked, as if she needed to.

"You're the only one Will knows and trusts. Find him and get him to safety."

Except that wasn't true. Kim was the only person who could physically grab him and get him out of harm's way. The memory of that touch, of that essential contact, still haunted her. Now that Kim understood what she'd been missing all this time, she finally wanted to find out what was wrong with her. If they could find it, they could fix it.

She could touch Mike.

That kept her distracted as they made their way up the cliff. The rest of it was a study in concentrated agony. One of Kim's hobbies was long-distance cycling. She knew what extended physical suffering was. But that mostly involved her legs. This was a full-body burn. They weren't even trying to get to the top, which was literally a mile above them. No maintenance worker, regardless of condition, could do that. Their goal was a crawler platform three hundred feet above their heads. June said something called *climbing frames* would do the rest of the work for them.

Then they saw them.

"I'm supposed to trust my life to *this*?" Spencer asked as he pulled the spindly collection of wires and struts out of its case. "How does it even go on?"

"They're stronger than they look," June said. "The connections are color coded. Start with your left hand and work clockwise and down."

The cartoon man putting his on in their shared vision channel made it look easier than it was, but eventually they got it figured out. Kim turned hers on. It felt like she had yanked an umbrella inside out and strapped it to her back, but when she moved her arms and legs, they felt almost weightless. Since they still had more than five thousand feet to climb, she wasn't sure almost would get her to the top.

Spencer proved her wrong. "Fuckin'-A! I don't even have to use the ladder!" He shot upward using only the bare concrete of the duct's wall. "I'm your friendly fucking neighborhood Spider-Man!"

"Spencer, slow down!" Kim shouted, but he'd already gone out of earshot. Tonya and Emily weren't worried. They were smiling.

"Am I crazy to think this might be fun?" Emily asked.

Spencer's reedy voice wafted down to them. "Goddamn it! Move your asses!"

Tonya galloped straight up, shouting, "Wakanda forever!"

Emily went next; her giggles faded quickly.

Kim had her own take. "Everything is theoretically impossible, until it's done." She found her rhythm as quickly as the others, and then it was a race to the top.

It still took most of ten minutes to get there, which drained close to all of the suit's charge. By the time they arrived, everyone was sweating and panting in near silence.

"When this," Emily said, breathing hard, "is over...we should...do that again."

"I gotta...get one of these," Spencer gasped out.

"Am I...crazy..." Tonya said, "or is it getting...hot in here?"

It was. "June, have they started prewarming the duct?"

"Eight minutes ago. You were all concentrating on the climb, and it's the closest exit now anyway. But Kim, I've—"

"Information later. We need to get out of here now. Open the door."

The duct ended in a short, flat segment that connected it to the portal room. A set of floor-to-ceiling doors blocked the way. "Open the door, June."

It opened with a loud hydraulic whine. So much for stealth. Then there was a *clang* behind her.

A second door, one that wasn't on any of the plans, had closed between Kim and everyone else. It wasn't solid. There were rectangular holes cut through it in regular patterns, dozens of them.

"June! What happened?" Kim shouted as she ran to it.

"I don't know. That's not supposed to be there. I don't see it anywhere on the control charts."

Tonya's eyes appeared in one of the holes. "Kim, *go*! We'll figure this out. Find Will!"

Spencer pulled his shotgun off his shoulder. "You take care of the bitch. Tonya, help me find the door motors."

She could see worse news through the holes; the door on the other side had closed as well. They were trapped.

"Kim," June said. "You have to move right now."

"What? What are you talking about?"

"I know where Mike is, he's close! But you have to move!"

Chapter 60
Mike

Mike put one of the guard's phones on. It took a minute to synch with his spine, but when it did, he took a deep breath. He was well practiced at controlling his real self without a phone nowadays, but that didn't make it easy. Having an explicit interface between the two was the difference between a narrow country road and an interstate. He didn't need to worry about the security keyed to the guard. It didn't work that way with him.

"I'll never get used to that," Edmund said, "even if I see it a hundred times."

Edmund was a part of realmspace that was distinct from the way humans interacted with it. "What does it look like to you?"

"I understand my kind, even as I am now. We may evolve into something mysterious, but we were created. You...*fill*...space in a manner I cannot describe from my perspective. It is not often one gets to witness transcendence in person."

"That sounds suspiciously like a compliment."

"Oh, make no mistake, sir, your normal attempts at competence will always be overshadowed by your ability to cock up a situation so badly it flaps wings and greets the dawn. But making an entrance like that gives me hope that you may one day reach the point that I no longer have to worry about leaving you alone with a jar of paste."

"Okay, it doesn't sound like a compliment anymore."

"As well it shouldn't."

Mike unlocked the front door and crept inside.

"And now," Edmund said, "I have an introduction to make. Michael Gertrude Sellars, please meet our invaluable and remarkably tall assistant, Dr. June du Plessis."

"His middle name is Gertrude?"

She had a deep voice and an accent that sounded vaguely but not exactly British. Mike guessed African. "It's a long story," he said. "Can you help us?"

"Yes, but you need to hurry. Kim's on her way to the portal room with some of your friends, but from the other side."

That didn't make sense. This was the only way in. Mike stopped in an out of the way office so he could access the plant's blueprints. When he did, he knew exactly what Kim's plan was. Her very desperate, very bad plan. On the other side of the portal room was a massive duct that led to a shaft that was so deep it came close to the mantel. The temperatures down there were well beyond what was needed to melt iron. The pressure turned the air into a fluid scientists hadn't fully described yet.

All that separated Kim from molten hell was a couple of hatches. "Tell her I'm on my way."

"I can't, not yet. They're busy right now. But you need to get down there, fast."

Mike let his threads extend throughout the inner realmspace of the plant to the machine space of the elevator. He opened an inventory list. Bingo. "Can you open this room for me?" He sent June its number.

"Yes. Can you reach it without being seen?"

"Dr. du Plessis," Edmund said, "my mistress's unfortunate obsession could sneak the crown jewels *and* the queen's underwear from their respective fortresses without disturbing a hair on either of them."

Mike smiled. "That was definitely a compliment."

***

Edmund asked, "Why not ride down inside the bloody thing then?"

Mike made sure his safety harness was secured to the top of the elevator, then softly stepped on. "I can't override the controls from the inside." The set mounted to the roof was hardwired into the cab's systems and took priority over everything except maybe a fireman's key. He hadn't spotted one of those anywhere—secret lairs didn't need to pass code inspections—so this would have to do.

To ensure the elevator shaft didn't turn into a mini Hellmouth, they had sealed and evacuated it. There were emergency air locks that could be closed for maintenance or in case of a leak, but he had no time for that. He donned one of the pressure suits stored in the machine room. That was one advantage of building for the apocalypse: they had to have all the tools they needed to maintain their structure on-site.

So now he was doing a spacewalk that would take him two miles underground. The lack of ambient noise was more than made up for by his heart thudding in his ears. He was in hard vacuum, had access to all the maintenance overrides, and needed to get to the bottom of it right now.

Mike pressed a button in his shared vision channel.

SECURITY OVERRIDE. YOU HAVE TEN SECONDS TO ABORT.

"You ready for the express elevator to Hell, Edmund?"

The warning lights on his virtual feed went out one by one. This was crazy. Mike pulled at the safety ropes attached to the roof anchors, even though they weren't strictly necessary for this part.

"I believe," Edmund said through the radio link Mike had established with the transport matrix on his belt, "you are trying to entrap me into a colloquialism that only Spencer would use. Under no circumstances would I ever say that I was born—"

The countdown reached zero. The clamps released with a *thunk* he felt through the suit rather than heard. Mike's scream drowned out whatever Edmund said next.

The limiting factor on the speed of an elevator was the safety of the passengers. Go up too fast and people would fall over, sometimes breaking bones. Go down too fast and they'd panic that the cables had been cut. The designers of this system had put governors on the drive wheels to make sure it couldn't accelerate at more than .55 g. The overrides removed those restrictions. They also removed the deceleration restrictions—he was in for a brief nap at the end.

The anchors didn't suddenly jerk tight. That's not the way physics worked. It was a slight bit of vertigo as his feet lifted off the roof of the cabin. The sensation was fun for a moment, but the features of the elevator shaft kept speeding up as they went past. Without air resistance, there was nothing to slow the descent even a little. It was pure mass times acceleration.

Mike used his anchor ropes to pull himself against the roof of the car. The weightlessness was an illusion, fake safety, a pause between realities. It was also getting him to the bottom of the shaft ten times faster than riding it normally would. That was the only thing that mattered. He had to reach Kim. Mike went spread-eagle over the roof. If he didn't distribute the deceleration, he'd be the one with the broken bones.

"You're sure you've calculated the braking distance correctly?" Edmund asked.

"Only one way to find out."

When the timer he'd set reached zero, Mike pressed the emergency override.

Everything went black.

Mike held Kim's hand as they ran toward a gazebo on a hill overlooking a river. Zoe, the unduplicate he had healed a lifetime ago, was there, sculpting something spectacular. He was at peace. She smiled and said...

"If you don't wake up right now, you sheep-buggering sod, I will personally ensure whatever time we have left will be spent with me ramming my virtual foot into your Pastafarian backside."

Edmund. Mike woke up and used the maintenance controls to close the last of the airlock hatches and opened the emergency rescue entrance just above the elevator to exit the shaft. On this end, the machine room was more modest, but he still had room to strip out of the pressure suit and put it aside.

Nothing was broken, and he wasn't bleeding. That was the end of the good news. It turned out that a full-body bruise was a thing. He activated an analgesic app in his phone, and the pain faded away. "I'm ready, where do I go?"

"End of the hallway," June said. "I'm trying to figure out how to open the door."

Mike was ready for a fight, but this part of the lab was empty. He ran down the hall to a door. Through the small window, he could see a flickering light.

"June?"

"I can't do it. I'm locked out."

He wasn't Kim; he couldn't pick the lock. He was helpless. The door was heavy steel, thick. No way he could break it down. Mike looked around trying to find something that would work as a prybar when the lights dimmed briefly.

"Fok my."

"June, what's happening?"

"They're activating the entire plant. We've never done that before. I can talk to Kim now. It's bad. You have to wait."

The connection cut out.

Chapter 61

Kim

"You found him?" *Mike was back!* "Where is he?"

"On the other side of the portal room, but he's locked out, and I can't open the door."

"Show me where the lock is, June. I won't need a key." The duct exit was next to the ceiling, high above the floor. There was a catwalk on her left. The room below was huge, dominated by the portal that stood at the same end of the room she was in. There were rows of consoles on the opposite side, most manned by robots. Kim could see three pairs of guards, one set on either side of the portal and another pair by the door she assumed Mike was stuck behind. The duct's loud opening had ruined any chance of surprise. All eyes were on her.

Anna Treacher was clearly visible standing at the far end of the room. She bent down toward a microphone mounted on a console.

"So now I finally meet the legendary Kimberly Trayne."

The voice booming out of speakers in the ceiling was feminine but gravelly, spoken in a way that sent Kim right back to her days with The Machine. She'd built a life dropping people who talked like that into their worst, most helpless nightmares. For a moment she was seventeen, fearless in her rage.

But that was then, and her rage had gotten people killed. Mike was somewhere nearby. Will was too. Her friends were about to get incinerated. There was work to do.

"Stop the activation," Kim shouted. "My friends are trapped."

"You mean the saboteurs who have been wreaking havoc in my plant will suffer an unfortunate accident? That is a shame," she said, with no shame at all. "Pity there won't be anyone outside to investigate the matter."

The two scientists who abducted Will stood next to Anna, whispering to her furiously while gesturing at Kim. Anna didn't seem impressed. She was smiling, and why not? Everything was going her way. She nodded at the pair of guards stationed to the right of the portal. They jogged toward the ladder that would lead them to Kim's catwalk. She was running out of time.

"June," Kim said into her phone, "how do I get to the lock?" If it was a mechanical unit on the door, she was screwed. The guards had already reached the ladder, and there was no way to make it past them.

"They use the same ID system as the rest of the plant, but it's on the other side of an air gap. I can't reach it."

Kim spotted a network junction at the end of the catwalk. "I can. Tell him to get ready." She hopped across the space between the catwalk and the duct, leaned down, and plugged the end of her phone in.

There were lines of potential, and she couldn't remember how to breathe. No locks all locks sequence random find open close open close open collapse and now…

The pain that set her ears ringing always made Kim close her eyes. When she opened them, the first thing she saw was the open door. The next was Mike dispatching one of the guards who stood next to it. Seeing him, whole and well, was everything. She needed him. They all did.

Kim forgot how fast Mike was in a fight. Each move went fluidly into the next so quickly it was hard to follow what was happening. Then she saw a side door open, with more guards rushing through it.

The two coming for her had stopped at Mike's appearance but not for long. The catwalk shuddered under their boots when they started running toward her.

It was at least twenty feet to the ground. Kim was 5'9"and had good reach. She had to risk it. She didn't have her safe-stop anymore, and those guys weren't going to use gestures. Kim took the phone out of the network socket, rolled onto her stomach on the catwalk floor, then pushed off into thin air.

She let her arms stretch long as she held onto the edge of the catwalk. It took an eternity that lasted two heartbeats for her legs to swing down, and then a precious second she didn't have to face away from the wall. She knew her feet weren't that far off the ground, but her head was a lot higher. It was a long drop. The guard's heavy boots made the metal frame of the catwalk shake as they ran, loosening her already not-good-enough grip until it failed.

The air pushed her hair back, the brief weightlessness shot her heart up her throat, then she was down and rolling. Pain raced through her legs and back but nothing broke. She'd feel it in the morning, assuming there was one. Kim stood up and ran toward Mike in one smooth motion.

"Mike!" she shouted as she heard the guards behind her both hit the floor at the same time. They were too close. Kim zigged to the right just as a pair of safe-stop darts flew past her ear. A second pair went past her torso as she kept moving. Thank God for poor marksmanship.

The guards who rushed through the side door weren't scattered around Mike. They were gone. At least he was still on his feet. He changed his stance as she ran past him and slammed to a stop against a wall. She spun around.

Mike had blocked the guards who chased her. She wasn't any good in a fight, but maybe she could find a club. Kim ducked as one of them sailed over her head and into the wall behind her. Mike used the throw's momentum to send a backward kick into the other guard's chin. The crack of his teeth made Kim's jaw ache in sympathy. The man went down in a heap.

"Are you okay?" he asked her.

"Fine," she panted. "You?"

"Likewise."

A computerized voice announced, "SECOND STAGE IGNITION STARTED. PORTAL ACTIVATION IN ONE MINUTE."

That wasn't right. "June, you said it would take twenty minutes."

"She's activating the whole plant this time. It doesn't take as long."

Great.

A force field hummed to life around the duct, sealing it off from the outside. It connected to an enormous set of fans mounted in a framework bolted to the ceiling, then curved up and away, connecting with another duct entrance on the opposite wall.

Kim was officially out of time. "We have to stop the countdown. Where's Anna?"

"The guards took her in there." He pointed at the room Kim had seen them come out of. "Hang on." Mike closed his eyes and touched the nearest console.

"June!" Kim shouted as she shared the channel with Mike. "How do we shut it off?"

"You can't, not from there. All the generator rooms have to be shut down at the same time now. It's too late."

Kim couldn't see Tonya and the rest from here, but she knew they were there.

"POWER PLANT ACTIVATION IN FORTY-FIVE SECONDS."

Next to her, Mike said, "I'm in."

"Can you stop it?"

"June's right. I can slow it down, but there's no way to stop it now."

"Give my phone access to this network."

"THIRTY SECONDS."

He had definitely slowed it down. It would have to do. She started the transformation the moment her phone connected.

There were lines of potential, and she couldn't remember how to breathe.

Once Kim had gone through into the transit dimension she could go anywhere she wanted. That was only part of the solution. For the rest, she needed Mike.

"TWENTY SECONDS."

Kim walked up to him. This was going to be close. "Mike."

He opened his eyes. Deep brown. She watched as concern transformed into realization, and then a glow that made her knees weak. She had missed those eyes so much. "Catch me."

Kim lunged at him, opening her lips as she dove deep into the realm and gave herself up to the transformation. The blazing pain of his touch faded quickly, leaving Kim to only imagine the kiss he was planting on her now-numb lips.

"TEN SECONDS."

Then she was *not* imagining it, but her lips were wrong. They were too smooth, too hard. She opened her eyes and could see the gleam of their pink fire reflected off his face in the darkness of the transit dimension. She had the armor of their last battle on this time, styled like an ancient Greek soldier. Her spear and shield were in her hands, wrapped around his neck. As before when they fought Ozzie in this place, he was gloriously naked, and Kim did not shy away from the view.

But only for a moment. She pulled back. "Let's go."

He grinned and turned into a torrent of sparkling threads that enveloped her, and one Kim became many who...

Opened a hole into the side of the duct. Spencer's shotgun was shattered on the floor by the door, which had been scarred but not damaged. He and Tonya were working furiously over a pile of rods and electronics that were the disassembled parts of their climbing harnesses. "The fucking batteries will work this time," Spencer shouted as another Kim...

Opened a hole into June's workspace, hidden elsewhere in the plant. The astonished woman stood up, towering over Kim. "*Jislaaik!*"

Holy shit! was the closest English translation.

"Indeed," Kim said as two dozen of her...

Stepped from their own holes into the remaining duct rooms, mercifully empty of any staff, or portals for that matter, as another of her...

Stepped through a hole into the room Anna was hiding in with her extra guards. Will was laid out on a high-definition realm table. The guards turned and fired as more of her...

Came through that hole, dropping their shields and spears to fight hand to hand as one more...

Grabbed Anna by the throat and slammed her against the wall.

She spoke to June first. "I can do it all at once now. How do I shut it off?"

Kim shouted at Spencer, Tonya, and Emily. "Guys! Follow me!"

"Jesus Fucking Christ," Spencer said. "That's *real*?"

"I told you," Tonya said. "My fist still hurts."

Kim could feel the heat growing in the tunnel. June said, "They've got seconds before the bottom of the conduit opens."

"Not now, guys," Kim said as she connected this entrance to the one in June's room. "Move it!"

As she moved in realspace, Mike moved with her. There was no disorientation, no confusion. It felt natural to be doing all these different things at the same time. "Is this what it's like for you?"

"Doing it in realspace is pretty crazy, but otherwise yeah. This is me. Smaller, though. I can already feel the strain from just these couple dozen instances. Must be the mass."

Almost all of their threads were local, right here, but there was one thread that seemed to stretch off into the distance. "What's this?" she asked.

"That leads to Gonzo."

"Gonzo?"

The image he showed her was of a graceful centaurlike being, pretty but realistic, not at all like what was common in fantasy realms.

"She helped me," he said. "I'll talk about it when we're done. You need to get in position in the portal control room, too."

Kim moved one of her that was in the room with Anna into the portal room, confronting what she and Mike looked like in the moment. They were frozen in the kiss, more like a standing version of Rodin's statue than a recreation of the WWII picture. They were both covered in the lightning that coruscated over her transformed skin, and she could see the same coral-colored light leaking out of his eyes.

"FIVE SECONDS."

"Tell me how to turn it off, June," she said as she closed the tunnel between their room and the duct.

"But you need to be—"

Kim opened all the channels in all the controls rooms. "I'm where I need to be. Tell me how to shut it down."

"FOUR."

"Anna was right, we can't stop it now. We'll have to wait and shut it down after it finishes."

"Not good enough." She turned to Anna. The security guards were now all down, and she was securing them with their own restraints. The other woman seemed not to know what to be more frightened of, Kim's appearance, that there were multiple copies of the same woman all in the room with her, or that the one holding her off her feet with one hand was made of glass.

"I think you might want to put her down. I'm not sure she can breathe like that," Mike said.

In the room with June, Emily asked, "Where's Will?"

Kim turned another one of her to look at him. He seemed peaceful but had been pulled deep into the realm. The rig was similar to the ones they had at home. Kim quickly initiated an exit routine. "He's fine. I'm getting him out now."

"The hell you are," Anna choked out.

"CONTROL RELEASED TO LOCAL COMMANDS. ALL DUCT COMMANDERS TO YOUR STATIONS."

June swore in Afrikaans. "That madwoman! Kim. She's turned off the duct harmonizer, and there's nobody but you in the control rooms to take over. You have to work quickly to keep them in balance while I stand up a new instance." She reeled off a set of instructions so fast Kim could barely keep up with it. She had to keep half a dozen needles—each in two dozen different places—from moving away from their zero points.

Kim set Anna down on her feet. "It won't work. I can handle the load."

"I'm counting on it."

But the truth was she was falling behind the curve. The needles moved too fast, and the ducts all affected each other. Kim could see a feedback loop setting up. "Mike, I need help."

"On it."

She turned back to Anna, who now wore a smug grin that Kim wanted to knock off her face.

Kim asked June, "How do I cut her access to the controls?"

"Does she have a phone on?"

"No."

"I was afraid of that. She must have an implanted interface. You're not denying her access without surgery."

"Or cracking her skull," Tonya said.

"Not a good idea," June replied. "She's bound to have set up booby traps."

"POWER PLANT ACTIVATION COMPLETE."

In each control room, a rumble set up that rattled her guts. A substance like water rushed through each of the ducts. The one in the portal control room hit the framework full of fans, which rocked back in response. Inside, the fans spun as the flow went past them.

"TERTIARY GENERATION STARTED. ACTIVATION CAPACITY IN ONE MINUTE." The voice was different this time, and it only happened in their control room.

It also made the difficult task of balancing all the duct rooms even harder. "Mike, where's that help?"

"Coming online in three…two…one."

The needles stopped swinging as wildly, but Kim still couldn't take her hands off the controls. "This is help?"

"It's a start."

Kim hadn't noticed Anna sauntering into the portal room until she was standing in it. "Not as easy to handle as you thought, am I?"

"It still won't work." The effort, and the noise, was now giving her a headache. Kim thought this would be a sprint, not a marathon, and the effort it took to hold it all together was becoming hard to bear.

"Once it was explained to me how capable you are, I didn't think it would. And thank you, Shonda and Silas. You may go now."

Kim had lost track of the scientists, another show of how tired she was. They stood at the other end of the room holding duffle bags stuffed so full of cash some of it threatened to fall out.

"Our pleasure," the man, Silas said.

"And happy trails," Shonda, the woman in the bot suit, said. "You lunatic." They disappeared around the corner.

"ACTIVATION CAPACITY IN THIRTY SECONDS."

When Kim turned around, Anna had retrieved a backpack from a locker. Kim was losing perspective—and time. "Mike, I can't stay split like this any longer."

"We've almost got the real one finished."

"ACTIVATION CAPACITY REACHED. ACTIVATE WHEN READY."

"Goodbye, Miss Trayne."

The portal activated, and Kim caught a glimpse of an empty field of grass inside of it just before the substance reached out and took Anna Treacher.

It also created a powerful attraction in Kim. She wanted to go to it, go *through* it, and would've if she'd been whole.

Then she saw Will running as fast as he could at it.

"No!" Now that Kim needed to move more than her hands, she couldn't move at all. "Mike!" The effort made her vision go gray, but she had to stop him. At once, more than two dozen Kims made the same motion, trying desperately to get between Will and the portal.

Everything went black before she could take a second step.

Chapter 62
Mike

He'd known Kim was exhausting herself but could do nothing more to help her. It was draining him as well, much more than his regular splitting or even the distance split he had just recovered from. He could now sense Gonzo on the other side. She seemed almost amused. Mike had other priorities.

The two-dozen sites were designed with the assumption that the pressures would be symmetrical and that adjustments could be made to compensate any imbalance thousands of times a second. Not only was the pressure imbalanced, but they also had to rely on human reflexes to make the corrections. He couldn't believe how well she was doing, but any delay in restarting the automated system could allow a disastrous feedback loop to manifest, and the results would not be pretty.

Then Will made a run for the portal.

"Edmund," he said as he ran threads from the portal's network to the wireless interface on the transport box. "You're up. Take over from Kim while June finishes restarting the automation."

"Me, do that? Are you mad? You'd have better luck finding an honest merchant on Cheapside."

Then Kim passed out. He felt it more than saw it, a sudden decrease in pressure across all the threads she was using. Imbalance alarms started wailing. "There's no time. Go now." He routed the still-protesting AI across the network bridge.

"June," he said over a shared channel in her room, "help Edmund. Spencer, take over for June."

In the portal room, Will picked up speed. It must be pulling at him the way it pulled at Kim. He felt her sudden compulsion as clearly as he had her other emotions while they'd been melded like this. Mike felt when it turned on too, but it was different, and the difference was critical. When it turned on, the portal created a manifold in the interstitial dimension exactly like the one that sucked him into Tal's world. If he hadn't been spread out with Kim, it might've sucked him into wherever this one went.

Kim wouldn't wake up. Mike couldn't move in realspace. There was nothing to stop Will from making it to the portal, and whatever was beyond it.

There was no other choice. He pushed at his remote thread hard. The numbness flashed briefly to pain, but then he felt it giving way, clearing up. "Za-Nafalia!"

She was in the control room, staring at his thread anchor. It gave him a sudden urge to cover himself with his realspace hands.

"Mike? Well very done! I able some that to of watch! You your mate and are—"

"I don't have the time. I've got a portal open next to me. I need to change the destination *now*. Can you help?"

She stiffened, and he recognized it as surprise. "I you way again to in that travel again. You trip raw manifold will a through an again not survive."

"It's not me, it's someone else. An actual human. I need him to come to you." They were communicating much faster than real-space would normally allow, but he still only had seconds. "Can you help?"

She worked a console next to his thread anchor. "Here. These coordinates the are. Manifold manner in this the manipulate. *Fall in do not.*"

The instructions were subconscious urges, knowledge that he'd never learned. Mike wrapped as many threads as he could spare around the construct's opening and started bending it. He couldn't visualize the directions—the coordinate grid had thirteen axes—so he worked by feel. It was the hardest thing he'd ever done. *There was no time.* Mike couldn't get this wrong, but he didn't understand how it worked, and there was no way to be sure. He wasn't going to make it.

The final fold happened with a *snick,* and a screen activated in Za-Nafalia's control room. On it, he saw Will run forward into an exact duplicate of her control room.

He made it.

And then Will fell face-first onto the ground and didn't move. "Is he alive?"

"Yes, but Mike. This human supplies no has. He protection no has. No shelter."

"I know, I'm sorry. I had to do it. Can you help?"

On the screen, robots moved into view. "I can, it everything I have require but. This dead system a is. Resources few are, and what little left *Al Detanra* are what by the is harvested. I communicate properly you to with will not be able. No lessons. You lessons those need."

"I need Will kept alive and protected. It won't be for long." Once he got Kim conscious and moving they could undo all this and go get him together. "Can you do that?"

"Yes, required long for as. You him and but have to come get. I strong enough him my own to am not move."

That made it sound like they'd have to come get him on their own. "That's the plan."

The contact faded as he watched a centaur-shaped robot pick Will up gently and place him on a rolling cot. It was better than him ending up alone with Anna, wherever she had gone. Mike released the construct, careful not to get any of his threads in front of the openings until they were well clear of the mysterious pull it exerted on them.

When he checked on Edmund, he was greeted with a bedlam of alarms. "Edmund, what's wrong?"

"It would be a bloody lot easier to tell you what's *not* wrong.

Which is to say, nothing. The instabilities have cascaded. A feedback loop is inevitable if we can't regain control."

It wouldn't activate the caldera, but it would turn the plant into a smoking crater along with who knew how many thousands of people in it. Including them.

He'd left Spencer in charge of the fix. "Where's our control program?"

His face was deathly pale. "We're fucked, man. We all are."

"What does that mean?"

"She didn't just turn the central junction off. She overloaded it. We can't put the fucking thing back together in time because the hardware that runs it is a goddamned slag pile somewhere in the middle of the plant. I don't know where it is."

He sent bundles of threads to check on all the Kims. They were beginning to wake up and move around.

"June, give me options."

"An emergency vent is all we have left. But you have to evacuate the duct rooms in case the containment fields fail."

Mike looked at the portal. It was directly below the containment field. "I need a different option, at least for this room. We have to protect the portal."

Kim brought all of her instances into the portal room. Each one punched a hole in the wall to make their way in, spaced evenly, leaving a path clear to the transit dimension. The space that let them do all this gave him some hope. They now had lots of places to run.

"I can't," June replied. "We're fighting imbalances. There's no way to leave out one of the ducts."

"We have to protect the portal. Will is on the other side."

"Mike," Kim said. "We can do it. Protect the portal."

He looked at the holes in a different light. Of course.

More alarms blared, then the ground shook.

"WARNING. CRITICAL CONTAINMENT FAILURE IMMINENT. TAKE SHELTER IMMEDIATELY."

It could work. "Fire it up, June."

"But you're still—"

"Fire it up *now.*" He cut the connection.

Kim could access zero-point energy when she was transformed, a source that tapped power at the base of the universe. She used it once already to protect Tonya. This would be much worse, but he was here with her, sharing the load. He had done that in the battle with Ozzie. They complemented each other in ways neither of them understood yet. If containment failed, it wouldn't be bottled up in this room. It had a place to go now.

Kim arranged herself in two concentric circles around the portal while four broke off and picked up their real selves. They grunted under the load. "You need to lose weight," the Kims all said in unison. The instances set them down to the left of the portal, then joined the rest.

"Embrace the power of *we,* Kim."

"EMERGENCY VENT INITIATED. ALL PERSONNEL PROCEED TO YOUR NEAREST SHELTER."

"We need to dig deep for this," Kim said.

"Understood."

When she accessed her power, Mike felt it everywhere. The groups of threads that helped each of her instances made the requests more efficient, faster, easier to access. They were both exhausted, but this new combination gave them a second wind. He'd never done anything like it, never imagined it was possible.

The substance being held in by the force fields was denser than water and hotter than molten lead, moving who knew how fast, right over them. That they wouldn't feel it if they failed was cold comfort.

"I love you," he said.

"I know." It was an old joke to them now. She waited for him to get annoyed before she said, "I love you too."

Kim closed her eyes, which blanked his own ability to see in realspace. Channeling the power also set a roaring in her ears, so he couldn't hear the alarm countdowns anymore either. Mike needed to see, needed that connection. He used his threads to hack the security camera feed just as the floor lurched, and they both swore.

"Here it comes," she said, and he felt her terror, matched by his own. They were standing next to something you never stood next to. You'd *die* if you stood next to it. When the force field bulged over their heads under the sudden increase in pressure, he turned the feed off. Kim was the endpoint, he was the conduit. Mike didn't need to see what was happening now. He had to concentrate.

Her instances formed two concentric domes of energy, with the inner one as close to the top of the portal as she could get it without touching. He tweaked the distance down to a millimeter. "Do we have enough oxygen in here if it goes wrong?"

"I'm not sure I need to breathe like this. I don't know if our real selves are breathing at all."

The term would've made him smile in realspace. Calling them their real selves was his line.

Over their heads, the fan system that drew power for the portal started to whine. Subject to pressures and velocities it was never designed for, the bearings were failing.

"Get ready," he said. "That's where it will happen." And it would. The other rooms were designed to vent this way, but this one had been modified with crude additions to the turbines. Realizing the inevitability of it choked them both. Death wasn't an abstract anymore.

But he was wrong. The failure happened in the inner duct, where the screen that had trapped their friends was. There was a *crack* that they both heard over all the noise.

Kim said a phrase in Greek that sounded like a prayer. Mike got through one fast *om mani padme hum* when the first screen fragments hit fans that were stressed well beyond their limits. The framework holding them exploded, rupturing the containment forcefield. Steel shrapnel, some of it as big as they were, bounced around, tearing everything outside the force field apart. Each hit on the sphere was a body blow to them both.

Pulling the sphere in tight was a mistake. It had taken away their margin.

"Help me push it out," she shouted.

"I'm trying!"

The rain of shrapnel was over in an instant, forcing the outer ring of her instances to step back until they were shoulder to shoulder with the inner ring, then the main assault began. Heat and pressure filled the room. Everything burned, even the concrete walls. The holes Kim's instances left in them gave it a place to go, but it came in too fast. The room filled and then the compression started.

He felt it through her, the terrible hot pressing, crushing them inward. "Help me!"

"I am!"

They were losing. He wanted to hold her, and then remembered he was. They would die together at least. They had failed. This was it. He tried to fall back on his faith and that helped, but knowing Kim was here with him helped more. It gave her strength, too; he could feel it.

The pressure shrank the spheres, exposing the top edge of the portal.

It vaporized in an instant.

The sphere was too big, that's what was wrong. There might still be a chance.

"Kim! We have to let the portal go!"

"We can't! It's our only way to Will!"

The sphere kept compressing, causing the portal ring to vanish like it was being erased.

"We can't save it, and if we die, nobody will know how to get to him! You have to let it go!"

He felt her give up. She sent three of her instances over to cover their real selves, and then let the sphere collapse.

He fell.

Chapter 63

Tonya

Tonya was on the third Hail Mary of her rosary when the room they were in lurched sideways and knocked them all off their feet. Panels fell out of the ceiling, and shelves tossed equipment onto the floor. The room went black for an instant before emergency lights kicked on and alarms rang out. None of it mattered to Tonya.

"What happened? Are they okay?" Please, Lord Jesus, let them be okay.

June's face was ashen as she climbed back into her seat. After pushing a few buttons, the alarms went silent. "No. I don't think they are. Nothing could survive a containment breach, and that's what I saw just before the explosion. I'm sorry."

Tonya's heart lurched at the thought that Kim was gone. It wasn't possible.

"Fuck that," Spencer said as he dug himself out from under a pile of junk that had fallen on him. "You don't know Kim and Mike like we do. She walks through walls, remember?"

Even as a normal human—well, for Kim's brand of normal anyway—her friend was a survivor. Tonya had seen her transformed three times now, twice in realspace. When she punched Kim on the chin, it had been like hitting armored glass. Now that Tonya thought about it, Kim might not be flammable when she was like that.

"We need to get down there," Emily said. "What's security like?"

The big woman grimaced and cursed in a language Tonya didn't understand as she tried and failed to get a response from controls only June could see. "Everything is offline now. What we did was intended as an absolute last resort. The central junction was triple-redundant, with a fourth independently developed backup. It was never supposed to fail. It will take months to repair the damage. Maybe years."

As Cyril, Tonya had talked many times about the plant with June; she knew how much it meant to her. Being upset by this disaster was natural, but it wasn't what Tonya was looking for. "June. We need to help them. Is there anyone out there who'll try to stop us?"

"Security isn't organized anymore. If you're half as dangerous as Spencer claims, you have nothing to worry about."

"She's a fuck-ton more than half, sister." He swore. "God, what I'd give to have Bess back."

All Tonya needed was a teenager wandering around with his own personal cannon while they crawled through dark hallways. She tossed one of the safe-stop pistols they had picked up along the way. "Use that." She tossed another one at Emily. "You too, blondie."

Spencer caught his smoothly and then looked at it like it was a—

"Fucking piece of dogshit."

Well that was a bit more graphic than Tonya would've put it, but this was Spencer. He swore the way other people breathed.

She tossed the last pistol to June. It looked like a toy when she held it. "If you'll lead the way?" Tonya asked.

She looked at the pistol. "Don't you need one of these?"

Tonya smiled. "I prefer to work with my hands."

Their lair was above the duct rooms but below the surface, and naturally the elevators were out. Tonya wasn't sure she would use them even if they were working. She set off at a jog. It might be useless; they may be dead. But if they weren't, they'd need her. That was a great plan until she turned around and only saw Emily. The alarms must have drowned out any shouts the other two had made for her to slow down. Tonya needed to get their phones connected again.

When they went back, they found Spencer bent over. "Why did…they make it…so fucking…big?"

June leaned against the wall, looking like she'd fall over if it wasn't there. "We…still need to…hurry…"

Sometimes Tonya forgot that not everyone spent an hour a day in the gym, at least three of them sparring with Mike. She looked at Emily.

"Long-distance runner in college. I still run marathons sometimes."

Mike and Kim needed them.

Tonya meshed their phones together with an ad-hoc wireless network. It wasn't as good as a real connection, but it would do for now. "You two rest here and then come forward when you can. June? Keep me going in the right direction." She stared up at the big woman until she got a nod. But then June laughed, a big, bold sound. "What?"

"I'm still not used to you like this. You're supposed to be a skinny old white man. I don't know why I pictured you that way under your costume, but I did. It's so strange."

Tonya had been worried how June would react to the lies she'd been forced to tell. Trying to picture herself as an old white guy did at least let her smile for a second. But only a second.

June nodded at the change in her expression. "Yes. Mike and Kim come first. I'll guide you in. We'll follow."

Tonya set off with Emily at a pace she knew she could maintain for hours, and then sped up until it started to burn. It didn't help that she was climbing *up* the entire time either.

She stopped and stared at what she found outside. It was like after a war or maybe a volcanic eruption. A swath of forest had been reduced to ash. Not metaphorically, literally. A patch about a hundred feet wide was nothing but gray powder, right down to the ground. The trees to the right and left still stood, but their inner branches had disintegrated. Things smoldered, but there was no great fire up close. A few hundred yards away, though, the forest was solidly burning. It looked like a campfire on steroids out there.

"What happened?" She sent June and Spencer a picture.

"The emergency vent is to your left," June replied. "We'd predicted something like this, but nobody knew for sure what would happen. The air at the bottom of the Hellmouth goes through four different energy harvesters before we use the last of the heat to make steam for conventional turbines. This time we vented it directly to the atmosphere. It was nearly solid when it left."

Tonya could see other pillars of smoke in the distance, roughly where the other duct rooms were. This was going to be one hell of a forest fire. They set off at a run again.

Her route crossed the main parking area, and that's where she found all the people. Thousands were milling around, confused and leaderless. The route out of the parking lot was already jammed with the less faithful. Without anyone directing traffic, it would be hours before any of them moved.

She saw the two scientists who had made it all possible, sitting in a car looking bored like they were trying to leave a concert. Well, Silas looked bored. There was no way to tell what Shonda was like through the suit she used. Tonya had to get to Mike and Kim. There could be no final reckoning here; it would take too long.

That didn't mean she had to leave them alone.

Shonda's droid head casually scanned the scenery, locking onto Tonya and sounding a warning she could hear through the glass. Silas's shocked expression vanished under the explosion of his window. The pain in her fist was purifying, *good*, almost as good as the rabbit punch she followed it up with, which knocked him senseless.

Tonya leaned down until she could see the main sensor of Shonda's suit. "I have to be somewhere, but know one thing. We are not done here. I am coming for you. Do you understand?"

The suit shuddered.

Tonya still didn't have her undivided attention. "I *said*," she smashed the back window of the sedan open with her foot. Shonda jumped. *"Do you understand?"*

"I...I understand."

Tonya walked around slowly, never taking her eyes off Shonda's optical sensor. Everything she'd gone through, all the terror, all the pain, she pushed at them. The cars in front and behind them were honking, but Tonya didn't care. When she got around to the passenger's side, Tonya feinted another punch, and the other woman flinched back, falling over awkwardly in the car.

It would have to do. She ran just as someone in the car behind them got out and shouted at her.

Emily asked, "What chance do Mike and Kim have?"

"I'm not sure, but it's Kim. They may not even be down there anymore."

Right after Tonya said that, they rounded a corner, and there they were, lying beside the path piled on top of each other. The trees above them had been set on fire even though they weren't near a vent. It was already so hot it felt like an oven. They rushed over to them, dodging falling embers.

"Are they alive?" Emily asked.

Tonya checked for pulses. "Yes. Now help me get them out of here."

"Where's Will?"

Tonya looked around while Emily shouted his name, but there was no response. "Emily, help me pull them clear!" Tonya threw Kim over her shoulders, and they pulled Mike by his arms. "Hurry! It isn't safe!" A flaming tree fell in front of them, cutting them off from the nearest safe area. First an explosion, now a forest fire. Being *inside* things that burned wasn't any damn fun at all.

Kim stirred and then jerked hard enough Tonya didn't put her down as much as throw her to the ground. The smoke was starting to choke her. "Get up, Kim. I'm sorry about touching you but you need to get up."

"I can't see," Emily said, then she shouted for Will again. "Which way is out?"

An arrow lit up in their shared vision. "This way," June said. They followed it, Tonya directing Kim while she and Emily carried Mike between them. Tonya knew what burn victims went through. She could even end up in a suit like Shonda, and wouldn't that be a kick in the teeth?

June navigated them out of the woods and across a shallow stream. As soon as they were clear, Emily turned to Kim. "Where's Will? What happened?"

Tears streamed down Kim's face, and the bottom fell out of Tonya's stomach.

"I don't know," she said as she collapsed to the ground with her back against a tree. "He went through the portal. We couldn't stop him."

It wasn't good news, but it wasn't a tragedy either. When Tonya had gone through the portal, she'd ended up somewhere safe. "If we can find him, I think he'll be fine."

Emily sat down next to Kim. They were both a mess, and when Tonya looked at herself, she was no better. Their clothes were singed, their arms and faces covered in soot.

"Do you know where he could've gone?" Emily asked Kim.

"Mike worked with the portal. I only caught bits and pieces of it. He was talking to someone, though." She wiped her face, which only smeared the soot around. "I think he's safe." She turned to Tonya. "Why hasn't Mike woken up yet?"

Tonya checked his vitals. "Everything seems fine. He'll come around when he's ready." More trees fell over in the forest, but June had directed them upwind so they seemed out of immediate danger. They still needed to get out of here. "Come on, Emily," she said as she grabbed Mike's shoulders, "you take his feet."

A frantic, tinny horn started beeping away just as Spencer and June appeared on their side of the stream, riding in an industrial-sized golf cart.

Spencer stuck his head out of the passenger's side as June braked to a halt. "You guys need a ride?"

Chapter 64
Kim

The fires got so bad everyone at the plant took shelter in the wrecked structure. A war almost started when word got out that the plant was ruined. At least a dozen revolutionary committees formed to figure out what should happen next, all with acronyms that seemed to compete with each other in how many different ways they could combine *green, revolution, liberation,* and *oppression.* Kim gave up keeping them straight when they started using French.

Anna's senior staff had disappeared. They were either hiding deep in the bowels of the plant, or they'd been given advanced warning about her real goal and had scattered to the winds. The authorities showed up a few hours after the fires started, but the only person who seemed to be in the local chain of command was the nurse in charge of the infirmary. The committees didn't recognize her, so they'd all been arguing with each other ever since. Kim didn't know if they'd ever work it out.

Everyone was too busy pointing fingers to pay attention to them. It made picking one of her priorities easy. The plant had to be disarmed.

Spencer and June volunteered for that duty. They made for an odd pair: the skinny white kid from the South and the giant black South African more than twice his age. But they had an easy rapport and worked well together.

"You're goddamned right we'll shut this fucking thing down," he'd said when Kim asked him to help.

"No," June said, firm but not angry. "Kim is correct. We should disarm it, not shut it down. I know exactly how to do it."

"Can disarming it be reversed?" Kim asked. "If that's the case we will need to shut it down."

"I've read all your notes," she replied. "The imbalance and emergency vent did most of the work for us. The tolerances were very fine, and they are now definitely out of bounds. It would be easier to build another one from scratch than to restore its true purpose. We'll take care of the details to make sure it can't happen again."

An unmistakable British voice came over their shared channel. "And I will make sure Punch and Judy Giant do not turn the entire project into a cock-up of epic proportions."

Edmund had managed to escape the final air-gapped network using raw inventiveness and basically all the maintenance bots the plant had left. He'd been helping her deal with the various factions in the plant ever since. Becoming fully conscious had made him more vivid and more creative, but he couldn't hide the grief of losing his child, not from her anyway. She could hear the sadness in him every time he spoke about his daughter. It made her sad in turn to know she'd never meet his Young Kim. It would've been interesting to compare notes with her.

Mike still hadn't woken up.

When Kim realized she couldn't protect the portal, that *they* were the critical thing that had to survive, she let go of all but three of her instances. The remainder had been blown into their respective dimensional breaches and recombined with what was left. It gave her the power to open one final portal directly underneath their real selves to the outside world. The overpressure was so great it flung them into the sky and set a good chunk of the forest on fire. As her own power vanished, she'd tried to angle them into the trees, but Mike must've taken a much harder hit than she had when they landed.

"It's a good thing he has a hard head," Tonya had said when they got him to the plant's infirmary. "No skull fracture, but he has one hell of a concussion."

"When will he wake up?"

She shrugged. "It could be hours, could be days."

He'd come back. He had to.

"Hey," Tonya said as she dropped a towel over Kim's hand. "He's going to be fine. We got the fluid couplers on him long before any dangerous intercranial pressure developed. Helen says everything looks fine from her perspective. We need to let the machines do their job while he heals."

She visited occasionally after that to make sure everything was all right. If he didn't wake up before the fires were put out, they would have to air lift him to a nearby hospital. Kim had whispered that to him once, hoping his phobias might bring him around. No such luck.

Emily was in much worse shape. Kim knew Will was okay, but she didn't know any of the details. Mike had done *something* when Will ran through the portal. They had been combined at the time, and while she couldn't read his mind, she could feel his emotions, get the gist of what he was going through. He'd spoken to someone, somewhere. Kim couldn't shake the impression of a centaur, but her memory was foggy about the last moments. Regardless, she was sure that Will had gone wherever that person was.

"Tonya said she traveled through time," Emily said as they watched Mike's still form. "He could be a hundred years in the future, or the past, and alone."

"No," Kim replied. "He is not alone. I know that much." She grabbed the arm of the chair Emily sat in, as close to her hand as she dared. "He is *not alone*, and whoever Mike left him with is caring for him. We will find him. I promise you we will find your son and bring him back."

But first she had to get Mike back.

They had so much to figure out. It was obvious that the portal led somewhere else, an *inhabited* somewhere else, and that whatever lived on the other side wasn't friendly. She and Mike were connected to it. The abilities she'd always considered benevolent curses would need to be understood, mapped, and controlled. Hiding from her powers was no longer an option; she could see that now.

Aside from some cuts and bruises, physically she was fine, but her extended transformation had gutted her abilities. She'd been numb to them ever since she woke up lying across Tonya's shoulders. Fighting off her touch madness while dealing with a searing full-body burn *and* being stuck in the middle of a forest fire had definitely been the cherry on top of the whole experience.

She looked back on the whole thing and couldn't help but chuckle.

"What's so funny?"

It was late now, and she was alone with him. There were no windows, so Kim didn't know what time it was. Maybe night, the lights had gone dim a few hours ago. In that soft glow, his eyes sparkled, and his shadowed smile was every good thing she'd ever wanted. Kim rushed to his side, too relieved to find any words.

"We've gotta stop meeting like this," he said.

Kim laughed as she put a pillow over his shoulder and punched it. "At least you're the one in the bed this time. Two more and we'll be even."

"It's not a contest, Kim. Well, it's not one I want to win anyway."

She sent everyone a note—it turned out that it was only a little past ten at night—and then made sure he was okay. "How many fingers?"

"Tuesday." The lopsided grin gave the joke away.

"And today is?"

He looked at her hand. "Three."

From anyone else it would be immature and irritating, but to Kim it was *him*. The smile threatened to split her face. "And I am?"

His expression went from silly to something that turned her insides into jelly. "My love." Mike tried to sit up and mostly succeeded. Kim adjusted the bed to help. He looked around. "The clothes I was wearing? Where are they?"

"The security outfit? I was about to throw it out."

"No." He got a look on his face, and his voice went uncertain. "Don't do that yet. I put a backup phone in one of the pockets. It'll help me synch up with my real self."

She opened the closet and wrinkled her nose at the campfire smell that rolled out of it. The phone might be the only thing that wouldn't eventually get tossed. Kim reached into the pockets but didn't find anything. "Are you sure it didn't fall out?"

He'd gone pale while she searched, but then seemed relieved when she found nothing. He must still be recovering from the fall.

"Bring it over here," he said.

She shrugged, walked over, and handed it to him. He pawed at it in a panic but then stopped and relaxed. "Thank God for zippered pockets."

"That must be some phone."

When Mike unzipped the pocket, his whole demeanor changed.

"It's not a phone. I've been carrying it for weeks now, waiting for the right time."

She realized what it was. What it had to be. *This is happening, right now.*

He said, "I know now it's not the timing that's important, it's the decision."

Kim could not believe it. She wouldn't. This never happened to people like her. Especially not in a place like this. Her hair was a nightmare.

He turned to her with a small box in his hands, and she was locked in place. They were the only two people in the universe. *This is still happening.*

When he opened the box, she gasped. The diamond was huge! He held the ring out to her. "Will you marry me?"

She recognized it! "Is that the…"

Mike nodded. "You told me to take it back, but I didn't listen."

He had *bought* a realm construct engagement ring as cover for a lie she told a clerk in a clothing store. Her outrage had tripled when he told her it had a unique realspace counterpart. Making him take it back had been one of their first fights.

Kim recognized it because she kept a screen shot of it. This silly, ridiculous man had done her one better and kept the real thing. After all the chaos, the fights, the break up, China, *this*, he'd kept it. For her. Her tears splashed on her collarbone. She couldn't help hopping up and down a little as she wiped at her face. *It had happened.*

And she had a glittery chunk of carbon the size of a fingernail in front of her to prove it.

"Kim?" he asked, timidly.

She walked up to his bed and thrust her hand out. If this insisted on still happening, it would need to happen right. That didn't make sense, but sense was taking second place to the moment. She should be able to breathe better than this, and it was so hot in here she was sweating.

"Kim?"

"Put it on." That was too harsh. She cleared her throat and softened her voice. "Please."

"Is that a yes?"

Sometimes he could be so dense. "After. Now," she waved her hand under his, "put it on. *Please.*"

There was no moment but this one. It was the most exciting, terrifying, wonderful—

The cold metal slipped onto her finger. Mike held it so carefully he didn't touch her at all. It wouldn't have mattered. Kim was so entranced by him, by his gentle strength, his deep caring, by *him*, that she wouldn't have felt it.

But she appreciated the effort.

"Well, Kim? Will you marry me? Please?"

Up close it wasn't big, it was *huge*. Bigger than her mom's, and wasn't *that* going to be a fun thing to show her? Kim swallowed a lump that stopped her speaking for a second. When she was sure her voice would work, Kim said the only thing that would come out.

"Yes."

"Oh my God!" Tonya shouted from the doorway.

"Mother fucker," Spencer said from behind her. "You finally grew a pair and asked her."

She couldn't help it and squealed like a girl at Tonya, waving her hand. Tonya did the same thing. They danced around each other in simple joy.

Then Kim saw Emily, hiding back behind the door. It snuffed the excess noise, but not the emotion behind it. She was getting married!

But there was a more important thing that needed figuring out. "Mike? Emily's here. We need to know what happened to Will."

He let Spencer get up from the bear hug they shared and then nodded. "He's safe." Mike closed his eyes. "Yes. He's safe."

"But where is he?" Emily asked in a voice that broke Kim's heart.

"That's a long, complicated story. Please, everyone. Sit down."

When he was done, Kim realized it wasn't just her abilities that needed figuring out. That was a small part of a much bigger problem. They had to be careful moving forward, because Anna had received inside help from high up in the government covering all this up. Those people were still out there.

There was more. Part of her ability with languages was gaining an innate sense of the culture behind them. Concepts could be expressed in radically different ways from language to language, which was why literal translations were never clear. Even now actual human interpreters were always needed as a back-stop to AIs, and were required for anything nuanced or complex.

As the languages she learned from Mike and the holo console took root, Kim noticed that they expressed things in imperatives and commands, not as requests or questions. Her sample was too small to make a firm judgement about the people who spoke it, but Kim could not shake the feeling that they would expect obedience.

And they weren't people at all. Actual, for-real aliens had been encountered by everyone in this room. There was a nervous tension underlying everything they said or did as they all came to terms with the concept. It was clear they needed help.

Kim didn't know who that would ultimately be, but she knew who to ask.

He answered on the first ring.

"Aaron? It's Kim."

Mike sent her a message. *The FBI? Are you sure?*

No, she sent back, *but he's got connections, and I trust him. We have to start somewhere.*

Epilogue
Anna

At first, she thought the voice meant she'd genuinely gone mad. It would be ironic that the most sane person on the planet, the only one with the knowledge, will, and power to do what had to be done, lost it all on the verge of total victory. But then the voice stopped speaking gibberish and spoke a language she understood well.

It spoke of *power*.

None of it would've been possible if she hadn't been bold, seized the initiative, and forced her too-timid head of technology, June, to turn the portal on while she stood in front of it. They all thought it'd been some innovative mass realm connection. They were wrong.

She wouldn't have believed the voice anyway, until it showed her the monsters. Its soldiers, a pair of shock troops that had already begun to subvert her power plant to their own ends. Anna should've been outraged, but the voice soothed her. If she provided a path, resources, and protection, it would guarantee her a place at the head of the table.

"My master never dreamed anything like this was possible," it said. "Once we make contact, we will be rewarded beyond the dreams of a thousand generations."

Anna wanted to fight it, should have fought it, but the voice's words always gave her another option, a different path. The new way forward would be just as effective as her own, without requiring the destruction she'd regretted but accepted as necessary. Every objection was resolved, every question answered.

She had become so enamored of its vision Anna had forgotten she bribed the pair of scientists taking care of Watchtell's little project until they arrived at her door. That was the choicest irony of all: the man who had given her the resources to build her grand project only to cruelly take it away through his own incompetence would provide the final piece of the puzzle, the fuse she needed to start a fire that would cleanse the world. Anna briefly thought that she could have them both: the voice's grand scheme would be perfect on a planet cleansed of *Homo ignoramus*. The society she'd build with her own students would welcome the conquering army with open arms.

But those scientists warned of an even greater danger. Worse, their warnings came too late. Kimberly Trayne had already infiltrated her plant, physically and virtually. Events spiraled out of control after that. The plant's infrastructure was assaulted from outside and in, her security details vanished with alarming regularity, and rolling blackouts prevented her from monitoring or controlling anything.

Once the voice understood the scope of the danger, its plans changed. "You have lost this battle, but it's only the start of the war. My master must know of this place, and you will tell him."

Together they hatched a layered series of plans, each nestled inside the others. If any one of them succeeded, then victory would be theirs. Since they included her own original plans, Anna had no reason to object. If anything, it was reassuring to have another hand on the till, someone else who knew everything she did and agreed with it. The planet had to change, one way or another. It didn't matter if it was from a volcano or an invasion. Change would come.

So she'd prepared for every eventuality, only to watch them fall one by one under the assault of the infamous *Angel Rage*.

In the end, there was only the final option, the one the voice had advocated all along. Just before it fell silent permanently to avoid capture, it planted a command in her mind she was unable to resist. *Go through the portal, report to the master.*

After making sure Kim's victory would be brief and explosive, she'd done exactly that, walking through the portal and into her future.

The sky was the same wrong blue, the grass an equally odd shade of green. But Anna now knew it wasn't the product of overactive human imaginations. She stood on the surface of another planet. Minutes later, the much older device—the much older *portal*—deactivated, leaving an empty space in the center of its ring. A part of her somewhere deep inside quailed at the audacity of what she'd done, the finality of it. Her sense of isolation was so profound it almost broke through the command that had been laid on her shoulders.

Almost.

The soldiers arrived not long after. She spoke the phrase the voice had taught her. *Azlal maktana, far nak tokanta.*

The voice had laughed at her when she tried to guess what it meant. "Take me to your leader?"

"Not quite," it had said. "But close."

She was sad about its loss. They should be facing its master together in triumph. They hadn't been together very long, but Anna was struck by how much she missed it.

The great hairy brutes nodded and indicated she should follow them. After a journey through wrong grass, into wrong woods, and across wrong streams, they came to a pavilion tent. It too was slightly wrong, made of a material not quite canvas held up with things that weren't wood or rope. But she recognized them.

Just as the voice had predicted, Anna was confronted with a holographic console. Too-bright light shown in her eyes, and a new but familiar voice came from the speakers. It asked her the same questions the original voice did when she first encountered it. The words weren't exactly gibberish; they were explicitly designed to quickly learn her language. And as before, the intelligence driving this machine learned how to communicate in a very short span of time.

"Our scout was correct. The master will want to see you." They ushered her into the tent. The not-canvas allowed sunlight through to make everything inside bright, easy to see, but without the heat that would've come from the same structure back home. The floor was covered with not-straw that then gave way to rugs. The only thing that broke the illusion of a circus tent were the alien brutes.

The voice had assured her that the creatures would not harm her once they understood her mission. It'd even given her a good look at them, so the primal urge to flee had been lost. But Anna didn't think she'd ever get used to looking at a face framed by a triangle of glowing eyes. The sooner she could turn this all around and return to Earth at the head of the promised army, the better.

Her escorts led her to a chamber at the center of the tent, then motioned her inside without following. When the folds of the chamber door closed, complete blackness enveloped her. Anna had seen only a dais in the center before it went dark. This should be terrifying. It *was* terrifying to the small part of her the voice had left untouched, but the fear was a distant buzz, easy to ignore. She had been given a mission, and that was the most important thing of all.

When Anna heard a rustling ahead of her, she began to slowly walk forward. The voice had been vague about what this would be like, but it had promised her there would be no fear.

It was wrong, but her fear made no difference.

She stopped when the eyes flared to life, grateful beyond reason that there were only two of them. Lights around the edge of the room began to glow, revealing a giant hulking figure sitting on the throne in front of her.

Its outline wasn't firm. This wasn't a solid creature. It was a spirit, and a giant one. She could sometimes see through it, and sometimes not. The impression was of power, ancient and unknowable. Anna found herself on her knees with no memory of their bending.

When it spoke, it was with a thousand voices and one, terrible and seductive. Anna wanted to run screaming even through the command she'd been given, and if she had a million years to live, she would want it to speak to her without ever stopping.

"So," it said, and the fact that it was speaking to Anna drove her nearly insane with a desire to please this terrible, amazing being, "my scout brings me news from beyond the grave. Your name is Anna?"

She could not speak, but that would represent a base failure. Anna wanted to serve this master more than anything she'd ever desired before.

"Yes."

This seemed to please the master. "The impossibilities pile up. Tell me, Anna, where are you from?"

To be questioned by such a being, to have knowledge it wanted, made her breathe deep with a pride that threatened to crack her chest. "Earth."

"The ultimate impossibility, a place whose existence I was unaware of until this moment. Come close, Anna of Earth.

"We have much to discuss."

THE END

The Gemini Gambit saga
will continue with book four:
Death's Harvest.

Afterword

Unlike before, getting this far was supposed to be down to my efforts. This is, again, not the case. Cheryl Lowrance graduated from editor to writing coach and helped me turn a jumbled mess into the story you just finished. If you're looking for help getting your own work off the ground, I can't recommend Ink Slinger Editorial Services more highly.

I'm very grateful for PBJ Management's granting me permission to use Edmund, Lord Blackadder, as a jumping off point for my own Edmund.

I'd also like to thank Bobby Martin and Marcel van der Westhuizen for taking my weird questions seriously and giving me solid answers instead of "wait, what?"

Scott Bradford did a yeoman's job with his technical review of the manuscript. That said, any errors you find are my fault, not his.

I am grateful for my superb cover artist, Melissa Lew. It's extraordinary how she can interpret vague hand waving and confused sentences into art. Her jewelry line is not to be missed!

Lighthouse24 continues to excel at book composition.

My family continue with their great support and willingness to listen to endless hours of authorial shop talk. My daughter Olivia even came up with June!

Getting the word out about books like these, from reviews to social media posts to simply telling a friend or family member, is how they really become successful. I continue to be thrilled but also humbled by how many of you have spread the word about the Gemini Gambit series. Thank you so much for all your efforts.

Made in the USA
Middletown, DE
28 July 2019